A GOD IN RUINS

BY LEON URIS

BATTLE CRY

THE ANGRY HILLS

EXODUS

MILA 18

ARMAGEDDON

TOPAZ

QB VII

TRINITY

THE HAJ

MITLA PASS

REDEMPTION

A GOD IN RUINS

LEON
A GOD IN RUINS
A N O V E L
URIS

Published by Harper Large Print
in association with
HarperCollins*Publishers*

HarperCollins books may be purchased for educational, business, or sales promotional use. For information please write: Special Markets Department, HarperCollins Publishers, Inc., 10 East 53rd Street, New York, NY 10022-5299.

A hardcover edition of this book was published in 1999 by HarperCollins*Publishers*.

FIRST LARGE PRINT EDITION

Designed by Alma Orenstein

This title is also available on cassette from HarperAudio.

Library of Congress Cataloging-in-Publication Data

Uris, Leon, 1924–
A god in ruins : a novel / Leon Uris.—1st ed.
p. cm.
ISBN 0-06-093304-6
I. Title.
PR3541.R46G63 1999
813'.54—dc21 99-11193

ISBN 0-06-093304-6 (Large Print)

99 00 01 02 03 ❖/RRD 10 9 8 7 6 5 4 3 2 1

This Book is Dedicated to
My Oldest and Dearest Friend,
HARRY KOFSKY.

Special Thanks to My Researcher, MARILYNNE PYSHER,
and My Assistant, JEANNE RANDALL.

Man is a god in ruins. . . . Infancy is the perpetual Messiah, which comes into the arms of fallen men, and pleads with them to return to paradise.

—Ralph Waldo Emerson, *Nature*

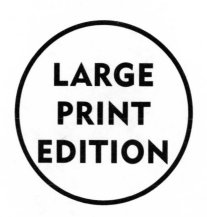

LARGE
PRINT
EDITION

PART ONE

ONE

Troublesome Mesa, Colorado
Autumn, 2008

A Catholic orphan of sixty years is not apt to forget the day he first learned that he was born Jewish. It would not have been that bombastic an event, except that I am running for the presidency of the United States. The 2008 election is less than a week away.

Earlier in the day, my in-close staff looked at one another around the conference table. We digested the numbers. Not only were we going to win, there was no way we were going to lose. Thank God, none of the staff prematurely uttered the words "Mr. President."

This morning was ten thousand years ago.

I'm Quinn Patrick O'Connell, governor of Colorado and the Democratic candidate for president. The voters know I was adopted through the Catholic bureaucracy by the ranchers Dan and Siobhan O'Connell.

My dad and I were Irish enough, at each other's throats. Thanks to my mom, we all had peace and a large measure of love before he was set down in his grave.

All things being equal, it appeared that I would be the second Roman Catholic president in American history. Unknown to me until earlier this day, I would be the first Jewish president as well.

Nothing compares to the constant melancholy thirst of the orphan to find his birth parents. It is the apparatus that forms us and rules us.

Aye, there was always someone out there, a faceless king and queen in a chilled haze, taunting.

Ben Horowitz, my half brother, had been searching for me, haunted, for over a half century. Today he found me.

Tomorrow at one o'clock Rocky Mountain time I must share my fate with the American people. You haven't heard of Rocky time? Some of the networks haven't, either. Lot of space but small market.

The second half of the last century held the years that the Jews became one of the prime forces in American life. Politically, there had been a mess of Jewish congressmen, senators, mayors, and governors of enormous popularity and power. None had won the big enchilada. I suppose the buck stops here.

Had I been elected governor as Alexander Horowitz, I'd have been just as good for my state. However, the discovery of my birth parents a week before the presidential election could well set off a series of tragic events from the darkness where those who will hate me lay in wait.

How do I bring this to you, folks? In the last few hours I have written, "my fellow Americans" twenty-six times, "a funny thing happened to me on the way to Washington" twenty-one times, and "the American people have the right to know" three dozen times. My wastebasket overfloweth.

Don't cry, little Susie, there *will* be a Christmas tree on the White House lawn.
No, the White House kitchen will not be kosher. My love of Carnegie tongue and pastrami is not of a religious nature.
By presidential decree, the wearing of a yarmulke is optional.
Israel will not become our fifty-first state.

To tell the truth, my countrymen, I simply do not know what this means in my future. O'Connell was a hell of a good governor, but we are in uncharted waters.

I'm getting a little fuzzy. I can see into the bedroom, where Rita is sprawled in the deep part of a power nap. Rita and our bedroom and her attire are all blended with Colorado hush tones, so soft and light in texture. At the ranch Rita liked to wear those full and colorful skirts like a Mexican woman at fiesta. As she lays there a bit rumpled, I can see up her thighs. I'd give my horse and saddle to be able to crawl alongside her. But then, I'd never finish my Washington's farewell to the troops speech.

On the other hand, Rita and I have made the wildest gung-ho love when we were under the deepest stress.

Write your speech, son, you've got to "face the nation" tomorrow, Rocky Mountain time.

Straight narrative, no intertwining B.S. or politicizing. Explain the O'Connell né Horowitz phenomenon. Truth, baby, truth. At least truth will not come back to haunt you.

Strange, I should be thinking of Greer at this moment. Rita is the most sensual soul mate one could pray for. We have loved one another without compromise for nearly thirty years. Yet, is it possible that Greer is really the love of my life?

I'd have never come this far in the campaign without Greer Little's genius. I would have been tossed into the boneyard of candidates never heard from again. She organized, she raised money, she knew the political operatives, and she masterminded my "miracle" campaign.

I was struck by the realization that Greer would leave soon, and I felt the same kind of agony as when we broke up years before. I had needed to see Greer on some business, and knocked and entered her room. She had been on the bed with Rita, passed-out drunk. Rita had held her and soothed her as though she were a little girl, and Rita had put her finger to her lips to tell me to be quiet.

Well, there was life without Greer, but there could be no life without Rita. Yet it still hurts.

I watch the hours flow in the passageway behind me like the tick of a suppressed bomb about to be released. I am through with a draft. I write another.

As the hours to dawn tick off, it all seems to come down to the same basic questions. Am I telling the truth? Do the American people have the civility and the decency to take the truth and rise with it?

Why me, Lord? Haven't I had enough of your pranks? Isn't slamming the White House door in my face just a little much, even for Your Holiness? I'm at the landing over the reception foyer of the White House. The Marine band drums up "Hail to the Chief" and the major of the guard proclaims, "The president of the United States and Mrs. Horowitz." Oh, come on now, Lord. Aren't you carrying this a little too far?

Well, all the stories of the good Irish lives are best passed on around the old campfire from *schanachie* to *schanachie*, and I'll not spare you mine.

In actual fact, my own beginnings began at the end of World War II, when my future adopted father, Daniel Timothy O'Connell, returned from the Pacific with a couple of rows of ribbons and a decided limp.

Brooklyn, Autumn, 1945

The war to end all wars had ended. The Military Air Transport DC–3 groaned as the cables stretched in a turn, and a piece of the plane's skin flapped against the pilot's window. The tail swung. A queasy contingent of soldiers, sailors, and a few Marines were losing the battle with their equilibrium.

Staff Sergeant Daniel Timothy O'Connell tried to suck oxygen from the wilted air as beads of sweat popped out on his forehead. The sergeant mumbled into his beard that he had come all the way from San Diego without puking and damned if he was going to puke in front of a planeload of swab jockeys and dog faces.

In the cockpit a pair of MATS women flew the craft, adding to his discomfort. "Guadalcanal," he continued mumbling, "Tarawa, Saipan, Okinawa, only to crash ten miles from home!"

Crossing the United States was no simple matter. There was no commercial air service to and from San Diego. MATS, which took as many discharged veterans as it could, had hundreds on their waiting list.

O'Connell had caught a train from San Diego to L.A. From there, two different airlines making nine stops over a twelve-hour period landed him at Wright-Patterson Field outside Dayton.

There was a delay of several hours before another MATS plane could get him to the East Coast. He checked in and segued into a bar just outside the gates and sashayed in with a sailor he had teamed up with named Gross. Marines seldom used first names, so Gross was Gross.

They entered the Blue Lady lounge to see a half dozen women lined up at one end of the bar.

"Could be a B-joint," O'Connell said. "Got your dough safe?"

"Money belt."

"You see," O'Connell went on, "they know a lot of GIs are coming through Wright-Patterson Field loaded with back pay and that we have to be out of town soon."

"I know you'll protect me," Gross said.

"Beer."

"Jim Beam with a Jim Beam backup."

"A couple of ladies would like to treat you boys."

"I'll bet they would."

"Hey, take off your pack and stand at ease," the bartender said. "I'm Army, myself. These are a lonely wives club. Some of them have been without for two years. Just women without men. They work at Wright-Patterson."

"You know," Gross said, "I might settle in here for a few days."

"Yeah, only after we find a Western Union and you wire home the money you're carrying."

"You going to stay?" Gross asked.

"No," O'Connell answered.

"I mean, look at them, their eager little bodies twitching."

"It's a duty thing," the Marine snapped.

"With me, too," Gross said. "God would never forgive me if I just upped and ignored His perfect works of beauty."

"I haven't seen my sweetheart in over three years," Dan said, becoming serious. "So pick a filly and let's get your money home."

With Gross on the way to wonderland on the arm of a happy/sad lady with two kids, Dan O'Connell returned to MATS at Wright-Patterson Field. He had been bumped by an officer.

In a race down the train platform he got aboard a train to Pittsburgh with no time to spare for the overnight ride to New York. Dan was up before daylight, a hundred dreams all fusing. How does one play out his homecoming scene?

Siobhan Logan rushed into Dan's arms while her brother, Father Sean Logan, remained a step behind. Sean smiled widely as they embraced. He had seen them as teenagers, young adults, same pose, only this time she screamed for joy.

Dan's testy hip and knee made itself felt when he dropped his sea bag to encurl her and spin her about.

"Oh, Dan, your leg, I'm sorry."

"I'm still big enough to hold up a drunk in either hand. Siobhan! Siobhan! Oh, you are so beautiful."

Dan spotted Father Sean advancing timidly. He wore a Roman collar. Ordained and everything.

"Father Sean."

"Just Sean."

The two men were the closest of pals, and they went

their separate ways—Sean to the seminary and Dan to the Brooklyn Police Academy. Both had prayed that Dan would get home. Dan didn't embrace men. A tough handshake, a couple of slaps on the shoulder.

"I'll take that sea bag," Father Sean said.

"I can deal with the weight."

"Oh, it's not the weight, it's your general awkwardness. See now, with your limp we'd have to attach the bag to your waist and have you drag it, or you could put it back on your shoulder and when you fall down I can pray over you and Siobhan will pass the plate."

"All right, all right—if you've no respect for a wounded veteran! Anyhow, I sent the big trunk home by Railway Express."

"I hope it finds its way to you someday," Father Sean said.

The Promenade along Brooklyn Heights rarely had enough benches and parking spaces these days. Dan was not the only lad from Brooklyn coming home.

"They're talking about putting a bridge over the Narrows," Siobhan said quickly and shakily, "to Staten Island."

"They'll never get a bridge over there."

This kiss was fiercely mellow or, as Dan would say in the Marines, "The price of poker has just gone up."

Siobhan straightened up and gulped a monster sigh. "We're all but married in name."

"Of course."

"Then you are behaving stupidly."

"What did I do?"

"It's not what you did. It's what you *do*! If we are virtually married, I want to do what married people do, now, today," she said.

"I've thought about it so much," Dan said, "that I want it to be utterly perfect, utterly. I want us to be joined by God first."

"That will take God two weeks. God may be patient, but I can't wait that long. I've got a key to a girlfriend's flat. Either we go there now, or I'm going to undress right here, right now."

Home! The grand illusion.

Everything you remembered had to be perfect to balance the imperfections. A cop from Flatbush. Now, that was a big man in Marine eyes. The only man who really came from a perfect place was his closest and eternal buddy, Justin Quinn.

Home! Dan had forgot that his mother's voice ranged between a squeal and shrill. Gooseflesh popped out on his skin when she argued, like someone had run chalk over a "singing" blackboard.

Home! Dan remembered those midnight-to-eight walking beats. It could be noon before he could get to the paperwork. The nights brought gunplay and gore. One of his backup partners had been massively wounded. A tot murdered in its crib, the mother's throat slashed, and a deranged boyfriend opting to shoot it out. ("That was a bad one. Take a couple days off, Dan.")

Home! Until he saw her again, he had clear forgotten about the wart on the end of his aunt's chin.

Or how small and crushing the streets were.

Or how tiny his room was.

The closeness of space and people led to a repetition of life.

Now, Justin Quinn had a real home! Justin Quinn had never returned. He had been killed in Saipan, but even the night before his death he had spoken of the beauty of his father's ranch in Colorado. It was the perfection sought by all but experienced by few.

A Marine's life can be boring, but there is always a jazzy sparkle when he is polishing up for shore leave. He and Justin blew through the camp gates. Justin would go to waiting arms. Dan played it straight with Siobhan for the entire time. But he was a singer and dancer and great teller of jokes. Well now, he did get into an awkward situation or two with the ladies in New Zealand, but nothing he couldn't tell Siobhan of, at a later time.

Home. Relatives and friends who spent most of their lives stirring the pot in each other's kitchens and salty old yarn spinners bragging about WWI, the "big" war in France and their blowout in Paree.

No Sunday came and went without a wedding or a christening. Hardly a week passed without a wake.

"How many Japs did you kill, Dan?"

"San Diego! That's the end of the earth now!"

"Go over your medals one more time, Dan. Which one was for getting wounded?"

"Is it true what they say about them Asian women?"

WELCOME HOME, DAN read the banner over the entrance of the precinct station. It was a happy event, indeed. The precinct had lost five men to the war.

A big cake had been baked and several cases of Coke hustled. (Can you believe it, Dan? Coke is up to a dime a bottle.)

Dan's new uniform came compliments of a grateful mayor. He was issued a revolver, a sweet .38 Smith & Wesson Police Special.

"You know, you can wear your military ribbons on your police uniform. Now, what's that one?"

"It's called a 'ruptured duck,' to signify you are a veteran."

The powers that be knew Dan would not be able to take up a walking beat again. He could handle it somewhat, but he'd lose too many suspects and arrests if he had to give chase. Well, no matter, Dan O'Connell was a war hero, and they'd talk about a desk job or perhaps a patrol car and, just maybe, becoming a detective.

A rookie named Kofski was on Dan's old beat. He put on his new uniform and holstered his new pistol for "the walk." Kofski was all thumbs. Dan preferred Irish cops to polacks.

"The walk" would be a sort of victory lap to reclaim the homage of his protectorate. It started as all walks started, with Dan taking an apple from the Italian vendor.

Farther along, they rushed up to a third floor to break up a marital. In the old days, Dan had been an arbitrator, along with the parish priest. Consultation fees, a cup of tea and a slice of pie. Jesus, Kofski, don't just burst in with your baton swinging!

A final cuff was made when they nailed a kid heisting hubcaps. Kofski shook the kid real hard and wanted to take him back to the station. Dan had to read quickly whether this boy was too far into the street scene or could still be salvaged. He opted to take the boy to his mother and dad.

This chase incident made Dan aware of his limited mobility. Kofski had to run the kid down, and it wasn't easy.

In the Corps, he'd been thrown in with all kinds of guys, Texans, farmers, and those wild lads from L.A. He'd only heard of such people and never believed he would live to see them. Won't the nation change at the end of the war? As they left "the walk," Dan wondered if his beat wasn't really the perimeter of a walled graveyard.

He sank into a mood of Irish maudlin. The pending mayhem of a large Irish wedding shaped up. A yard filled with clucking hens writing invitations, pinning up, pinning down. A band and step dancers and a tenor and a poet were hired, and even the mayor might make it.

As the kitchen calendar was X'd, Dan entombed himself in his tiny room, awaiting his only respite, the daily visit from Father Sean Logan, his forthcoming brother-in-law.

"Looks like you've had enough of the women, Dan."

"Egh."

"Well, marriage is the one moment in life that a girl can make a kill. It's bound to test your patience. But some fine news! Permission to use the big cathedral came from the cardinal of Brooklyn himself. I've waited for near on three years and have never performed a marriage ceremony. I wanted you and my beloved sister Siobhan to be my first."

Dan said it must have cost him a fortune in fees.

"Never to mind. You don't wear this collar to make money. You appear to be having normal prenuptial jitters."

"No doubts, Sean. I love Siobhan fiercely."

"Almost as much as you love the Marine Corps," the priest retorted.

"It's so damned hard to let go!" Dan cried.

"I'm counseling veterans a good part of the day. Lots of lads are stumbling around. It was for most of you the first taste of life beyond Brooklyn, and no matter what happens, the war will always remain the big event of your life."

"It passed through my mind to reenlist."

"One of the chaplains from the Sixth Marines was with me at a retreat a few months ago. He told me that your battalion lost four commanders in the first day."

"Saipan was a shit kicker. So were Guadalcanal and Tarawa. The worst foxhole is the one you happen to be in when the shit hits the fan."

"Did you find something along the way?"

"Yeah, right in the beginning. On the train on the way to boot camp in San Diego. In Buffalo there was another train of recruits. To join them we had to walk through the station to their platform. The station in Buffalo was scary, high and icy and silent, a walk to the unknown. When the two trains merged they were so full, some recruits were sleeping on the floor. I ended up in a lower bunk with another guy. That's the way fighting for space had been back home.

"Later in the trip we slowed down at the tip of daylight. I had the window position that night and rolled the shade up. Outside was a huge green lawn before a beautiful, newly painted station. Douglass, Kansas. Beyond, I could see nice houses, like Mickey Rooney lived in when he played Andy Hardy."

"Weren't you trying to deceive yourself, Dan? Pretending there are perfect places outside Brooklyn? If you knocked on any door in this Kansas place, you'd find Brooklyn once removed."

"Well, what have I got here? There are still five of us in our home on top of each other trying to ace each other out of the bathroom. My parents are arguing.

Everyday ordinary conversation is argumentative. Some fifteen-year-old niece is knocked up, someone is stitched up from a fight, and the friggin' bed is lumpy."

"It sounds like you've been making a plan for a long time."

"I want to see Douglass, Kansas, and a lot of the places my men came from."

"That's not a bad idea, but you'll not drive far enough to escape trouble. The virgin you saw at dawn may now show you some pimples on her ass in the midday sun."

Dan became excited. "After Douglass, Kansas, we'll head for Colorado and visit the parents of the one great friend of my life, Justin Quinn. It drives me, Sean. I can't rest until I see Justin's mom and dad and let them know what a powerful Marine their son was. Justin Quinn was the man among us, winning any broad with a glance, winning the division rodeo. Ah, the fucking fool, trying to win the battle of Saipan by himself. Maybe after that I'll concentrate on settling down. I'm too restless now."

"Well, you should be. Your war has been taken away from you. When do you plan to go?"

"After the wedding."

"Does Siobhan know?"

"Ah, Jaysus, I can't face the tears now."

"Has it occurred to you that she might not want to go? She's very tribal."

"Yes, but I have to take the chance."

* * *

The bachelor's stag party was but three nights away. There would be nearly a hundred cops boozing and relatives all the way from Jersey and just maybe one of those weasly guys with an 8mm projector and dirty films.

Siobhan was picking up puzzling vibrations from Dan at a rapid rate. Did he truly want to marry? Was it coming back from a war too emptied out? He spoke little of vicious battles or malaria or dengue fever. From a strange, secret place he'd mutter the name of one of the boys in his platoon. Except for Justin Quinn. He'd talk about Justin.

"Two more days and I've got you," Siobhan said. "I understand the boys will have a couple of strippers at your stag party. Just remember, you're an officer of the law."

"Ah, geez, Siobhan, the captain himself is sending them."

"How does Mrs. Jane O'Connell sound?" she asked. "Or should I continue to use Siobhan?"

"You use Mrs. Daniel Timothy O'Connell. If it was good enough for the liberator of Ireland, it's good enough for the likes of us."

"Oh, thank you, milord, but I'll be using my own Christian name."

"Look at what the war went and done," Dan retorted. "All you ladies got liberated to work in the defense factories. That doesn't give you the right to throw your husband's fine name out with the garbage."

It was wonderful. Dan knew new ways of defusing his woman. The official engagement had many advantages. He could touch her breasts any time he wished. Every damned time, she liked it! She'd put her hand atop his to make him stay awhile. Having petted her into a weak state, he sprang forth.

"I've got something of great consequence to tell you," he blurted.

"We're not going to get married!"

"Of course we're going to get married. Sunday we're getting married. I'm addressing you on a matter after the wedding."

"We are still going to Niagara Falls, aren't we, Dan?"

"Definitely, but not by train," he croaked.

"I'm not walking!"

"Will you let me get a word in edgewise!" She became silent. He paced. All of his airtight arguments disappeared in a dim puff. "Well," he managed, "I was of a mind that when we leave Niagara Falls, we continue directly to San Francisco."

"Sacred Heart! I may faint!"

"Siobhan, I tried to hint to you in my letters. I've met too many men from too many places not to realize that this is a great land and life could be wondrous in a way that it never could be here."

After a time she whispered, "I've been thinking much the same. Brooklyn is an island. Islands dull the race after time. Maybe I should have told you, but I would say nothing, ever, at the risk of losing you, Dan."

"Jaysus, now, isn't that something."

Siobhan pulled off her blouse and unhooked her bra. "Kiss them, Dan."

He did as told and took her on his lap.

"There will be a better life for us. You remember the Romero kid over in the eyetalian street? He put his car up on blocks for the duration of the war. He was killed at Iwo."

"I know."

"My brother Pearse knows cars as well as Henry Ford, went and inspected it from bumper to bumper. It's in perfect condition. Father Sean said if someone bought the car, it would help Romero's old man get over his grieving. It's a '41 DeSoto."

"Forty-one! Aren't we hoi polloi! Did you steal the money?"

They stopped for a little personal entanglement. It couldn't get too serious in the middle of the day.

"Anyhow, I got the car for a pittance. Old man Romero wanted me to have it, his son being a fellow police officer and Marine. I, uh, paid seven hundred dollars for it."

"Seven hundred dollars! Besides, I never heard of anyone driving across the country. Where would we sleep? Where would we eat? We could be attacked by Indians."

"Let me explain, let me explain. I went to the AAA and, being a veteran, they gave me free maps and a book listing motels."

"What the devil are motels?"

"Well, they're not exactly hotels . . . they're motor hotels."

They digested it.

"Do they have toilets?"

"Yes, toilets and private showers, and we're apt to run into one every hundred miles or so."

"Are we coming back?" she whispered shakily.

"If we don't find something better. But we'll never know unless we try."

"Are we fooling ourselves that there is something better than here?"

"From what I've seen, there is every chance."

"How will we live?"

"I have a New York state bonus, plus severance pay from the Marines, and I've got disability compensation. I've been sending money home, which Dad deposited. Then, you know, gambling is not illegal in the Marine Corps, and I got this knack for poker."

"Poker! You used to raid poker games!"

"And some dice."

"You used to raid such games. You got a citation for it!"

"In the Corps it's perfectly legal, so when you're in the Marines you do as the Marines do."

"How much dirty money did you take from them?"

"We have over nine thousand dollars in total, including the bonus and stuff like that. And don't forget, I get two hundred a month from the government for my wound."

Siobhan fumed a bit at the revelations.

"I've been too many places, Siobhan. I don't want to be another Irish cop all my life."

She snapped her brassiere shut and put on her top. "I suppose," she said, "I can always find my way back to Brooklyn if I have to."

TWO

Fall 1945

Their honeymoon became a sort of pioneer epic. Daniel O'Connell continued to wear his Marine Corps uniform with the "ruptured duck" over his breast pocket, and he speeded up his pace every time they walked past a men's clothing store.

Siobhan O'Connell lost her newlywed nervousness. At the end of the day's drive they either found a motel or the usual four-story brick hotel used by traveling salesmen, occupying a corner of the main cross streets of whatever town they were in. The similarity of rooms, the fishy-eyed desk clerks, and stuttering bell boys was striking. They were mid-range, six- to eight-dollar-a-night rooms.

Siobhan usually waited in the car while Dan signed in at the registration desk. The fishy-eyed clerk guarded the gates to the kingdom like a true centurion. By the time they got to Cleveland, Mrs. Siobhan O'Connell opened her purse and slapped their marriage certificate on the desk.

They glowed each morning and even more so when the correct safe dates appeared on the calendar. Siobhan realized that there might be other channels of gratification during the abstention part, but she had a whole life ahead to work on it. For now, though, abstention was hell.

CHICAGO!

A married buddy, Cliff Romanowski, lived in Chicago. Cliff had lost an arm in the earlier battle of Tarawa. Beautiful reunion. Cliff's wife, Corinne, was six months pregnant and all popped out. Good omen, Siobhan thought.

After a homemade dinner featuring Polish sausage, the four went out to paint the town. Dan mustered his bad leg into duty and did a sort of polka, which seemed to be the national dance of Chicago.

The wives were deliciously tolerant of their lads' drinking and subsequent hell-raising. They all crashed with the daylight.

Next day, noticeably slowed, Dan took them to a Greek restaurant, the anxiety of their first meeting converted into nostalgia. At Cliff and Corinne's apartment, they ended up sitting on the floor in a circle, propped up by pillows, and Siobhan's toe trying to creep up inside Dan's pant leg.

The Marine Corps. Reminiscence began with the

sweat of a double-time hike, then drifted into their patented tomfoolery and sophomoric behavior. Beer busts were recalled with kindness.

"And me and O'Connell and Quinn hit the railroad station just as the last liberty train was leaving. Everything was full, the seats, the floor, the platform where you could sleep standing up. So the three of us climbed into the overhead luggage rack, where there was already men laying end to end. And an hour out of Wellington, the luggage rack comes crashing down! The lights went out and I've got to tell you, I felt a lot of Marine ass!"

New Zealand had been a never-never land with the bursting scenery, Maoris, flocks on the skyline, colonial ways. Siobhan was tempted to ask about the New Zealand women but held her tongue. It was the night to let their men erupt.

Now came the war.

". . . remember that little runt?"

". . . yeah, Weasel from Arizona."

". . . nobody thought he'd hold up."

". . . great fighter."

". . . little Weasel."

". . . remember . . ."

". . . geez, I forgot about that bout of malaria."

. . . remember . . . remember . . . for God's sake, remember me, Marine.

"I was in the Oak Knoll Naval Hospital near Frisco when you guys hit that beach at Saipan. I finally found a guy, remember Prentice in Intelligence?" Cliff asked.

"Yeah, sure do."

"He told me what happened to you. All the casualties on the beach. But I think the worst was the day I heard about Justin Quinn," Cliff recalled. "You don't figure a Marine of his quality would catch a stray bullet."

"He got hit because he had to deliver a message and there were no phone lines connected yet. It was his own bloody fault. He should have waited."

Thump, the visit was wearily ended.

Dan and Siobhan and Cliff and Corinne would never forget it. After two devastating hangovers, the O'Connells packed the '41 DeSoto and pointed it toward the corn and wheat fields of the Great Plains.

Even though it cost a long-distance phone call, Siobhan always made certain there would be food and lodging at the end of the day. Ahead, they moved into an infinity of two-lane roads.

It was here that Siobhan learned to drive. When stopped for speeding, she became Everywoman, coyly explaining their newlywed status, and what with her husband home from the war . . .

"Never mind, lady, just slow down."

They drove through Kansas City, then chose the E-Z Inne on the road out of town because it was offering half-price rooms for veterans. There were a lot of big trucks about and a steak house right next door.

Fooled them! Dan thought to himself as he took a long drink from his purchase from a state bottle store.

Actually, a dry state, can you imagine? Must not be many Irish about.

He set the glass on the floor and submerged to the bottom of the tub. "Ahhhh!"

Siobhan answered his moose call and scrubbed his back as he kept diving and coming up exclaiming "Ahhhh!"

At the steak house, the two stared at the extraordinary size of the meat. "Sure, I've never had a piece of meat like this in my icebox," Siobhan said in wonderment.

"And it cuts with a fork. I wonder what they do to the meat?"

"It's not what *they* do," Siobhan said, "it's what we do after we get it."

Dan quickly shifted his brown-bagged bottle of bourbon as the sheriff strolled in and took a stool at the counter. In a few minutes, their waiter came and presented them with two bottles of beer, compliments of the sheriff.

Ah, now this is living, Dan thought.

"Notice how nice people are out here?" she noted.

"Yeah," Dan said so sadly he croaked. "Yeah."

"Dan, I'm trying to be patient and understanding. It's not a case of merely getting rid of the war. It will always be with you, but it can no longer dominate our lives. We've big tomorrows to think about, and you have to shift the Marine Corps and hold it in a place close to your heart but out of the mainstream of our marriage."

Dan nodded and watched the big trucks speed past, their sound muffled by glass.

"Why are we driving south tomorrow?" she asked.

"I went over and over and over a picture in my mind of you and me standing before that make-believe little rail station in Douglass, Kansas. Me, with my arms about you, looking past the lawns to those beautiful dollhouses."

"You can't move your hometown because you don't like its location. You are going to great lengths to fool yourself. If we don't go, the memory of it will remain perfect."

"I'm afraid to reach Colorado," Dan blurted. "I'm scared of seeing Justin Quinn's parents. My visit might bring them nightmares. They don't know we're coming. I avoided writing them. There is something so final about it."

"Yes," she said. "It means you are closing the cover of a book. Not that you can ever forget Justin Quinn."

"We were so close, almost as close as you and me, Siobhan. You cannot say or feel that you actually love a man because that is sinful and unhealthy. But you know, we enjoyed horsing around, jumping each other, goosing each other. Strictly correct, you know. With my baritone and his tenor, we could strike our tent silent. And with the two of us . . . well, no one ever did anything to my boys. We cleaned out one bar that was clipping. Busted them down like lumberjacks."

Her hand slipped into his, and she nodded for him to continue.

"Damned shame. His family has this tremendous spread, as they call it, beyond Denver. Justin Quinn, being the oldest son, was due to take over the ranch. First he was going to the University of Colorado, where he had won a football scholarship."

"Calm your fears, Dan. Justin's folks will be eternally grateful for your visit, and we'll be totally comfortable there."

No pilgrim's ride up to Jerusalem was ever more ethereal than the one they experienced as Dan piloted the '41 DeSoto around their first taste of an unpaved, washboard, rutted, cliff-side excuse for a road. Every switchback brought more stupendous scenery. Siobhan took her hands from her eyes to look at the vista, gasp, and then take cover again.

At last the township of Troublesome Mesa welcomed them. The West was there. All they needed was a pair of gunmen to face each other down in the dirt street.

"M/M Ranch?" the gas station owner said.

"Yes, sir."

"Huh. Don't hear too much about it these days."

"How far is it?"

"About fifteen miles . . . up. Probably take you better part of an hour. Sure you want to drive it today?"

"Yes."

"Well, now," the attendant said, shading his eyes to ascertain the time, "if you get past five o'clock and haven't reached the ranch, turn on back. Otherwise you'll be in stone cold darkness, and we'll probably have to pull you out of a ravine tomorrow."

A crude map was drawn, and Dan thanked the attendant profusely. Half numb, Daniel Timothy O'Connell girded himself as the attendant filled his water bags.

"If you come back tonight, I have a bed for you over the garage. Damned hotel folded when the molybdenum mine closed."

Half greeting and half guarding, a pair of border collies held them at bay until a man emerged from a large, fancy house.

"It must be the place," Dan said. "It's exactly as Quinn described it to me."

"Hello, Marine," the man said, shooing the dogs back. "Can I help you?"

"Is this the M/M Ranch?"

The man laughed. "Used to be a long time ago."

Dan studied the man. His skin was dark and he certainly was full of Mexican blood, but he spoke with no accent.

"I'm looking for the Quinn family. See, uh, Justin Quinn was in my company. He was killed at Saipan. My wife, Siobhan, and I have come to pay respects to his family."

A nice-looking woman in her mid-twenties emerged from the house and came alongside her husband. He spoke to her in Spanish, and as he did, her face became grim.

"I am Pedro Martinez, the caretaker. And this is my wife, Consuelo. Will you please come in? Your name?"

"Sergeant . . . rather, Daniel Timothy O'Connell. My wife, Siobhan."

"Siobhan is a beautiful name," Consuelo said.

"It's Irish for Jane. Oh, what a lovely room."

The ranch house living room was timbered and high-ceilinged, with a river stone fireplace to match. The Pedro fellow seemed concerned as he checked his watch.

"Can I offer you drinks?" Consuelo asked.

"No, thanks. I mean, I want to know about Quinn's mother and father."

"I have to take you to another part of the ranch," Pedro said. "The problem is that it will be dark before we return, and I won't let you go down to Troublesome on that road at night. You are most welcome to stay here overnight."

Siobhan smiled and nodded to Dan.

"Perhaps, Miss Siobhan, the sergeant and I should make this visit ourselves," Pedro said. "Uh, there is a stream to cross."

Pedro was not very good at covering his uneasiness.

"Certainly," Siobhan said.

Dan and the foreman jeeped down a winding dirt road inside the property until they could hear a faint rush of water. They parked at a tentative wooden bridge across the stream from a ramshackle miner's cabin.

"Is this what I think it is?" Dan asked, sinking.

"I'm afraid so," Pedro replied.

"I may not be able to cross," Dan said suddenly. "My leg might give out on that narrow beam."

"I understand."

"Like hell you understand! Like hell you do!" Dan told himself.

"Shall we go back to the ranch house, then?"

Dan did not answer. His choice was to turn and go, but he was unable to. If he walked away, he'd come back. "Let's cross," he whispered.

The shack reeked of mold. Everything inside was broken. Newspapers had been stuffed in the cracks to keep the cold out. The roof was half down, the windows broken and thick with sludge. Outhouse turned over. It was altogether a place for rats. Dan's eyes studied a place of disemboweled human life. He could not speak, or barely breathe. Dan staggered outside and stared at it, crazed pain in his eyes.

"The ranch never belonged to the Quinns," Pedro said.

"Tell me!" Dan cried.

"There is a large settlement of Serbs between here

and Crested Butte. This ranch was property of the brothers Tarka and Sinja. Tarka Malkovich was the only man I ever saw who could beat an Irishman to the bottom of a bottle. He and his brother were at war with everyone, and each other. They were troublemakers. It was hard for the valley to live with them. Everyone had a beef going with the Malkoviches: the doctor, the sheriff, the feed store. Tarka died of a heart attack, undoubtedly from drink. That was right before the war. Sinja ran the place into the ground in no time flat. The bank evicted him, and the ranch stood unattended for over a year. The bank made me a deal. I was to get the ranch up and running in good shape. When it was sold, the bank promised to stake me to three hundred acres, my own little ranch."

"I want to know about Justin Quinn!" Dan interrupted sharply.

"You should only see the way the water gushes down in the springtime after the winter snowmelt," Pedro said.

"I want to know about Justin Quinn!"

Pedro sighed and said a soft "*Amigo.*" "His father was Roscoe Quinn, a bad, bad *hombre.* For a time the Malkovich brothers let him sharecrop and mine a claim. Roscoe was a pig," he spat. "He beat his wife and children, and played with his daughter, you know how. Anyhow, Justin was the oldest and grew to be able to handle his father. They say their fights were vicious."

"He was a fighter, all right," Dan mumbled.

"Roscoe went into Denver to the cattle show and got piss-assed drunk and ended up raping a woman and trying to rob a bank. He's in the state penitentiary in Cañon City. Twenty years. The wife and kids went to relatives in Arizona. Justin joined the Marine Corps."

Dan's voice cracked, but he knew he had to keep talking, keep thinking. "Well, too bad he didn't get to play out his scholarship at the University . . . or . . . have all the valley girls falling all over him."

"Sergeant Dan, Justin never had a scholarship. He never completed high school. As for the girls, no one wanted to come near the Quinn family."

Dan sat by the window all night. "Fucking liar," he said under his voice.

Siobhan felt for him in bed, then propped herself up on an elbow. The betrayal had left Dan robbed of his sacred moment. Nothing had ever clutched him so, not even the word of Quinn's death. "Fucking liar."

"Why can't you feel for the pain in his life that forced him to live a lie?" she challenged.

"I do! Poor Quinn! The sonofabitch! We all lie, but nothing like this. Me? Brooklyn cop. Sure, I exaggerated about cuffing gangsters. We all lie. Impressing each other is a craft. But this was a big fucking lie!"

"Justin had a lot to lie about."

He felt her hand on his shoulder. Oh, Jaysus, that felt fine enough. He turned around and found her breasts for his head to rest on and breathed uneasily to hold back sobs.

"He lied from day one about his grand house and prize beef. About his football scholarship. Maybe he wasn't even American. He had kind of dark skin. The Corps was taking in Mexicans and Indians. We had three Navajos. But we never had no blacks in the Corps!"

"Dan, that's an ugly word, I don't like it."

"Well, you never had to walk the beat in the colored neighborhood."

"Shut up. You sound like a bigot."

Dan wept.

"I feel for your sorrow," she said. Siobhan slipped on her bathrobe and went out onto the veranda. For the first time she saw the moonlight up a string of mountaintops. Troublesome Mesa lay at the bottom of a glen in a steep, winding valley. Snow blankets and a silver sliver of a stream. What a land, indeed. She'd never known of a place like this.

"Jesus, I'm sorry," Dan said, coming from the bedroom. "I'm really sorry. That Martinez fellow has been a good, sensitive man. I guess they import a lot of these people from Mexico. It's nice to see a good one, I mean, not just another Mexican who would multiply and go on relief."

"Consuelo told me that Pedro served six years in the Navy. He is from an old Colorado family, and he was wounded at Pearl Harbor, or maybe you didn't notice that he's blind in one eye."

"I seem to have everything upside down," he said softly.

"That is because your world has been set upside down. We'll have to set it right, then."

"Can I touch you, Siobhan? The blow goes away."

She knew now how to fit into his big, strong arms. "Quinn knew that you would come here," she said.

"You really think that?"

"Yeah," she said.

"What does it mean, then?"

"Hard to say what might have gone 'round in his head. But I know he wanted you to come here."

THREE

Late 1945—Onward

The banker's chair from the turn of the century was worn through in several spots, just as the decrepit First National Bank of Troublesome Mesa had survived the land rushes, the silver crash, and ever-present drought.

Mr. Dancy, a Mormon, knew every tree in the valley and beyond. He was strikingly direct. "I was able to close on the Malkovich boys just in time. Frankly, I couldn't have sold the M/M if I threw in the Brooklyn Bridge. Anyhow, Pedro there comes home from the war, one eye and all, and marries the most beautiful girl on the western slopes. I knew his yahoo days were over, right, Pedro?"

"I don't even miss it," Pedro answered.

"Pedro talked me into letting him run the place until after the war, when I could find a buyer. We're going to stake Pedro to a couple hundred acres somewhere."

"I'll let you two gentlemen have at it," Pedro added. "I'll be down at the diner, Sergeant Dan."

There was talk between Dan and Dancy about the size of the ranch—well over two thousand acres with bits and pieces all over the mountain, and the water rights were clean. The house, worth at least eleven thousand dollars, would be part of the deal. They shillied and shallied, Dan's service and decorations making their own impact. Dancy had hoped to save the ranch for some Mormon boy returning from the war, but this had a hopping good flavor to it.

"What're the numbers?" Dan gulped.

Dancy studied the ledger. "It's a good ranch and expandable, except for where those crazy Slavs started fencing each other off and cheating with the water."

"How much?"

"Can't tell precisely. There's almost thirty thousand still on the books. I'd have to research the county records, particularly the government land abutting the south. Forty-some thousand would swing it, I'd say."

Dan's heart became a cannonball.

"You were a cop in New York?"

"In the three days I've ridden with Pedro, I find I can ride a horse without too much discomfort."

"Wounded?"

"Yes, sir. Saipan."

"How much can you put in?"

"I have over nine thousand cash and probably can raise another four or five from my family."

"But you don't know doodly egg roll about cattle."

Dan lowered his eyes and shrugged.

"I have an idea," Dancy said. "Do you like Pedro Martinez?"

"I'd have him in my platoon anyday."

"He used to be a hell-raising kid, too generous with money he didn't have, and Mexicans have no inherited family money. Fact is, Sergeant, we have already turned him down for a large loan. They are not too dependable, if you know what I mean."

"He's honest, isn't he?"

"Honest as Jesus. He was in the hospital for almost a year, mostly blindfolded with sandbags holding his head still. If you don't find God that way, He isn't there for you. Right now I pay him ten percent of the net and housing. If you were to, say, give him twenty percent, you'd have one of the best cattlemen in Colorado."

"Let me talk it over with the wife."

"Confidentially, Sergeant, you and I can make a deal, but only if you have someone to train you." Dancy leaned over close. "I'm a man of God," he said, "and God tells me the two of you together are well worth the risk."

It took time for Daniel Timothy O'Connell to transform from Brooklyn cop to rugged Coloradan. All of about a week. His attitude was a force, a force that wakened him every morning, led him to his knees to thank God for bringing them to this place.

Dan loved boots and cowboy hats and leather chaps. He loved to rope and brand and train his new border collie. He loved life during a challenging blizzard.

Dan loved the rodeos and the B.S. that went with cattle trading. He loved the respect. He was a tough man in a tough valley.

Saturday night in the old mining town, Troublesome Mesa came to life at the Bottomless Mine Saloon. For all the hurrahs, it was peaceful enough to bring the women folk. Dan taught the band a repertoire of Irish ballads to augment the sad-ass country and western songs.

"It's Irish time!" and Christ, Dan O'Connell moved you to tears with his "Danny Boy." If he only had Justin Quinn singing with him, he always thought.

As trust developed between Dan and Pedro, they made a hardworking, clever, aggressive team. Dan had been a platoon sergeant, and men learned to listen to him. He did not have to be told to listen to Pedro.

For several months the families lived together. Cautious at first, there was space enough to grow easy with each other. Siobhan in particular was ecstatic about the entirely new ways of cooking, and she adored Consuelo.

Come springtime, the top priority was to build onto the caretaker's cabin a mile toward Troublesome Creek. To add to the urgency, Consuelo was due to have a second baby.

They finished the house in a rush. In the next month or two, every man in the valley pounded nails, making a charming lodgepole log cabin. The Mexican part of the valley pitched in, as did some Mormons and Catholics and Protestants as the finish drew near. A fiesta exploded when they raised the roof! In this time and place they all seemed less threatening to each other. Dan caught the sight of some of the Mormon men nipping booze out of view of their wives. From then on Dan kept a "Mormon" bottle in his cupboard.

The Martinez family no sooner moved into their place than Consuelo went into labor and gave birth to wee Pablo. The joy of a new child was tempered by Dan and Siobhan's situation.

Once settled, every month for three years Dan waited for her to tell him the good news that she had missed her period. It never happened.

As they grew prosperous, the O'Connells became total Coloradans. Both of them flew the ranch's twin-engine Cessna, inched out their ranch boundaries, sent money home, were magnificently generous to the church, the school, and even the Mormons. Dan was elected state assemblyman. All that was missing was a baby for their waiting nest.

Joy gave way to an ever-present sense of sorrow. Their bed grew colder and colder. When he sang "Danny Boy" these days it was maudlin, and the Bottomless's owner had to caution Dan about getting mean. The day after an apologetic sheriff dumped Dan off, after putting him in the cooler for the night, Siobhan reached the breaking point.

Their bed held a half-full suitcase, the French one of the set he had bought her for Christmas.

"What the hell's going on here?"

"I'm going into Denver. I'll be at the Brown Palace."

"What for?"

"To get a complete fertility examination."

"It's about time," he said. "I pray to God they are able to find out what is wrong with you and cure it."

"I want you to come with me," she said.

"Me? You mean, me?"

"Yes, you."

"I'll have none of that voodoo black-magic quackery."

"Very well. I intend to continue on to New York. I've been missing everyone sorely. I haven't seen Father Sean in over three years."

"Is this a threat?"

"No, I want to see them. But I think it's time you face up to the fact that something serious is the matter. Are you scared to go to Denver with me? Is that why you've never suggested it before?"

Dan started for the door.

"One of these nights you are going off one of the hairpin turns, the way you're guzzling."

Dan opened the door.

"Sleep in the guest room," she commanded.

He slammed the door but remained in the room.

"Are you going to a Catholic hospital?" he asked.

"Of course."

"Then maybe, well, pack a bag for me, too."

The eminent Dr. Leary at St. Anne's Hospital put Siobhan into a regimen to chart her ovulation. It could be months before they had an accurate reading on her.

Meanwhile, Dr. Leary got access to Dan's Marine Corps medical records. He had had the usual Marine ailments, cat fever in boot camp, jaundice and malaria after Guadalcanal, dengue fever at Tarawa, and a blown hip at Saipan. Dan was shocked when Dr. Leary asked him for a specimen of his semen.

"It couldn't possibly be! I mean, I, the cause?"

"This is routine, Mr. O'Connell."

Dan grunted in displeasure but did as he was told.

A time later, he was called by Dr. Leary and asked to come to Denver alone.

"I've some difficult news," Dr. Leary said. "It's taken this long because I had to be certain."

"She can't bear children," Dan moaned.

"Your wife is healthy as a heifer."

"Then . . ."

"I want to check something here in your medical record. Camp Matthews, January of 1942," the doctor said.

"Camp Matthews was the rifle range, a long drive from the base. We stayed there several weeks on weapons training."

"Did you get sent to a quarantine tent?"

"A bunch of us got sick, and there was no regular doctor at Matthews. Yeah, I sure remember now. I had to finish boot camp with a new platoon."

"All that jibes with what we feel was an outbreak of mumps."

"My face was swollen, funny-like, and I had a lot of pain around my, you know, private parts. Yeah, it was hard to walk."

"Did anyone diagnose it as mumps?"

"We'd had all this cat fever and dysentery; we may have joked about mumps, but you know, it's a kid's disease. I thought I had already had it as a baby."

"The record here says, 'Possibly mumps.'"

"Isn't that a kid's disease?"

"It usually is, with no after effects. With an adult there can be. Your semen is sterile."

When was it ever more terrible than the day he learned he'd never sire children? No jungle, no lagoon at Tarawa with the Japs shooting at you and you in chest-high water holding your rifle over your head, not Red Beach on Saipan watching your battalion blown to shreds, not even Justin Quinn dying . . .

It would be a double slam against Siobhan, for Consuelo had had another perfect baby boy. Carlos was the beauty of the Martinez family.

God! What of poor, dear Siobhan! How crude I've been not realizing that she has suffered even greater than I.

He talked it over with a priest in Denver before returning to Troublesome Mesa.

"Forget about God for the moment," the priest said. "What did they do during your worst moments in the Corps?"

"I always told my lads, when you're scared shitless, you're in such pain that death would be a pleasure, or no matter the catastrophe, the only thing you can do is 'Be a Marine.'"

"Then be a Marine for that woman of yours."

Dan found Siobhan at the Martinez house. She was in the rocking chair, yakking with Consuelo, who was putting up a dinner for the O'Connells as well as her own family.

He looked in, but they did not see him. "Be a Marine," he told himself.

Siobhan sat in the chair Consuelo used for nursing. She had handed little Carlos to Siobhan to hold while she filled the oven. Siobhan put the child's head on her breast with a longing not to be realized. Then she saw Dan.

Dan's hand was never so firm, so filled with meaning, as it grasped her shoulder. "It will be all right, darling," he said.

FOUR

Washington, D.C., 2008

Yes, it's your president, Thornton Tomtree. A year ago I was considered unbeatable for a second term, but as George Bush and James Earl Carter learned, there is a fickle bent to our voters.

At this moment we stand a week before the 2008 election. A bizarre series of events has damaged my candidacy. Lord, is there a man more dismissed than a one-term president?

Anyone can pinpoint the time and place when the tide turned against me. It was the Six Shooter Canyon Massacre.

Immediately following the disaster, my rating bottomed out, then climbed back up as I traveled the country ceaselessly and was able to placate some of the national trauma. I was successful in divorcing myself from direct responsibility for the massacre, in the eyes of most of the people.

During those hard days, my vice president, former Texas senator Matt Hope, held in line that massive group of voters of the Christian conservatives. Taking on Hope as V.P. meant I did not have to personally deal with those pompous preacher men guarding the kingdom. Vice President Hope quickly convinced the Christian constituency they had no place else to go. Certainly, Governor Quinn Patrick O'Connell, a Catholic liberal, represented an unthinkable alternative.

It is election day minus seven. Perhaps I'm grasping, but I sense that the sudden dry-up of news out of O'Connell's headquarters means something. Although we are separated by two thousand miles, I sense a tension and quandary.

I had given O'Connell a hell of a run. Whatever hope I had was squashed at our "great debate" at the New York City Public Library. During an intermission at the end of the first hour, I was informed of treachery that would send me packing out of office.

Well, Thornton Tomtree, how did you get here? How did I get enmeshed in a tragedy that was not of my making? Why have I had to live to the great betrayal?

Even back in the 1950s, I never wanted to be much more than a junkyard dog, like my daddy, Henry Tomtree, who knew every scrap of metal, every bale of newspaper, and every dead battery and doorknob in his yard, and who could carry on business without calculator or ledger because he kept everything in his head. Henry Tomtree was the greatest junkyard dog the Northeast states ever had.

How old are your first memories? Vaguely, around kindergarten or first grade. I loved the yard so, I didn't have many friends on the outside. Suddenly, I was in big classrooms with them, boys and girls. One day I was standing before our long hall mirror in our hallway. I remember finding it hard to look at myself. I was different from the other kids. Even looking in the mirror I wanted to defend myself from outside inspections of me.

In my early grades I had a terrible time in school. Studies were fine and simple. It was lunch period, the cafeteria, and the playground where I was not spared perpetual taunting.

And as they taunted, I ran to my safe place in a corner of the junkyard. It was here that I began to build my empire. I studied my daddy's ways. I fiddled endlessly with physics problems. I became able to play both sides of a chess game in my mind.

If you can't crack a problem through logic, you make an end run. I developed an auxiliary to standard mathematics, my own methods. I slipped in and out of quantum math.

All this I had in me, but I could barely hold up my hand in class or engage in conversation or, God forbid, approach a girl. I was interesting, but nobody knew the things I was interested in.

I was storing so much data and so many formulae that I had to have a place to hold it all. So I created a fantasy place. It was called Bulldog City, although it was really a nation, in an isolated place with mountains encircling it and mountaintop guard posts and missile emplacements. I invented a super laser to knock out incoming missiles and spy planes. I could even hit a satellite when it spied on Bulldog City. Boy, nothing could get in and out, and I commanded the armed forces and quarterbacked the football team and sang concerts and all the stuff I couldn't do.

My daddy's partner was a Negro named Moses Jefferson. Moses was a spiritual gentleman who did odd jobs until he proved his true worth. Moses entered a secret bid to demolish the old Williams Hotel. His bid was lower than Henry Tomtree's.

Moses didn't have the money for a crew and equipment, but subcontracted everything and put them on a profit-sharing plan. He ended up with an enormous cache of sinks, pipes, toilets, bricks, fine old turn-of-the-century urinals, chandeliers, railings, and everything a petit grand hotel could yield.

Henry Tomtree had been skinned, but he got the message. Moses Jefferson possessed the keen mind of a junk dealer. As messy as the yard might appear, a good dealer had it organized in his head, down to a button.

Hell, better to have Moses in as a partner than as a competitor.

Sorry, that's my phone. "Yes?"

"We've hit up everybody, Mr. President, but we can't find out what the hell's going on with O'Connell."

Tomtree mumbled "Shit" under his breath. "It's two A.M. here, what's that mean in, what the hell you call it, Mountain Time?"

"I think I'd want to keep some people here to cover the monitors and phones and the rest of us pack it in," Darnell said. "The instant O'Connell calls for a news conference, we assemble top staff, watch the conference together, and immediately whack out a counterattack."

"No inkling of what the Democrats are up to?"

"None."

"Right," the President said, disappointed. "Darnell, bunk in tonight here at the White House. I, uh, need you to be close by."

FIVE

Pawtucket, Rhode Island
Late 1950s to Late 1960s

Henry Tomtree's junkyard occupied a full block in a semi-derelict industrial zone. Long past its heyday. Stacks of crushed autos and chopped-up tires mingled with the new pop harvests of soft drink and beer bottles, broken glass bins, plastic, and the junk dealer's mainstay—baled-up old newspapers and magazines.

"A cacophony of smells," Henry would note, breathing in the fumes from the fuel trucks, smoke from a nearby landfill, and oil from the grease pits. Every night the garbage truck fleet parked in a nearby lot, the sky maddened with the mean wings and frenzied yowls of seagulls.

When Henry discovered Mo's true worth, the two entered a life-long relationship which was to be carried on by their sons, Thornton Tomtree and Darnell Jefferson.

Moses and his family lived in Pawtucket, a very decent lower-middle-class city. It had a little less of everything, except for the Pawtucket Red Sox.

Henry Tomtree lived a few blocks from Mo in Providence, which was considered to be middle-middle. Providence was a good-sized little city, lovely to look at as it rippled up and down the hills to the sea. Houses seemed newly painted, and the town was filled with educational facilities and boasted a strong cultural life, so as to be a kitchen community for both New York and Boston.

Twenty miles down the bay preened Newport, which ranged from tourist all the way to upper-upper. Setting aside the beach town aspects, and other summer garnishments, Newport was a world-class port of yacht racing. Here, the main thoroughfare was named America's Cup Way after the trophy won by Yankee sailors for over a century.

Moses Jefferson's American ancestry went back further than Henry's and even further than many of the mansion owners of Newport.

Mo's family originally came from a Portuguese colony in the Cape Verde Islands off the west coast of Africa. They were never completely slaves but made their livelihood servicing the hundreds of ships plying the Atlantic routes. Mo's wife, Ruby, continued to clean houses for a few years after he began to work for

Tomtree. Oftentimes, she had to leave little Darnell with his daddy at the yard.

Thornton Tomtree was a shy lad. Hanging out at the yard was his main form of recreation. As Darnell grew to waddle around on his own, Henry was in an endless checkers war with Mo. No one knows the exact number of boards they went through until Ruby gave her husband a wooden one for his birthday.

Throughout grammar school Thornton's attraction to the yard increased. He'd pillage everything before it went to the crusher or was shipped out: instrument panels, washing machine motors, boat props, lawn mowers, and more used fan belts than GM would need in a year.

In the inner-inner area of the yard stood a warehouse where the good stuff was stored: stained-glass windows from derelict mansions, statuary, copper hardware, scrolled woods, once gleaming banister rails.

Inch by inch Thornton and his little helper, Darnell, pushed things around in this warehouse, so he was able to establish a work bench.

When Thornton was eleven and Darnell merely nine, Moses and Henry put up a basketball hoop. In the beginning the two daddies had a notion they were more skilled than their sons. The notion was quickly dispelled by Darnell, and there was a swift return to their checkers.

An unmentionable thing drew Darnell to the yard: stacks of old *Playboy* magazines. Darnell got a whooping when Ruby found one under her son's mattress, but that didn't deter him. He thought there was something strange about the magazine—strange as well as invigorating. All the women in the photographs were white women, and none of them had pubic hair. Darnell long believed that this was normal. Years later at a midnight skinny-dipping party, he realized that *all* women, black and white, had pubic hair. That was about the time the magazine took a courageous position and flat-out showed it.

Darnell Jefferson was a born point guard and remained one: quick, graceful, deceptive, and cool, momma, cool. He had a face full of sunshine and was blessed with a silk tongue.

Thornton Tomtree grew gangly like his father, with a permanent aura of nerdiness about him, although he was wiry and very strong from slinging bales of newsprint and handling scrap metal. It seemed early that shaping Thornton's personality—or lack of it—would become a lifetime mission for Darnell.

They went their separate ways to school and were pushed into different social circles, but always they rushed to return to the yard where their joint kingdom lay.

Then came the training of Thornton Tomtree, unlikely basketball player. Darnell ran hours of films, depicting how the great centers of the game operated as a hub.

Darnell snapped the ball to him a hundred times a

day until his reflexes and coordination were brought to their limits.

"Catch the ball! Pass to the open man!"

"How about me getting some shooting time?"

"You ain't no shooter, Thornton. Them that can, does. You are a trench warrior. You're a white maypole with guys hanging all over you. But you are junkyard strong. Plant your ass under the basket and disembowel anyone who tries to get *your* rebound."

Thornton Tomtree was awkward, not dumb. Once he understood the niche Darnell was creating for him, he studied the complexity and possibilities of the game and his particular value.

Darnell invited kids into the yard for pickup games which were nonstop verbal assaults on his student, to move his feet, leap, dunk.

By the end of the summer Darnell had created a player out of bits and pieces. His strength was under the basket, elbow and knee land. Only one problem. The two were going to different high schools.

Thornton changed his address from his home to the junkyard, which allowed him to transfer to Pawtucket High.

There were only two white boys trying out for the team, and they became the target of bad intent. At six foot three, Thornton was a nice-sized center for a small school. He closed his ears to the jiving. His physical strength tested and proved, Thornton became a legitimate second-string player. Darnell Jefferson's "Frankenstein."

Competence on the basketball court was a hard-earned grace. Less difficult was Thornton's quick mastery of all the school's curriculum in math and science.

Darnell drilled him in social skills, particularly girls. In time he joined Darnell in reading old *Playboys* in the yard.

"How come white women don't have pussies?" Darnell wondered.

"I never saw a pussy," Thornton said. "Do your women?"

"Oh, hell yes, but they've never had a picture of a black lady in *Playboy.*"

These sessions ended more quickly than Darnell wished. Thornton would always end with a sigh and a shake of his head and make for his workbench.

Without saying it aloud, or even knowing it, Darnell was becoming an intricate part of Thornton's ability to function in the outside world. Darnell preferred shooting baskets, *Playboy*, fishing and pussy-speak, but Thornton's enormous devotion to the workbench lured Darnell in. An electronic ding-dong of some sort was explained as a Rube Goldberg-type invention. As he learned enough just through proximity and contact, his large vocabulary became punctuated with scientific terms.

A new day of science wizardry was arriving, and

Thornton Tomtree was at home with it. Thornton's ding-dong invention was a kind of computer which he called the Bulldog. He never shared the secret of Bulldog City with Darnell, or anyone.

Thornton tweaked the curiosity of the technical colleges that loomed large in the region. He established contact with MIT and played complex physics games. Whatever the Bulldog could do, it seemed to mop up the opposition of renowned institutions.

When Thornton Tomtree graduated Pawtucket High, they named a science medal after him. But it was a bad day for the odd couple. Thornton would leave for college, and Darnell had two more years to go at Pawtucket High.

For a time it was feared he would be drafted for Vietnam, but he was given an exemption as an only son.

On a late summer's night in Newport, a thousand and one tourists strolled up the street looking at curios, and another thousand and one across the road strolled down the street looking at curios. Macho sailors, who manned the yachts of the rich, partied. Petitioners looked over Brown University, which had an open night for applicants. In the drawing rooms of the great mansions, string quartets played for charity at a thousand dollars a pop.

Thornton parked the junkyard pickup truck in Darnell's driveway and waited on the porch swing for him to come home from a date.

"Darnell."

"Yo, Thornton?"

"Yeah, how'd you make out?"

"Not too bad, I guess but those Jamaican girls have an agenda that has something to do with American passports. So, what's going on?"

"You haven't been in the shop most of the summer," Thornton said.

"All right," Darnell said, seating himself opposite on a rocker. "I mean, you're going your own way. I hear my daddy talk about all the schools after you. MIT, Harvard, Carnegie Tech. How many scholarships have you been offered? They've got you mistaken for a quarterback."

"Well, what's that got to do with our friendship?"

"Everything," Darnell said. "Man, you're in solo land. A couple of years of college and we'll need a translator to be able to speak to each other. Hey, man, you're going to take off like a rocket. You and I just ran out of time and space. I mean, we can always be friends. Good friends, but you're going north and south and I'm heading east and west."

"I've made a decision," Thornton said. "I'm not taking a scholarship. I'm not going to college. Why should I spend four years learning something I already know? My time would be better spent continuing to develop the Bulldog."

"What the fuck you talking about?"

"I'm not going to college."

"Your daddy know?"

"My daddy's smart," Thornton said. "He looked me over like he was bidding on ten tons of metal and asked me if I knew what I was doing. He trusts my judgment."

"Because Henry didn't need a college education to run a junkyard," Darnell shot back.

"He needed more. He was born with stuff you don't learn in school. Don't you get it, Darnell? You'll be at Pawtucket for two more years and I'll be at the yard."

"I'm not married to you, man."

"No, but you're the only person in the world I want helping me. The Bulldog is going to do some awesome things, once I figure it all out."

Darnell stopped the rocking chair.

"I thought you would be really happy about this," Thornton muttered.

"It seems to be about you and what you want," Darnell answered. "What about me? So, let's go a couple years down the road. I'll be heading for college. Columbia Law School. They have encouraged me to come to them first for a basketball scholarship. Like man, we're talking New York City."

"I hate stupidity," Thornton said in disgust. "I mean, I truly hate stupidity. Look at me. Four left feet. I can still catch the ball and pass the open man. How come you can't smell shit in a cow barn?"

"Columbia is no barn. Get used to it."

"So waste your life for a law degree and end up as the

house darky for one of the insurance companies. Everyone's looking for darkies, especially point guard darkies. You are the dream minority package, Darnell."

"Why are you doing this, Thornton?"

"By the time you pass the bar, the Bulldog computer will be the standard of its field. And you'll have bupkas. That's Jewish for zero."

"Let's just talk about putting leverage on each other," Darnell said. "Hey, man, you're arrogant. I've got my own life. What do you want me to be? Your little nigger boy?"

"Maybe you don't get it, Darnell. I'm going to the top. I need somebody out there in front of me to take care of things so I can stay at my workbench."

"That's arrogant."

"Is it? I live in a funny world that has me in its grip. I'm past most mathematicians in the world. It's something I didn't learn. It's just there. But when I look into a mirror, I see ugly. I see this broken clay statue with fingers missing and a shoulder missing and a leg missing. I am incomplete, and there is nothing I can do about it. You're the only real friend I have or probably will ever have. Maybe, going to the yard day after day this summer, alone, I maybe got scared without you."

Oh, Tomtree, Darnell thought. In the middle of a game he'd read Thornton's eyes on the court. The guy would be working on a physics problem. The pretty little cheerleaders in their pretty flaming red satin shorts way up on their sweet little black and white legs. Thornton's head was somewhere else while they were cheering him. He was always so far away, most folks were afraid to speak to him, to interrupt that siren song that Thornton alone heard.

It had not been all that great a summer for Darnell, bikinis notwithstanding. Too much of the uniqueness and lore of the junkyard had invaded his being over the years. He'd missed Thornton. Thought he was free of him at first, but ended up lonely for him. Why? What he wants from me, Darnell thought, was to be a junkyard dog's junkyard dog.

"So, you want me to come in with you the minute I graduate high school? I don't know business. I don't know how money works. I don't know nothing."

"Yes, you do, Darnell. You've got instincts about . . . people . . . and that's number one. Nobody in this state is smarter than you."

"It's a small state."

"Well, if we went in together, you could still go to one of the colleges around Providence."

"I'm going to Columbia."

Thornton left the porch fuming and harangued the pickup truck into starting.

Darnell turned at the slam of the screen door to see his daddy shuffle out.

"Sorry, I overheard," Mo said.

"That be okay, Daddy."

"You've got two years of high school left. That gives you all the time in the world to make up your mind."

"What are you thinking, Daddy?"

"Listen to what he is saying, real good."

"Daddy, I love you and I respect your judgment. But one thing I know better than you is Thornton Tomtree. His whole life is like a chess game where he's four moves ahead of Bobby Fisher. If I let Thornton collar me, I'll walk behind him with a broom and dust pan."

"You ready to shut up for a minute?" Mo said.

"Yes, sir."

"You're going to be real good at whatever you do, son. Let's talk a little black-ass reality. We're still pushing against the door for equality. No matter how incredible a young black man may be, the road for him is still going to be torture. You'll become the house nigra and you'll be forced, all your life, to try to act and live in a white world. No matter what profession you choose and no matter how good you are at it, you're still going to be thought of by the color of your skin."

"Maybe the blacks aren't going to take it anymore, Daddy. I'm talking about the civil rights movement."

"That's going to be a long, bloody struggle, and in the end it's still the white man who's going to be boss," Henry answered.

"Thornton Tomtree might not make all the high-and-mighty plans he has. He wants me to be his doo-doo bird. I think I'd rather struggle through and have my freedom."

"Or learn one day how you missed the boat."

"Why you so high on Thornton, Daddy?"

"Because I've never seen a genius like him. It's the

kind of genius that has to be served. If he stays out of trouble, if he learns his right foot from his left, if he learns everything you can teach him, he's going to end up one of the most powerful men in America. I've been watching you young men most of your life, Darnell. If you become indispensable to him, you're in for a real ride." Now Daddy Jefferson came down with a pointing finger. "In my opinion, you'll always have a boss. A boss that you can control is the best one to have."

For two years Darnell kept a sharp eye on Thornton Tomtree's invention. The Bulldog was doing spell-binding work. Thornton rebuffed a dozen offers to join the top national electronics companies.

He did not exactly know what he ultimately wanted from the Bulldog. More and more electronic research and product appeared around the country. Thornton concentrated on understanding an overall pulsation of the computer phenomenon.

Darnell was lured in. With the way opened for anything, he started his own collection of data to try to find an indispensable niche where the Bulldog would fit.

Columbia came courting, to no avail. Darnell was now in his corner in the junkyard. Backup point guard for the elegant Providence College team might better suit his future.

For the next couple of years he wanted to collect and analyze every bit of business information he could get his hands on. Providence would serve him well.

* * *

"Henry, don't take the boat out today. I don't like the direction of the wind. Could kick up some rogue waves."

"Moses, that hole is full of sea bass, and they're boiling with lust," Henry said, tossing his fishing gear into the rear of the pickup.

Mo grabbed his arms. "Don't go out today. It just don't feel right."

"You get the head and tail."

When the bass were running, the best fishing was at Noah's Rock with its nasty little riptide that ran between the rock and the beach, a quarter of a mile away. When the incoming tide overpowered the outgoing tide in the rip, fish came in like a blizzard.

But this day the power of the churning and surging sea proved too much for the old converted lobster boat to outrun. A rogue wave a dozen feet high bashed the rock, then sucked the water out of the inlet until one could see the bottom. Behind it came swells that literally hurled the boat into Noah's Rock, where it burst apart.

Henry Tomtree was so bashed up, he had to be buried in a closed coffin.

Thornton did not weep at the wake or funeral. He did not hear or have a remembrance of Darnell's entreaties. The numbing pain of his first great loss plunged him deeper into himself where he worked 'round the clock, hunched over his maze of wires. After a month he allowed himself a single groan of pain.

Like new, he showed up at the yard to go over the accounts with Moses.

"The books are a mess, Mo," Thornton said.

"Those ain't the books. The books are up here," Mo answered, pointing a forefinger at his forehead.

"Well, I've got to get them in some kind of order. We're in probate. I don't just inherit. I inherit what is left. Mo, I'm scared of losing the yard."

Mo rubbed Thornton's hair. "You won't lose the yard, son. Henry was very good to me. I've put away a creditable sum for just such an occasion."

A month later, a very lonely Moses Jefferson took a last look around the kingdom of tortured metal. He stood by the basketball court. "Catch the ball! Throw it to the open man!"

The light was burning in Thornton's shack. Seemed like it was always burning.

Mo felt he was waiting around these days, just waiting around. He knew he'd be going off to sleep soon.

SIX

Troublesome Mesa, 2008

Quinn, I told myself, keep it simple. Literature is not appreciated these days. Say your piece and get off the stage. What is this! Only 2:14 A.M.

What would Rita and I and the kids do after the election? If we were defeated on the campaign issues, we'd suck it up and go on with life. To have come within touching distance of the White House and have the door slammed in your face, rejected, is another matter. I could take some solace in the fact that it was Alexander Horowitz who was defeated and not Quinn O'Connell. Reality says this will go with us to our graves and largely dictate the lives of our children.

I scan the speech. Well, it needs some more touching up, but not now.

I feel a glow. Rita is near. I'd know her presence from

a half mile away. Driving up to the ranch house, I can tell by the feel of it if she is home or not.

She floated in from the bedroom without me hearing, but I knew she was there, behind me. Her fingers are at my temples. Nobody groans like I groan.

"How does it look?" she asked.

"No matter how I put it to the American people tomorrow, it doesn't sound real. Winning the Democratic nomination didn't seem real, either. But this, it's unabashed madness. Want to wake up Greer, honey? She's got to set up the press conference."

"Greer is in la-la land. I turned it over to Kohlmeyer before I hit the bed."

Quinn phoned out.

"Kohlmeyer speaking."

"Pete, it's Quinn. How are we looking for tomorrow?"

"The saints are marching into Troublesome Mesa, boss. They're buzzing around like sunset gnats hunting for a piece of dead skin. Quinn, if I can push this into the noon spot in Denver, we'll break at eleven on the coast right before their noon news and at three in the afternoon on the East Coast, giving us a flying start on the evening news."

"It will make no difference this time, Pete," Quinn said.

Peter Kohlmeyer, as everyone else on the staff, wanted to know what Quinn was up to. Pete held his tongue with a gnarl between his teeth.

"Pete, this is largely in the hands of President Tomtree. His reaction could change the entire election."

"Sonofabitch is too smart to shoot himself now," Pete said.

Give up, Quinn. Surrender to Rita. She offers everything to comfort you. Lord, I no sooner hit the pillow than I'm streaking through space. Rita knows what is lovely to me. I feel the warmth of protection, and relief in knowing I'll still have her when all of this is over.

Christ, I can't sleep, but at least the atmosphere is comfortable.

The details of my birth have eluded me all my life and never fail to grate on me.

I try to remember back, some tiny connection with my infant life, but everything I recall began in Troublesome Mesa.

Dan and Siobhan had gone through a half dozen winters of discontent when I came onto the scene.

Troublesome Mesa, 1953

Dan was a Marine, the most tender and loving of men but faced with the most sorrowful of circumtances. Siobhan, equally comfortable in jeans or behind the controls of the Cessna, found Dan's faith and understanding giving them the power of many.

In the springtime the snowpack in the high mountains melted and let go its cargo, the journey turning it into great, gushing rivers. The roar of it created quivers in the ranch house.

As water poured into the valley, it left little lakes and tiny beaches filled with hungry but wise mountain trout in the high country.

The ranchers read the winds, predicted the rains, knew the value of crop by touch.

In came the hummingbirds, skinny and exhausted from their flight north. Consuelo put up several pieces of red glass to attract them and tell them they had a free handout at the O'Connell ranch. Feeders of sugar water and red dye were set out, and by twilight hundreds of hummers had arrived. A bully, the rufous, larger than the "ruby throats," spent hours near the feeder chasing off the little ones. They went into WWII dogfights and battled to get to the food.

With little light finding its way up from town at night, the O'Connell ranch sat in darkness, allowing a star-gazing extravaganza. And one would have to wonder if the earth was truly the center of the universe.

Now came the ballet dancers: showers of yellow, red, and purple columbines, each mass filling its own hill or meadow or cliff side to radiate its vibrance and then leave, far too soon. Dan and Siobhan chose their own magic meadow and made love in the grass. And he laughed at the white-capped demigods hovering above them.

Dan did whatever a good man had to do to ease the heartache of their life. With Pedro Martinez firmly in control of the operation and Siobhan doing the books, Dan was able to win a seat as state senator.

From Pedro, Dan learned to hunt and fish and canoe, how to survive if lost in the mountains, how to mend fences, drive and buy and sell cattle, read the fast-moving weather fronts roaring down their valley.

The fine warm weather didn't last long enough, though. It didn't have to, because stands of millions of aspen trees, propagated through their roots, covered the slopes on both sides of the valley. Their translucent pale green leaves trembled at the slightest breeze. The Mexicans called them "money for the pope."

In the second or third week of September came the announcement that winter was not far behind as the leaves turned solid gold with the occasional dark green spike of a conifer piquing the stand.

Spring and autumn were muddy and sloppy from snowflakes holding too much water. Around Thanksgiving, as the real cold snapped in, the flakes became so light you could blow them off a branch with the slightest breath.

Father Sean was coming!

For three years he had been in one of those godawful places in Africa where only a Catholic missionary would go. Ravaged by ailments, he had been recalled to the States. The three years in Africa had earned him the respect due a full and sacrificing priest in the eyes of

Paul Cardinal Watts, archbishop of Brooklyn. The cardinal sequestered Sean.

The priest needed healing. A light course of duty was set up in which he could spend part of his time at nearby St. John's in study and teaching.

Cardinal Watts agreed that a month off in Colorado would put some roses back in his cheeks. Father Sean was picked up at the Denver airport and whisked to the small aircraft side of the field. He nearly fainted with fear when his sister, little Siobhan, took the controls of the Cessna. She had waited long for this golden moment and flew it high and down into Troublesome's dirt runway flawlessly.

Another surprise—an apartment, Sean's apartment, had been added to the ranch house! It had everything from his own vehicle to a futuristic sound system, to a mighty fireplace, to a veranda which afforded a grand vista.

At the fire, Father Sean's initial fire, they gathered around. Siobhan unlaced her brother's shoes and slipped his feet into a pair of woollies. He groaned with delight, and soon the smoke of his pipe danced with the smoke of the fire.

"How's it going to go?" Dan asked.

"Cardinal Watts is the kind of man you want to work hard for."

Sean sipped a rare velvety cognac, audible in his contentment, then stared from one to the other.

"Siobhan, you've been back to Brooklyn how many times?"

"Eight, ten. I don't know exactly."

"Everyone glories in the life you've made in Colorado. But that room at the end of the hall stays locked."

"You know what happened," Dan said. "For a time I traveled to God knows where to see fertility doctors. I even dropped my pants for Jewish doctors. They all said sterility from mumps is rare, and there is a chance I may become whole again."

"How long do you plan to wait?"

Dan's paws fell into his lap, and he lowered his eyes. "We may be ready to adopt," he said in a whisper.

"We looked into our Catholic agency. Somehow, it seems very risky, getting an ill child, and after months, maybe years, of waiting," Siobhan said.

Father Sean tapped out his pipe. "I did some investigating of my own," he said. "Cardinal Watts' closest aide is a Monsignor Gallico. He is the diocese fixer. When I told the cardinal of your situation, he said, 'Why don't you talk it over with the monsignor?'"

Both of them tensed noticeably.

"You don't have to do much more than meet Monsignor Gallico to realize he is a wheeler-dealer, a real Jesuit. In the past few weeks he showed me a number of infants, but I just couldn't square any of them in terms of the ranch and the mountains. Just before I was to fly out here, Gallico called me, very excited. One particular baby he had been tracking was found. The child had lived with his birth parents for its first year and was placed in a convent with special attention told to be given. I have a suspicion that the monsignor might have known about this child all along and showed me the others as a straw man. You know the church, we've got to play out our mysteries and secrets."

Siobhan roused herself more than once. Father Sean filled and lit his pipe again.

"What do you know about this child?" Dan asked tentatively.

Sean shrugged. "The church has a massive bureaucracy for handling orphans, welfare, and foster homes. I am sad to report that most of our infants up for adoption are from unwed and often underage mothers. Fathers gone. The trick is," he went on, "if you don't take a newly born, you should know as much as possible about the child's first year."

"How so?" Dan asked, puzzled.

"In the first year human-to-human touch is paramount. It is nearly always the key to future behavior. I do know that this was a wanted child and the object of great affection. He trusts the nuns, who do a great deal of fawning over him."

"Sounds to me like the monsignor might have known this child from the beginning," Dan said. "Is he the father, Sean?"

"I don't know. I am barred from asking. However, when Gallico brought this child to see me, there was no further reason to wonder why he is so special. He's handsome, he's smart, he's cuddly. The child is wonderful with the infants at the orphanage, a little gentleman. There is a glow about him I can't put into words."

Sean dug into his worn wallet, torn and with green spots from African fungus. Siobhan reminded herself to get him a new one tomorrow. Sean held the billfold up to the light and drew out a photograph.

"Oh, God, he's beautiful!" Siobhan cried. Dan knew, from her reaction, it was a done deal, beyond his input or personal reaction. He took the photograph and he, too, melted.

"I'm going to have to ask you, Father Sean, are we to know nothing about his parents?"

"Nothing."

"How was Monsignor Gallico mixed up in this?" Dan wondered aloud. "I love my church. The ranch is filled with shrines. But I don't fancy getting mixed up in secrets and deceit. Are they covering the child so because it was conceived by a priest or a nun?"

"Dan!" Siobhan snapped. "You know the rules."

"It will be pretty much the same with any child you adopt," Father Sean said.

Dan took the photograph again. He never again wanted to see the anguish on Siobhan's face when she had learned her husband was sterile.

"It may sound cruel, but the more you and a child know of its past, the more you open your doors for strangers to come and live in the house. I've been there when children meet a birth parent, and it can shatter a life. It wrecks dreams that should be left as dreams."

"And who makes that judgment?"

"Centuries of a priesthood charged with men's and women's most sacred and secret problems."

"Secrets to the grave. Lies to the grave."

"If you don't know and tell your son you don't know, you'll be telling him the truth."

"God damned, Gallico's Jesuit double-talk."

"Dan," Siobhan said, "what is tomorrow night and the nights thereafter going to be like if we turn this down?"

"I can't tell you how many times I passed the fishing hole and saw myself with my son. How many times we were at the ball games together. How many times . . . these things are always complicated, aren't they, Father?"

"Life is complicated."

"All right, Siobhan, we have a son," Dan said.

"I'm glad, and let his life begin the moment he steps foot on the ranch. I caution you that sometimes a child's drive to find his birth parents is insatiable. The only thing you can do is raise him with wisdom and love. His life can be made so full, his need to know may simply fade. Make it so he won't want any parents but you."

Dan leaned against the fireplace. The mantel, the picture gallery of all Irish homes, was empty.

"God has given us everything," Dan said. "We can't take our failings out on the child. What is his name?"

"The sisters call him Patrick."

"That's Irish enough."

"Patrick O'Connell," Siobhan said three times over.

"You know," Dan said, "in the Corps we almost entirely knew each other by our last name. Do you suppose we might call our son Quinn Patrick O'Connell?"

"That was in my line of thinking as well," his wife said.

SEVEN

Washington, D.C., 2008

It is nearly three o'clock. Nothing makes time pass more slowly than waiting for a cold pot to boil.

"Get me Whipple," I ordered over the phone.

"Whipple here, Mr. President."

"What's going on?"

"Just a few minutes ago the O'Connell people called a news conference for tomorrow at one P.M. Rocky time."

"Sounds like O'Connell is burning the midnight oil."

"Yes, sir. The press corps is heading for Troublesome Mesa en masse."

"Contact my staff advisers. We'll watch the press conference in the Situation Room. Christ, what's going on?"

"A lot of rumors. One here is interesting. A *New York Times* correspondent, June Siddell, spotted someone she knew debarking at the Denver airport. She got to the manifest and confirmed the passenger was a fairly well-known police detective by the name of Ben Horowitz. He was met by O'Connell's staff, and they headed from the airport in the direction of Troublesome Mesa. Reporters at Troublesome confirm Horowitz's arrival, where he was taken straight up to the O'Connell ranch."

"How does all this fit, Whipple?"

"Haven't got a clue, Mr. President."

"Have the FBI in New York find out who this Horowitz guy is." Before Whipple could complain about using the FBI for this, I tried moving on quickly: "Now, where is the veep?"

"Uh, sir, are you sure about the FBI?"

"We've got no goddamned time to fiddle-fart. Do it! Now, where's the vice president?"

"Dallas."

"Get him."

Senator, now Vice President, Matthew Hope was my major concession to a very vocal Southern Christian coalition. Matt Hope was one of them, body and soul. Through him I could control that bloc. During the last stage of Clinton's reign, several Christian denominations, Presbyterian, United Methodist, as well as the Catholic and Jewish clergy had come out with thorough anti-gun proposals. After Clinton left office, the gun lobby awakened and gained back most of their rights. Central to this was Matt Hope's unquestioned hold on sixteen million Southern Baptists.

"Matt Hope speaking."

"Matthew, what's the rumor mill saying down in Dallas?"

"Not much, Mr. President."

"We've got a little change of plans, Matt. Get back to Washington immediately. Be in the Situation Room by two P.M. Before we sign off, I want you to be thinking about some disturbing numbers I received from our pollsters a few hours ago. Since the big debate there has been slippage all over your territory."

The vice president cleared his throat. "Oh, just a surge. There will be a more favorable adjustment picture as the line flattens out."

"Bullshit!" I informed him. "There has been a two-point swing to O'Connell in South Carolina and Alabama. A two-and-a-half-point swing in Louisiana, Georgia, and Mississippi. That's a fucking trend, Matthew."

"Hell, the Presbyterians are *your* people, Mr. President."

"That's my point, Matthew. The Southern Baptists are your baby. There are sixteen million of them. We are losing ground in Baptist land. Maybe their women haven't submitted graciously."

Matthew Hope, my would-be deliverer, waffled and spoke Potomac gobbledy-gook. I hung up. The door to the adjoining room was open, and Darnell came in.

"I thought I heard a lark singing," he said, "so I supposed you were up."

"I sent for Matthew. If I can win without the Baptists and get that Baptist gun off my head, I'll have Matthew Hope shoveling horseshit like a vice president should."

"My hunch is that what O'Connell announces is going to be a national issue. The South may only be one player."

"You're usually right, Darnell. We'll use Matthew this final week to lock up Texas and Florida."

Darnell knew my discomfort.

"We're in very gray territory, Thornton. However, we've been in gray territory a good part of our lives. Talk about getting through by the skin of our teeth; we didn't have a slice of baloney to put in the middle of two slices of bread when we hit bottom. We were sharp, we were bold. We were unethical and bailed ourselves out by our wits. Do you miss those days, Thornton?"

"Hell, no."

"This election is not over. Something is in the air. I can almost smell O'Connell's blood from here."

I sent Darnell to get the latest updates.

No use of me trying to fall back asleep. I never had trouble sleeping before I became president. I tried to set up a physics problem in my mind, but I simply wasn't clicking in.

It is strange how Darnell sees our lives in two sweeping cycles. He's right that the early days set the tone of our toughness and resourcefulness. Can you believe that the nineteen seventies were nearly four decades ago?

Do I really miss it? Hell, no! Well, maybe.

Pawtucket, the 1970s

Thornton Tomtree clung to the square block of the junkyard by the hair of his rinny-chin-chin, so absorbed in his work he scarcely differentiated between light and darkness. He handmade a fleet of prototypes with their own bells and whistles and exotic functions.

The great electronic revolution that had growled and growled now burst through the top of the volcano.

Because Thornton did not study the wizardry of his future competitors, he was alone in a technology of one. Yet, how would the Bulldog fit into this brave new world?

Darnell, who was supposed to market it, wondered even more. To what avail was the Bulldog? Darnell did not return to Providence College in his senior year but joined Thornton in the yard. Darnell had already chucked in his entire inheritance, a hundred thousand dollars, which Thornton had no trouble eating up.

The yard had ceased to trade in junk. The bank account—nonexistent. Darnell organized a fire sale.

As the various piles of scrap and paper disappeared, they ended one life and entered into another. Neither of them had inherited Henry and Mo's love of trash.

Finally, the good stuff went. The stained glass and antique embellishments were carted off, and all that remained was a single shacklike warehouse building and Thornton's rat's nest of wires.

Darnell charted the most likely paths the new enterprises would take. Much of it was happening too fast to comprehend. The top new inventors and marketers could not give a rational answer as to where it was all heading. Some companies soared, some crashed. They bashed into one another in merciless attempts to have their product become a standard item.

Darnell and Thornton spoke throughout more than one night trying to evolve a strategy. They knew they would not take the Bulldog into the middle of a battlefield. They also knew they had to remain free of outside control.

It came down to a purpose of being. To what avail was the Bulldog? What road could they take with the Bulldog that others could not follow? What unique niche would this system fill?

Simultaneously, they had come to a dark place. The darkness held the secret. Speed is the seed of greed, Darnell had said.

As each new innovation reached the market, Thornton's "purpose for being" opened wider. He followed inroads in his mind where Darnell could not follow.

"We must keep the darkness dark," Thornton said at last. "What's happening, Darnell? Every computer is trying to outfox every other computer. High-wall technology is trying to turn back invaders. A mad hunt is on to keep security and integrity of a system. This eats up half a researcher's time. But! What are they doing but reacting to something already taking place? In my own modest way, I can break into almost any line and decode any message."

"We can't market that."

"We can build a system that's impenetrable. We can have that system in place and grab our corner of the market while the others are playing catch-up. We'll have it going in."

"What?"

"Unbreakable encrypted messages and transactions."

"You sure?"

"I am positive," Thornton said, holding up a small black box called the Growler, an accomplished high-line code and decoder. The Growler also came from a place deep inside Thornton Tomtree, his versions of math, his flirtation with quantum. His natural penchant for secrecy!

"Wouldn't we be better off just selling the Growler?"

"No way."

"But it may cost millions to set up one network for one company."

"We place our small terminals at Harvard, MIT, Cal Tech, Georgia Tech, Stamford, and with the Army, Navy, and Air Force and let those people break their balls trying to decode us. You, my dear friend, will sell the results to, say, three hundred companies in the Fortune Five Hundred. Three hundred corporations installed and paying monthly fees for absolute protection starts to add up to billions . . ."

Thornton was right, but even so, he was wrong, Darnell thought. What had he said: *keep the darkness dark.* As Darnell studied the meaning of the system, he assured himself that they would be clear of antitrust violations, unfair competition, and other government interference. After all, they were only going after a very small piece of the market.

However, Thornton would not stop with three hundred Bulldog networks once it had become the Rolls-Royce of the computer world.

Banks, insurance companies, car manufacturers, oil companies, police, airlines, mercantile chains, medical networks . . . all in secret.

A great central mainframe to be built in Pawtucket could drive thousands of networks. The senders and receivers could not operate unless both were positively identified through fingerprints, photos, and a DNA scanner.

Darnell did not go in fully convinced, but followed his own part of the work. He set up the university and military network, exciting and challenging the listeners. The military was particularly sought out, for any system installed for them would open the door to a hundred corporations. The bright people in his new thinking would exercise their minds achingly trying to break the Growler. To no avail.

Thornton growled in content as his friendly adversaries threw in the towel. The Growler flipped to one of several million code algorithms so that the sender and receiver had to be "married."

But that was out there and this was down here. In the real world they were a long way from the financing to build mainframes.

Darnell had lingering doubts. He always held out hope that a universal benefit could be found somewhere in the system. It was Darnell's upbringing, a matter of the soul to answer dirty questions. As Thornton went in, seemingly without scruples, Darnell wondered if he would be able to follow.

"What we are doing, Thornton, is tapping into man's paranoia. Half the energy in a computer is to mistrust, and the walls go higher until we come to the ultimate weapon, the Bulldog. You see, mistrust begets mistrust, and the fucking computer industry is being built on greed. So, we'd be building a buffer around the corporate elites to carry on in total secrecy. That is the dark space, and we will control the night. The government eventually will make us give up the Growler."

"Think about this, Darnell, because you plotted it. In another decade there are going to be millions of individual terminals and business networks, and a damned good part of them will be scamming the public. They are the ones the feds will go after, to clean up smut and thievery."

"They'll get around to us . . ."

"By the time the government does, much of the world's commerce and defense will run on Bulldog networks. We will be too integral a part of the world's being to fuck around with."

"Keep the darkness dark," Darnell mumbled.

"You've got it. All we do," Thornton said, "is supply the technology. It is up to our clients to supply the morality."

Refining the dream was slow going. Getting a full-sized network up and running was galactic in reach.

Ping, went the checkbook.

"I'm going to need twenty thousand dollars by the end of next week, Darnell."

"Maybe we're going to have to go to the bank or take in a partner."

Thornton pondered long enough to empower his database of broken codes.

"Thornton, I don't like you doing that!"

"Let's see, First Union of Providence. It's drug money. They launder it by transferring it to 'Reserve Building Funds,' which the bank invests partly in new construction. Bundles of cash come in. Checks are cut by the dozens."

"Man, we're dealing with some nasty dudes."

"Well, how the hell do you think we've stayed alive? Besides, we're not dealing with real bright people. Those stupid-ass bankers lend money to Mexico. Anyhow, they don't question transfers out of the Reserve Building Funds. All I do is bill them for consulting fees, pick up a check at a post office box, and deposit it. Darnell, they're sending out checks to dealers all the time under the guise of consulting fees."

"Ahem," a voice behind them announced. A proper gentleman entered the shack and handed Thornton a card which read DWIGHT GRASSLEY. It was one of those top-echelon business cards that need not carry an address, phone number, or type of business. Dwight Grassley was it.

The Grassley pedigree in Rhode Island went back over two centuries when they landed as Quakers on Block Island. The Grassley dynasty, once a towering insurance and banking power, had peaked, but mainly through too much inbreeding, it had fallen to a lesser plateau, as factory after factory shut down, plunging New England into a manufacturing and economic crisis.

Indeed, the Grassleys were a diminished power, but a power nonetheless.

The Grassley before them was short, round-faced, apple-cheeked, with the pasty smile of an unfavorite son. He would not have been heard from again, but the patriarchs and matriarchs all seemed to die about the same time, leaving him a primary heir.

Dwight got kicked up to first vice president and COO of the Grassley operating entity.

"Sorry to barge in on you without an appointment."

"Well, that doesn't seem to be a problem," Darnell noted.

"I was looking over Hell's Acres here to see what we can do with it. We own most of this land, but there's no money in parking garbage trucks."

"Hell, I didn't know they did that around here," Darnell said. Mr. Grassley was miffed over this fellow's smart-ass comments. "If we had your parcel, we would have over twenty-five contiguous acres and could certainly draw interest on the market. Otherwise, it would have to go in two pieces, which makes it a very hard sell. Now, we'd build in a handsome premium for you."

"And it just so happens that you have some parcels between Harmony and Chepachet you'll swap us for a song," Darnell said as Dwight Grassley grew aggravated.

"You selling or developing?" Thornton asked.

"All, nothing, or part and part," Dwight answered. "There are a variety of options. . . ."

"Yeah," Darnell chipped in, "a shopping mall but too close to Pawtucket, a marina hotel but too far from Newport, a senior citizens' development. Costs to build old folks' condos are too far out of line of prospective receipts."

Dwight now underwent a different reaction, one of shock. "How did you get this information?"

Thornton started to jibber-jabber, but Darnell held his hand up. "We got the data on the land sell off your computers."

Well, well, thought Dwight. Well, well, well. He cleared his throat and leaned toward Thornton, dropping his voice. "May we speak privately?" he asked.

"'Scuse me," Thornton said. "This is Darnell Jefferson, my vice president, sole employee, and nigra confidant. Sure you must keep a few nigra lawyers around so's they can translate to the nigras in the low-rent district."

"I did it," Dwight said, folding his arms on the desk and laying his head in them. "Even great men like me make mistakes," he said, trying to make light. "Now that we're past introductions, you got a cold Coke?"

"If we still have electricity," Darnell said. "What's your thinking, Mr. Grassley?"

"The land will sell for enough to clear our books."

"Let's see, you can then put a Woolworth's, Jacques Penne, Sears, Filene's Basement, and maybe a hundred-thousand-seat stadium made entirely of luxury boxes to attract an NFL franchise. Al Davis would be interested."

"Dwight—may I call you Dwight?" Darnell queried.

"Certainly. And you're Darnell and you're Thornton."

"Let's go up on the roof," Darnell said. It afforded a view of the dump site and was rather depressing. "Mr. Grassley—Dwight—you're from one of Rhode Island's great families. This state is known for beads, bracelets, and costume jewelry, probably taught to the Pilgrims by the Indians. It's no longer a growth industry or a major financial winner. This land, reclaimed, could hold a modern industrial park that could help revive the economy of Rhode Island."

"With your plant as our anchor," Dwight retorted. "Look, fellows, we've also done our research. Nobody knows what you're doing, including yourselves."

No sun would burn off the haze this morning. They returned to the office.

"Give me a figure for your land. We'll attach it to our parcels and get you, say, twenty percent of the total sale."

At that moment Darnell and Thornton looked at one another, completely locked into each other's brain. Thornton gave a tiny, tiny nod. Darnell was on. He picked up a Growler and handed it to Dwight.

"This little devil makes our Bulldog network totally secure."

Dwight burped out a laugh, excused himself, and waved them off.

"The computer environment is now being invaded by every con artist, cross-dressing sicko, porno pervert, thief, monster banks, stock manipulator, secret arms and trade dealer," Darnell said.

"And you boys must have God on your side," Dwight mocked.

"In a manner of speaking," Thornton said. "The First Union Bank of Providence, your bank, dips freely into ten numbered cocaine accounts and 'reinvests' through your building funds. Accurate records are hard to come by. You've got a sweet, clean seventeen percent skim-off."

Dwight paled. Suddenly he was looking at a pair of

young men, eager of purpose and filled with frightening information. He told himself to remain calm. After casting about for a reason, he realized there was no explanation.

"Are you going to blow the whistle on us?" Dwight asked.

"Of course not," Thornton answered. "You're just doing what any respectable bank would do. But get yourself a new security system."

"Like the Bulldog and Growler," Darnell said.

It was a fortunate day for Dwight Grassley. Thornton Tomtree and Darnell Jefferson had long envisioned the extent of their own greed. It was plenty, and it converted to the computer's mistrust of the computer, or more succinctly, man's mistrust of man.

First Union of Providence, their insurance company, and their real estate holdings used the initial Bulldog/Growler network. It was filled with bugs, but no one could tap into its secrecy circuit.

Then came the Air Force after one of its most vital and secret networks had been broken into by a hacker.

Teams of geniuses in many universities and laboratories went into exercises with the Bulldog/Growler, each coming out with incredible praise of attaining absolute secrecy.

The greening of Thornton Tomtree began when a row of bulldozers moved in to reclaim the land. The first building would house the mainframes, a pair of electronic wizards hand-created by Thornton.

Darnell made certain that every set of tests was covered by the media. With much publicity, the system sold itself and there was soon a waiting list for installations. Darnell came up with the great name and logo, T3 Industries.

In a few years T3 Industries had set up networks for over a hundred industries listed in the Fortune 500.

If demand were to be met, manufacturing capacity had to be increased by several hundred percentiles. Flushed with a generous deal with T3, Dwight Grassley knew he had a cash cow, an endless, endless, endless cash cow. He even got rid of his drug-money accounts.

As the system built, Darnell Jefferson took it upon himself to push the parameters of Thornton's personality. It was slow, mushy going. Meeting the press, using wit, building a comfort level into local business and fraternal lunches. Darnell brought in a speech coach, and Thornton responded, slowly. At first, when he went to the rostrum, there was an awkward dry-mouth trembling and jokes that lay flat. A mild beta blocker calmed his trembling. The challenge was great, and Thornton stuck it out and became reasonably proficient.

The more he spoke, the more those elusive thoughts would clear themselves in his mind and then on his lips. He began to toy with words and got a grip on what was humorous.

Thornton moved up to college commencements, guest appearances at business and professional power conventions, and learned that stumbling in mid-sentence could be endearing. A moment of trembling could make the audience tremble, his shy charm brought smiles, and that old humor, which he scarcely understood, made others howl with laughter.

Meanwhile, Darnell saw to it that Thornton's appearances were plentiful and important.

Darnell understood immediately that this was another page being opened to him in the now-and-future Thornton Tomtree Book of Revelations. Why is he trying to get people to adore him? Darnell wondered. What was his curse, his sin, his burden? He did not seem to return the warmth but always positioned himself as the wise father figure.

One night at the ultraliberal and prestigious 92nd Street Y in Manhattan, everything fell into place. About three or four minutes into his speech Thornton realized the audience was mesmerized. He crossed the enormous chasm that made an ordinary speaker into a speaker who absolutely controlled his listeners: an orator, an actor.

To step down from the lectern and shove his hands in his pockets "home style," to wipe his glasses or remark he'd lost his place, to relieve drama with a funny quip, to drop a curse word.

Well, Thornton was a sound sleeper, but he didn't sleep for three days after the 92nd Street Y speech. He was top-of-the-line, just a notch below Kissinger, as an attraction.

* * *

Expand they must. It was Darnell's baby. The Pawtucket Central station would be a state-of-the-art home of two mainframes capable of transmitting and receiving tens of thousands of messages simultaneously.

A factory would make and assemble the computer and the encryption box. No employee worked on more than a fourth of a Growler. Another building would hold the research lab and the repair and installation division.

A final building was to be a modest four-story office.

Darnell brought Thornton all the blueprints, including some T3 had never seen.

"What the hell is this?" Thornton spread the last several sheets on his workbench. "Do I read this correctly? Employees Health and Recreation Center? This your idea of a whiz-bang knee slapper?"

"The architects," Darnell answered, "and I hold no brief for architects, say that every progressive new factory has workout rooms, TV room, dance hall, and so forth and so forth."

"This dispensary here looks like the Mass General Hospital."

"Think in terms of the days we won't lose to illness."

"Bullshit! Quality restaurant, travel office, beach club, packaged tours . . . *what!* A nursery for preschool children!"

Thornton ripped the pages from their moorings, tore

them into six parts, crumpled them and put them into his wastebasket and lit a match to it.

"I take it you're not in full agreement," Darnell noted.

"This is fucking, and I mean fucking, socialism. Baby-sitters! We'll end up with a Russian labor force, complete with a portrait of Lenin in the Comrades Meeting Hall."

"You do know why I'm pushing this," Darnell said.

"No, unless it's to be your last words on earth."

"I had to fight you like hell to skim off the best personnel in the country. We have the best. But you can't pay a man a six-figure salary to work in a junkyard. We have a golden opportunity to take future labor troubles off the table. The public relations aspects are dynamic. If they ever vote a union in here, if absenteeism doesn't drop and production per worker doesn't rise, I'll kiss your ass in Macy's window at the Thanksgiving Day Parade."

"Not a single Republican CEO, which make up ninety percent of the CEOs worth their salt, will support this. You're crazy if you think you can buy employee loyalty."

They had both reached their side of the chasm. What had started out as one of their friendly debates had sunk quickly to the very reason of their being.

"Are you giving me an ultimatum, Darnell?"

"Yep."

"And spend the rest of your life blackmailing me?"

"Only when you're going to fuck up, Thornton. The investment now will be a pittance. Later? A week on the picket line will cost us quadruple. Goddammit! You're still living in the Industrial Revolution."

"What if the business world turns on me?"

"The odds are that the better business world will follow you."

The laying of the cornerstone for the employee recreation building turned into a joyous occasion and huge public relations coup.

A band, a picnic, the governor, Miss Rhode Island, *and* the Boston Pops orchestra sparked a gala. Two thousand one hundred and four steaks were devoured.

While the band played "Yankee Doodle Dandy," T3 himself broke the ground for the cornerstone.

EIGHT

Troublesome Mesa, 1953

The nun, Sister Donna, set the little boy down at the Denver airport and pointed at Dan and Siobhan across the hall. He ran to them. "Momma! Daddy!"

Siobhan hugged him first. "How on earth did he know us?" she sniffled.

"We've been showing Patrick photographs of the two of you and telling him you are his father and mother."

Quinn arrived with one small bag of clothing, a stocking doll, and eyes filled with wonderment.

During the changeover period, Siobhan was always at Sister Donna's side, and each time the baby was passed to her she squeezed and kissed him, and every time Dan held him, he looked for an O'Connell or Logan resemblance.

As it came time for Sister Donna to leave, Siobhan

inched around her with abstruse theories of the boy's origin.

"Siobhan," Sister Donna finally said, "I do not know where Quinn Patrick came from. As they say, I'm only the messenger. This child's first years are a closed book. It is the passage you and Mr. O'Connell have to pay for such a blessed child. Vows are vows, Siobhan."

"But Dan is so proud, so Irish, so generational. And Quinn Patrick. God rue the day Dan finds out the boy isn't Irish."

"All I know is that he was brought to the convent, and he made us all very happy," the nun said, staring directly at Siobhan.

Siobhan showed wisdom, Dan was ecstatic. All families have their secrets and closets and things to be whispered. Yet two ghosts—a man and a woman who had given Quinn life—were now part of their life, of the unsaid extended family.

During Quinn's growing years he was rarely away from hand in hand with his daddy. The great hand held the little one; he rode on Daddy's horse with Daddy's arms about him.

Dan was tough, ran the posse, was crowned king of the valley, and won elections, twice as a state senator. Once a Tammany Hall Democrat, he turned into a ranching Republican, detesting . . . loathing . . . hating government regulations. Troublesome Mesa was his territory, and he didn't want anything to do with those bearded hippy pot-smoking scum who called themselves environmentalists. Shit! Telling me I've got to move my stream! The day came, an environmentalist, dressed like a normal man, sat down at the table with Dan to work out a small dam that would save the beavers left in the mesa. Dan changed his mind slightly in their favor.

As for little Quinn Patrick, once his novelty had worn off and once he had shown that he had a temper and could be naughty, the calendar of parenthood caught up with them. Almost all the time and on almost every occasion, the boy made them proud.

Siobhan realized that a very clever Quinn was making better adjustments than Dan. When it came time to finesse his dad around, Quinn could side-slip and waylay an argument, or if things tightened up, he'd do something to please Dan.

Yet Quinn and Dan could be stubborn, so much so a fear crept into Siobhan when they were abrasive. As the result of Dan's frustrations, he often blamed it on the mystery of Quinn's birth.

Unraveling happened, as it does most times, by accident, a random and thoughtless remark.

"Hey, Quinn," Frank Piccola said, coming up to the school bus stop.

"Hey, Frank, going to play ball today?"

"Naw, old man's got a ton of work."

"If we ever get nine men on the field, we're going to have some kind of ball club."

"Hey, Quinn," Frank continued, "I heard my dad and mom talking in the kitchen, in Italian, like they talk when they don't want me to hear. I heard them. My dad said he remembered the day the nun brought you to the ranch."

The element of love was so deeply embedded, the secret disarrayed them but did not break them.

There would inevitably be this day of reckoning.

"Dad and I have talked about this a thousand times. When is the right time to tell you? Secrets don't stay buried. They come up at the craziest times. At a school bus stop," Siobhan said.

"Frank Piccola didn't say it to be mean," Quinn defended.

"I'm glad it is on the table, son," Dan said. "We waited too long, but long enough to know we belong to each other. You are Quinn Patrick O'Connell, named for a brave Marine, and you are our son."

"I was adopted?"

"Yes," Siobhan said, and went through the entire story, as much of it as they knew.

Quinn took their hands with utmost maturity. "I love you," he said. "We are now and forever a family. This answers so many little questions that have popped up about me that seemed to have no answers . . . but I love you . . . I love you."

Dan and Siobhan knew the pain of pain. Quinn got up to leave the room. "What about my real—I mean, my other parents?"

"We don't know!" Siobhan cried.

"In God's name. In Mary's name. We were told never to ask or we'd lose you! I swear to you, son, Mom and I don't know," Dan pleaded.

"The Church knows," Quinn said, leaving.

The waters did not separate entirely. The three of them hung on to one another. Yet two ghosts lived in the house. Who were they? They were always lurking. At times it was sharply painful. At other times it drifted easily on through.

The years were good to all of them. Long fishing trips with his son . . . trips to L.A. to see the Dodgers . . . shooting the rapids . . . firing on the range. Dan's hip kept him from running after a ball, but Quinn's accuracy didn't make it necessary very often.

Quinn's great friendship with Carlos Martinez, son of the ranch foreman, formed early. Carlos was the non-rancher of his family. He liked chess, serious reading, and fine music. He also had a macho attitude of a Latin leading man. His conquests began in his mid-teens.

Quinn's life, on the other hand, dealt with nature and cattle. Thus, each boy and, later, young man, brought gifts to the other. They reminded Dan somewhat of his own love for Justin Quinn.

The only young girl in the area was Rita Maldonado, daughter of the famed portrait artist and sculptor Reynaldo Maldonado. Reynaldo had built a magnificent A-frame home and studio on a plateau a mile down from the ranch. A widower, he had raised Rita with the help of a Mexican nanny.

Although Rita was considerably younger than Quinn and Carlos, she persisted in breaking into their two-person club. She rode with the wind, played ball, and helped build a monumental tree house. She hung out around the O'Connell kitchen. She learned chess well enough to beat both of her "brothers."

By high school, Carlos Martinez knew where he was going and how to get there. His ambition became to gain admission to a law college, pass the bar, and become a great lawyer. The posh Eastern universities were beyond his reach, but he wanted to specialize in immigration and that could not be taught better than at the University of Texas.

While Carlos had direction, Quinn sort of treaded water, mainly honing his ranching skills.

Dan O'Connell watched Quinn with intent. Dan didn't have college because of family economics.

He kept track of Quinn's growth and skill on the fields of play. Quinn would stand five feet ten inches and weigh a hundred and seventy pounds, most of it brick hard.

Troublesome Mesa High School put weak teams on the field, fortunately, to play other weak teams. Quinn was a nifty first baseman in baseball. He played ice hockey and ski raced in a rather mediocre manner.

Dan harangued him into football. Quinn played fullback on offense and linebacker on defense. He was average to everyone except Dan O'Connell.

Dan worried about the growing bookshelves in Quinn's room, some on subjects he did not comprehend. He saw it as a symbol of the boy's desire to leave home permanently. For Daniel O'Connell it would be the ultimate nightmare.

As time went by, there was less and less interaction between Dan and Quinn. It seemed that Dan had an agenda, hitherto unseen goals he was slowly uncovering.

To make matters very lonely, Carlos Martinez went off to the University of Texas in Austin, where he loaded himself up with courses.

The two boys wrote quite often at first, but as Carlos went into a new atmosphere, mail time lengthened. Carlos simply studied and let women chase him.

Their first meeting back at the ranch was tinged with sorrow, for they knew that what they had once had was faded and would not return. Carlos even looked different, what with his mustache and all.

Quinn had his little pal, Rita, who seemed very content in being nearby. Almost into her teens, her body was beginning to bloom. Still a kid, unfortunately, but Rita was going to be extremely beautiful.

Quinn found himself pondering the issues of his Catholicism. School out, Carlos gone, and even Rita away with her father in Mexico. He had time to find a boulder by a stream, throw in a line, and think. The spark of his meditation was the devoutness of his parents, which often led to dead-end attempts at explanations.

Carried to somewhat of an extreme, the ranch and formal garden carried a dozen shrines, and every bed in the house was guarded by a cross.

Quinn knew better than argue the subject with his parents.

The arrival of Father Sean came on a good wind. He was a wise observer of the family progress. A certain quality of conversation was now possible on a hundred subjects Dan and Siobhan knew nothing about.

On the porch of Father Sean's apartment, Quinn became an evening guest.

"Lonesome, Quinn?" the priest asked.

"In a manner of speaking. There's plenty to do, and I've a bushel of great friends. What I seem to be missing is someone to talk to. Carlos is staying in Austin this summer. He's maniacal to complete his courses. I had wonderful hours with Reynaldo Maldonado, but he and Rita are in Mexico till school starts."

"Your dad tells me you're a natural for a football scholarship to one of the smaller colleges."

"My dad looks at me and sees Gayle Sayers. He's never really asked, but I don't like football. Not that I mind mixing it up. I'm pretty good at ice hockey. Football doesn't excite me like, pardon the expression, baseball. But Dad seems obsessed with getting me a football scholarship."

It was not the football scholarship, it was control of his son. Father Sean knew what he had suspected, that Dan was setting the boy up as an alter ego. It wasn't working. Every time they grated on one another, Dan feared it was Quinn's desire to bolt, to search for his birth parents. His fear became unreasonable.

It worried Quinn as well. "Uncle Sean, I can't control certain insatiable desires. I can't fathom why God has taunted me with the secret of my birth. So I look deeper into my Catholicism to find comfort from my frustration. Please know that my loyalty is to Dan and Siobhan, but I have lost some trust in the Church. I'm sorry."

"Oh, I've pondered on the same thing," Sean said. "The system must be doing something right; it's the oldest and strongest non-military organization ever known to man."

"How can I find solace in so many alcoholic priests? Or a virgin birth? I almost died when I found out that Saladin, the Moslem, was the true hero of the Crusades, and the Crusaders were mindless butchers. And the Inquisition and the Holocaust. All of these were done by primarily Catholic nations."

Father Sean held his hand up. "There are many paths to God; we are only one of them. We must put on a show for the wealthy who identify with the pomp and gold and splendor. The Church's power is their power.

"The same show is performed for the hopeless. Human fodder. They use Catholicism for their own purpose, for survival. They sacrifice chickens on the cathedral steps in some cultures. Each group's needs twist Catholicism around to fill those needs.

"Evil men attend church," he went on. "Evil men pray in synagogues, and evil men perform mutilations on women to the glory of Allah. Evil men pay large sums for us to renew the leases on their consciences. Men invented the system because they needed it, and the system, faulty as it is, works."

Wise man, his uncle, Quinn thought. His wisdom made him realize how lonesome he was for the rich food of ideas and conversations.

"There is one bottom line for me," Father Sean said, "and that is the message of love from Jesus. All the rest of it, miracles and saints and whatever we've contrived or distorted, doesn't matter. Love is the bottom line. Find something in that message you can weave into your life."

Even as he spoke, Father Sean realized that Quinn would always inquire, always challenge a Church that did not promote inquiry and challenge. But no other religion would work for him, either, because he could never truly accept what was unacceptable to him.

It seemed that each turn in season, particularly coming out of winter, the divide in the father-son stream widened. At Troublesome Mesa School, with four hundred students from kindergarten through high school, Quinn was one of the campus heroes. A charming personality beamed from a charmed spirit. He was a nice person. Kids gravitated to him.

Father Sean, with great care and diplomacy, got Dan to thinking: Quinn's quest for his birth parents was a natural human drive known by every orphan. It would not endanger his relationship with Quinn.

Moreover, Quinn was an intellectual. Yet they had the Dodgers in common and Duke Snyder and Jackie Robinson and Camp and Pee Wee Reese and Gil Hodges and Preacher Roe. But the Dodgers upped and left Brooklyn.

Maybe, just maybe, Dan began to think, there could be a real mending instead of the growing aggrievement if he could think along the lines of a great scholastic university for his son.

Constraint took over. When civility has to be practiced with caution, it becomes a draining way for two people to communicate.

They ceased doing things together. Fishing or the rodeo or canoeing or riding their dirt bikes. With graduation from Troublesome Mesa School, the time had come to make a decision, perhaps the first life decision.

Carlos Martinez wanted Quinn to come to Texas, but it was a selfish request. At the speed Carlos was pushing through college, they'd be together for only a year or so.

Dan O'Connell applied to a number of universities for Quinn, some "just for the hell of it." In a moment of magnanimity, and to prove to Quinn he had his interest at heart, he sent Quinn and Siobhan back East to look over some of the great campuses. Not that anybody ever gave Dan O'Connell this kind of golden chance. I'll never, Dan thought, get him to understand that sports is where a young man sets his mark for life. But his life is his life. If he gets into a fine Eastern school, then he'll be morally indebted to return to Colorado. Dan was wrapped up in scenarios, and none of them thought through seriously.

Mother and son drove about New England, in a journey of realization. The East was not the West. In New York, during the second act of a Tennessee Williams play, all the characters on stage were crying out their misery and no one heard the other. If truth be known, Quinn wanted New York City and Fordham. But no one would hear the other's misery.

Quinn knew if he went East, he might have serious trouble returning to the ranch. It would devastate his parents. Further, no one leaves Colorado without having inflicted a wound on himself. It was Quinn's life, but he could not turn away from Dan's legacy. Wanting a brother had long come and gone in Quinn's fantasies. Quinn was it, alone.

Quinn and Siobhan made a drive from Washington state through Stanford and into Los Angeles. Quinn was awed by the greatness of America and felt his first urges of desire to do something of value for everyone.

They returned to the ranch to find Dan elated. In their absence something good had gotten to the man.

"Which school was your favorite, Siobhan?" Dan asked.

"I personally liked Berkeley."

"Commies," Dan retorted. "They eat protest flakes for breakfast. As for UCLA, it's a brothel."

The moment was at hand for Dan to pass to them a half dozen letters of acceptance, all fine schools. Dan held one out, then slapped it on the table and broke into a wide, wide grin and awaited the howls of joy which never arrived.

Siobhan could see Quinn's stare become troubled as Dan read, *"Harvard!*

". . . That's Harvard, in case you didn't know. Harvard! The first O'Connell to go to Harvard, the first to do anything but night school. Harvard. My son goes to Harvard!"

"Mom told me to apply through my school. I didn't think I had a prayer."

"Prayers have been answered. Along with my Silver Star, this is the proudest moment of my life."

"Hold up, Dan," his wife said. "You don't seem to be pleased, Quinn."

"Shouldn't I have something to say?" Quinn asked.

"Well, didn't you and your mother visit enough campuses? I mean, we're talking Harvard. The greatest university in the world. Do you know how many applicants they turn down?"

"Dad, I agreed to take a look at Harvard to confirm I'm going to make the right choice."

"What's your point, son?" Dan asked with a touch of meanness in his voice. "You could even make the baseball team."

"For God's sake, Dad, I'm a marginal athlete."

"Not in baseball. You have a real talent."

"Stop trying to make a Brooklyn Dodger out of me. Students go to Harvard for scholastics. I don't want to get involved in the rat race until I know what I want to study."

"Quinn, you're the first white man ever to turn down a Harvard education. Have you got any idea how much it costs?"

"That's enough, Dan," Siobhan said angrily. "Forget what he said, son. God has been gracious to us, and I've got plenty of money put away."

With direct insults falling now, Dan unloaded bottle into glass. Quinn made him uneasy by not backing down.

"I want to live my own life, Dad. I saw enough of the country with Mom to know how wonderful it is. I don't want to be lured, yet. I want to stay near here. Dad, you don't need a Harvard education to operate a ranch."

"So what is it, then," Dan said ominously.

"He's only a boy," Siobhan said. "How many times did you come in off of your police beat cursing your father for setting up your life?"

"I'm going to the University of Colorado," Quinn said. "No ice hockey, no football. Maybe I'll play baseball if the team is bad enough. I'm going to study a general liberal arts course and the humanities. I want to study with Reynaldo Maldonado. I hope it leads me to something I can be passionate about."

Dan arose, came to Quinn, and slapped him in the face. Siobhan was between them instantly. Quinn turned away and made for the door.

NINE

Troublesome Mesa, 1968

It was mud season. The tracks and washboard of the dirt road went from slop during the day to a thin coat of frost through the night. It was a slippery go from the ranch to the town, two miles of switchbacks and steep grades. Walking was slippery. One was off one's feet every twenty steps.

Quinn left without a jacket, a flashlight, the Jeep he never really felt was his. Go to Carlos in Texas? No. That would bring Consuelo and Pedro into a family brawl they had no part of.

Call Uncle Sean? He laughed aloud at his own misery. There were no phones for over a mile. Headlights hit him in the back. He stopped in a rut with slush running over the top of his boots.

"Quinn!" Siobhan called, stopping the Jeep. "Son,

come home! Please! Your father is beside himself with sorrow. Please! Quinn."

All he did was shake his head.

She pleaded to the mesa and the valley, for he did not hear. Her arms went about him. He pushed her away firmly. She was a mud woman, a streaked mud woman grotesquely crying with mud running down her face.

"Take the Jeep," she gasped. "There's money and credit cards in the glove compartment. Please phone me, son, please!"

She turned and staggered back toward the house. After a time, Quinn grabbed the steering wheel and, in an automatic move, slid into the driver's seat. The windshield was half ice, half water. He wiped away a spot of fog so he could see through, then put the vehicle into four-wheel low and inched down the incline.

Between his tears and the frost he could hardly see, but he knew the turns of the hill and he understood it could be his last moment on earth. His caution told him he did not want to die and gave him a tiny relief from his pain.

The Jeep skidded. He had to lay off the brakes. It stopped abruptly down in the roadside ditch, barely kissing a great old pine tree. He'd stay here. Town was still two switchbacks away. Well, what's the difference? he thought, I don't belong to anyone. I'm no one.

A flashlight beam hit his face.

"Holy Mary, is that you, Quinn?"

"Ugh."

"Are you hurt?"

"No, no, I'm okay."

"Oh, my God," she whispered when she saw the agony worn like a Pagliacci mask.

"Who are you?"

"It's Rita Maldonado."

She found a rag and wiped his face carefully and put handfuls of snow on the rising lumps and bruises.

"What the hell you doing out on a night like this?" he groaned.

"I was at the movies and, if memory serves me right, you were the one in the ditch trying to climb this tree. I'll take you to the hospital."

"No, I swear I'm okay."

"Looks like you've just seen the abominable snowman."

"Yeah, maybe I have."

"All right, then, I'll run you home," she said.

"No. I have no home."

"Oh, God," Rita mumbled. "Come on, now, I'm taking you to my house. I'll call the sheriff and tell him where your Jeep is. Come on, now." She half dragged him to her pickup and plopped him on the seat and buckled him up, then got behind the wheel.

"What are you doing driving? You're only thirteen years old," Quinn growled.

"I'm going on fourteen and I'm very mature for my

age. Besides, I baby-sit the sheriff's kids. He just doesn't want me to drive during the daytime."

Rita was right about one thing, she was mature.

They sputtered on the slick track up to the next shelf and turned into a one-lane road affording another fabulous view down to Troublesome Mesa. The Maldonado spread was highlighted by a few acres of level lawn filled with wild sculptures and a flying-wing house.

Reynaldo Maldonado, only a seven-year resident, had brought a measure of fame to Troublesome by selecting it for his studio and home.

He had done it all, from picking cotton in Texas to doing prison time in Cañon City. He did it by being a roustabout, by smuggling on the border, by boiling booze, by selling peyote.

His early primitive drawings were of the usual Mexican rage against exploitation, and he worked to become one of the nation's foremost portrait artists and sculptors. Although he was always thought of as being Mexican, he was actually third-generation American. His only marriage was to a fair, blond Minnesota girl who died of breast cancer and left him with a six-year-old daughter.

Her death settled his wild ways, and for the sake of Rita he found Troublesome Mesa.

Maldonado's home had become a sort of sanctuary for the high school children of the area. He spun rapturous tales, he sang and played the guitar, he had lots of nudes on his walls and pedestals. For years Maldonado was an in-and-out figure at the University of Colorado, where he taught to small groups, at random, about an array of worldly subjects. He was a Colorado "treasure."

Rita helped Quinn up the back porch steps. Mal flicked on a light for them. "What you got there, Rita?"

"Quinn O'Connell."

"Quinn, you look like a yard of dirt road."

"I'm all right. I mean, I'm not hurt. I mean, I'm hurt but I'm not hurt . . . nothing's broken or anything."

Rita unlaced his shoes, gave him a big robe from the hot tub, and ordered him to take a shower. Each time the icy fingers brought him closer to awareness, the whap from Dan hit him again. All right, he told himself, pull it together.

"I'd better call your home," Mal said a few minutes later.

"No."

"What do you mean, no?"

After a time he said, "We had some words."

"I'm calling him. If Rita was out in this weather, I'd want a phone call no matter what had transpired."

Everyone knew, Quinn thought, that Mal was an artist with an eccentric leaning. He heard Mal's muffled voice from the next room.

"You'll stay with us tonight. Eaten?"

"I wouldn't mind something warm."

As the soup brought chilled nerves and circulation back to Quinn, he came out of his half-frozen trance.

"Did you know I was adopted?" Quinn asked.

"I didn't know," Rita said.

"Nor I. You didn't just find out tonight?" Mal asked.

"No, I was about ten."

"We've only been in Troublesome seven years. Quinn, if I had known something like that, I personally would have confronted your parents. Your mom was in it, too."

"Nobody knows anything about my birth parents. The Church is all mixed up in it: secrets, lies, God's will."

"Well, that's Church business. A priest once brought me back from hell. Win some, lose some. You're too beat to talk. Stretch out. I'll sit with you and maybe sing a little song or two."

Quinn's head fell on Mal's chest, and he sobbed softly and allowed himself to be walked to a guest room, wishing at this moment for his dad.

He was damned near asleep by the time Rita turned down the lights, lit a candle and a night-light in the bathroom. Mal sang about a poor little dying dove. As he drifted, Quinn thought, where do the Mexicans get their magnificent voices?

Mal set his guitar aside and looked at Rita with a bit of apprehension. She adored Quinn, always had. At thirteen and counting, those galloping ovarian changes inside her—no way. Quinn would never take advantage of his lovesick puppy, despite her attributes.

Last summer Rita had tried to have Mal do a nude

study of her. What the hell, they skinny-dipped with those who would and took hot tubs in the altogether. But as she posed, Mal couldn't even look at his daughter. Both artist and model began laughing until they were hysterical. He burned the beginnings of the sketch and told her to come back after she'd had a couple of kids.

"I'll be turning in," Mal said.

Rita fished for some kind of permission.

"Why don't you sit with him for a while? Make sure he's out for the night. Something terrible must have happened."

"Thanks, Papa," she said.

Oh, Quinn . . . flower of my heart . . . why is it you have never noticed me? Don't leave our valley, Quinn. If you do, I'll die . . . You're going to belong to me someday, and I'll take care of you. Nothing will ever hurt you again . . .

TEN

University of Colorado, Boulder

The result of maternal rage happened fast. When Siobhan left to take her mother and sister to Europe, Dan got the message.

He prayed. He offered penance. He paid. He confessed. He felt like the dumbest cop in the universe.

He spoke by phone endlessly to Father Sean.

"Now, Dan, God's finances are in relatively good order. You have got to make the gesture to Quinn."

"I was thinking of sending him a Mustang—"

"Send yourself instead."

Dan had felt badly for some things he had done as a cop and a Marine. Bullying from behind his stripes. In the past, a slap on the back and the problem was over.

But now? It sat like an undigested cabbage under his heart, day and night.

Siobhan brought her son a used Jeep and set up a moderate but ample bank account for Quinn to rent his own apartment. Enfolded by a peaceful campus unlike Kent State, he danced through two years of humanities courses, still wondering, as one is apt to do at that age, where the road was taking him.

The sting of the fight with his father faded somewhat, until the day that Dan entered a Boulder bar where Quinn worked one day a week covering for a pal.

Dan strode to the end of the bar, took a stool, and shoved the cowboy Stetson back on his forehead. "I'd like to talk to my son. If there was a million ways to say I'm sorry, I'm saying them now."

"Coors?" Quinn asked.

"Lite."

"You, Lite?" Quinn said.

"Fucking doctors."

As Quinn wiped the bar, Dan's hand shot out and covered Quinn's. Quinn looked into a face that was beyond pleading.

"I'll be off my shift in an hour," Quinn said. "Why don't we try the steak house?"

By the end of the evening, Quinn had forgiven him and Dan's face instantly gained color. "Thank God, we're not like an ordinary Irish family to carry something like this to the grave. You set up okay?" Dan asked.

"Yeah, I went for a two-bedroom apartment. Professor Maldonado comes down every two weeks to teach an arts ethics course. He camps out at my place, pays part of the rent."

"Professor? What do you mean, professor?"

"Well, Dad, go into a gallery, any gallery, and tell them you want a Reynaldo Maldonado."

"I'll be damned. I thought he was just painting naked women down there."

"He does those, too."

"I'll be go to hell. Are you after coming home, Quinn? It's been a long time, over two years."

"I want to," Quinn said with a shaky voice. "I uh, have lots of friends here, sometimes a new girlfriend."

"I see what you mean. Christ, kids are advanced these days. I mean, shacking up isn't any more sinful than drinking a beer. That's part of my problem, son. It's hard for me to equate my, you know, squeaky-clean life with all this stuff going around. I mean loose women, the kind you don't marry."

"We'll cross that bridge when we get to it, Dad."

It worked somewhat. Quinn didn't come too often and brought home a girlfriend even less frequently. Quinn and the girl of the moment usually jeeped up to Dan's Shanty, a lonely cottage on the ranch at the tip-top of Ivory Pass by some hot springs. On those weekends anyone standing close to Dan could see him look up the hill to Dan's Shanty and hear him emit a gurgle of displeasure.

However, when they all sat down for dinner, Quinn's

girlfriends were pleasures. Imagine, this one studying law and that one studying engineering. Brave new world, they call it. Father Sean says even Catholic kids shack up.

Well then, maybe Quinn will find a *good* girl, one interested in her personal dignity. Holy Mother!

Quinn fungoed fly balls to the outfielders. A potbellied Coach Hoy stood with hands on hips, bellowing to his fielders to peg the ball home.

When Quinn changed buckets of balls, he realized he was putting on a tad of a show for the same girl who had been watching practice for three days now.

She wasn't all that much to look at. She was thin but moved in a manner that said that being lean didn't cost her too much. She moved it all in concert when she walked. That was good stuff. Cute, about a seven on the female scale. Date? Maybe.

Coach Hoy called an end to the outfielders' drill, and as they jogged toward the dugout and locker room, Hoy whistled and waved for the girl to come over.

"Quinn, I want you to meet this young lady, here."

"I'm Greer Little."

"Greer writes for the *Bison Weekly* and is doing an in-depth piece on someone from each of the teams. You're the baseball interview." His bow legs disappeared into the dugout.

"All yours," Quinn said.

They took a front row seat in the stands, and she took down the vitals. Junior year, rancher's son, general humanities courses, some politics, some lit. He seems a little light on drugs, sex and rock 'n' roll. Close personal friend with the illustrious Professor Maldonado.

Vibes! Quinn thought. I'm getting vibes.

The first thing Quinn noticed was a very light olive skin that seemed too smooth to be skin. She let her clothing work for her, enfolding her little highlights with a drifty material that picked up her salient points. Knockout jewelry, not expensive but explosive. Her body language was speaking but not tauntingly. Aware but not aware.

"I'm going to need at least another two or three sessions," she said.

"Anything for my country."

"Men's locker rooms smell," she said. "My apartment has two other girls in it who are messier than boys. Library?"

"How about a working dinner?"

"Yes," she said, "and yes again. The damned football players think you can suck on a beer all night."

"Let's go off campus," Quinn said. "There's a restaurant a little ways up the valley."

With a nearby motel handy, Greer thought.

Greer ate more than her size would indicate. And afterward. Three milk shakes. "Let's see, Daddy's a state senator. Mind if I say, off the record, he's a terrible reactionary?"

"He'd be the first to agree with you. He still undresses with his clothing on."

"Tell me about the orphan business?"

Quinn's eyes instantly became moist, and he shook his head. "Pass."

She simply stared as he worked his way through his discomfort. "Greer, I don't think your readers need an Oliver Twist chapter."

"All right, then, let's go off the record," she answered.

"Why are you doing this?"

"For Christ's sake, Quinn. I like you. I like you a lot. Coach Hoy gave me the pick of the litter. I saw your tush doing all those little first baseman ballet steps and the long stretches. Then you examine the ball and whip it to the third baseman in the same motion. The first baseman's moves are unique."

"I leap, too, for overthrown balls. You want me to leap for you?"

"Depends on where you land."

"The only thing is," Quinn said, "I'm a nonentity until I know who my parents are. Was I born in a lady's room? Have I got a sister in Dallas? The people who adopted me were sworn by some kind of Catholic voodoo to silence, and they have suffered from it as much as I have. My dad told me last weekend that a lot of the anger against me was not that I wasn't his son, but that I could do most things better than he could. Dad's your basic Brooklyn cop. He's tough and knows the territory. So, this little squirt here is found under a rock, shoots better, rides better, reads books he's never heard of, repairs cars, and loves the Mexicans in the valley whom Dan is never quite comfortable with."

Greer flipped her notepad closed. Quinn looked so smooth and easy on the ball field she'd thought she'd gotten a pudding. Six hours into a relationship and it was void of vulgarity and snappy rejoinders about feminists and bras.

She slurped the bottom of the milk shake as though it was a dying man's last supper.

"One more?"

"Pass."

"How do you stay so slim?"

"Sex," she answered.

"Here, you've got a mustache," he said, dabbing her lip with a napkin.

"I want to thank you for the dinner, but I have bad news. You hit two-seventy last year because you're loaded with bad habits. I could get you up to three hundred."

"Excuse me?"

"My pop played double-A ball for Des Moines, and being the son he didn't have, I have intimate knowledge on everything, including jock straps."

"You wacko?"

"Yep, but I can raise your batting average. You've got me, afraid to say, 'in more ways than one.'"

"Explain."

"You're either a batsman or a gorilla. Nine out of ten college players are gorillas. Quinn, no offense to your macho, but I could throw you sliders and split-finger fastballs all day, and you wouldn't hit one past the pitcher's mound."

"You're serious, aren't you?"

"Tomorrow's Sunday. See you after noon mass?"

"I don't go to mass."

"Neither do I. I think I'm like a Lutheran or something Scandinavian."

They loaded up the ball machine and took a dozen bats from the racks. Greer stood at the pitcher's mound, set the machine on medium speed, and the iron arm began hurling missiles.

Quinn was a right-handed batter who got a piece of most balls and cracked a few that sounded like a hallelujah chorus. After thirty or forty swings she stopped the machine and came to the plate.

"Ski?" she asked.

"Half-ass racer."

"Golf?"

"Few times."

"How about tennis?"

"I love it, but I'm a real hacker, a lefty."

"All right," she said. "We've just thrown a club to a cave man, and he's going after a lion. Most of his moves are natural. Put a bat in your hand, and most of your moves are what you feel comfortable with. There is one basic movement in tennis, skiing, and baseball. Drive your hip."

She swung in slow motion, the forward step natural, and that set off the sequence. The hip turn and change of weight must be fluid and part of the whole swing, or everything goes out of synch.

She drilled him as though he had never held a bat. What was astonishing was her reasoning.

"You bat right-handed but play tennis left. Now, I want a back-handed swing, hold the bat with your left hand only. Don't let your backswing fall too low. Now loft the ball like a backswing, loft it this way, loft it that way."

Quinn found himself seeing more of the ball than he ever had. His swing had been jerking his eyes and thrusting his bat out a millisecond too late. She came to him and backed up into him. "Here is the part of the movie where the instructor gets fresh," she said. "Arms around me, get against me as close as you can. Now, let's go through some swings."

"I can't," Quinn said.

"Why?"

"You've given me a hard-on."

"Well, I do declare, Mr. Quinn Patrick O'Connell."

They teetered thusly for a moment, and Greer stepped away. "I know I'll forget this. Don't line your fingers up on the bat. I want you to move the knuckles of your left hand about an eighth of a turn. All kinds of control falls into place." She went back to the ball machine.

Sonofabitch! Whack! Whack! Whack!

"Go down with it! Lay off it! Step in the bucket and pull!"

She smiled, and her eyes were big brown muffins.

"Oh, that last batch of swings felt sweet. How many little boys have you lured to the ball field?"

"Dozens. I had to learn to play ball or starve. My daddy's Little League team, the John Deere Tractors, won one state and two local championships."

Quinn debated with himself as he came to the verge of doing something really stupid.

"You still need fixing," she said.

"I was afraid you were going to discharge me. Greer, you scare the hell out of me."

"And you make me hot," she said.

"Nobody from Grand Junction gets hot."

Quinn's apartment was a very desirable two-bedroom flat, but it didn't brag. It was startlingly tidy, jammed with books and filled with touches.

"That's Mal's bedroom at the end of the hall."

"Hmmm."

"His daughter comes in often. When she does, she sleeps on the air mattress in the living room." Nice. It was covered with an embroidered *bushkashee* spread, and every place was inundated with fuzzy and leather pillows.

"You could use a few mirrors. We can't have an alcove without mirrors. Hark, what's this? *Madame Butterfly, La Bohème*?" she said, thumbing through his LPs.

"My buddy, Carlos Martinez, taught me this."

"Mozart, Glenn Miller, Satch. Neat, but no Beatles?"

"The beginning of the end of music in this century."

"I hate to say it, but I agree. Between the frantic tribal ritual and the pot and an obvious lunatic shrieking at you; hey man, maybe you and I are not tribal. Had many girls here?"

"I've got them marked off and graded on a calendar somewhere. I'll see if I can find it."

"I want something serious to drink," she said.

"I keep a few bottles for the priests." He opened the cabinet. Ah, here was something to shiver her timbers. Lemon Hart, a Polish paint remover sold as liquor. *Plunk, plunk* and some grenadine so she wouldn't have heart failure. Greer, cowboy style, said, "Here's lookin' at you, pardner."

Her eyes widened as she tore to the sink and filled herself with water.

"You son of a bitch!"

"Sorry, ma'am," he said, taking a nip of the Lemon Hart and purring, "Ahhh, smooth!"

She threw her arms about him. "Oh, boy, you're fun. You should have seen that hairy Iranian left tackle I had to do a bio on."

"Best seat is on the mattress," Quinn said. "It's also the safest. I don't make passes. I just put on my Sunday best manners and wait to be invited."

Greer flopped on her back and stretched in every direction as he fixed her a sweet, humane gin and tonic. "I feel wonderful. You got a rich daddy?"

"So-so."

Quinn fixed some of the little pillows around his back to full comfort. Greer sat up, tried her new drink, then tucked her knees under her chin and wrapped her arms about them.

"So, where do you go from here?" she asked.

"Into my senior year. I'm a Maldonado junkie for sure. Aside from his class he does a semi-private ethics course with four students. He has a great way of explaining the human condition in relationship to civilization and Eros. And you?"

"Me?"

"Uh-huh."

"Just a skinny ole gal from Junction on a pit stop en route to New York. I'm going to the top in the media. I'm going to be a boss, a giant. I was born with all kinds of wigglies driving this little engine. Maybe Professor Maldonado can explain them to me next semester."

"You try to shock people with your jock talk. What are you covering up?"

"Ninety-eight pounds and a lot of other wigglies, horny ones. Next year is my dirty year. I've read every book and seen every porno flick I can get my hands on.

Let me say, I do not exactly come chaste. Unfortunately, there have always been cowboys practicing roping and branding. Anyhow, there was enough of an appetizer in it to tell me good things are ahead."

"Well, lucky guy."

"Could be you," she said.

"Include me out," Quinn replied.

"Uh-uh. Every day a new day and a new way. We'll buy out all the candles in Boulder, incense, mirror the nooks, clothing fit for a whore, tattoos. I'm having a one-year blowout before I go conquer New York."

"You're really a friggin' nutcase," Quinn said.

She flung her arms about him. "I know! And I know something else. You've got a thing for that Maldonado chick."

"Come on, stupid. She's only sixteen years old."

"But oh, my. You ought to see her watching a ball game."

"Don't call me, I'll call you."

The "I'll call you" macho talk didn't last long. Quinn was annoyed that Greer didn't show up for practices and a game where he hit three doubles, one to each field.

He caught a glimpse of her in the deli in the company of a tank-topped beanpole crowned with a bush of hair that could give shade to a regiment. He was the star of the basketball team. It occurred to him that an animal like Greer was the ultimate colorblind woman; in fact, she might just pursue her curiosity. Quinn always ended his sermons to himself with, she ain't nothing but misery.

The ball club played a respectable .500 season. Quinn O'Connell became a .294 spray hitter, moved from eighth to second in the lineup.

As a matter of fact, the professional A-team out of Bakersfield tried to woo him for the summer. Coach Hoy held his breath and put on his hound dog look.

"Hey, don't worry," Quinn told him. "I owe my dad a big summer's work, and I want to get reacquainted with the ranch."

"You coming back for a senior year?"

"Funny. Professor Maldonado lives down the road from me, but I've got to come to Boulder to hear his lectures. I kind of think I'll be back."

"The skinny broad?" Coach Hoy grunted.

It hit! Quinn shrugged. "Her game is just a game. Big mouth trying to cover little boobs."

"They called it cock teasing when I was a young man," Hoy said.

The conversation ended with Quinn holding a pair of trembling hands down by his sides.

He saw her alone again cuddled in a chair in the reading room of the Norlin Library.

"Howdy, pardner."

"Oh, hi there. Sit down, it's public."

"I was hoping you'd see what your student did in the last three games."

"I saw you. You hit nine-for-fifteen against the best pitchers Missouri and Kansas had. God, if Colorado had one more pitcher."

"Why haven't I seen you, Greer?"

"Same reason I haven't seen you. I felt so good and open with you, I guess I went over the edge. I painted you a picture of a tawdry whore, and actually, all I want to be next year is a tawdry whore. I thought it could be kind of crazy with us but . . ."

"What?"

"What! Hey, Quinn, you got it all going for you with that handsome, steady, skilled silence and you ain't Elmer Fudd, not with the titles on your bookshelf. You've got a few dozen girlie tricks up your sleeve, but you're just not as loud about it as I am."

"Movies, Friday night?"

"Why don't we pass?" she said.

"Are you ashamed of yourself or something like that?" he asked.

"Feel silly."

"Christ, woman, I envy you from head to toe. The way life bursts out of you and puts bright colors on everything around you," Quinn said.

"You stealing that from some poet?" she replied.

"Movies, then?"

"No."

Quinn gnashed his teeth to head off in some different direction. He was trying to decide which. A frustrated fist on the table brought "shhh" and "ahem" from around the library. His squealing chair brought the required raised eyebrows from the librarian.

"Look," Quinn said, speaking softly and smiling to those seated nearby. "See, I know how to talk barely above a whisper. Let's go outside."

She pouted a moment. He loved to see her pout. "Okay," she said.

They found a place on the library steps. From there the campus was guarded by a picket of mountaintops on the other side of the Great Divide. Many were old white-headed boys gushing their winter snow, soon to fill the downslopes with great mountain daisies.

"Is it me?" Quinn asked. "Is it me—Quinn O'Connell's personality or belching habits or nose picking that puts you off? Just say, 'I don't like you, Quinn,' and I'll split."

"No, it's me," she said. "I threw you all that raw meat, and you've called my bluff."

"Hey, Greer, baby . . ."

"Quinn, I'm not in my right mind about you, and I know what I know and what I know is that once I put my hands on you, we're going to go for the championship."

"We can start slowly," he said. "Lots of weekends to know each other up at the ranch."

"Dammit! I don't want to go to the ranch with you. I don't want to fall helplessly in love with you. Nothing is going to keep me from going to New York."

"Well, can't I visit?"

"Quinn baby, I've got a ten-week internship with a producer-director at Crowder Media in New York. If you're there, it won't be fair to me."

Quinn digested it grudgingly. Her whole life had been geared to this opportunity. As a couple in Manhattan they could barely learn the bridges and tunnels in ten weeks. She was on a sacred mission. Quinn? Going nowhere, doing nothing. Since the trip East with his mother, Quinn had a mountain of second thoughts about that human blizzard called Manhattan, but he could see Greer relishing it, all right. Not himself.

"You plan to come back to Colorado?" he asked.

"Scenario one, yes. Scenario two, no. Maybe I'll forget you, maybe I won't. Maybe New York is going to grab me."

"You're gone," he whispered.

"Quinn, maybe you don't know how desperately I'm holding myself together at this moment. I want you, man, but I can't stay home the rest of my life and bake cookies." She thought. She had been thinking of it. The time had come.

"I'll make you a deal. I swear I'll come back from New York and take my next year in Colorado and live with you. Then we go our separate ways."

"Why come back?" he asked, a bit acidly.

"Twenty years from now I don't want to curse myself for passing this over."

"Sounds a little Faustian to me. How free can we be knowing there is a time clock ticking away?"

"If it's not for you, Quinn, I don't come back. I'd go to NYU. God knows, a TV station might want me—no, wait, don't butt in. Even if I get the scholarships and even if I see myself advancing, I'll come back because I'll know I can make it there. I'm not afraid of swapping my place in line for a year with you."

He pulled her up to standing, and they walked tightly together. She cuddled so close he felt better than at any moment he could remember. "How about us making love tonight?"

"Oh, God!" she cried. "Don't dangle wisps of paradise over me, driving me back to Colorado before my time."

"You're right," he said. "I was trying not to be fair. Baby, when I think of you, I just forget to remember what I was supposed to be thinking of. It's more powerful than anything I've known," he said.

"Me, too."

"I'll be at the airport to meet you on Labor Day."

It was the summer of great hurting and healing. Dan tried to hold his feelings of fear and urgency and to take their lives back ten years when peace and love prevailed.

Quinn realized how much it ran against Dan's

Marine Corps grain to take this path of compassion and was glad for it. They had a fine time together, the best, a retreat to Langara Lodge up on the Canadian-Alaskan border, where the salmon were an honest yard long.

Quinn read a lot and hung out with Maldonado, always coming out brighter than when he went in. Mal didn't preach, he just spoke and a twisted U-turn in one's brain suddenly straightened out.

Rita whipped through her seventeenth birthday looking twenty and feeling ridiculous with some of the pimple-faced young men she was dating. Quinn was a man! A man in his twenties! Her spirits dropped when she considered her chances.

In the first two weeks of vacation, the phone lines burned up between the Village in New York and Troublesome Mesa. These times were difficult for Quinn because Greer was hiding the thrill of her New York experience. He slowly brought himself around to the realization she might not come back, even for their fantasy year.

Dan and Siobhan met Greer by telephone. Dan felt it was rather serious because Quinn was spending the summer very much alone except his visits to Maldonado and a long week when Carlos came home.

Was Dan more desperate to know more about Greer—or more desperate not to rock the boat?

"She Catholic?"

"Nope. Why?"

"Well, you know it's better if everyone's the same religion."

"Why?"

"You know, kids and all."

"Dad, we're not that serious about each other."

"Sure, good," Dan would say, relieved.

"Greer a good cook?"

"Pizza Hut's finest."

"She a Nixon person?"

"She's a Kennedy liberal."

"They say most of the girls at Colorado are on the wild side."

"You mean, like Mom?"

The feeling was forlorn as August ended and Labor Day led to the new semester.

Greer had not returned as promised, and he could feel the apprehension in her voice. Phone calls had slowed to a trickle. Greer told him she'd be working on late shifts or have to cover something out of town or would be a second teamer on a big event in Manhattan.

No calls for ten days. Quinn didn't complain as he braced for the fall.

"Son," Dan said with great empathy, "why don't you bring one of your girlfriends up to the ranch and head up to the cabin for the weekend? You've been getting calls from everyone else all summer."

"Except from Greer."

"You haven't smiled much this summer, either."

"Appreciate your sympathy, Dad, but let's call it for what it is. You'd be just as happy if she stays in New York."

"Yes and no. I don't like to see you this unhappy. I'm your father, and I'm entitled to an opinion. Greer Little will never give you what you need. The pain of losing her will diminish. It simply wasn't meant to be."

"Never truer words spoken," Quinn said with a saddened voice.

Siobhan's foot kicked the screen door open, and she set a pair of grocery bags on the counter.

"Any more groceries?"

"Yes."

As he went out the back door, the phone rang and Siobhan took it. When Quinn returned, she handed him the phone, appearing somewhat dumbstruck. Dan had his face halfway down his coffee cup. Siobhan smiled very weakly as she left the room with Dan.

"Quinn," he said.

"I'm on the way back to Colorado," Greer said at the other end. "Baby, I haven't been laid all summer. Can't fight you, man."

Quinn's sigh was complete with vocals.

"Here's the skinny. I'm flying to Junction to see my family. I'll be at your apartment sometime Sunday."

"Me, too. We've got a round-up in the high country

and a branding, but I'll be in Sunday as well. Baby, is this for real?"

"Changed your mind?"

"No way."

Greer arrived first, bursting with Manhattan stories she wanted to share but afraid they'd bother as much as please Quinn. Like the madness in the increasingly strong gay community and women's lib, she had said she had not had sex, which was virtually true, but the dancing until four, the party refreshments and the speeded-up scene . . . the vastness of the New York Public Library, the height of the Empire State, the whiz of graffitied subways. One night dancing, one night maudlin. She didn't let on about the staggering pain of his loss.

Whatever! Greer Little did not go unnoticed anywhere!

Quick, she said to herself at Quinn's apartment, before he arrives from Troublesome. She opened the first of two suitcases. Out came a trapeze to hook over the beams above the mattress in the nook. A whip, but mercifully covered in velvet, handcuffs, and . . . candles: big candles, little candles, smelly candles, floating candles, Christian candles, Jewish candles. There were enough undergarments to outfit a small chorus line—or a chorus line of small women. The balance of the suitcase held a variety of adult toys.

The second case held the artist's paraphernalia. Greer undressed and stood before the bathroom mirror. First on went an orange-colored wig; then she painted her face down the middle, violet on the left side and orange on the right. She encircled her breasts with a swath of green on the right breast and red on the left.

"Bottoms, bottoms," she said to herself. White thigh boots. Now, let's see, here we go. Across her midsection she painted the words and spread sparkles on it, reading: PRAISE THE LORD.

Greer heard a car parking outside. Holy moly—not a second to spare. She caught her breath and stood a few feet back, so he would have to get full sight of her.

A knock on the door. "Use your keys, I've got my hands full," she called.

The key was tight from its summer's rest. Finally, the door popped open.

"Fuck me, man!" Greer cried, holding arms and legs spread-eagled.

A number of beats of silence were required for everyone to get rearranged. Siobhan held a pair of shopping bags.

"Excuse me," Siobhan said, "I was looking for the brothel. I'll try down the hall."

"Mrs. O'Connell?"

"Yes, lovely meeting you in person at last."

"Oh, *God*!"

Siobhan set the bags down and went to the kitchen cabinet. "I think I need a drink," she said, and belted down some Lemon Hart before Greer could stop her, staggered to the kitchen table as Greer pumped several glasses of water into her.

Suddenly, they looked at one another and burst out laughing and replayed the grand entrance and went hysterical.

"Thank God Dan wasn't here!" Siobhan screamed.

"Or Maldonado!"

"Or Maldonado's daughter!"

"Or Father Sean!"

"Or the dean of admissions!"

"You weren't exactly expecting this, were you, ma'am?"

Greer was up front with Siobhan. She and Quinn were classical sad ships passing in the night.

"Fifteen weeks is a long time, Greer. Life isn't going to stop, a million things can happen."

"You want me to go back to New York?"

"You're going back," Siobhan said. "I just don't know how it would work if Quinn followed you there. When we traveled together looking for colleges, New York lit him up for the moment, but he's not a lit-up man. I'm glad he knows there is a New York. I'm glad we are able to keep him studying. He's not heading for oblivion, and he's not a loser. But unlike you, he does not know what he needs."

"He knows. He desperately wants to find his roots.

No one other than Quinn can control that hunger. Listen to me, Siobhan, maybe I'm the only one who has understood his intensity. He wants peace, which I could never give him. He wants, how do I say it, the man wants to make things better for every living thing."

"Will you stay for a year?" Siobhan asked.

"A year is a long time. I'm a pretty crazy number to nail down."

Having gathered the bazooka, washboard, bones, Jew's harp, kazoo, and four horn brass band, Quinn burst in with them playing, "Don't Roll Them Bloodshot Eyes at Me."

ELEVEN

Boulder, 1971

Greer Little was a lover whose mind never strayed far from the scene. All the power pieces concealed in Quinn responded fivefold. Their open boldness of speaking out and then usually acting it out was astonishing.

It got so that the mere touching of one another while walking past each other could set off a conflagration. As apprehensions faded to trust, a cool sweetness settled over them. Time, thank God, stood still. The inevitable parting at the end of a year seemed far away, way down the runway.

When out of kissing distance, they rushed back together. And the humor was salty, raunchy, and very high. Neither of them were out to make the dean's list but read voraciously when too exhausted to make love. They learned what their schools could give them, mostly learned on the queen-size mattress in the nook, where she went to read, with the kitchen chair for himself.

Once a week was party time. The place overflowed with happy, frustrated, angry, bewildered, and scared campus kids. Drugs were minimal, not so sex. It was the kind of campus where Nixon's visit to China might get as much discussion as a new psychedelic drug. Oh, if they only had something going like Quinn and Greer.

Little bits at a time, Greer felt all right about giving him little pieces of New York. She did not want him to think she was heading back to some kind of subway or Central Park murder. She understood that Quinn was only partly interested in their trips on the wild side, and this gave her a sense of peace that the city was just not his thing. She'd often think, "We met in the wrong century, darling, but praise the Lord, we stopped and went a little way, hand in hand."

During the past summer, Greer had cruised the scum holes of Eighth Avenue, purchasing books and magazines and checking out the porn films. The New York Public Library offered another trove. Crossing out and combining, she came up with a list of a hundred and six ways for them to make love.

"Done that, done that," Quinn said, reading the list. "So, what's new?"

"Us. Keep reading."

"*What!* You found this in the New York Library?"

"In the same section with *Mary Poppins.*"

"You didn't get this at the library. You have a fertile and diseased mind."

"That's beautiful, Quinn. You make a girl cry."

Sometimes they smoked a joint, mostly at parties. Quinn felt he was in control, and she went wild with lust. The best times were three in the morning, waking up drowsy, downing a big glass of o.j. and having a few tokes on the bongo.

Quinn set the drug limit. After seeing two men on the team smash up on LSD and coke, he drew a line. She broke the rule once with cocaine, and he moved out for two weeks until she swore, and kept her promise of, no more coke. "Coke is the devil, baby. The devil is at his smartest when you don't believe there's a devil. Chrissake, when you were cruising Eighth Avenue, didn't you see what it did? How about coke at work?"

"Yeah, some girls and fellows at the studio really busted themselves up. Thank God, I've got you."

The honey kisses—passing a syrupy ice cube into each other's mouth and letting it melt and run down their necks and licking it off. Daring, risking, they opened each other up entirely.

The touch, the touch, the touch. That's all it took as a forerunner to a full night's journey or a quick leap off the pier. They read each other perfectly.

After a few visits to the ranch Dan softened considerably. Siobhan's usual loveliness was always tempered by the hidden fear that Greer might not return to New

York. These two kids were filling up huge storage tanks for a lifetime, for a hundred and twenty years.

The first chill was at Christmas, which they had to awkwardly split between Grand Junction and the ranch. However, it was a good thing they went outside and got some fresh air. Quinn liked her father, a double-A shortstop . . .

"Dad could have made it to the show, but he could never hit a motherfucking slow curve inside," Greer explained.

"That was the first thing you taught me," Quinn said.

"Too bad she was born of the opposite sex. But you know, she sure can manage a team. Little Leaguers. One kid was pushing her button the year they won the state. She soaped out his mouth in front of the rest of them and made him apologize . . . well, in my estimate Jimmy Foxx was the greatest power hitter of them all because he was right-handed."

Joyful and Triumphant.

After a gallop through the low meadow Quinn had to carry her into the house and set her in a tub. Roping was out of the question.

O Come Ye, O Come Ye.

New Year's Eve, 1971

New Year's. All the apartments opened their doors. Sad revelers and happy revelers wondered what it meant.

Nuclear devastation was all the talk. A downer ran through the land.

But most of those on downers had each other. The New Year's kiss was always a kiss of hello. In that instant Greer and Quinn knew it was a kiss of good-bye; the awful countdown had begun.

At a late-winter indoor baseball practice, Quinn was whacking the ball as though he had Superman's eyes. He had crossed a magic line where his psyche could slow the ball down.

She watched him now as though she had turned a page forever and it didn't read like the old madcap joy of the other page. Although they still had months left on their odyssey, a residue of discontent had begun in the pit of her stomach.

Quinn was, as usual, hunched over the kitchen table, far away, into Joseph Campbell, when she came home rather draggy. She mussed his hair and turned on the teakettle.

"How was your day, honey?" Quinn asked.

"Oh, fine except for one little thing," she said, sitting opposite him.

"You're pregnant," Quinn said.

"How did you know?"

"I can count to twenty-nine."

She shook her head. His hand pulled her over to his lap. He rubbed her stomach. "Not too much room in there."

"You don't seem too upset, Quinn."

"The way we've been going at it, we don't keep throwing a dare at God. Anyhow, I thought about it early on. Last few days, I've thought about it much. We've gotten down a lot of road. Let's talk, Quinn-and-Greer talk."

"Oh, Jesus, you're wonderful," she said, resting her head on his shoulder and allowing herself to sob.

"I love you, Greer. We decide, I'll abide."

"My own Reverend Jackson. It's not that big a deal these days. They're happening every day on campus. When I found out, I was just going to have it fixed, have an abortion and string you along. I, uh, even made an appointment. I couldn't do it. I love you, man. We won't marry and I'll go on to New York with the baby."

"That's got a bad downside, baby. My daughter, my son, I want to raise it. Single parent in Manhattan for a twenty-two-year-old woman? Not when you are set to launch a dynamic career."

"Adoption?" she whispered.

"No!" he cried. "No! Greer, have the child. I'll raise it in Colorado, and in time it'll meet its mother."

"You're ready to take on something like this?"

"Very much so."

Greer wept. "You're too good for me. I'm a selfish

bitch." She grabbed his hands and pleaded. "You know I can't start out in New York with an infant."

"We've blown out the lights, Greer. In five thousand years no couple has enthralled each other more. We're way ahead, baby and all."

"Suppose we marry other people?"

"He'll have a mother and a father, and it will be up to you what kind of relationship you want to make. At least he'll always know where he came from—or she . . . the thought of a baby girl . . . really makes me smile."

After his nap, Father Sean came down from his apartment to a room seemingly sticky with wet tar. Siobhan, Dan, and Quinn were wearing their Eugene O'Neill faces.

"Am I family or am I the priest?" Sean asked.

"I've written and talked to you about Greer Little," Quinn began. "Unfortunately, I didn't take your advice. You're right, Uncle Sean, the piper must be paid. Greer is not your ordinary *hausfrau*, no offense, Mom. She's one of the most brilliant communications students this university has ever put out. She's also a wild woman. She's graduating and has three or four jobs waiting for her in New York. We thought we'd like to do one year in paradise before we got on with the nuts and bolts of our lives."

"And she's pregnant," Father Sean said, "but wants to continue on in New York?"

"That's right."

"They weren't normal!" Dan cried.

"That's what they wanted," Sean said, "not to be normal. Were you quite wild?"

"Yes, sir," Quinn replied.

"Were other people involved?" Sean asked.

"No, just the two of us."

"Drugs?"

"One or two joints a week. Nothing else."

"I felt," Siobhan said, "Greer was not right for Quinn from the beginning. I also knew if he went to New York after her or if we disapproved, we'd lose him."

"She can't cook," Dan said, "she can't sew, she can't ride, she's not a Catholic."

"Shut up, Dan. You love this girl?" Sean asked.

"Yes. We . . . we . . . we . . . won't marry. That would be a farce."

"What do you want to do, Quinn?"

"I want her to stay here, carry the baby to term, and have the child. I want to take care of it for the rest of my life."

"Slut!" Dan bellowed. "Dirty, skinny, rotten slut."

"Dan, stop it!" Siobhan cried.

"Dad, never say that again! Dad, don't *ever* say that!"

"Are we so damned certain it's Quinn's child?"

"That's enough, Dan!" Sean commanded. "My Roman collar is off! No and no! You can't bring a child here into this hatred. Yes, Quinn could leave and this time for good. You are a very decent man, Quinn, but you are innocent of what is required to raise such a child whose mother is alive and in all likelihood might never contact him. Haven't you had enough of that, Quinn, than to pass down your own misery?"

"You're not suggesting an abortion," Siobhan wept.

"Yes, I am," Sean said, "and God help me."

"The only way," Dan mumbled, "is to have her get her abortion and I'll give her ten thousand dollars."

"You've just told me everything I want to know, Dad. Greer doesn't want the baby here, same way you didn't want me here! Too bad my parents let me be born. Go on, man, throw the fetus in a garbage can."

"Dan, I'm on my hands and knees," Siobhan cried, "and it will be Quinn's son."

"I'm out of here," Quinn said softly. "Pack my things."

"Oh, go ahead! Getting to be a routine," Dan said. "Every time you've looked at me since you were ten, Quinn, you've blamed me. You've looked at me in that way that said, you're not my father. What about *my* feelings! I took it all, but this is it. You and that tramp!"

Siobhan was speechless, clinging to Quinn.

"And you, Father Sean, advising me to kill my baby. Have it in a public toilet and throw it in a Dumpster," Quinn cried.

"Yes, I did," Sean said meekly.

"Before you go crawling back to that little whore, take this with you. Greer's a whore just like your birth mother. Your mother was a nun and a whore!"

"Is that true?"

"No," Sean said.

"My church . . . my church telling me to spend my entire life with a lie. My priest, my uncle saying murder it."

Quinn walked out without looking back.

A sense of urgency, a need for clear thinking, enveloped Quinn as he sped back to Boulder. The idea of fatherhood swelled up in him like Billy Bigelow in *Carousel*: my little boy . . . my little girl. . . . This kid will know love. This precious little life will not be wasted by human haggling over commas and semicolons. "No nightmares for you, honey."

He arrived at the apartment knowing what he must do. Whatever, however, she would carry the baby to term. Whatever, however! The door was unlocked. He flung it open.

"Greer!"

He saw her cap and sunglasses on the table. "Where the hell are you?" He flung open closet doors, tried the bathroom. Empty. A faint sniffle caught his ear. She was curled up against the wall beneath a long worktable.

"Baby, come out of there, come on."

She crawled out, fell into him, and became hysterical.

"I had it taken care of!" she screamed.

All one could hear was painful breathing and a sudden return to calm. "The minute I had it done, I realized what I'd done. I love you, man. I can't leave you! To hell with New York, Quinn. I'll stay. Marry me and we'll make another baby!"

He provided comfort and shelter and soft, sad smiles. Their time had passed. And every night as he held her he felt her pain growing smaller and smaller and then the urge to be Greer again, fly away Greer, took over.

And she left.

TWELVE

Troublesome Mesa, 1973

It had been a long time since Carlos Martinez had come home. On the last occasion, they'd had his graduation from the University of Texas and he took night school in law. He had been taken by a prestigious law firm in Houston which handled masses of Mexican business.

Although very much of a junior partner, Carlos quickly established he would earn his salt. He spent much of his time in legal work below the border and often in many places in South America and the Caribbean.

Carlos wore the best. In a short time he knew he would be driving the best, sailing the best, and perhaps even flying the best. He was clever and brilliant and forceful, a rare combination for one so young.

Coming back to the ranch was a mixed blessing. His father and mother, Pedro and Consuelo, had reduced their workloads and enjoyed the comforts of coming age.

Juan, the youngest of his brothers, was the rancher. Under the watch and direction of his father, Juan evolved to take over as foreman.

The Martinez family was a twenty-five-percent partner in the ranch, so the generations were doing their proper thing. At least one son in the Martinez family would remain.

The O'Connells? Quinn was gone, out of contact with everyone except Reynaldo Maldonado and his daughter, Rita. A permanent pall of dusk had fallen over Dan and Siobhan.

Fiesta!

The entire valley, including Mormons, came for the spice and feast. Carlos devoured the female attention as well as the awe of the ranchers' boys. "See who I am!" his manner said. "I will drive a Corvette next year! You didn't think Carlos would be so great, did you?"

The valley girls seemed rather heavy and frumpy to him. Their best clothing was drab. Ranch girls were for ranch boys, who were not so particular.

It was all a great victory for Carlos, the return of the triumphant son!

And then he saw Rita Maldonado and her father wending their way through the crowd to him.

"Jesus," he whispered to himself.

How old would she be now? Seventeen. Reynaldo had never painted or sculpted a woman as beautiful as his daughter. She was Aphrodite with dark hair and just enough of her mother's Nordic genes to refine her features.

"Carlos," she cried, throwing her arms about him. "You've grown up."

That included an observation of her bosom and everything else. They remained standing and looking at one another until people around them became uncomfortable.

They rode their horses on the familiar trails they had ridden as children and young people. Only now Quinn was missing. Quinn's absence hovered over the homecoming and dampened their joy.

They dipped their feet in an icy stream near big boulders a thousand feet above the ranch.

"It's not the same without Quinn here, is it?" she said.

Carlos shook his head. "I saw him a few times when I was in San Diego on business. He didn't talk much about why he left Troublesome."

"I don't know, either," Rita said. "He had this girl, her name was Greer, whom he loved very much. When she went away to New York on an internship, he moaned on Mal's shoulder almost every night. Then she came back, and after a year they broke up and Quinn left. Neither his mother nor father will speak about him. I know he doesn't write to them. Some kind of Catholic thing, I think."

"It's not the same," Carlos repeated. "See, even though I was the older, it was Quinn who protected me in the school yard and taught me so much."

"And you taught him, too, Carlos. Anyhow, we exchange letters every month. I would write him more often, but I don't want him to owe me letters. You know what I mean."

"Funny, he's always been a sort of hero to me," Carlos said. "I think I've come to learn his lessons by practicing law now. So much of law is rotten and lies and cheating. I realized, only recently, that Quinn was never that way. If he promised you something, it was done."

Carlos stared at Rita, hard, found a large sitting rock, and put on his boots. He was numb from the sight of her. When she had stepped into the water, she had held up her wide, twirling skirt and showed her magnificent legs, and her scooped blouse showed her magnificent bosom. Rita came to him pensively.

"I suppose we've both lost him," Carlos said.

"What do you mean, Carlos?"

"I remember the day you and Mal moved into your house. The day after that you were in love with Quinn. What were you? Six or seven?"

"Did I show it that much?"

"I saw it. The three of us were together a lot."

"Well, Quinn Patrick O'Connell has never had eyes

for me. I am still his baby sister. I cried alone a lot when he fell in love with that Greer woman. And when they broke up, I can't say that I was unhappy. I sent him photographs to indicate I wasn't a little girl anymore, but he didn't seem to notice. I suppose he must have a hundred women in San Diego."

Carlos said nothing, which said everything.

"I was a fool, Carlos. No more. I want to get into things."

"What things?"

She put her arms around his neck and drew her lips to his and pressed her body against his as a punctuation mark. Carlos held her at arm's length in amazement. She kissed him again, but he spun away.

"Is this your way of getting even with him?" Carlos asked.

"I don't know," she answered.

"What do you know?" Carlos asked.

"I know that for the last three years you have had a yearning for me. And I sent you photographs because I wanted you to yearn for me. When I knew you were coming to Troublesome, I also knew that the time had come for me to enter the society of womanhood. I know," she went on haltingly, "how gentle you are and that I trust you and I want you to be gentle with me."

They flung themselves at each other and held on and rocked . . .

"So unfair to Quinn," Carlos cried.

"No! He made his choice. It is not unfair to Quinn. You can't feel guilty for a man who has spurned you as a woman. Guilty of what? Discovering my lover was you all this time?"

Their bursting forth let loose torrents of restraint, a restraint of younger years. Rita and Carlos were as wild as the giant boulders and icy stream and needled ground. During the week of his stay, they went off each day, mesmerized.

When the end of the stay was at hand, both of them were sad. "How hard is it for you to get to Denver?" Carlos asked.

"I can, on weekends."

"What about Mal?"

"I'll tell him I have a boyfriend in Denver."

"That part of it is true, but what about the other?"

"Quinn is gone from my life," she said. "So, why do we have to lie?"

"I don't know what I don't know," Carlos said, "only that you and I as lovers would further poison the well with the O'Connells and my parents. Rita, I have never known days like these. I love you. I want you to be mine always."

"But?" she asked.

"I am only starting my career. I am not so far along that I can take a wife. I travel endlessly. We have an office in Denver I can work out of once or twice a month."

Reluctantly, Rita had to come around to his way of thinking. "Papa's heart would be broken if I did not finish my schooling," she said at last.

"We'll see each other in Denver," he asked pleadingly, "until the way becomes clear for us?"

"Something is going to happen, Carlos, something bad."

"Don't be superstitious," he said.

Carlos Martinez would be a fine choice, she thought. I'm glad he was the first man. Yes, a fine choice, if she could not have Quinn.

THIRTEEN

Pawtucket, Rhode Island—Late 1970s

The personal greening of Thornton Tomtree began with spring's warm breezes hushing up the immaculate lawn of Dwight Grassley's yachting club, a somewhat tattered royalty that once had defended the America's Cup. With T3's name gaining coin about the country, Dwight sponsored Tomtree into the elite world of Newport.

Scion of the old Grassley family, Dwight had the duty of seeing that his female siblings made suitable marriages. He had three sisters: one barely coherent, in a Tribeca loft, one who did everything right, and one who was a problem. Penny, the barefoot, skinny-dipping *contessa,* was not a bad artist, but she loved the many men who passed her way. Three of them had left her bearing three quite different children. It bothered

Dwight that she was the happiest of them all, give or take a suicidal incident or two.

Nini, on the other hand, did everything right. A Newport Yacht Club wedding to be forgotten as soon as the ice sculpture melted. The couple were both homely but produced beautiful children.

Pucky was the problem. She was a long streaker, a tall, thin girl of five foot eleven. She had a pleasant face, though her teeth were a mite large. Pucky knew from her first boarding school what her route would be in the airless, closed Newport society. She'd leave the race car drivers to Penny.

Looking closely at Pucky, one would see a personality bubbling like a newly opened bottle of Perrier. Her body was thin but made the right slow turns at the right places, giving her a tall flow which she knew how to use.

What seemed to be a shallow inlet was very deep, filled with disarming knowledge of a wide range of subjects. Somewhere along the line Pucky became very comfortable with herself, and she stopped the bull-moose monetary charges of a number of the yacht club's finest who tried to court or seduce her.

Thornton Tomtree's appearance immediately drew her interest. He seemed even taller than he was because of his growing stature in the national community.

T3, as he came to be known, didn't like the yacht club scene, but neither did she. Those qualities, deep down, unspoken, got to her. She saw him as a great big Newfoundland puppy, not quite coordinated, but a lonely man needing a compassionate woman, wife, lover.

Pucky, whose short list usually ran to actors, writers, and artists in Providence, suddenly found herself taken by an industrialist!

She was far from invisible. She sailed splendidly, was a charming hostess, a charity workaholic, and mainly—a force in the cultural life of the state, including the great jazz festival.

Providence had become a strong satellite community for the artists who couldn't quite cut it in New York. Pucky's long suit was her quiet but very serious help for the creative. "'Tis told" she was very romantic.

When all was said and done, Pucky wanted Thornton Tomtree's magnificent mind, or enough of it to take her to places where she might get a chance look into his ethereal world.

Penny set Thornton up by sending him to the family's beach cabana to get Pucky a towel, and he entered to find her naked. Totally unexpected, she appeared as a tall, beautifully proportioned Greek statue, particularly her breasts, from which he could not remove his eyes.

T3 Industries netted a billion dollars the day they were married. He purchased Nanatuck Island, built a twenty-thousand-square-foot home among the climbing rocks and flat level plateaus, and he helicoptered to and from Pawtucket.

The early years were palatable enough. Pucky gave birth to the required son and daughter a few years later.

His premarital introversion which she had found so charming did not hold up. The bloom fell off the rose. *Clunk.*

The ensuing twenty years was a catalogue of Thornton's indifference to her and the good things she did.

Pucky Tomtree never did travel very far into her husband's mind. He had a built-in walled city of a brain, connected mostly to speak the new language of the computer.

The fork in their road ran in opposite directions, and that was the way they evolved, away from one another. He showed up at a few baroque string quartets played at the Newport mansions for high-scaled charity events. Pucky was more at home with the jazz trumpets at the people's festival.

Their children, CiCi and Thomas Carmichael Tomtree, grew up flatly within the required Grassley-Newport framework. They were flat in ambition, flat in achievement, great sailors and peacefully took their places in line on the inheritance ladder and went on to live flat wealthy lives with flat wealthy mates. But before taking that flat voyage as permanence in life, both drifted into the flower-child, hippie scene and had to be retrieved from Haight-Asbury on two occasions.

Pucky simply had too much vitality. Unable to plumb her husband's mind or excite him physically, she endured for a time as indentured chattel. For Thornton, sleep meant working out a problem in his dreams. Lovemaking meant working out a manufacturing glitch.

New York? Theater? A waste of time. Those puffy-cheeked clarinetists blowing out "Saints"? Good Lord, Pucky, what next? Conversation? To what avail if not to advance your business?

After two decades and out from under child rearing, Pucky threw in the towel. Her confidant was—who else but Darnell Jefferson?

"T3 is more a piece of technology than a human being," she had told Darnell over and over again.

Even knowing the two were too far separated ever to have a fruitful and peaceful relationship, Darnell sideslipped the discussion until he saw a woman coming on fifty nearly totally melancholy.

"You knew what you were getting into, Pucky."

"I knew and I never complained."

"You went into the marriage with Thornton thinking you could change him, fuck him into compliance. Too many wives fling open the refrigerator on their wedding night and say, you don't need those hot dogs, but you should have more yogurt. Nobody in the world can change Thornton Tomtree. He's an original."

"You can," she challenged.

"Pucky, I can't produce his testosterone for him."

So, on she went with her good works in the arts, traveling to and from Washington on national committees, patronizing the theater in her region, supporting young artists. It was all very Grassley. And Pucky was to be congratulated for stabilizing her son and daughter so ultimately they were neither hippies nor druggies.

* * *

The master bedroom at Nanatuck faced the sea, complete with a hot tub and a play area. Thornton slept in the dark-dark because too much light hurt his eyes.

About five in the morning, most mornings, Pucky was awakened by the sound of Thornton in his bathroom, urinating and brushing his teeth. She quickly went to her own bathroom, and he knew exactly how long it took her to prepare and get back under the covers.

A very low-key ritual dance began with a peck of a kiss followed by certain wigglings and allah-kazam, they were in the missionary posture. Give or take, the entire drill lasted around fifteen minutes. It was impossible for Pucky to confront him with his sexual inadequacy. He simply didn't get it, require it, or see that there should be more to it.

The woman kept it to herself, had herself tied off after the daughter was born, and lived with a low tide of sadness always near.

Darnell always had business in New York and Washington, where T3 maintained offices. It was a wild time of happenings from the *Challenger* explosion to the Chernobyl disaster to the fall of the Berlin Wall. He and his present wife often accompanied Pucky to Broadway theater, Lincoln Center, or the wild bright spots in the Village.

At the end of the night she often did not go back to

the T3 apartment on Park Avenue but drifted down to the Village alone to her sister Penny's loft. Darnell did not know that anything was amiss but suspected it.

He did not want such a tight relationship with Thornton's wife. It put him on the middle of a fault.

A time back, Darnell had convinced Thornton that he should establish a charitable foundation. The monster bill was tens of millions; its guiding philosophy was a support system for engineering, medical, and scientific research.

"Over my dead body," warned Thornton when Darnell proposed a five-million-dollar research grant for AIDS. T3 was alive and well when the gift was made. It grabbed national attention, and suddenly over a hundred gay employees of T3 Industries came out of the closet.

Darnell worked the boss like he was playing a fine violin, so Thornton got credit for putting Pucky on the foundation board. It was a brilliant move, one that put a light into her eyes again.

Dr. Hans Neucamp, president of the Tomtree Foundation, was tired and sported squinting red eyes. "Grant number one hundred twenty-two," he said, "thirty thousand dollars to Utah State for finishing ponds for the rest of the freshwater fish experiments."

No objections.

"And one more. The Peterson brothers in Toledo.

Their battery will drive a Jeep three hundred miles without a charge. They're onto the right system for a breakthrough," Dr. Neucamp said.

Thornton nodded his head.

"Well, that's it," Neucamp said.

"If I hear no objections, I propose we vote to pass the grants unanimously."

"I object," Pucky said. *Emerge from your long darkness now,* Darnell had pleaded with her. She caught a glimpse of Darnell on the right side of T3.

Come on, baby, Darnell thought, kick ass.

"Mrs. Tomtree?" Dr. Neucamp asked with a crooked smile and a voice that leapt just a few notes higher.

"What the hell is this all about?" Thornton snapped, looking at his watch. He leaned closer to Darnell, and Darnell nodded. "This being the case, we've had a very long day. Why don't we adjourn till tomorrow? I'll see what's on Mrs. T's mind, and it will only take a few minutes to wrap it up. See you here at ten."

Dr. Neucamp wanted to hear what transpired, badly, but Darnell took his elbow and guided him through the leather door. The other board members, a cross section of intimidated silence, slunk out.

Darnell phoned the press office and told them to hold up the fund announcements.

"My goodness," Pucky said, "'I object' were the first two words I've spoken in ten board meetings. I object, I object, I object."

Darnell started to leave.

"Come back here. You're not leaving me alone with this crazy woman."

"MIT, Cal Tech, Carnegie-Mellon, are going to be drenched in joy tomorrow," she said.

"I know what my bride is up to," Thornton said.

"When I came on the board, you agreed that a portion, not specified, would go to the arts. A portion of zero is zero."

"Correct! Nothing of nothing is nothing. And nothing is where the arts are going in the next century. Playwrights have abandoned the stage, and novels will become relics. They prefer to spread crap thinner and thinner on a hundred and fifty TV channels."

"Hold on, Thornton," Pucky commanded. "We woke up from a war singing, 'Oh, What a Beautiful Morning.' It was the nation's song of hope. Brilliant and talented people carried this through the middle of the century with golden plays, golden novels, and golden theater. They were as good as any in American history. Richard Rogers, Tennessee Williams, John Steinbeck . . . Lord!"

"The people have made their choice, Pucky. I'm only following their orders," Thornton answered.

"Their orders! To conceal corporate greed?"

"Oh, Jesus, Pucky. People have gladly traded their freedom for a web site. Everything, everything is going to be packaged and merchandized so they won't ever have to get up off the couch again. You've heard the rappers . . .

Oh, woe is me,
Cop on the beat, mean mother,
I'm in pain without gain,
So, listen up, brother,
And listen up, dykes
I'll slash you for yo
Nikes!

"You want me to support this noise?" he continued. "You want me to support so-called artists floating livers in bottles of urine and calling it art? Where are the men and women who write for the stage? A single American play a year might get through to Broadway. Not a single goddamned play in twenty-five years. *Jesus Christ, Superstar* . . . that's a musical?

"Listen up, Pucky, they are going to do up Broadway soon. Down with the hookers! Down with the pimps! Down with dealers! Down with the storefronts going out of business every week! Down with all the freaks! We are going to have us a sanitized, packaged, merchandized Broadway. When they run the faggots out of Forty-second Street, we're gonna have Walt Disney's itchy-clean Broadway . . . a place where a man can take his wife and kids into itchy-clean T-shirt shops."

For the first time Darnell had heard his boss passionate about something other than his computers. Thornton knew he was on the leading edge of a revolution for the minds of the people, one where instant gratification and not knowledge dug from deep places was going to be the rule. Thornton was dedicated to some kind of sterilization of society.

"I heard a golden-voiced man sing at Juilliard last night," Pucky said as if in a trance. "He's no chance without a scholarship because the tuition doesn't cover a crippled wife and two children, and unless we provide it, we may have lost a new Pavarotti."

"We've already got one. Who needs another one?"

"Thornton. Musicians and writers and most artists are the least greedy people in the world. Because they cannot function without support, what do we do? Every culture since man began has supported its creative heritage."

"Can't you see, woman, we've been shedding this past year by year. It's a new scheme of things. So what is it, Pucky? Have we abandoned the writers or have the writers abandoned us? Revivals are going clear back to the *Student Prince*—à la mode. Or would you prefer a British tête-à-tête? The writers are all making more money filling up time desperately on a hundred and fifty channels. Money is good! Writers never had money. So, my dear, give unto Disney what is Disney's and sweep Times Square clean and have little fairy princesses passing out gumdrops on Forty-second Street."

Pucky was ashen. He had too much truth in his words, but damned if she would stand by quietly watching during a cultural collapse.

Now Darnell Jefferson jumped in. "Wait! Wait!" he

cried. "I'm getting a vision. Pawtucket has just opened a ten-plex movie house. I go to the movies. What picture? Eight of them are buddy-uddy cop bang-bang films that must gross twenty million on the first weekend or die. Ah, at last a picture I want to see, *badly.* Passenger plane, a 747, off course, transatlantic flight. Somehow a half dozen terrorists get aboard with breakdown plastic guns. There is a case of deadly virus stored in the luggage compartment. If, oh God, the canister is found and opened by the vile terrorists . . . good-bye East Coast of America. The president of the United States is informed in his bad left ear while dozing in a reception line. Call a scramble to sitcomm.comm.comm.org, orders the president *over* the head of his chief of staff, Field Marshal Stoopnagel. Scramble the fighter planes of the famous Asshole Squadron. Shoot the motherfucker down if it gets closer than fifty miles off the coast. A sweet, innocent little girl in row twenty-two brushes the hair of her Barbie doll. 'I'm going to see my daddy in Sing Sing.'"

Pucky and Thornton caught their breath and waited for Darnell to quit ranting. He didn't. "Wait a minute, is this the movie where the poison was going to destroy the East Coast, or where it was carrying a load of kudzu seeds to strangle every tree in the South? Well, we know one thing, don't we? *Only one man can save the situation,* Sylvester Ford Harrison, who has played in sixty films without smiling. He is lowered into the 747 toilet by a jet helicopter. You know, brother and sister, I left the ten-plex rather disappointed, so when I got home I turned on the TV to get a breath of quality. They had an uptown audience of fourteen- and sixteen-year-olds and on the stage in front of the camera a lot of fat people. Jenny Degenerate, the hostess, asked Hydrangea Flapjacks if she'd had incest with her brothers and father. The audience squealed! 'Yes, ma'am, till I married my uncle.'"

"All right, enough, Darnell. We have been patient. What are you trying to say?" Thornton demanded.

Darnell leaned over the table, and tears welled and perspiration dripped. "Thornton! For God's sake! These pissy-ass movies and that pissy-ass television eat up more material in one day than was written by all the English authors during the entire Victorian era. Pucky is only trying to hold back an avalanche of ignorance."

"All right," Thornton said softly. "I want you to listen to something, and you tell me."

He put a disk into the Bulldog's CD-ROM and punched the required keys. In a few seconds music came over the speakers. It was sweet, melodic, dancy and teasy. It was pure Mozart.

Thornton changed the setting to what was obviously Beethoven. Pucky was caught up in trying to identify the symphony. It occurred to her that somehow, some unplayed and unpublished Mozart and Beethoven had been discovered. My God, it was world-shattering.

"That's the future of music," Thornton said. "It is already the future of writing, as you have just documented so well, Darnell. The Bulldog was programmed to log fifty hours of each composer, then compose something new using the composer's structure."

"The computer composed that!" Darnell cried.

"That's the future. Want to see some non-paintings by Rembrandt or some non-statues by Michelangelo or maybe read a little non-Hemingway? Alas, the Bulldog is a little weak on Hemingway."

Pucky looked around the office until she spotted the Ming vase she had bought at auction, snatched it from its stand, marched to his desk, lifted it over her head, and flung it into the monitor of the Bulldog.

FOURTEEN

Marine Corps Air Base, El Toro, California —Late 1970s

Throughout the history of the republic, military mavericks have popped up, some with innovations that changed the nature of war. After World War I, an Army Air Force general, Billy Mitchell, demonstrated the impossible, that airplanes could sink a battleship.

The Navy's most renowned off-horse appeared in the form of Admiral Hyman Rickover, father of the nuclear submarine, who gave nightmares to his superiors and Congress.

Marine Major General Jeremiah Duncan was a lesser maverick, but a maverick nonetheless. By the time of the Great Depression the American military had fallen into a pathetic state. There was congressional pressure to disband the Marine Corps or reduce it to giving concerts on the Capitol steps and serving as embassy guards.

It was incumbent upon a group of Marine officers, including Duncan, to reinvent the mission of the Corps and thereby save it from extinction.

Their thesis was simple but unique. In future wars, global in nature, tactics had to be developed to land men from the sea against fortified land positions.

The major test in World War I had taken place against the Turkish peninsula at Gallipoli. British naval gunfire bashed the Turkish forts and emplacements for weeks prior to a landing by Anzac, British, and French forces. The Allied troops were cut to pieces, and ultimately the campaign ended in a disaster that resulted in Winston Churchill's removal from the Admiralty.

Away from probing eyes on the island of Vieques, off the east coast of Puerto Rico, the Marines went about developing the tactics that would become a key to victory in future wars. Naval gunfire was moved in close and concentrated on a single beach or two, forcing the enemy to retreat inland temporarily. The Marines would then land infantry, set up a perimeter, and dig in to ward off the inevitable enemy counterattack. The key was holding a piece of turf, then moving inland.

All that was needed was a war to prove the thesis. It came along in good time.

It has been said that Jeremiah Duncan's first words as an infant were "Semper Fidelis." He became the first fighter pilot ace when he shot down five Japanese Zeros in a single day over Guadalcanal, but was shot down in turn and somehow escaped alive. An ace, but he could fly combat no more.

As a battalion commander in Korea, when he was advised that his men were surrounded, he said, "Good, that makes the tactical situation simpler." Duncan led his mangled forces back from the Chosin Reservoir on the Chinese border to the sea in the dead of an icy winter.

In Vietnam he was moved from field command to staff to develop and improve new tactics against a tenacious and resourceful enemy.

Jeremiah Duncan's chest bore a Congressional Medal of Honor, a Navy Cross, and three Purple Hearts. Known with affection throughout the Corps as Dogbreath, he now longed to retire to the Eastern Shore, where he had a big old house, a dandy fishing boat, and scads of children and grandchildren.

His wife of thirty years upped and died tragically in a house fire, leaving him devastated and debilitated. The Corps hung on to him to get him through his bereavement.

Jeremiah never got to the Eastern Shore. He ended up with a vague title as adviser to planning at El Toro Marine Air Base. There on the outskirts of Los Angeles, he worked another innovation, the lightning strike force.

The Corps, along with Bell and Boeing, was developing a hybrid aircraft—the SCARAB, that could take off and land like a helicopter, then fly like a turbo-prop. It was designed to carry twenty-some Marines with medical, electronic, and specialty personnel.

As was his wont, Jeremiah was soon bucking heads with the top brass. As a lady colonel inched into his life, he finally requested his belated retirement.

It was no surprise when the commandant, General Keith Brickhouse, a gnarly specimen not unlike Duncan, showed up at El Toro. With a name like Brickhouse, the general had a reputation akin to Dogbreath's.

"So, it's you and Colonel Dorothy, eh? Getting hitched, Jeremiah?"

"If the Marine Corps wanted me to have another wife, they'd of issued me one. Cut to the chase, Keith, but let me advise you in advance—after Nam it took me six months to be able to write my name. Who sent you, Keith?"

"The President."

"Well, you've got my attention."

"As well as Defense, State, Joint Chiefs, and the CIA," Brickhouse continued. "I didn't assign you to El Toro to play with the SCARAB by accident."

"Any damned fool could tell you we had to develop a rapid-strike force. The SCARAB is interesting. Helicopter turned airplane turned helicopter and carrying more firepower than anything ten times its size, with the exception of nuclear weapons."

"It's more than that," the commandant said. "Jeremiah, we're heading into an era of an entirely different kind of warfare, vomit warfare."

"Like?"

"World terrorism. We must get a leg up. This Palestine Liberation Organization is just the tip of a gigantic iceberg. Playing by no rules and operating covertly, they can multiply like roaches. Every dingy little organization with a beef will feel free to call themselves Heroes of God on Tuesday and blow up a civilian aircraft and rename themselves Liberation Unit Twenty on Wednesday and take a classroom of kids as hostages. The bad news is that the Warsaw Pact nations and the Islamic states are giving them sanctuary, training camps, money, diplomatic passports, weapons. Thus far terrorist activity has been outside of the States. At the moment there is no way we can make the American public believe we are not immune. But something's going to happen inside America, and sooner rather than later. It's up to us to have something in the ready."

"Let me finish this for you," Duncan interrupted. "The President wants me to create a small, secret, lightning strike force. Once we identify a perpetrator of a terrorist act, we will hit a preplanned target in reprisal."

"You heard that from you, not me," the commandant retorted. "How do you think the SCARAB would fit in?"

Jeremiah did not have to stretch far to grasp that one. "The SCARAB could be a big part of the Marines' future."

"We're thinking of ordering five hundred of them," Brickhouse retorted.

* * *

Jeremiah had enjoyed playing with the SCARAB in the tightly guarded hangar. It brought him back to a first love, aviation. He had already surmised what the craft's future role might be. The notion of marrying a lady colonel and retiring did not entirely appeal to him. The alternative was staying in the Corps.

"The SCARAB has potential. To do the rapid-force mission I want something faster, lighter, and with high-end missiles. I could soup the engines up. I'd want a titanium wing and install the new TAD laser bomb-guidance system," he said.

"I'll get the funding," the commandant said quickly.

"I didn't say I'd do it, Keith. I said I'd think it over."

The commandant knew that either Jeremiah would agree or he would have to be retired. He waited.

"I want to build my own team," Jeremiah snapped, "and I don't want a fucking congressional oversight committee buggering me—"

"Deal," Keith interrupted.

"I'll give you a list of the key people I need," Jeremiah said, already caught up in the venture.

"If we're staying top secret, it has to be an all-volunteer force," the commandant said.

"Sure, fine. I'll volunteer them," Jeremiah answered.

Master Technical Sergeant Quinn Patrick O'Connell was the man to see at the El Toro helicopter command.

He received new craft, oversaw electronic installations, personally ran all serviced 'copters through their test drills, kept the manuals up to date, and pulled the best safety record in the Corps.

Quinn's relationship with Major General Jeremiah Duncan formally began when the general's personal 'copter pilot took ill. He knew Dogbreath was playing around with some kind of flying egg crate in Q Hangar and 'coptered often to Camp Pendleton, a skip down the coast and over to a semi-mysterious Marine Corps facility near Barstow in the Mojave Desert.

They flew together so often, a confidence between the two came naturally and was cemented when Quinn flew the boss to Vegas for a rendezvous with Colonel Dorothy.

Shortly after General Brickhouse's visit, Jeremiah called the commander of El Toro. "I need to borrow a 'copter pilot for a month or so. Send me Sergeant O'Connell and put him on detached duty."

"I can't spare him for a month, Jeremiah," the commander retorted. "He's key personnel."

"Then I'll appreciate it doubly."

"Don't you Dogbreath me!"

"Shall we put this down as a request and not an order?"

"I hear you, I hear you."

"Sir!" Quinn snapped, coming to attention before Duncan's desk.

"Sit down, son."

Oh, Christ, Quinn thought as the general reached out to shake his hand, I'm going to get my pockets picked.

"My 'copter pilot has the crud. I'm going to need you for a month or so. Detached duty has been cleared. I trust you have no objections."

"I understand your words, a month, but I don't understand how long 'or so' might be."

"Or so means or so."

"I'm checking out a half dozen new men. A couple of them are real joy-stick freaks. Let me pick you a gung-ho man," Quinn said.

"I don't think so."

"Can I have four or five days to brief the new NCO at the 'copter compound?" Quinn asked.

"Take two."

"Sir, uh . . ."

"What, son, what!"

"On your 'copter, sir, I'd like to select the copilot."

"In actual fact," Jeremiah answered, "I'll copilot."

"Ohh."

"I note a drop of enthusiasm in your voice," the general grumbled. Receiving no answer, he bellowed, "Well!"

"General Duncan, this here Corps holds you in the same reverence as Joe Foss, Marian Carl, and Pappy Boyington's Black Sheep. Sir, it was a glorious day in our aviation history when you became the first American ace in a single day. However, General, World War II ended thirty-five years ago, and with these new systems you couldn't hit a bull in the ass with a bass fiddle."

Duncan's voice went from grumble to gurgle to rumble.

"Sir, there is a new poster on the far wall. Kindly read the top line of it from here."

Duncan squinted, and squinted, then drummed the top of his desk ominously.

"What's this all about, sir?"

"I need you," Jeremiah said dead-on. "I'm putting together a special all-volunteer force, about two platoons' worth, and I want you to volunteer."

"Volunteer to do what?"

"I'd rather not have to explain," he finally said, simmering down. "The nature of our mission requires utmost secrecy. I can't tell you unless you volunteer."

Quinn browsed back over their relationship, the Corps, and the present conversation. "Sir, my hitch is up in five months."

"Then I'm asking you to ship over."

"Sir, I love the Corps. It salvaged my life. When I find out what I'm good for in this world, a lot of my strength will have been born in the Marines. However, I'm not a career man."

"Somehow, I prayed that you would be," Jeremiah said somewhat sadly. "You're as smart as they come, O'Connell. You'll be a wild-ass success and make a great fortune on the outside."

"I don't believe that money is my motivation," Quinn said.

"And that's why I thought you'd choose a career in the Corps."

"You've a great way of choking my windpipe, sir."

"Sorry. You told me you were orphaned at birth."

"Yes, sir."

"My old man," the general said, "worked Texas ranches and, believe it or not, was a Baptist preacher on Sundays. We're all looking for our father, one way or the other. Always trying to do something to make him proud of us. My father never made it big, nor did he live to see me get the first star pinned on my shoulder. First time I was supposed to retire, a long time ago, I got offers for positions not only from every defense plant, but from an airline, an oil company, a chain of ice cream stores. I received over thirty job offers, some at the kind of money I didn't know existed. I just knew I couldn't taste ice cream flavors for the rest of my life. What the hell could I do with money, anyhow?"

"With your permission, sir," Quinn said, standing.

"Sure," he answered with a wave of the hand, "go."

Quinn could not open the door. He tottered. "Sir."

"You still here?"

"Sir, tell me the truth, just this once," Quinn said.

Jeremiah grunted a smile. "I'll try."

"This mission?"

"It is the highest priority at the command of the President. I consider it about as important as anything any Marine alive could become involved in. And moreover, it's a Marine's fantasy."

"I, uh, could extend my enlistment for two years."

"You've made old Dogbreath very happy," the general said. "First thing is to get those stripes off your sleeve. I'm skipping you over second lieutenant to first lieut."

"I don't want to sound ungrateful, sir . . ."

"But . . ."

"There's too much, too much . . ."

"Back-biting, regulations, kiss-my-ass?" the general volunteered.

"Something like that."

"You're a mustang," Duncan said in reference to enlisted men who always stayed enlisted at heart, no matter their rank. "When I hit the same fork in the road," he continued, "I sure as hell didn't need regulations on how to bow on lady's night. So, they made me a Marine gunner," he said in reference to a special warrant officer rank above the enlisted men but below the officers, like a bridge between the two. The exploding-bomb insignias on their epaulets were highly respected.

"Marine gunner," Quinn said. "I like that, sir."

"Gunner O'Connell it is," Duncan said. "And thanks, Marine."

Quinn knew what Jeremiah meant.

Thus, Jeremiah Duncan's Recreation and Morale Unit was formed. RAM Company occupied a remote space at Pendleton and in the desert, and its fighters endured a regimen that would make the Navy Seals and Army Rangers cringe. These were light men so as not to add too much weight to the SCARAB load. Major Hugo Grubb, another mustang, honed them to a razor's edge.

Cherokee Cottrell, who claimed to be half Sioux, had been on the wagon for five years when Jeremiah pulled him from obscurity to pilot the SCARAB.

A Harvard failure, Todd Wetmore IV, a super talent with something to prove to his family, came in as co-pilot and navigator.

A weirdo, Captain Novinski, without whom nothing electronic was purchased by the Corps, found and installed and tested every system now in use or on the planning boards.

Dogbreath got his titanium wing. It was six feet longer than the production wing of aluminum composite. Stronger and more rigid, the black wing made the craft faster, lighter, and able to carry more weight.

The Allison turbo-prop engines were pushed, then pushed again.

Marine Gunner Quinn O'Connell wore many hats: backup on the electronic board, bombardier, Mayday pilot, and mostly logistics expert. He was given twenty potential worldwide targets to prepare for a counterinsurgency attack.

All the members of RAM Company doubled as medical corpsmen.

Jeremiah attached bomb racks to carry a mix of sixteen missiles, ultra-light, laser-guided, with explosive capacity not yet seen in combat.

What was created was a dual-capacity roto-tiller that could fly as a helicopter and convert in seconds to a standard turbo jet aircraft. She had a decent subsonic speed of 500 knots and, with spare fuel tanks, a range of two thousand miles. She could carry two dozen men plus pilots and topped out at an altitude of twenty thousand feet.

Every square inch and every pound allowable held a basket of systems, from laser-targeted lock-ons to ground-view.

She carried her own ordnance, crafted to fit her limited space and weight capacities. Her demonstrations were awesome, a lethal bombardment followed by a landing or ground hovering as twenty Marines debarked out of a rear ramp.

Nearly a year passed. The SCARAB was worked into higher levels of performance, as were the men of the RAM team.

In Europe in particular, terrorists kept upping the level of violence with increasing daring. Outside America, her buildings, businesses, and citizens were targeted even though the nation itself had not undergone an attack. This, everyone agreed, was only a matter of time.

The inevitable happened. An Air Force Lear jet crossing the Atlantic from Germany and carrying an American ambassador and an American NATO general blew up in midair.

A series of incredible breaks linked together . . .

In Frankfurt, an Israeli Mossad agent identified Iranians entering Germany and followed them to a run-down hotel in the foreign workers' part of town. The Mossad informed the CIA.

Air Force Lieutenant Sumner Smith was officer on duty at the small-craft section of the Rhein-Main air base. Contacted by the terrorists, Smith had agreed to plant a briefcase bomb for a hundred thousand dollars.

The pilot of the Lear jet was able to send a Mayday call at the time of the explosion.

In a heightened state of alert, German police were able to catch the terrorists, six Iranians, at the airport and the *autobahn* hastening to leave Frankfurt.

Lieutenant Smith's wife, a German national named Helga, discovered the hundred thousand dollars. In a nasty marriage, she took the money to the police.

Four of the Iranians confessed, as did Lieutenant Smith.

The president of the United States clamped on a lid of secrecy. There would be no public announcement. If pressed, they would say an aircraft was missing and they were investigating.

With confessions in their pockets and further confirmation, the President saw a window of opportunity to strike back!

FIFTEEN

"Jeremiah Duncan here," Duncan growled.

"Hold up one minute, sir, for the President."

"General?"

"Sir."

"One of our Lear jets carrying Ambassador August and NATO General Marplade blew up over the Atlantic about five hours ago. We scored the biggest break in the world by unbelievable apprehensions and confessions. Double and triple verifications are coming in. It was Iranian terrorists."

"Yes, sir."

"With this news in our pockets," the President said, "and the Iranians in the dark, we feel we might pull off a counterstrike even before our plane is reported missing. Now, has your team done virtual practice on any specific Iranian sites?"

"Yes, sir, four or five of them."

"How fast can you get to Washington?"

"I'm on the way. Do I have permission to do a little commandeering here and there?"

"Carte blanche. As soon as you're in the air, establish communications with the Situation Room. They'll be looking out for you."

The Situation Room—The White House —Several Hours Later

In the basement of the White House, the Situation Room was no futuristic phantasmagoria of a Hollywood intergalactic set, but a conference table ringed with brainy men. Gathered in, the Joint Chiefs of Staff, the director of the CIA, the secretary of Defense, the ranking man at State, the President's defense adviser, and numbers of indispensable aides.

In the deep of night, Jeremiah Duncan arrived with a single aide, a Marine gunner. The two-man team accounted for the commander, chief planner, bombardier, and emergency copilot.

When the President assumed his seat and nodded to Major General Duncan, the animus about the table was tempered by a reluctant respect for the old Marine. It was merely a year ago that the Joint Chiefs had pleaded with Duncan to remain in the service for just this sort of eventuality. But, and it was a big but, at this table Duncan could be a rogue.

Jeremiah's long tenure served him well. He played his

presentation, knowing the President had to give Iran a whack or terrorist activity would ooze all over the European continent.

"Gentlemen, as we know," Duncan said, plunging right into his remarks, "we have received a break that happens once in a lifetime. A German *frau* has ratted on her lieutenant husband, an American rat, and the Israelis in Frankfurt had the terrorists fingered before they could get out of town. A Lear jet is missing. The Iranian government does not know what we know. We can nail them."

"But a lightning strike without rehearsals leaves a big margin for error."

"Moreover, Duncan, we don't know enough about your SCARAB's capabilities."

"Moreover, Duncan, we are going to lose precious time getting the SCARAB to the East Coast along with your RAM team."

"Gentlemen, Mr. President, I used my discretionary powers and commandeered a C-5 jet cargo plane from Long Beach, folded up the SCARAB, and put it aboard along with twenty-some Marines of the RAM team. We are ready to go."

Pencils as sharp as daggers, pressed on foolscap pads, now lightened up. Assistants behind their bosses exchanged quick whispers.

"Have I got it straight? You brought your attack team and your airplane with you?"

"Yes, sir."

Now there came a sincere clearing of throats and rapt attention.

"Marine Gunner O'Connell here has worked up plans for four potential raid sites in Iran. A Teheran power grid, a dam, and an oil terminal. Yet they won't work in this situation."

"You said there were four."

"I'm coming to that. We learned as we went on to eliminate any plan which would require months of intelligence and massive use of resources. It defeats the rock-bottom mission of a lightning surprise attack."

Gunner O'Connell asked for the screen to be lowered and operated a slide carousel of maps, photographs, tactics, and stat sheets.

"The genesis of this attack is to hit them in the next fifteen or twenty hours, in the middle of the night. RAM will be on its way to Iran even as Washington wakes up yawning tomorrow. Around noon Washington time, the Defense Department will report an American Lear jet is missing. A flash in the sky was seen. Some of our ships in the area are investigating. Gentlemen," Dogbreath said, "I shit you not when I tell you the Iranians will still be squatting over their holes with their pants down."

"What is your target, General Duncan?" the President asked.

Quinn clicked on a map of Iran. "Here," Jeremiah said, pointing, "in the dead center of the country between the Great Salt Desert and the Persian Gulf. As you know, it is a wild, bitter, mountainous region. Quinn?"

Click, click.

"This is the area around Mount Shir. It stands at around twelve thousand feet and is commanded by an overlook fortress. The fort is a couple centuries old, of mud brick, but from it the military is able to control an enormous, sparsely populated area. For generations Fort Urbakkan commanded the area, collected taxes from peasants and herders, decapitated smugglers, and exhorted tolls from caravans. It also contains prison cells for sabbath buggering. The garrison consists of about two hundred troops with a major in command. Since the ayatollahs have gained power, the fort has been used to detain high-ranking members from the shah's regime while the ayatollahs decide their fate."

"Who do they have there now?"

Duncan nodded to Charlie Bethune, the CIA chief.

"General Duncan contacted us as he flew out of California. We gave him the data we had on Fort Urbakkan. At present it is holding Bandar Barakat."

Bandar Barakat! The name resounded off the walls of the Situation Room.

"Jesus Christ!"

"Barakat!"

"Charlie?" the President asked.

"If you can figure Bandar Barakat out, then you can figure out the Middle East. He was one of the top intelligence people under the shah. He smelled the ayatollahs taking power and turned double agent. Because of his Western intelligence contacts, he could still deliver information to the new regime. On our side of the equation, we thought we had buried a valuable mole in the new government. This source of Western intelligence would dry up if they whack off Barakat's head. So, they imprisoned him and moved him up to Fort Urbakkan, where the VIP prisoner or prisoners are housed in a specific tower."

The room hummed in admiration at the preciseness of the CIA data.

"Go on, Charlie," the President said.

"Barakat is probably making like Scheherazade, giving just enough new information to remain alive."

"What do we want this bastard for?" Admiral Clearfield, chief of Naval Operations, inquired.

"Good question," Bethune answered. "Barakat had worked his way in Iran to becoming chief coordinator for terrorist activities. Moreover, the ayatollahs aren't going to get rid of him until they find the money he's skimmed from the Saudis, who are financing a major part of his operation. In our hands, Barakat can give us the names of terrorists, their aliases, cells, organizations, training sites, bank accounts, future targets being planned—"

"Do you mean to say," Air Force Commander Hoyt interrupted, "you intend to take him out of this fort?"

"Precisely," Jeremiah Duncan said.

"How do you know he'll cooperate?"

"Read my lips . . . M-O-N-E-Y."

Drawn smiles.

"Believe it or not," Bethune said, "he still has friends in Western intelligence. That cautiously includes the CIA."

"How does that figure?"

"He has more money sitting and waiting in the States than in Iran. It includes a prime building on Fifth Avenue. With the ayatollahs breathing down his neck, Barakat has to figure they'll find and extort his fortune in Iran and Europe. On the other hand, we feel that he's picked us as the winner and wants to run for it. One more thing, Barakat is an Arab. The Iranians don't trust Arabs."

"Are we all on the same page?" the President asked.

"With reservations," General Bellicek, chair of the Joint Chiefs, noted. "Always with reservations."

"And you think you can snatch Barakat?" the President asked Jeremiah Duncan.

"I sure as hell like the odds. If he is killed, the raid is still a success. If we spirit him out, we've won the lottery."

"How do you envision this?"

"Quinn."

Click, click.

"Here, we've an extended map that includes the NATO base at Tikkah on the Turkish border next to Armenia. We take the SCARAB out of the C–5, unfold the wings and blades, arm it with bombs and missiles we've designed, fuel it, and go."

"Hold it a minute, Jeremiah. Are you suggesting we are going to avoid Iranian radar?" Hoyt of the Air Force asked.

"Yes, in two ways. We're going to take a page from the Israeli attack on the Egyptians in the Sixty-seven War. The Israelis flew out to the Mediterranean away from Egyptian radar, then came in and attacked them from the rear. We will go back door ourselves. The SCARAB will follow the coast of the Caspian Sea and enter Iran at the Turkoman border."

"You said there were two reasons."

"I had this SCARAB prototype built with composites. It is not an all-aluminum plane, and the radar cross section is very low."

Now came an hour of caution, nitpicking, alternate ideas: we haven't thoroughly tested the experimental missiles and bombs, the SCARAB has to be refueled in midair, we need a diversionary attack or a carrier hit from the Persian or Oman Gulf . . . air cover . . . the condition of the Marine RAM team will be exhaustion after flying fifteen hours . . . and finally:

"No disrespect, Jeremiah," General Bellicek said, "but aren't you a little too enamored of those Israeli wing-and-a-prayer raids? They have to win. We have to plan it so as not to take losses."

"Yeah, but they work," Duncan retorted, "and the one goddamn reason they work is because they aren't cluttered up with all the Yankee bells and whistles. One plane, in and out, twenty fucking Marines."

"But does the SCARAB have the legs, Jeremiah?" General Hoyt pressed. "You are going to fly under enemy radar in rocky terrain. These are gas-guzzling tactics."

"Quinn."

"Yes, sir," the gunner said. He clicked the carousel forward several slides and spoke. "Using a bad-case scenario, we can reach Fort Urbakkan, pull the raid, and fly out for a few hundred miles. We have called for a fuel tanker from Diego Garcia to rendezvous at thirty-one degrees, forty minutes latitude, fifty-eight degrees, twenty minutes longitude. That will give us four hours till daylight to scramble south to the Arabian Sea and land aboard one of our container ships."

"How many tanker-to-SCARAB refuels have you tried?" Admiral Clearfield asked knowingly.

Duncan looked away, miffed. "Two," he peeped.

Back and forth, back and forth. It was the kind of plan that made the American military clutch. One mistake would mean a catastrophe. To let go of this opportunity could be a sign of overcaution, or a fear of casualties. The terrorist would remember an American balk.

Keith Brickhouse, commandant of the Marines, broke his silence. "The PLO, the Iranians, and the rest of those terrorist bastards will increase their activities. They are going to say that America just doesn't have the capacity to stop them. We are capable of this mission. We will be in and out of there before the muezzin calls the Moslems to prayer in Teheran."

"And you'll wish to hell you had had fresh troops going in," General Hoyt said.

"Fresh troops is an oxymoron," Duncan answered. "I have never known men to reach battle or who fight battles as fresh troops. Wars are won by men less exhausted."

Silence. With the specter of American casualties and a failure, the Joint Chiefs and the President were overburdened.

"From time to time, war to war, Americans have shown the utmost ingenuity and courage. Such a time and place is right here now," the commandant said.

Fourteen hours and twenty-two minutes had elapsed since Iranian terrorists had taken an American Lear jet out of the sky.

Overhead a giant C–5 jet transport carrying RAM and its sleeping SCARAB pressed toward the Tikkah Air Base on the far reach of Turkey.

SIXTEEN

Aboard the C–5 each member of the Recreation and Morale team was issued a packet of maps, personalized for each Marine's participation in the raid.

The mission and the importance of Bandar Barakat was explained. Jeremiah called for map blowups and went over the plan, minute by minute, inch by inch. Many the day and week they had drilled in specific maneuvering that was now fitted inside the scheme of the raid.

Every Marine had secondary and tertiary duties. All of them could double as corpsmen. Nicknames and personal names only spoken now, no calling a person by his rank. This they had also trained for, and it was hallelujah time when they got to call Major General Jeremiah Duncan "Dogbreath."

Gunner Quinn O'Connell was the Mayday pilot, bombardier, second backup on the electronic systems, corpsman, and backup navigator behind the pilots.

Grubb, the field commander, and squad leaders Ropo and Marsh, Novinski on electronics, and the pilots, Cherokee and IV, were networked through their helmets to Dogbreath and Quinn.

More intelligence photos. More weather information.

Now a weapons and ammunition check. The twenty Marines were going in with serious firepower.

Duncan snarled time and again, he had pressed the President so hard to make an instant strike, he might have bought a pig in a poke. Would it not have been better to have practiced a virtual raid for a week? They'd find out.

A mere sixteen and a half hours had elapsed since the terrorist attack. The C–5 flew quite close to where the Lear jet's scattered bits and pieces floated on the waves below.

The plane veered off course, following international waters so as not to fly in an air space where permission would be required.

They did aerobic exercises in the C–5, hard, hard, hard, hard. Major Hugo Grubb was a monster for conditioning. He could make a man's hand fall off with finger exercises.

Chow included beer! Three per Marine. It would slow down the heart thump, drown out the jumping nerve ends.

One more time they went through a step-by-step account of the coming strike.

Two films were set up, one straight and one porno. By dawn light everyone was in their canvas bunk, dead out, snoring so loud their sound nearly drowned out the jet engines.

Nato Air Base, Tikkah, Turkey

RAM-A arrived ahead of schedule and was whisked to an isolated hangar, where they were sealed in.

The men stretched, yawned, belched, scratched, and passed air, cracking their bones into alignment. Quickly awake, they unloaded their gear from the C–5 and laid their packs and weapons against a wall.

A hushed moment among the gathering as the SCARAB was rolled down the C–5 ramp. Lord, it looked so small and fragile, an infant being born from the gigantic cargo ship.

The wings had been turned on a pivot for travel, running from tail to cockpit. They were rotated into normal flying mode and clicked in.

Cherokee entered the plane and hit the thumb switch to raise the nacelles housing the engines and propellers. He set them at 75 degrees so the blades would be well clear of the deck. The long and powerful blades had an upside and a downside. Downside, all takeoffs and landings had to be made in helicopter mode. Downside, when firing missiles from under-wing racks, they also had to be in helicopter mode. Upside, the plane was hushlike quiet in flight and unlikely to be heard by the enemy.

Showers!

Slabs of beef for breakfast with pasta and gallons of orange juice and high-voltage chocolates.

Captain Novinski and his backup man, Master Tech Sergeant Roosevelt Jarvis, entered. They set up a mini-display and command console, directly behind the pilots, activated and checked out systems and the display panels.

"SMAC?"

"Pretty as a picture."

"SMAC locked in."

"Matching area correlation?"

"A-Okay."

"NOE?" Jarvis checked the digital tracking map system.

Novinski and Jarvis were joined by the chief American navigator at the Tikkah Air Base. The three of them programmed in a flight plan. They activated the terrain-following multifunction radar that would take pulsations from the ground and compare them to their database and display their position to within a hundred feet.

The chief navigator pointed out choppy air corridors, hidden peaks, radar stations, and myriad dangers.

In the radio shack, the pilots received their radio frequencies as well as Russian and Iranian frequencies.

"Fellah?"

"Yo," Corporal Anwar Fellah answered, taking a headphone set that would include him in the command network.

"When you get the red light, it will indicate that we are being contacted by a tower or, God forbid, a fighter plane patrol. If they are speaking in Farsi," Quinn said, "I'll signal you to talk to them. Positive of the drill?"

"Gotcha."

"Volkovitch, the same goes for you in Russian."

"Aye, aye."

Bomb carts rolled in sleek baby missiles. The "Duncan" missiles were short, light, but could penetrate a heavily resistant bunker. At Fort Urbakkan they would be shooting at a mix of mud and stone.

A second set of bombs were little fat ones, murderous against personnel, ugly cluster bombs to shower the enemy with thousands of razor-sharp steel squares and ball bearings.

The nacelles would remain at 75 degrees so the SCARAB could fire from helicopter mode without fear of hitting the propellers. Space under the wing was limited. The laser guidance system looked fine.

The bombing run, in Gunner O'Connell's hands, had to be executed accurately and surely. To hit the targets dead-on, the SCARAB would be maneuvered as close as possible. Would the hovering SCARAB take Iranian ground fire in this period? Were the bombs squirrely? Could they be held fast during what had to be a wild, shaking flight?

In the rear of the main cabin of the SCARAB an operating table and supplies of blood, surgical tools, and medicines were secured on the ceiling. A pulley rope allowed them to drop easily into place. Dr. Wheat checked over his supplies. Christ, keep the casualties down. The table was again stowed and secured to the roof.

Jeremiah Duncan and his pilots went over the exterior of the SCARAB, an inspection that lasted an hour and a half. In that time a tanker truck entered the hangar and filled the plane with fuel. This was a dicey moment. With this size load and full gas tanks, there was a remote possibility of fire during takeoff. Jeremiah had spotted the danger months earlier, and hoped he had beaten the problem with the Bell and Boeing engineers.

"Gentlemen, the SCARAB is ripe!"

The Marines went to their combat packs and weapons, waiting for the command to fall in.

"You will first evacuate your bowels and bladders. No one will be permitted to leave until he takes an airsick pill."

Groan! Boo!

"You *will* take the airsick pill because the Marine Corps says you need an airsick pill. We'll be riding some nausea-causing waves of air, and we will bounce until your gut humps up into your throats. Puking is not an option, but if you must do so, vomit in your evacuation bags."

When all had evacuated who could, they fell in near the boarding ramp. Personnel were loaded forward to aft, so Jeremiah did a round of handshakes and entered behind Cherokee and IV.

Directly behind the pilots and a step higher than their heads, Duncan had a mini-console installed. Duncan, with Novinski on one side of him and Quinn on the other, could read a number of displays from it, to monitor the speed, fuel, terrain, communications, as well as the systems that would come into play at the time of their attack.

"Intercom, we all hooked up?"

"Yo, Quinn."

"Yo, Cherokee."

"Yo, IV."

"Yo, Grubb."

"Ropo, on."

"Marsh, yo."

"Novinski here."

"All troops present and accounted for, sir."

The hangar door yawned open. A tow cart inched SCARAB out into the dying light. With the nacelles at 75 degrees, the SCARAB could be rolled a short distance on the runway in a fuel-saving maneuver for take-off as compared to full helicopter thrust.

"Dogbreath, this is Cherokee. Shall we go for a rolling start?"

"This is Dogbreath, let me think. We've got a monster load on. Any half-power stunts promulgates six or seven risks I can think of, none of them pleasant. Ninety degrees and full thrust, get this son of a bitch up in the air."

"Yo."

Cherokee switched on the engines, a whine and then the SCARAB's whispering thunder.

"Thrust," Cherokee ordered.

IV took the long handle to his left and levered it down. The SCARAB hesitated an instant, rose, hung, then popped up.

"We're at a thousand . . . eleven hundred," IV said.

"Beep the nacelles down."

Cherokee's Fred Astaire feet tickled the rudders as his hand on the joystick held the nose still.

"Nacelles at forty-five degrees."

"Let's do some flying . . . but first I want to sing you all a little song."

Arrayed at the cramped console behind the pilots, Novinski engaged the FLIR to be able to see the ground at night.

Jeremiah and Quinn hovered over the displays depicting Fort Urbakkan's layout. The fort's main installations stood three hundred feet down a courtyard next to a headquarters building with radio and telephone capacity. Next to headquarters, an enlisted barracks and mess hall, next the officers quarters. Across the back wall, the supply building and arsenal.

Opposite this, a stable for mules to negotiate the

final miles along the cliff-side road to Urbakkan. Then a small prison and punishment court.

Quinn took a radio message and decoded it. THERE IS NO EVIDENCE OF COMMANDING OFFICER BEING BILLETED IN MOSQUE.

"That makes the cheese more binding," Dogbreath said. "Quinn?"

"Yo, I read it."

"Do you think we should save a rack of missiles in case the mosque is armed?" Duncan asked of Quinn.

"No. This intelligence gives us the advantage of entering right over the main gate with no potential enemy able to get behind us. This baby flies so quietly, we'll make our entrance without being detected. I say we come in and over the main gate, hover and unload our missiles and bombs right down the bowling alley. As soon as the buildings and their munitions go, we come down right alongside Barakat's tower."

"Let me think about it," Dogbreath said. And he did, until his eyes washed out from glaze and concentration.

"Cherokee, this is Dogbreath."

"Yo."

"We're probably going to scratch the mosque as a target. That means we can fly directly over the main gate."

"No problem."

"Novinski, this is Dogbreath."

"Yo," answered Novinski, sitting next to the general.

"Any of those gadgets give me a reading of how noisy it is outside?"

"Yo," Novinski said. "Whispering Jesus, singing a lullaby. Under eighty decibels."

Dogbreath shook his head in amazement. The SCARAB was eight times more quiet in the turbo-prop mode than as a helicopter. Should we make a bombing run or hope that the Iranians are totally off guard? We need a few minutes to get into the fort and for Quinn to squeeze off his missiles. I vote for Quinn.

Dogbreath turned and smiled and waved to RAM in the rear. They sat knee to knee in hard-ass bucket seats, their combat packs, helmets, and weapons crammed on the deck in the center aisle. Dogbreath found something else to fret about: the main cabin was not pressurized, and they'd have to go on oxygen if the SCARAB went high to save fuel.

The first point of the flight was to fly into the northernmost tip of Iran, avoiding Tabriz radar. The SCARAB took to her zigzag preprogrammed course like an old pro. Although the entire mission was made more difficult by mountains, she cruised unexcitingly.

No calls from Tabriz!

Sensing that radar coverage was poor and feeling the SCARAB might not be picked up at all because of her composite materials, Dogbreath ordered her up over the mountaintops to save fuel.

They flew close to plan toward the Iranian-Armenian-Azerbaijan borders.

"Volkovitch and Fellah, this is Dogbreath."

"Yo."

"Yo."

"Are you scanning your frequencies?"

"Fellah here. Tabriz tower is speaking normally. Apparently, they didn't see us or hear us."

"Volkovitch?"

"No news from the Russians in Baku."

"Novinski?"

"Yo?"

"Anybody's radar suspect we're up here?"

"Sure doesn't look like it."

"Dogbreath to Cherokee and IV. We're looking very clean. Let's make a run for the Caspian Sea just south of Arbail," Dogbreath ordered.

The SCARAB descended as she approached the Caspian Sea and banked right to follow the coast. A high mountain range along the coast would give them cover from inland installations. Intelligence had the mountains well photographed. A dodge here and a twist there would keep them from being spotted.

Those not eating candy bars slept sitting up.

At the Iranian-Turkoman border, Dogbreath ordered the pilots to stay north and cross a deep marsh that would allow them to come around the back door into Iran and give a wide berth around Teheran.

Into a mad swirl of clashing hot and cold winds, the

SCARAB chopped and chopped and dropped suddenly, then dropped into a wadi with her tail almost completely whipped around. Cherokee quickly took her off automatic pilot.

The craft was sorely protesting her load and altitude.

"Novinski, this is Cherokee, how is your terrain following?"

"We're in a tight-ass valley. The cross winds are too crazy. We may not be getting accurate readings," Novinski said.

"I'm going visual. You stay on the multifunction radar," Cherokee said.

"Yo," IV said.

Cherokee put on his night-vision goggles, whispered an "Oh, Jesus." "I'm going up a thousand feet and clear that ridge."

That ridge didn't want to be cleared, hurtling wind into chainsaw mountaintops. Debris spewed up, some of it pelting the SCARAB.

"Shit!" Novinski noted as the bottom fell out on the far side of the ridge. Another roller-coaster wadi compelled Cherokee and IV to fly by the seat of their pants.

During the violent weather and turbulence, Dogbreath kept his mind on his display panels, unaware of the tension about him.

Should I have taken a spare pilot from El Toro? Damned, how could I? We only have a total of twenty men with arms. Marginal, marginal, well, hell, can't do anything about it now. What's that? he asked himself as perspiration beaded over his forehead. Goddammit, I should have taken an airsick pill. I cannot puke in front of these people!

"Quinn, this is Dogbreath."

"Yo."

"We've scratched the mosque as a target, so let's examine your frontal assault plan."

SCARAB dropped into a long, flat valley, and the air became dirty, woefully dirty. Quinn looked back and saw RAM tossed up and down, like a film with broken threads. Yelps!

"Congratulations, men," Cherokee said, switching on the loudspeaker system, "we made it again."

Quinn gave a fuel reading to IV. The bitch was drinking up too many calories. IV fine-tuned the angle of the prop blades.

"Quinn to front cabin. We're cleared of Teheran radar."

"Dogbreath to Cherokee."

"Yo."

"We're using up too much fuel. It is touch and go if we can reach the tanker plane or not. Since we're cleared of major radar and there are no patrols in the area, shut down the terrain follower and take her up to twenty thousand and look for some smooth air."

"I'll see if I can run into a tailwind going our way," Cherokee said.

"Attention, all hands," Dogbreath said. "We will be climbing, looking for better air. Prepare your oxygen masks for deployment over your ugly faces."

Bad time for humor. The rear cabin looked like carcasses hanging from hooks in a butcher's freezer.

SCARAB climbed happily.

"Satellite report coming in," Quinn said. "A few commercial flights to and from Teheran."

"Time?"

"We are sixteen minutes behind."

"Here we go," Cherokee sang as his engine mellowed, caught a tailwind, and lifted her speed to a respectable five hundred subsonic knots per hour.

. . . Dogbreath's head nodded as he joined his men snapping out a thirty-second nap.

"Novinski, this is Dogbreath."

"Yo."

"What will the wind be doing at twelve thousand?"

"One-forty at twenty-three knots, but definitely swirling over Urbakkan."

He clicked on the SCARAB's loudspeaker. "This is Dogbreath. The wind doth bloweth, too strong and from iffy directions. I'd like your input. We scratched napalm as one of our ordnance and replaced it with phosphorous. We are now considering the idea of a direct courtyard landing after dispensing missiles and bombs. If we drop a phosphorous curtain, as we have practiced, we will have to fly out and circle the fort. I likewise fear that the courtyard mud might be flammable, and a fuck-up wind shift send the fire right back at us. Of course, the phosphorous could well insure our success . . . if it goes perfectly."

"This is Grubb. I don't like working with fire, it doesn't cooperate."

"Novinski here. How about something like this: ditch the phosphorous about ten miles downwind from the fort. It will save us nearly seven hundred pounds."

"This is Quinn. Can't ditch it all. We need some to have flare capacity when we rendezvous with the tanker plane."

"IV."

"Yo."

"No phosphorous drop. If we light up the fort too soon, it could give the Irans several minutes to organize. We may need the flares on the way home."

"Yo" confirmations. Dogbreath pulled down his night-vision goggles and peered from one display panel to another. The phosphorous was a damned-if-you-do, damned-if-you-don't decision. "What character this plane has," he thought. "If we come through this, it will be a big player in the Marine Corps' future. How do you feel, Jeremiah Duncan?" he asked himself. "Pretty good, I believe we've got everything covered."

"Attention, all hands, this is Dogbreath. We are making a variation of the landing. We will not make passes over the fort but fire our artillery from the hover position, then drop right into the courtyard. Marsh, Ropo," he said, calling the squad leaders.

"Yo."

"Yo."

"This is Dogbreath. We will pick up twenty minutes, and Cherokee will reduce speed so that we hit our target precisely on the minute."

H-hour minus twelve minutes . . . eleven minutes.

"All hands, check your weapons, ammo clips, and gear. Do not carry anything out of the SCARAB you can't shoot or eat or wipe your ass with. Keep your oxygen masks on until you debark."

H-hour minus seven minutes.

The front cabin people were all wearing night-vision goggles, and the FLIR gave a pretty picture of what was passing beneath them.

"Jesus!" Dogbreath thought. "What if we just put the SCARAB down in the courtyard and loudspeaker to the Iranians that we are an Iranian plane dispatched to take Barakat away to Teheran! No . . . if we landed and set up a perimeter, we'd get into a nasty fire fight when they caught on. No, we've got to knock out our targets. But what an idea! Never will get a chance at it . . . Okay, Dogbreath, scratch that one . . ."

H-hour minus three minutes.

Holy shit, Mother McGee! IV saw it first in the sallow green, grainy glow that lit up their screen. Further glows flashed on the display panels.

"The minaret is sticking up like the hard-on I had

this morning," Cherokee said. "IV, start lifting the nacelles."

"Forty-five . . . fifty . . . sixty . . . seventy-five . . ."

"Nothing moving down there, Dogbreath," Novinski said.

A slight engine and propeller thump was smoothed by Cherokee's hand.

"We are in helicopter mode," IV said.

"This is Dogbreath. Quinn?"

Quinn O'Connell took a reading from his display screen, then locked on to the far end of the courtyard with a laser beam. Its light could not be seen by the Iranians. There it is! The communications tower. The beam further lit up the installation buildings.

"I am locked on the headquarters building and need minimal adjustments to target officers billet and enlisted barracks. Give me ten seconds between racks."

"Jesus," Dogbreath said softly, "they're all asleep down there."

"Cherokee, this is Quinn. Take her up another few hundred feet so I can get a better visual."

"Rotors at eighty-five degrees. We are in helicopter mode."

As the SCARAB drifted over the fort wall, Quinn's fingers unlocked the bomb-rack releases. If Dogbreath's bombs were working, they'd follow the laser beam into the target.

Quinn squeezed the bomb release. "God forgive me," he whispered. Even as the missiles hurled down on the first sleeping target, he had lined up his second target.

Everything turned into slow motion, as if moving in a dream—clouds billowed, thunder, blinding light, and madly careening air.

The pulsating waves of air billowed before a stiff wind.

"Quinn, this is Cherokee. Hold your second rack. I'm taking her up some or we'll start shaking like a dog shitting peach seeds."

"Yo."

The SCARAB caught the tail end of the blast, and it shook her. Little bits of the mud buildings sent up a shower of debris, pelting the craft.

"This is Quinn. I'm locked on the arsenal."

"This is Cherokee. I need another minute and a half—"

"Novinski, this is Dogbreath. Can you confirm that there is only a little panic activity near the installations?"

"Novinski to Dogbreath. They're running around in circles, not even armed."

"Cherokee to Quinn. You are free to release the balance of your racks."

"Two fired . . . three fired . . . four fired."

Fort Urbakkan jumped and rocked and broke apart, leveled to the ground, a deep hole gouged from the site of the arsenal.

One end of the courtyard filled up with pajama-clad,

screaming, kneeling, quivering men, like ants trying to scurry from boiling water.

"Novinski, Quinn, IV . . . how many Irans down there?"

"Fifty, maybe more."

"They're still climbing out of the rubble. Seventy-five," Quinn reckoned.

"I'd say fifty," IV said.

For the first time since the mission began, Dogbreath blinked. He froze time to get the words out of him . . . "Dogbreath to Quinn. Fire all cluster bombs."

The scene below became a horror of Irans being showered with hundreds of thousands of razor bits of steel and exploding ball bearings.

"Dogbreath to Cherokee. Land her as far away from those people as we can and as close to that tower as we can get."

"Aye, aye."

"Attention, all hands, this is Dogbreath. We are descending to land. It appears that we have neutralized our primary targets."

The RAM people were so glad to be getting out of the SCARAB, they forgot fear for the moment. The plane touched down softly, sending up a small billow of dust. Ramp down!

"Let's go!"

Twenty Marines poured out at high port and split off. Marsh's squad made for the tower while Grubb set up a perimeter in front of the SCARAB. Meeting no opposition, Grubb moved his men carefully down the courtyard.

They saw the enemy! Survivors crawling out of the rubble—some fell to their knees and pleaded not to be killed while others held up white flags of surrender.

"Grubb to Dogbreath."

"Yo."

"I've got maybe forty, fifty Irans trying to surrender."

Dogbreath grunted, about to give an order to kill them. There were no contingency plans for prisoners. Unless we take them down, they might organize for a suicide charge . . . a couple of lucky shots and the SCARAB could be hit in a vital spot.

"Dogbreath to Grubb. Have your people fire over their heads and advance down yard. Try to herd them back into the far end. If and only if you detect hostile gunfire or they make any gesture toward us, cut them down."

The Marines moved their perimeter a bit farther, then a bit farther.

The raid had reached its critical moments. It was going too smoothly, Jeremiah thought. Nothing can shoot and maneuver like this! First blip. An Iranian machine-gun squad was creeping atop the west wall. Grubb ordered his night-vision, shoulder-firing TOW gunner to lay one on. He did. Out in the courtyard the Irans seemed to get the RAM communication and backpedaled.

Moment of truth.

"Dogbreath to Ropo. What's going on?"

"Ropo, can't talk."

Dogbreath now tensed from the torture of not knowing if Bandar Barakat had been located and was alive.

Ropo crept up a circular staircase that must have been built for midgets. His team struggled behind him like a toy train taking a sharp curve. Muffle the fucking grunts!

Ropo's hand reached for the next step. No step there. He patted the floor. He had reached a landing. Ropo wormed himself onto it in a sitting position, back against the wall; he held his gun at the ready and flicked on a flashlight to locate the apartment door. He felt a presence. Ropo looked up to see a fat man standing over him with a pistol a few inches from his head, and caught a glimpse of the man's face as the flashlight was kicked from his hands. Barakat!

The man said something in Farsi.

"Barakat," Ropo said loudly, "if you shoot me, you're dead."

"Israelis?" asked the fat man.

"We're from Mars," Ropo answered, tempted to grab Barakat's ankles and dump him.

The conversation could be heard over the command network. Those in the SCARAB sweated. The Marine below Ropo had inched to the platform but could see next to nothing. Barakat's uneven breath became ponderous.

"Where are your guards?" Ropo asked.

"I shot them the instant I heard the bombs."

"Can I turn on my flashlight and talk?"

The Marine behind Ropo shined a light into Barakat's face. Ropo slammed his forearm into Barakat's knee, sending him crashing. He fired.

"Oh, God, no!" Duncan whispered as he heard the report of the bullet.

"We've got him! We've got him. We'll be back in seven or eight minutes."

Jeremiah Duncan allowed himself to decompress for the first time since receiving orders to fly to Washington. No joy, no elation, no sense of final victory. Duncan, a religious man when unseen by others, nodded to God in thanks for seeing things his way this time. Novinski, Quinn, and IV reached over and squeezed his shoulder. Jeremiah accepted the touch, hunched his shoulders, and cracked his neck.

The old Marine allowed himself a moment of self-satisfaction. Jesus, he thought, all the years of planning, how many years? Forty? Planning maneuvers, raids, battles, campaigns. Now at last was a close-to-perfect operation. At least, up to this point. It seemed like something went always awry after the first shots were exchanged, and it usually boiled down to every Marine improvising with the man on his left and right to win their piece of turf. This was sublime!

"Quinn to Novinski. What kind of read can you get on your display of the courtyard?"

"Novinski here. Marsh's squad at ten o'clock from west wall to one-third of courtyard. Grubb's people making a move back toward SCARAB. Separation between Marines and Irans is at least sixty yards. Hold it, hold everything, something's lying on the deck about twenty yards behind Marsh's squad."

"What?"

"Quinn to Dogbreath! I see it, too! Unexploded bomb!"

"This is Grubb. I see it loud and clear."

"Dogbreath to Grubb. Can you read the stripes?"

"Black and blue, a cluster bomb!"

"Dogbreath to Grubb. Stop! You are ordered not to throw yourself on that bomb. It won't help. Pull Marsh's squad back, dump your ammo and missiles as planned for weight reduction. Marsh."

"Marsh here."

"Cover Ropo's and Grubb's people. Do not, repeat, do not fire near that grounded bomb, but keep those Irans pinned back. Allow no forward movement."

"Marsh here. I've got it."

Half of Grubb's squad ditched their ammo clips, laid their missiles down, and ran up the ramp. They had to jam their way around the operating table and dispensary that had been lowered from the ceiling.

Ropo's five-man squad burst out of the tower dragging a dumpy captive whose legs would not keep up. Into the plane! Marsh pulled his men back . . . back . . .

"Dogbreath to Grubb. We've got the fat man. Keep bringing your people back, but softly and at the ready."

Gunfire cracked and echoed throughout the yard. Either some Irans had regrouped, or maybe there was a patrol outside the fort that had rushed back.

"Dogbreath to Grubb. Barrage them with TOWs. Do not! Do not fire near that bomb laying out there." As the missiles zipped and struck, the end of the yard choked in blood and agony.

Bandar Barakat was shoved forward toward the front cabin, tied and gagged. Grubb and Marsh remained outside of the SCARAB as their men went up the ramp.

Jeremiah Duncan looked it all over quickly, seized Quinn's arm. "If anything happens to me, it's your command, Quinn."

Quinn protested. "Don't like it."

Dogbreath repeated, "Yea or nay?"

"This is Quinn. I'll do it."

"Dogbreath to Cherokee and IV."

"Yo."

"Yo."

"Prepare the SCARAB to go."

"Aye, aye."

"Yo."

It happened neither violently nor loudly, but with a powerful *womph*! Outside, Marsh went down. The left-side bubble of the SCARAB's windshield popped in, followed by a roiling hiss of air and a shower of razor-sharp metal squares and explosive buckshot. The top of

Cherokee's head was sliced clean off; behind him, Jeremiah Duncan's and Novinski's faces were blown away. IV caught a ricochet boring into his left side. He was still alive!

Quinn had been kneeling over Barakat, tying him up, and was out of the direct line of the bomb's wrath. *Oh, Jesus!* Quinn's head screamed! He doubled over, his forehead opened and bleeding down his face. He fought his way back from unconsciousness with an unknown power keeping him alive and awake.

"Corpsman," Quinn called softly, "I'm hit, when you've got a chance."

Outside the plane, Grubb ran to Marsh, flung him over his shoulder, and ran for the SCARAB. Marines jumped out of the plane to cover and assist them. Marsh's leg dangled by a cord of sinew.

Dr. Wheat went forward. "Three body bags! Dogbreath, Novinski, and Cherokee are dead."

Ropo's men tugged the bodies and laid them out in the center aisle, then fished for the body bags.

"IV and Quinn," Dr. Wheat called.

"I'm all right," Quinn gasped. "Are you hit? I just have a little trouble seeing."

IV was alive and groaning. He pointed at his side. Wheat ripped his shirt in half to get to the wound and applied a pressure pack, hard now, hard. "Now, don't you go into shock on me, IV. You're going to make it if we can stop the bleeding. Talk."

"That's better, count me in," IV rasped.

"Doc! We got a mess back here."

"IV, press hard. Quinn, I'll send Corpsman Lew up for you."

"Yo."

The doctor got Marsh on the operating litter and examined the mangled limb and mapped a course of action. He applied a tourniquet and sent Corpsman Lew forward.

Lew had Quinn sit, then knelt alongside him. "Hang on, bubba." He wrapped a large cloth over Quinn's head and wiped the blood from his face. It was very difficult to move, for the cabin ceiling was dripping with the blood of the three dead Marines and the floor was slimy with it.

"Talk to me, bubba. Where did you get hit?"

"I think the back of my head and the front of my head."

"How's your attitude?"

"I'm okay, goddammit."

"Talk about shithouse luck," Corpsman Lew said. "Back of your neck is ripped, and it looks like a mole furrow right around to your forehead . . . and that's got a nice hole in it. You gonna be all pretty again, Quinn. I'm taping the gash together and wrapping your head tight. We'll get that bleeding . . . yes, sir."

"Whew, Lew, be gentle, mother."

Corpsman Lew gasped for breath after finishing a very rapid binding.

"Who got hit?" Quinn cried.

"Cherokee, Novinski, and Dogbreath are dead. IV is hurting. Marsh's wounded. We'll have to go into IV's belly and take a look."

Quinn's mind bolted through bashings of pain. He gave himself a few seconds more to align with the situation. Think, son, think. He dared open his eyes, and the first sight of the cabin caused him to vomit. That was good. The puking was over with.

It became clear. IV was the only one who could fly the SCARAB. Quinn called for Doc Wheat and Grubb.

The doctor checked Quinn quickly. "You'll last for a while. Corpsman Lew. Shot of penicillin in the ass for Quinn and prepare some plasma. I've got to get back and take Marsh's leg off."

"No," Quinn snapped. "IV is the only one who can fly us out. He has priority on medical attention. Grubb."

"Yo."

"Dogbreath told me to take over. Do you have any problem with that?"

"I heard him," IV rasped.

"Hell, no, Gunner," Grubb said.

"As I understand it," Quinn said, "we've got two emergencies, Marsh and IV. IV is the only one who can fly us out. Keep him awake and out of shock."

"What about Marsh?" Dr. Wheat asked.

"Corpsman Lew is assigned to Marsh till you can get back to him."

"But I can't fly, I can't move," IV agonized.

"You can tell me how to fly. Remember, I've logged a few hours' flight time on this plane," Quinn said.

"Can you see at all, Quinn?"

"We'll work that out. No choice. Kindly stay alive, IV. I need Jarvis front and center."

Master Tech Sergeant Roosevelt Jarvis had been seated close to the front cabin. He wormed his way in.

"Novinski has bought it," Quinn said.

"Shit."

"Take Dogbreath's seat and run down our systems."

As Quinn cleared his eyes of blood, Jarvis came up with death-notice news. "All the systems are inoperative. The display panels have been blown away. I don't think we've even got radio."

"Quinn to Grubb."

"Yo."

"I need some paper maps and a pair of field compasses. I'm keeping Jarvis here with me."

Quinn turned to the blown-in window. "IV, any way we can fly with the window out?"

"No."

"Mercer, this is Quinn. Get your tool kit and come up here."

They moved with unerring grace through the slippery carpet as Quinn gave orders between thumps of blood spilling down his face.

A break! The window frame was made of titanium and intact. Mercer measured the hole.

"I think the back of my seat is titanium," Quinn rasped. "Remove it and see if you can use a piece."

"No way we can attach it in the frame."

"All right," Quinn said, "do you have any clamps?"

"Yeah, four or five."

"How's this: wrap the piece with plastic from the spare body bags and canvas from the litters. We clamp it all together, put it inside the plane, and tie it with rope wire through the struts. Anybody got a better idea?"

The odor of dead parts now mingled with a waterfall of sweat.

"Jarvis. Help me into Cherokee's seat," Quinn ordered.

"Yo."

Grubb took off Quinn's soaked bandage and replaced it.

"Grubb. I want you to stay up front. Turn the back cabin over to Ropo. Then snuggle in close to Jarvis. Jarvis, you read the instruments and point. Grubb, take my hand and place it on the proper levers. IV, you still there, buddy?"

"In a manner of . . ." IV gasped.

"Have you got the drill? Stop me if I'm making a bad move," Quinn said.

Quinn made the mistake of reaching to give IV a pat. IV's stomach seemed bubbling to explode. "If we can't get this SCARAB up and away, I think we fight it out to the last man," Quinn said to himself. "I'm not taking these men to an Iranian prison." He punched the makeshift window. May not hold.

"Mercer, make a brace or a cross over the window out of a couple of machine-gun barrels."

"Got it."

No Iranian had crossed the "I dare you" line in the courtyard, but distant curses could be heard from the survivors, reaching to their depths for valor, collecting weapons amid the devastation, and craving a rally.

The first shots rang over the courtyard, kicking up dirt near the SCARAB.

"Ropo! Get all your TOW men out of the plane and give the Irans hellfire! Shoot up everything you've got! We need to buy ten minutes."

IV grunted the checklist to Grubb, who quickly located the switches and levers and moved Quinn's hand to them.

. . . Doc Wheat had screwed down the tourniquet on Marsh's leg, turned him over to Corpsman Lew, and skidded on blood to the forward cabin to ease the pressure bandage off IV. He probed. "I need a bigger flashlight here!"

"Coming," Mercer answered.

"Holy *Mother*!" screamed IV.

"Sulfa powder! Sulfa powder!" Wheat called, probing with forceps and fingers. "Geez peese," he cried, pulling out a piece of buckshot. "Sorry, buddy, I've got to cauterize you . . . don't go into fucking shock on me. Who's holding the flashlight?

"Give me the light and tell Corpsman Lew I need the hot needle, and a couple slugs of brandy, then put this clamp in his mouth to bite on."

Outside, the Marine shoulder missiles laid rubble on rubble and broke up the Irans' attempt to rally.

"We're running low on TOWs!"

"Fire your clips till empty. There's ammo ditched on the ground, right side of the craft."

"In like Quinn," Mercer said, pointing at the unconventional window brace.

"Kick it, hard," Quinn ordered.

It held.

"IV."

"Oh, piss, what?"

"If the ship doesn't hold pressurization, how low do we have to fly?"

"Under ten thousand . . ." he groaned.

"Hot needle coming up!"

A barrage of automatic fire wiped out all other sounds. Quickly, everyone clamped on earphone sound deflectors.

"I've got your belly deadened best I can, IV, now drink this, then bite on your clamp. Go."

Wheat applied the needle. IV arched up, screamed. Held in place by strong hands, he settled down and a smile crossed his sweaty, bloody, tortured face.

"Hey, Marine, good going," Wheat said.

"Jarvis, can you punch in an alternate system and try to bring up the CDU?"

"All the display panels and LED readouts were shattered by the cluster," Jarvis answered.

"Do we have a radio?" Quinn asked.

"Negative."

"Oh, Lord. Well, let's see." The head pain came on like a torrent until he had to bite his tongue and lower lip, hard. Come on, Quinn, for Christ's sake, this is no time to pass out.

"Jarvis."

"Yo."

"Jarvis, wipe the blood out of my eyes, then have the closest two men to Barakat remove his gag and get his face up here. What's our fuel reading?"

"No reading."

Quinn quickly ran through the problem. He had ledgered the weight of each piece of equipment. If he subtracted all the missiles and bullets shot up, subtracted the approximate weight of the fuel used, he might get a round figure on remaining fuel. He gave the problem over the intercom.

"No questions, just answers," he ordered.

It appeared they could get off the ground and fly . . . how long was moot . . .

Quinn mulled taking a run down the courtyard with the nacelles at seventy-five degrees to save fuel. No . . .

madness. What if, out of fear of running out of fuel, we flew in helicopter mode and made a soft landing somewhere in Iran when the fuel ran out?

Fuck it! I'm going to take her high, put her into turbo-prop, and hope to God we can find the tanker. The decision had been made by Quinn. It would be better to crash than be captured.

Barakat's sweating face was pushed close to Quinn. "Stop trembling, Barakat."

"Am I friend or foe?" Barakat asked.

"Damned if I know, but your ass belongs to us now. You going to help us get out of here?"

"I try, I try."

"I've got a totally FUBAR display and systems."

"Try your altimeter," IV moaned.

Grubb switched the dials on. "Got a reading."

"Barakat, we've got two field compasses and a paper map. The altimeter appears to be working. I am going to fly by the stars. I want you to draw me a flight route for a rendezvous with a tanker at thirty-one-forty latitude and fifty-eight-twenty long."

"I try, but even if we reach it, how do we contact them?"

"Phosphorous. Take the seat behind me and go to work.

"All hands, everyone in?"

"This is Ropo. All present and accounted for. Ramp is lifted."

A horrendous shriek from Marsh as his leg was cut away. For an instant the action diminished, then a resumption.

Quinn pitched the blade angles. He wiggled his feet on the rudder controls, daintily almost, as though he were stepping into the batter's box. He maneuvered the joystick. It felt solid. We'll find out.

"Barakat."

"Sir."

"How high do we have to go to clear these mountains?"

"About nine thousand meters."

Fourteen thousand feet! It would be borderline on oxygen use. Oxygen would help them now at any altitude. What the hell. No use saving it.

"All hands! This is Quinn. We've got every chance in the world to make it home. Prayers will help. Try to stay off oxygen, but use it if you feel like you're going under."

Random gunfire popped around the plane. Quinn checked to see if the rotors were properly engaged and whatever preflight instructions he could get from IV, who was sinking and rallying.

Quinn speeded the rotors to maximum, kicked off the hover brake, and reached for the thrust control on IV's side. He could not properly reach it.

"Jarvis! Crawl in and push the thrust control forward. Try not to touch IV."

"Aye, aye."

The SCARAB shot straight up.

"Oh, God, my leg is gone!"

"Quinn," gasped IV, "trim the nacelle to forty-five degrees . . . ugh . . . fool with the blade angle, you'll hear it when it's right."

"Grubb, put my hand on the nacelle or roto-tilt levers."

"Yeah."

"This is IV," he said, with his stomach half opened. "I feel like I'm in good shape."

The doctor scribbled a note to Quinn. "IV needs morphine."

The weight of one terrible decision after another fell on Quinn as Jarvis added more bandages to his head. If IV took morphine, IV could go ga-ga and incoherent. On the other hand, IV was going to have to go through excruciating pain without strong medication. Sorry, IV, Quinn said to himself, we need you coherent.

Quinn lifted his hand and gave a thumbs-down to Dr. Wheat.

Fort Urbakkan grew smaller and smaller, its great courtyard filled with survivors, now firing aimlessly.

SEVENTEEN

Rhein-Main Military Clinic, Frankfurt

It was a rare non-dank day. A kiss of sunshine flowed over the solarium. Quinn aimed his wheelchair at the warmth and held his face up. Oh, that feels good. I'll be out of the darkness soon.

The heavy bandage kept him from scratching at the itch across his forehead. How many stitches did the doctor say? More than four hundred invisible stitches to close the underlayers of skin. You lucky bastard, he thought.

The rest of it? Strange stuff, but for shrapnel head wounds, his lasting damage would be minimal. The right eye had escaped injury, the migraine headaches would simmer down in time, and the scar would smooth out to a thin line. He'd even be able to grow hair back over the seven-inch trail from the back of his neck to his temple.

Dr. Llewellyn Comfort, an eminent plastic surgeon, had been flown over from London for the operation. Dr. Comfort's skills were apparent as he softly hummed arias from *La Bohème* and *Tosca* as he worked. Quinn had remained conscious and exchanged banter with the doctor.

Quinn tightened up and emitted a pained wince of remembrance now, under his wrappings. He could think outside of the raid for a time, but the cycle always closed: Jeremiah Duncan dead, Novinski dead, Cherokee dead, Marsh dead, their faces and body parts blobbing off him, his vision blinded by his own blood . . .

Nightmare! How in the name of God had he managed to pilot the SCARAB to rendezvous with the tanker plane with Barakat reading coordinates on a map, a pair of field compasses, IV rasping out instructions, and Grubb and Jarvis placing Quinn's hands on the controls. Rocking and thumping over mountainous desert with a Marine-load of sallow green-skinned men deep in prayer.

"Hey, Gunner." Someone interrupted his memory chain. It was the nurse, the kindly nurse who rubbed against him whenever the occasion presented itself. She wanted to baptize him in waters of compassion. "It says on your chart that Dr. Comfort is going to remove your bandages today."

"It's going to be nice to unglue my eyes."

"The doctor immobilized them so you wouldn't inadvertently tug on your stitches."

She patted his face, old Mandy did, and sighed a companionable sigh, then set his wheelchair into motion.

"Where we going? I don't have to whittle yet," Quinn said. "The sun feels good."

"There's someone here to see you," Mandy answered. "There's a quiet little room off to the side."

The big door bumped open, and as Quinn drew a breath, he knew. "Greer?" he whispered, barely audible.

"How in the name of—"

"It's that stuff you're wearing, aroma of boys' locker room."

"It's Arpège, and you started me off on it. Too bad you can't see me, I look great."

After all the bloody years, boom, in she walks, just like that. Hi, stranger, remember me? "Well, now, let me guess," Quinn said. "How did Greer know Quinn was in Frankfurt? What is it that you own? A radio and TV network, forty-six papers, seven magazines, and satellites-o-rama?"

His heart speeded when her lips found his cheek.

"Well," he said, "there's good news. My dick just tingled. It's still working. How's Vampira, the media queen?"

"Hey, man, I'm just a salaried employee of Warren Crowder—"

". . . of We Own the World, Inc."

"I'm, in fact, the CEO of a medium-large division."

"I heard you've elevated the face of television and radio programming clear up to semiliterate."

"Did you know that the *Great Symphony Orchestras of America* series draws more than arena football and women's fight-night combined? Might I say I'm friggin' proud of the fact that I can still find a civilization breathing under all the sitcoms and sludge talk shows. How do I do it? I find subjects on the ad nauseam channels and packages culture. Shakespeare sells corn flakes."

"Yeah," Quinn said, "Disney makes dirty adult pictures now, too. But here we are talking shop. How did you find me?"

"I never lost you, Quinn. I always had an eye out."

"What do you know about my recent past?"

"Marine Recreational and Morale team raided and flattened—no, obliterated—an ancient mountaintop Persian fort near the Great Salt Desert, snatched Bandar Barakat, and made a clean escape."

"So, news of the raid is out?"

"No, not exactly," Greer answered. "A few rumors, mostly wild guesses. Barakat's banker gave me the first tip. I took it from there."

"Then it's not out . . ."

"The President called me in and asked us not to run with the story," Greer said. "He realizes he can't sit on it too much longer. So the White House wants to call a press conference and put Barakat on display. Major antiterrorist coup."

"You agreed to give up a scoop like that?"

"Sounds a little corny, but even though I'm in the media, it doesn't mean that I can't make an unselfish gesture for the good of my country."

"Ah, but your colleagues will chastise you. They will squirt you with witch's bile for denying the public's right to know."

"After which we'll hold panels on all channels about media overkill and media responsibility . . . until the next big story comes up. Yeah, bud, but try to have democracy without us."

"So, when does the public learn about the Urbakkan raid?"

"Day after tomorrow."

"What's going to happen to RAM Company?"

"They're trying to decide whether to disband RAM, integrate it into a larger strike force, or just continue to keep RAM at the ready. There will probably be a congressional investigation. Anyhow, Quinn, you're above it all. We got us a genuine American hero."

"Everyone on the raid was a hero."

"Aw, shucks, gee whiz, ma'am," she mocked.

"Greer. You were born with a cynical hair up your butt. I couldn't even try to make you understand."

"Yeah," she said, "boys' bonding stuff."

"All right, we have established the following: You are a big hitter with Crowder, multi-global double universal, simultaneously broadcasting twenty sporting events, including inline-skate cliff jumping. What I want to know is why you returned to me eight months of unopened letters and why you fled New York when I came to see you."

"You know why, dammit!"

"I'll tell you what I know. A broken heart is not a metaphor. That whack I got in the back of my head never gave me the pain I had over you."

"Baby . . ." she whispered, and touched his cheek. He reached out to grab her hand, but she took it way.

"Okay," Quinn said. "You've shown me how clever you are and how you have filled your responsibility to our president by giving up the scoop of the year. Anything else?"

"You son of a bitch," she snapped.

"That's more like Greer."

"You son of a bitch. If I had opened a single letter from you—if I had seen you in New York—Quinn, I opted not to spend my life baking cookies for the St. Patrick's Day church supper. I've done what I set out to do."

"Why are you so fucking happy, then?"

"I don't know what happiness is supposed to mean. I love the money, I crave the power, I adore my Fifth Avenue apartment, I sweep in to chauffeured limos. But I don't know what happy is. I don't know. I don't know."

"What is it you don't know?"

"It ain't your body that's in my bed anymore, man, and I pay that bill every day of my life."

It was getting to be vintage Quinn vs. Greer. Did they adore it or what?

"Did you nail Crowder?" Quinn asked.

"To the cross," she answered. "He never had a chance. Nor could he dust me off like I was one of his bimbos."

"Warren Crowder's moll."

"The one who came to stay, and let me tell you, buddy, he needs one."

"Why, he's just like a wee little hapless puppy if you peel back that veneer of crusted tycoon. He's a little lost soul when he hasn't gobbled up a competitor, closed down a factory. He's destroyed and pained when the government doesn't let him pull an end run around a monopoly."

"He's no puppy," Greer said bluntly, "but neither is he some sort of latter-day phenomenon. He was in a toga in Roman times and led a Mongol horde across the steppes. Power men like Warren have been running the show since the beginning of time."

"The two of you must set off volcanos."

"Yeah, yeah, that's right."

"And you've got control of the monster."

"I see a future in it."

"Well, drop by again if you're in the neighborhood."

The bell gonged, and he went to his corner and she to hers, and they snarled across the ring at each other.

"It still hurts, baby," he rasped at last.

"It still hurts," she whispered. "Quinn, I flew here to talk over another matter with you. It's about your father."

Quinn reacted as she knew he would, in tight-lipped, tight-jawed, teeth-clenched confusion.

"It's been five years since you contacted them. Isn't enough enough?"

"This is weird," he answered, "Greer speaking on behalf of Dan O'Connell."

"You haven't been out of their sight. They read every letter you've sent Rita and Mal. They have spent enough tears to re-star the universe. When you joined the Corps, I was a basket case. Dan came to New York and pleaded for me to give him forgiveness. He was wasted over the abortion. I forgave him. See? I'm not as stubborn as you. I forgave him."

"I don't want to hear any more," Quinn said.

"Well, you're in no condition now to impose your wishes, so you're going to listen. Dan knew that you and I would never end up together, but he was extremely kind. He and your mother insisted on watching over my well-being, as though I was their child. I forgave him and, later, I accepted help. I went to a number of shrinks, but they all turned out to be mind fuckers. It was your dad, Dan O'Connell, who taught Greer to return to being Greer, and that I had to continue playing Greer's game in life. The man grieves for you with a passion of kings. If there is such a thing as redemption, they have redeemed themselves."

Quinn turned the wheels of his chair in a sightless circle, stood, and fished for the door.

"Let go of your rage, Quinn! God has punished them enough! Stop this goddamned silence of the Irish! Stop this goddamned Eugene O'Neill play!"

Quinn was unable to speak coherently under a deluge of bursting floodgates. She eased him back into the wheelchair. He attempted to stuff his agony back inside him.

"Quinn," she said softly, "Dan has had a stroke. He needs you, buddy."

"Oh, God!" Quinn cried and stuttered and mumbled, more tears coming under his bandaged eyes. Greer attended him until his trembling subsided.

"How bad's Dan?"

"Half and half. It's certainly not a full recovery, but he isn't crippled. He has some trouble walking and talking. The pain is in his chest, just as it was in mine and yours."

"Mom?"

"She's also devastated by her sin to her church. And you are the only son she'll ever have."

They sat silently for ever so long until day turned to evening. "I have to go now," she said. "Can I tell your parents to be expecting your call?"

"Yes."

"And thus closes another chapter in the splendid adventure of Quinn and Greer," she said.

"Baby . . ." he pleaded, "just once."

"Please don't ask me," she cried.

"Baby . . . baby . . ."

Greer lifted her skirt and straddled his lap, facing him. He lifted her top. He knew she would wear her clothes that way. Those little breasts were just the same. One kiss, two. "Baby . . . baby . . . go now," he said.

Quinn O'Connell was empty, but filled. The anger was gone. So was the affair with Greer.

There were people who loved him fiercely, and he could love them again. Yet can finality truly be final even so? There still lingered the haunting of his birth mother's name—and his father. Would this bloody nagging ever come to a close? He was beginning a process which might allow him to spend the rest of his life with the mystery. In doing so, then perhaps he could allow Dan and Siobhan to come in closer and for him to give what was due them.

He sensed the nurse entering to wheel him back to his room, then asked her if she would write a letter for him.

Wanting to be near Quinn as much as she could, Mandy took the letter, which was written to Mal. It didn't reveal anything of the raid, because he'd have to remain silent until the presidential press conference.

And how was Rita? No lack of letters from her. Every year brought new batches of photographs. How old was she now? Twenty-two, maybe twenty-three. Every photograph lingered in his wallet until it was eventually replaced by a newer one. She was magnificent. Her letters to him were powerful in what was left unsaid.

Later, Dr. Llewellyn Comfort came with a small platoon of lesser physicians and interns trailing behind him. He nodded to Mandy to remove the bandage, and he hummed an unintelligible aria as she did his bidding.

The room was darkened as she rinsed his eyes with a solution that set them free. Quinn squinted, then saw a half dozen smiling faces arrayed behind Dr. Comfort.

"Bravo," said one doctor.

"Lovely, lovely, lovely," agreed Comfort.

Mandy was faint with Quinn's beauty and power. She realized it was the end of her unrequited love, because he'd see her in daylight soon.

"So, that's what you look like, doctor," Quinn said. "Hi, Mandy."

The doctor examined him, happy with the results.

"I like a man who loves his own handiwork," Quinn said. "Can I have a look?"

Not much more than a thin line of the path of the shrapnel and a small mark where it had made its exit. "A dueling scar," Quinn said, allowing his fright to bubble out of him.

"We'll get most of that cleaned up," Comfort said. "Keep your shades drawn, just use the dim lamp until you adjust. You'll be fine in a few days. I've done every wound in the book, but you take the gold, Gunner. A one-eighty between your skull and skin and hair."

"Thank you, doctor."

"In my line of work we don't see too many breaks from God. He must have you lined up for something big."

When they left, Quinn held Mandy's hand, kissed it, and thanked her for her kindness. What the hell! Mandy wanted some memories. Why not?

"How about dinner when they let me go out?" he asked.

"You don't have to," she said, reddening.

"I want to," Quinn retorted strongly. Once said, he saw a certain loveliness in her. Every woman is beautiful, he had often said to himself.

The phone broke the awkwardness. "It's for you, Gunner," Mandy said, and left the room.

"Gunner Quinn," he said.

"Hi, son," Dan's voice rasped.

"Hi, Dad."

"What the hell are you doing in a German hospital? I thought you were at Pendleton."

"I got a little messed up on a training exercise. Just some scrapes and bruises. Greer was here. Thank you for taking care of her in New York."

"She's a wonderful woman," Dan said.

Quinn stepped in to stop the coming apologies. "Dad, let's start anew. Let's just put the past behind us. I want to come home, soon as I can."

"Do you forgive me, son?"

"Of course I do. You're my dad."

"Marine gunner, huh?" Dan said. "Now, you just had to go and get a higher rank than me, didn't you?"

Quinn laughed. It hurt his scar. "Is Mom there?"

"She's right here. I'll put her on. I love you, Quinn."

"I love you, Dad . . . I love you."

EIGHTEEN

Quinn spent a restful night, the sleep of the reprieved. There had been many women since Greer, but none had put out the Olympian flame he held for her. He felt now that there could and would be life after Greer.

How well he slept after he had spoken to his mother and father! They slept well that night, too.

There was a knock on Quinn's door.

"Come in," he called from the easy chair.

General Keith Brickhouse, commandant of the Marines, entered.

Quinn came to his feet. The general waved him back into his seat, hung his hat and riding crop on the door peg, turned a chair around so he could lean his arms on the back.

"Army treating you okay here?"

"Everyone's been great, sir."

"That's a pretty damned good job Dr. Comfort did on your head."

"I'm lucky I still have a head."

"We need to talk a few things over. In another day you're going to be very big news. Please speak up now, and let's keep it informal. You're up for a big medal. I'd say the Congressional Medal is indicated, but it's peacetime and there's politics. So you'll have to settle for a Navy Cross."

Quinn shook his head. "Sorry, sir. I cry a lot these days, more in the past week than all my life combined. I can't accept a medal."

"Why?" Brickhouse demanded, then added, "As if I didn't know."

"If you know, then don't ask."

"Gunner, the RAM team, to a man, wants you to wear it on behalf of all of them. The President is going to issue a special unit citation medal for the rest of the men. The raid was one of the great chapters in Marine Corps history."

Quinn spoke nothing in return.

"You've a brilliant career ahead, Gunner. Before all the hoopla starts, I wanted to thank you personally. Will my smoking bother you?"

"Not at all, sir. As for my future, I've reached my capacity as a Marine. General, I cannot live with such violence. Funny to say after Urbakkan, but I'm not made of the stuff to take more hits like that. The cockpit was filled with brains dripping from the bulkheads and roof. Someone's eye was pasted against a window and stared at me all the way back. And I must add, sir,

I got no sweet feelings about the Iranians I killed. I must have gotten over a hundred of those poor devils in their sleep. General Brickhouse, I'm grieving far too much for Jeremiah Duncan and the others. Sorry, sorry."

Brickhouse followed his cigarette smoke to the window, sat on the deep sill, and commented on the nasty weather of middle Europe. "We all reach a saturation point, all of us."

"But there's a difference. You know—and General Duncan knew—what to do with your saturation points. That's why you're a general."

"You think so?"

"I know how Jeremiah Duncan was all but destroyed by Nam, but he had the guts to—to gut it out. The Corps is in my being, and I can take its spirit with me. I'm starting to get some idea where my future worth may lie," Quinn said.

Brickhouse weighed the proposition of cajoling, arm twisting, sweetening the pot. Gunner O'Connell was one powerful man. Guts enough to cry. God, the times he'd wished he could weep. God, the times he'd turned away from his wife's breast. Go till you fall, that's what.

"It will be a great loss to the Corps," the commandant said at last. "But we have some other business on the table."

"Yes, sir."

"Everything surrounding the formation of the RAM Company and the SCARAB was secret. The raid was of extraordinary importance in proving we could retaliate virtually within hours at any point in the world. It also proved the great stamina of that aircraft. Now then, Gunner, you are aware of the nature of the raid being a military operation and *not* a CIA operation, which would be under the surveillance of a congressional oversight committee."

"General Duncan trained me very carefully."

"How so?"

"He schooled me on the political ramifications of the military in a democracy. He drilled it into me that the Corps does not drop their pants and bend over before the other services or Congress. Democracy's daisy chain, he called it."

"You've heard of Senator Sol Lightner of North Carolina?"

"Mr. Powerhouse, undefeatable. Heads the intelligence oversight and is the hit man on armed services. Not friendly to the Corps," Quinn replied.

"That's him. He's been in the Senate over twenty years. Well, he's on the way to Frankfurt with one of his dobermans. Senator Sol is pissed off that he wasn't advised of the raid in advance. Our position—the President's, that is—is that it was not only a strictly military affair, but that the need for security overpowered the need to share. The inference is that the senator's office leaks copiously."

"But, General," Quinn interrupted, "the President didn't ask *me* if it was okay. He said raid; so we raided."

Brickhouse smiled. "Just giving you the gist. What the senator is going to try to hit us with is twofold. One, the raid smacks of a massacre. It was overkill. Second, there's a big no-no. Autopsies performed on our five dead show them all to be riddled with shrapnel from an American cluster bomb."

"What the hell were we supposed to do, sir? Sit down and hammer out the rules of engagement with the Iranians?"

"Senator Lightner has the magic buzz word to create a media feeding frenzy, namely, our men were killed by *friendly fire*! TV goes apeshit interviewing the weeping loved ones of the deceased. The print people will unlimber their big verbs on the 'We didn't play fair' theme by using cluster bombs, and the Marine Corps is going to get busted for our blood lust."

"What the hell's this all about?"

"It has its origins with the American people, who want to wage war without casualties. When the words *friendly fire* emblazon the headlines, half-truths will tarnish one of the great moments in our military history. But we had to advertise to the terrorists that we will hit them again and again."

"The truth is, sir, our people were killed by one of our cluster bombs. That's the truth."

"We are not playing semper fi and buddy-buddy, Gunner. Remember that your hero, Jeremiah Duncan, as well as myself, has had to feed the Congress a little."

Quinn wobbled to his feet. His head throbbed now.

Horseshit! The Corps comes first. He tilted his carafe of water, spilling it, missing the glass.

"You're telling me to lie, sir?"

"Oh, hell, no. Just be creative with the truth. We weren't raised that way, but our countrymen expect us to be saints, to be sparkly clean and pure. All the shit you had to go through to train and carry out a raid against terrorism. Now you've still got to justify it. And the press can be as bloodthirsty as the enemy. From what Jeremiah told me about you, you'll know how to handle it."

Keith Brickhouse troweled on the mortar of honor and duty and set the bricks of responsibility on his shoulders. Quinn had a sense of capability, a calm feeling of his own capacity.

Although Quinn wanted to walk to the conference room, Mandy would not let him. She wheeled him in. It was not only the wound, but he had expended blood and stamina unconditionally, and his entire body needed revitalizing. The flight from Urbakkan had demanded his final ounce of strength. He had borrowed too much strength from his own willpower, and it had debilitated him with recurring migraines.

The commandant and Senator Sol Lightner came in and took seats at the conference table. The committee lawyer looked up from the table, half rose, and nodded.

Quinn detected an adversarial relationship at once.

V. VINCENT ZACCO, his card read: SPECIAL COUNSEL. The card was undersized but expensive, as was Vincent himself. Form-fitting suit, Hoover collar, and the big mustache that small men of the world wear to send a message of their macho. The handshake told Quinn that the counsel had not made his way up through hard labor.

Senator Lightner was honored, honored, honored. He purred on, "We ought to have this little visit before the President's news conference tomorrow to see if we are all on the same page. I think informality is the order of the day. Now, you do understand, Gunner, that hearings are a usual way of life in the Congress, and you might be asked the same questions later, under oath."

Jesus, Quinn thought, the last clone of Senator Claghorn on *Fibber McGee and Molly*, or was it *Fred Allen*? A senator's senator, with honey-drawn banter. Hearings that ensure legislators a role in the separation of powers.

Lightner returned to his seat, lit a cigarillo, and nodded to Zacco, whose papers were rustling in anticipation. Zacco cleared his throat repetitively, tuning up. He oozed out a question or two to give a false impression of gentleness and feigned innocence. Quinn's guard went on alert.

Vincent led Quinn through his acquaintance and relationship with the late Major General Duncan, his joining the RAM unit, and an "understanding" of Quinn's role in the raid.

Quinn explained that there were separate entities within the company: namely, the fighting section, the front cabin men and command, and the aircraft itself. Quinn's job had been to coordinate the three and oversee the training schedules. In addition, Quinn had worked on the logistics of possible future targets. Quinn had also had his voice in all meetings and a hand on every piece of equipment that flowed to the Marines and had been tested for the SCARAB.

"In actual fact," Zacco said, "you were not only second in command, but the general's complete staff."

"In a manner of speaking," Quinn answered. "This was his manner of operation, to travel light. Likewise, every man in the unit had a second, third, and fourth skill. Everyone knew how to handle every weapon we carried, and so forth."

"But a drop in rank straight down from major general to Marine gunner? No disrespect, but shouldn't there have been a stronger chain of command? Perhaps a colonel directly under Duncan?"

"Well, unfortunately," Quinn said, "the man who could answer that is no longer here. However, and fortunately, it worked so well that we were right."

Brickhouse allowed a meager smile to form up.

"'Kiss,' General Duncan would say."

"'Kiss,' indeed!" Brickhouse retorted.

"It stands for, Keep It Simple, Stupid," Quinn retorted.

The corners of Brickhouse's lips smiled higher.

"I know you are hesitant to give an opinion, but wouldn't you agree that Duncan was a maverick and played a maverick's game?" Zacco asked.

"I'll give you my opinion," Quinn replied. "In my opinion, Jeremiah Duncan was the greatest Marine I ever met."

"And men tended to follow him blindly." That was V. Vincent Zacco's first mouse turd, Quinn thought as he stared at the counsel's beaver-squirrel-rat glint. "Let me take that a bit further. Didn't he have the officers' helmets wired so he could move you around like robots?"

Quinn laughed out loud. "Duncan made suggestions. The man on the scene made the decision. Our network gave us unity. We moved like a chorus line. Blindly? Hell, this was one of the best trained and informed group of men in any of the services. As far as the missing colonel in the chain of command was concerned, we obviously didn't need him."

Lightner's cigarillo ash grew longer on his frozen face. Zacco switched quickly to the savagery and overkill of the raid.

"The facts on the ground were clear," Quinn said. "We were compelled to fight in a walled-in, tight area. Our first strike was not only to take as many of them out as possible, but to inflict confusion. We weren't high on enemy blood, sir. We just didn't want anyone to get a lucky shot at the SCARAB."

"So," Zacco shot back quickly, "many Iranians came

out to the middle of the courtyard and tried to surrender."

"Yes, but maybe you'd like to tell me what we were supposed to do with prisoners."

"So you massacred them!"

"Not exactly, sir. We were ordered to shoot over their heads and drive them away from the plane, then keep them pinned down."

Christ! Quinn thought, how could Duncan have made decisions *knowing* he'd be grilled by Congress later on.

Sol Lightner's ever kindly Kris Kringle expression was tainted by his warthog eyes above his hanging jowls.

Zacco then attacked the speed at which the raid was put together. Was it not a sloppy affair, throwing in men not trained properly for the particular mission?

"The very cornerstone of the unit was advance preparation and development of a line of skills. This was guaranteed by drill after drill after drill. Duncan and his pilots checked out the SCARAB for nearly two hours every time it was flown. The systems were pushed every which way in training. The great strength of the SCARAB herself has been proved by her murderous flight to and from the target."

Quinn had warded off every attack with the ease of a fencing master.

"Shouldn't we take a little break?" the senator said, knowing his doberman had worked the questioning in to the critical areas, ones that Quinn could not talk around.

"I'd like to continue," Quinn pressed, "as long as I feel okay."

He felt that even in his state he had more stamina than the lawyer, who was near yelping in frustration.

"I take it that you and General Duncan were quite friendly."

"We worked very closely. A lot of formality was dropped. However, our relationship was by the book."

"You visited his home often?"

"General Duncan's office traveled with him, in his head, in his briefcase, in the trunk of his car. The office was open for business twenty-four hours a day. He called, I came."

"And you had dinner together?"

"He fed his dogs as well."

"At the table?"

"What the hell has this got to do with the raid on Urbakkan?"

"I'm coming to that," Zacco rumbled, sensing his first taste of blood. "You saw movies together, shot a round of golf with him now and then?"

"May I intercede?" Brickhouse interceded. "General Duncan found Quinn O'Connell to be the best young prospect for a high command that he had ever seen. I'd say, with the amount of responsibility Jeremiah laid on, probably they were closer as friends—and don't forget, in this kind of unit, the very fine line between officer and enlisted man often blurs."

"I am suggesting," Zacco said, "you two were close enough that if you survived him, which you have, you'd do anything to protect his record."

Quinn saw foul men and their foul tactics. He could do little but glare as he watched Senator Lightner cock his head waiting for his attack dog to strike.

"You wouldn't lie for General Duncan," Zacco said, "or cover up out of your deep respect and personal friendship?"

Quinn felt his hands grip the arms of his chair, and he started to rise. Sit down! he ordered himself, sit fucking down, Quinn!

"Like flying to Vegas in a government helicopter to keep a hot date?"

"That is most disgusting," Brickhouse exclaimed. "Don't answer it, Gunner."

"Now, gentlemen," cooed Lightner, "I do believe it is within counsel's purview to establish that if, in Duncan's position of unlimited power without accountability, he might have crossed the line and taken advantage—"

"Of what?" Quinn snapped. "Taxpayers' dollars? It's clear what you two are trying to do. I don't know how low you plan to take this, but I don't rat on a fellow Marine on matters that are none of your fucking business."

They had him.

"I've only a few more questions," Zacco said eagerly. "These homemade cluster bombs. You helped Duncan concoct them?"

"We worked with the finest munitions and ordnance people in the country. The weight of the men, the weight of the bombs, the titanium wings, were all factored in to make the plane lighter."

"This was not a safe bomb," Zacco accused.

"It was as safe as we could make it. We tested over a hundred of them successfully."

"But it was not a safe bomb because it exploded at the wrong time and killed five Marine officers. Gunner, they were killed by an American cluster bomb, were they not?"

"They were."

"And you were wounded by the same bomb."

"Yes."

"Friendly fire," the counselor snapped.

Hang on, Quinn, he compelled himself. Look at him in his rat's eyes. But stay calm, bubba. Quinn shrugged. "That's a stupid expression. It's the biggest oxymoron in the language. There is no such thing as friendly fire—safe bombs."

"It is a term commonly used to denote death at the hands of one's own people."

"The bomb was my responsibility," Quinn said. "I will take the blame."

The ash fell from Senator Lightner's cigarillo.

Zacco looked confused. "Would you care to explain that?" he mumbled.

"Sure. From the design to the installation to the firing, it was my baby. I checked the bomb racks at the Tikkah Air Base. They appeared secure. That was proved by the wild flight to Urbakkan. We flew at various altitudes, and the plane was nearly shaken to pieces. No bombs went off. If one had exploded, it would have been the endgame. You see, Mr. Zacco, you work with your people and your equipment to the best of your human capability, and then you have to trust. The Marine Corps is built on trust."

A silence followed. Quinn was dead calm, his eyes fixed on the lawyer. The lawyer didn't like it.

"Shall I continue?"

Vito Vincent Zacco nodded cautiously.

"Between Tikkah Air Base and Fort Urbakkan, some glitch developed in bomb rack four. Could have been the plane shaking violently, drastic changes in temperature, perhaps a little ping of some sort of debris which was flying at us as we crossed closely over the ridge tops. I got no indication of a problem on the display panels or gauges."

Lightner was transfixed. Zacco was confused.

"We positioned ourselves to fire," Quinn said. "I had under a minute to unload the missile racks. One bomb obviously veered off course and fell short in the courtyard. It was too small for our FLIR to pick up, and we didn't even sight it until the end of the raid. We moved our people away from the bomb, but she went off. Next half hour, forty minutes, was spent in ankle-deep blood, brains and guts on the ceiling, an amputation and a copilot with his guts about to spill out . . . we needed to patch a window . . . with Barakat's knowledge of the terrain and IV's courage, we made our rendezvous with the tanker plane . . . and after that . . . IV stayed alive and instructed me for over two thousand miles . . . that was five and a half hours from the time we left the fort. When I touched down on the helipad of our container ship and cut the engines, IV died instantly."

Zacco knew that when the fourth version of this insane story was told, Quinn would riddle himself with contradictions. He had the goods now to blame Quinn for the friendly-fire bomb.

"The bomb was my responsibility," Quinn said, entirely taking the wind out of both inquisitors.

Senator Lightner had a rare moment of shame and disgust for himself. Zacco had been stripped of his congressional right to bully. He knocked on the table in successive knocks. "I have a feeling you have something more to tell me, Gunner."

"Yeah, I sure do," Quinn said with a lowered voice. "You're a necrophilic, a corpse fucker. Now, get out of my sight."

"Mr. Zacco," the senator creamed reflectively, "the

gunner has been through a tremendous ordeal. I suggest his remark was made in the heat of the moment. Kindly wait outside."

The senator crushed an empty cigarillo box, tried but was unable to say something to Quinn. Quinn called for Mandy, waiting just beyond the door, who wheeled him away.

Now the scornful eyes of Commandant Brickhouse fell on Lightner. "I don't think we'd better have a hearing on this," the senator said. "I'm not going to tangle with Gunner Quinn."

PART TWO

NINETEEN

Troublesome Mesa, 1980

Oh, what a glorious valley. It echoed in a sound that said, "peace."

Dan O'Connell was neither able to drive a car nor ride in the saddle. The first time Quinn swooped him up into his arms and set him in the passenger side, the two looked at each other, wordless but rich with joy. Neither of them ever said, "I'm sorry." Dan was at his son's side a good part of the day, at the chessboard, or the movies, or being wheeled into Mile High Stadium for a Bronco game.

Quinn said to himself, over and again, "This is what life should be all about."

Dan O'Connell ceded his seat as state senator, and the governor selected Quinn to finish the term, even though it was a switch from Republican to Democratic.

Dan had made dramatic changes and lost some of

his Brooklyn cop mentality, broadening his base and finally getting a keen and compassionate understanding of other people.

He had been confused by the roiling student protests of the Vietnam War, by the ruckus called music, and by the decline in the basic morality, yet he'd grown enough to understand the meaning of the civil rights movement.

It was good to have a son as knowledgeable as Quinn, who seemed to have a grasp on all kinds of events and was a student of human history and behavior.

With Dan and his son so close these days, Siobhan was able to free herself to take a path she longed for. Siobhan had always been a stalwart of the church. She had to make peace with Greer Little's abortion and finally concluded that her church made mistakes. The mistakes usually came from men asked to give more than they had to give.

Siobhan soon represented Colorado as an upper-middle national committee woman. She and Dan traveled a lot on church tours of the cathedrals of grandeur in Italy and France, or they would cruise to the Alaskan glaciers, visit Buddhist temples, or charter for the Greek islands.

Quinn took over more and more of the ranch operation, bringing him into daily contact with the Martinez family. Consuelo and Pedro had four children, three of them university graduates, settled in cities as professionals with careers.

The remaining son, Juan, evolved into what seemed a natural passage from his father.

The Martinez family were twenty-five percent partners in the ranch operation. The changing of the guard from Pedro to Juan continued the close relationship with the O'Connells.

The families accorded one another the affection and respect of people who had spent a long time in one another's kitchens. And this, too, was good. Dan had overcome a good part of his bigotry as the Martinezes largely replaced his own family back in Brooklyn.

The older people were delighted that Quinn and Juan would continue to run the ranch. Juan, in particular, was a cowboy's cowboy, born to ride and rope, a mountain man with a graceful work ethic.

The clinker was that Carlos was missing. Quinn and Carlos had buddied so well, playing the games, dancing the music, riding like fury over the range, chasing girls, and tiptoeing into drinking and carousing when they felt manhood in their groins.

Carlos had gotten through law school in a blaze and been snatched up by a major Houston firm. His speciality, immigration. Whatever it consisted of, the family knew that Carlos would be good. Carlos was always flying off to the South and Caribbean and seemed prominent in his firm early on.

Quinn had only seen him once in the five years he was gone from Troublesome Mesa. They met in San Diego, mostly by happenstance, when Quinn was in the Corps.

Carlos had carved a hell of a life for himself, but why didn't he ever return to Troublesome? Consuelo and Pedro visited him every year in Houston and wondered why their son remained a bachelor or why he didn't let them know when he was traveling to Denver.

It had an eerie slant to it. Well, Quinn thought, I sure as hell didn't get Carlos's approval to join the Marines, and Carlos was certainly not indentured to the ranch. But he had loved the ranch. What made him divorce himself from it? In Quinn's fantasy of the future, Carlos had always been riding alongside him.

Quinn's homecoming brought a heartwarming letter from Carlos. He would come to the ranch for the first time in five years. When Carlos showed up, he and Quinn met each other as strangers.

Carlos wore an Italian suit, a wristwatch worth thousands, and was altogether a wealthy young dandy. It seemed that his reputation as a lawyer grew by the day.

Quinn's thoughts of them riding and howling at the moon and tying one on fell awkwardly by the wayside.

Carlos's visit was brief. They bumbled through their litanies, each realizing that they had outgrown one another and now lived in different worlds.

Carlos was dark and secretive and decorated like an

expensive crown prince. What of his love life? Many ladies to love but none to marry, Carlos told him.

Something was strange, out of kilter with the homecoming. Carlos never mentioned the third member of their childhood club, that little pest, Rita Maldonado. After she had graduated from Wellesley, she had stayed on in the East to do postgraduate work in creative writing and some teaching at the endless writers' conferences.

Why had her letters to Quinn suddenly ceased? Why hadn't she returned for Quinn's homecoming? Well, now, all Marines freeze a part of their childhood, a perfect part. Life evolves and Quinn had made no provisions in his dreams for the adulthood of Carlos and Rita.

The rewards of his new life with his parents was countered by an emptiness over his pals.

If Carlos and Rita were Quinn's disappointment, Reynaldo Maldonado mellowed it. They came together strongly, swapping tales of the Corps and tales of the road, conversing half the night away.

Maldonado remained unmarried but still had a collection of great beauties, particularly in Mexico, where he kept a studio in Cuernavaca. There was always a waiting line of magnificent creatures who wanted to model for him, and Quinn thought it wondrous how Mal had evaded the wrath of some jealous husband.

Each time Quinn came down to Mal's, he was halted

by the array of photographs on the mantel depicting Rita's growth from a little girl to the present. Quinn studied the photographs each time with growing interest.

"Jesus," he muttered one evening.

"You didn't expect she'd stay in pigtails," Mal said, carefully charting Quinn's interest.

"She is really beautiful. I mean, unearthly beautiful."

"Devastatingly so," Mal said. "Give or take a little more of this and a little less of that, Rita is probably one of the most beautiful women in the world."

"And she writes a lovely letter," Quinn said. "Her letters were never repetitious ad nauseam. She could relate any story about the wiggle on the end of the nose of one of your models, or maybe Saturday night in the old mining town, or the sheriff being the fattest gun in the West, or her walk through the wildflowers. You know, she was awfully pretty walking through a field of flowers, even when she was a kid, and then holding her skirts up to cross a stream."

In contrast to his own catting around, Mal had raised Rita as a protective father with great intelligence. Rita had developed into Rita, and that was what he had prayed for.

Rita was a constant child, quietly off with her poetry, quite sweet, and quite charitable about her father's wicked ways, for he also was a source of her growth.

Mal knew, almost from the beginning, how she had ached for Quinn from the time they first had come to

Troublesome Mesa. It was something a father could do poor little about. Watching Rita progress and develop, and after Quinn broke up with Greer Little, perhaps he would notice her. Their age difference was not that awesome, but the years of separation put them on different plateaus.

She's fully grown, Mal thought, and the homecoming fiesta is over and Siobhan and Dan are off to Florence. Well? What about it, Quinn? How many hearts were broken during your hitch in the Corps?

"What was Rita," Quinn said, "sixteen or seventeen when I left?"

"She's not seventeen anymore, Quinn. When you hooked up with Greer, Rita grieved as only a teenager could."

"Oh, come on, Mal. I never gave her an improper look."

"Yes," Mal said, "and I felt very good about that. Even a roustabout artist can have lionesque protective instincts about his only daughter. Rita was always a holy light to me. She tried to model for me a couple of times, but she was too beautiful to ruin in stone or oil."

"Why are you suddenly telling me this?" Quinn asked.

"She made a loud noise by her absence."

"I missed her, too," Quinn said. "I've loved Rita all my life but never thought of her as more than a little sister."

"Exactly the point," Mal retorted. "Rita is terrified that you'll reject her as a woman."

Quinn wanted to argue, but Mal's pronouncement had too much sting to it, too many years of wisdom.

"Do you want to see the Quinn O'Connell shrine in her room?" Mal led him by the arm and opened her door. The walls were adorned with photographs of Quinn the ball player, Quinn the rodeo rider, Quinn the Marine. There was a torn football jersey hanging off a rafter, a scrapbook.

"How do you feel about this, Mal?"

"You can't tell a person to change the longings of her heart. But now, well, you are back to stay, and I believe Rita wants to come back to stay and to write. I would like to see this part of her life resolved. In the drawers there are short stories and poems. Rita trying to prove to you and me that she is worthy of our love. That's why little girls twist themselves in pretzels in ballet class, to win their father's approval. That's why big girls write erotic poetry, to win their lover."

"And me, Quinn Patrick O'Connell?"

"Don't you know how much I love you, amigo?" Mal said. "It has been no pleasure knowing her secret and having to remain silent all these years. Will you stand up and tell her now?"

Mal's words chilled him. He was frightened. "Suppose I don't . . . can't love her that way?" Quinn asked.

"You'd have to be crazy not to love Rita, but it's your heart, man, just tell her the truth."

Quinn stared at her photographs and blended them with his own memories of a quiet little sloe-eyed, raven silk-haired being, tickled by him but hardly laughing to show him the stuff she was made of. Even in her early teens she had been scrumptious, classically round, voluptuous in a bikini.

"I've done something dreadful," Mal said. "I knew she kept a drawer of secret poetry, and I went in without permission." He opened the drawer and handed Quinn a paper. "She wrote this when she was sixteen."

Our first night together after dark
you never caught me
following at reaching distance behind you
on your way home from the river.
Had you looked back
you would have seen the same child
whose spare, uncharted body
you would instinctively shield with yours
against the sudden loss of passing time.
Twice you paused,
as if between movements of a symphony
the secret panicked crackling leaves
under my feet
and artless rhythm in the audience of your forest.
An aspen tree marks the place
where your land begins.
Its infinite shadows like fingerprints
of the moments I have stood beside it
confusing your arms with its firm extended
branches,

the deep cedar color of your skin,
the bark white corners of your eyes,
the sap which in unnatural light fills them,
runs down the ordinary roughness of wood,
your unshaven cheek.
For the first time, this night,
I stayed longer to watch you walk
toward the lit windows of your cabin
saw your two halves split at the roots:
wood and flesh
bark and skin
the veins of dried leaves the greener veins
across your wrists.
You never knew
but we fell asleep together
half of you beside me,
the other half locked behind a lit window,
all silent until the dark noisy grass woke us,
rousing itself with thoughts of its own fallen dew.

"God," Quinn whispered. "Her stories? Have you ever read them, Mal?"

"She read to me once in a while, or used to. I never wanted to be in judgment of her. Suppose she has no talent. I don't want to be the one to reject my daughter. Quinn, I've seen enough of her writing to know she isn't going to make it. I'll be there to pick her up when the realization comes to her. I'm a mediocre artist. I get through by being a Mexican tit man. I fart around with this modern bullshit because nobody, critics or clients, knows what it is but wouldn't dare say so. You can't get away with my shit as a writer."

"Mal, no sale. You're great."

"He's great," Mal said, pointing at an original scribble by Van Gogh.

That night Quinn's letters from Rita came out of his sea trunk. There were well over a hundred of them. Seen from letter to letter, their continuity was soon understood. Not exactly veiled words of love, but more of missing him as a part of the mountains. Nothing about boyfriends or her own growing maturity. She let the photographs do the talking.

Quinn had gotten one of two monkeys off his back. The resurrection with his parents was a great blessing. The other? Greer Little. He clung to a diminished, unreal thread. Hadn't Rita done the same thing? The women who loved Marine gunners were plentiful, but . . .

Quinn was puzzled by his own soul opening up. He didn't know if he loved her and wouldn't know until they stood face to face.

Quinn quivered every time he thought of Rita. All the way to the upstate New York Writers Conference, he sighed constantly. A powerful uncertainty it was whose moment of truth had come.

In the splendiferous woods bordering Lake George, the great old novelist Christopher Christopher held forth for ten weeks in the summer for serious aspiring writers. Ten weeks to feed the dream.

One had to go back a bit to remember Christopher's last great novel. He had outlived his mediocre talent but knew the whens and hows. He became a legend.

Actually, did old Christopher have any masterpieces? His name wove in and out of a generation of magnificent American writers, from the expatriots in Paris between world wars or in Pamplona, where he chased the bulls with Hemingway. Hadn't he actually been a cub reporter who got an interview with Hemingway and after Papa's death became a Hemingway "close friend" and aficionado. He wrote of visits to Cuba to arm-wrestle Papa. Never happened.

What about Sinclair Lewis? Christopher Christopher's *New Yorker* portrait of "Red" was certainly quintessential. Of course, not that many things had been written about Sinclair Lewis.

Christopher Christopher really made his big hit in American literature with an article for *Esquire* entitled "Chrysler Airflow—The Great American Car."

A Broadway producer of zingy revues thought it had a catchy ring to it—*The Great American Car.* He named one of his annual follies after it, and eight hundred performances later, Christopher Christopher was made for life.

These days he was an American icon (who once had tossed a chilled martini into F. Scott Fitzgerald's face).

Now thatched with wild silver hair, he held forth at Lake George with a dozen "master" students conducting the eternal hunt for the great American novel.

"I've done my little bit, made my small contribution," he would say as his eyes misted to the students of mixed gender. "As Pearl, Pearl Buck, God rest her, said just before she passed on upstairs, 'Christopher,' she said, 'keep the flame.' "

As he stared at the new students, some of whom had long since ripened, he wondered which of them, male or female, would become his bed mate for the summer.

"It is time to pass the torch," Christopher whispered.

Rita Maldonado realized in less than two weeks that she had bought an ultimate con. Or she faced an ultimate reality about her writing. No one can teach writing sitting in a happy circle barbecuing each other's writings. The criticism sessions could have killed a budding Shakespeare. Christopher drooled and dozed as his students had at it.

Rita was packing to leave when Quinn held up the brass knocker on the Jack London cabin. He was suddenly stricken with a notion that Rita might be in the middle of . . . well, a scene.

He used the knocker and took a step backward.

Rita opened the door and squinted through the screen.

"I've come to see you," he said.

The screen door squealed open, and he inched into

the cabin. She was so beautiful he had to lower his eyes for fear of blushing. Rita took his hand to her lips and kissed the joint of one finger at least a dozen times. Then she reached behind him and slid the bolt.

Their foreheads came together gently. She began to tremble.

"I don't want to hurt you anymore," Quinn said, "but I feel like . . . this here, now is the great beyond . . . and we're floating . . . Rita, I don't want to hurt you anymore."

She brought Quinn's hand to her blouse and unbuttoned the top button with him, never taking her eyes from his, button by button.

"I love you, Rita."

"Yes! Yes!"

She wore no bra.

"God, you're beautiful. I've been a real fool."

"Yes," she said.

"I'm worried that—"

She pressed a finger to his lips. "Don't worry. Quinn, you're never going to want to leave me."

"I think you're right," Quinn said

"Shall we be lovers?"

"I want you so bad."

"Bad or badly?"

"Both," he said.

She turned from him and went to a big armchair. "Just enjoy," she said, "I want to undress for you." There wasn't all that much to disrobe, jeans and panties.

She did it deliberately, as she must have practiced the moment a hundred times in her fantasies.

Rita sat on the big arm of the chair and struck a pose, handed him her panties. Quinn rubbed it against his cheek, then tried to eat it, drink it, bite it.

The dinner gong sounded for those for whom the gong rang.

TWENTY

Troublesome Mesa Early 1980s

Events, both sorrowful and joyous, befell Troublesome Mesa. Father Sean Logan, the gentle priest, passed away. He had never forgiven himself for his counseling an abortion for Quinn's sweetheart; nor had he fully accepted the vows that imposed secrecy in the matter of Quinn's biological parents.

Siobhan O'Connell, a church functionary with high mid-level contacts, began a quiet probe at Sean's funeral about locating the mysterious Monsignor Gallico. It was fruitless. He had disappeared, leaving no footprints.

A few months later, Daniel O'Connell had another more devastating stroke that almost totally debilitated him.

A moment of unabashed bliss happened for the wedding of Quinn and Rita. Over three hundred people from all over the state gathered to celebrate. The wedding vows were performed at Dan's bedside. Dan died shortly after with his wife holding one hand and his son holding the other.

So let it be. A bombastic wedding celebration and wake took place together with a party that Troublesome Mesa would never forget.

Quinn grieved for Dan in his long walk through the darkness. For all their being at odds, for all the mistakes, he and his father had ended up on the same road. Quinn realized that he and his father had been cemented by the same sense of honor and love developed in the Marine Corps. No matter Dan's flaws, these were overwhelmed by loyalty and honesty and courage.

After three months of intense mourning, Siobhan said, at the end of a meal one night, "We have to go on with life. I'm going to make an offer you can't turn down. Why don't you and Rita take a few months off just, just to follow your bliss? Meanwhile, back at the ranch, I'll take care of everything."

Their bliss led them to Venice. They arrived just a pinch before dawn and boarded the only gondola to be seen on the Grand Canal as a feeble sun arose, casting pastel glows mixed with foggy dew as in an Impressionist painting.

The honeymoon had been worth waiting for.

Glide, glide, glide skimmed the ornate boat; splish-splash whispered the gondolier's rudder.

Under the little footbridges, *click, click, click* sounded the women's heels.

The luring alleyways twisting and trapping as in a maze.

And not to forget the pigeons of San Marco Square.

Their corner suite of the Gritti Palace was mellowed by the smooth music of the Italian jazz saxophones and tapes of the San Remo Festival . . . and Pavarotti!

They did their initiation to Venice by making great love in a gondola. The rest of it was powerful, so powerful they seemed drugged and weary by daylight until the great blinds were opened and the sounds and light of that fairyland out there reached them.

At the end of a week, Quinn realized he had not thought of Greer Little since they arrived. Rita, him, Venice. A lifelong plan that absolutely thrilled him. Realizing he had not thought of Greer caused him to think about her. She was now locked away in a place in his memory. His desire for Rita was nearly crazy.

Yet, in the odd moments Rita seemed to stray. She could go from uncontrolled passion to a chilling, languid sadness.

It took six weeks for them to have their fill of Venice and find themselves flying back to America, starting to get homesick.

Once home, Rita dared her great challenge. The ranch and its divergent sounds, from bleating cattle to zooming pickup trucks and the general activity, threw her attempts to write off kilter.

She sought Quinn's blessing and set up a studio at the Maldonado villa a half mile below. Her bedroom was huge, had a fireplace, and was isolated.

Rita put a small wardrobe for herself and Quinn down there. If she worked late, if he needed a break from the ranch, if they wanted to make mad love, the studio was perfect.

Now there was a commitment to write, but the plushest office is no guarantee for lush pages. Rita was alone with Rita, with nothing between her and her typewriter.

It was serenely quiet.

Mal was gone a good part of the time, sculpting or painting some gorgeous body. Jesus, Mal, all those rich married ladies who want their boobs aggrandized! Some of his clients were older ladies, not of the sturdiest stuff but defiant and flouting their sensuality.

Rita had seen a lifetime of her dad working them. Anyhow, he always seemed inspired, no matter their sag.

Mal settled into his studio down in Cuernavaca in order to give his daughter thinking space.

Quinn had some apprehensions about Rita's studio. He did not want it to become the scene of her heartbreak. He traveled back and forth to Denver as a senator, or on ranch business or flying about the country to Democratic Party meetings. Ordinarily, he'd want Rita with him, but she was entitled to follow her own bliss and make her own life.

She wrote her Venice pages and read and corrected them, lured by the soft-scented fire. Thoughts which had been so clear in her mind had terrible trouble finding their way onto paper.

It was perfect here, she knew. Peace and isolation had been achieved. She had a wonderful, understanding husband. God, she thought, does God want writers to go to hell to write?

For all the ethereal wonderment, Rita began to feel she was in a trap, a cage. Why did the story stop suddenly?

Quinn was due home from San Francisco late. She admonished herself for not going into Denver to meet him and stay over at their condo. She didn't like him flying into Troublesome at night.

She closed her eyes and thought of him, and the stirring between her legs went on automatic. She'd while away the hours thinking of Venice, and then his Jeep would vroom into the driveway. Hearing his voice was like eating chocolate. Rita purred and stretched and ran her hands over herself.

Her tummy felt squiggly. She made a pitcher of margueritas, which she never did when drinking alone. As she licked the salt around the top of the glass, her forehead broke into tiny droplets of perspiration. Now came unfettered fright.

The level in the marguerita pitcher lowered.

Quinn knew something was awry when he arrived a few hours later. Rita was slightly listing, and their kiss was punctuated with salt.

"I'm a couple of drinks up on you," she said. "How did the meetings go?"

He related the business of the trip. Dinner was sitting on the floor before the fireplace at the coffee table and afterwards, a sink into soft pillows with softer sax over the hi-fi.

Rita appeared misty-eyed, hardly taking her eyes off him. Quinn loved what he saw. It seemed that they were unable to pass each other without some kind of touch. Painted-on leather pants, bare midriff, an open blouse knotted under her breasts, glowing lipstick. He watched her clear the table . . .

"Quinn," she said, meandering to her desk. "I'd like you to read my pages. I realize some of them look like they were written between the sheets. Look, I think I might need some help."

Quinn was about to go into his standard evasion, but on this night the air had something different drifting on it.

"I'd be scared to death," he said.

"Scared of hurting me? Scared of rejecting me, telling me I stink? Mal has played that game with me for years."

"Rita, it isn't as though Mal was telling you that you made the bacon too crisp, try to get it right the next time. Writing has been at the center of all your longings most of your life. I don't have the proper credentials. I don't want to screw around in a place I have no right to be."

"I've heard all that before," she said with a tart edge rising in her voice.

"Don't be pissed at Mal for wanting to protect you from his ignorance. He was smart not to make that kind of mistake. Damned if I want to sit in judgment of you."

"You're both convincing. Frankly, I think you're copping out. Between you and Mal, you've read every piece of literature written since the Middle Ages."

"That doesn't make me an expert."

"Who is an expert? Christopher Christopher? I've reached that stage where anyone with a license to steal is a self-promoting prick in business to keep the wannabes coming back for one more writers' conference. Quinn, do you know what it's like making a submission for publication? You're dead, rejected before you put it in the mail. 'Your story is well-written but doesn't fit our needs,' signed 'The Editors,' who will remain nameless."

"Rita, nobody forced you into writing."

"Thanks, I really appreciate that. I'm twenty-five years old. I've been doing this since I was nine. I need a break. Mal takes my work to the literature professors on campus. 'Shows a lot of promise, but needs work.'"

"Haven't you just answered your own question? What professors at the University of Colorado, or all the universities in Colorado, have published anything of major note in the past fifty years?" Quinn argued.

"I want a straight answer. I want to hear cold-turkey truth from one person of literary integrity. Just one person. If I can't get that from my husband, who can I get it from?"

Rita would not be deterred. She had drawn the line, and Quinn had to cross it.

"Are these the pages?" he asked. "All right, but I wish to hell I knew better about what I am doing."

He knew enough.

Some of her earlier poetry had danced and leapt and was filled with cunning and grace and metaphors. Down through the years, as each new piece of non-poetry grew longer, it strayed. She was unable to organize the work, keep it under the central command of the writer. The dialogue came from pickled talking heads, not people of wit and observation.

There was a list of commonplace pitfalls, no sense of when a sentence could be expanded into a paragraph or a chapter shrunk to a few paragraphs. Her first chapter was front-loaded with information, a fear that novice writers have about leaving anything out of the manuscript.

What about the prerequisites? Writing required both enormous motivation and enormous drive. Rita had only enormous desire.

The baffling part of it was that lesser writers had succeeded. Rita could glow in spots. Some writers were ready to cut off their arms and legs for the title of writer. Was it possible she could rally her gifts, enhance them, and then make the commitment to enslave herself at the typewriter?

Perhaps Rita's life and Troublesome Mesa and her beauty and her father had all been too perfect to arouse a bit of rage. Rita had been too protected, and her craving for expression could only carry her through a half dozen verses of a psalm.

Quinn set down the Venice pages deep in the night. He was dog tired, too tired to be intelligent about it now.

Rita had fallen asleep atop the bed, adrift in self-deprecation. She was curled up tightly, her perfect hair askew and an odor of tequila lingering. Rita couldn't drink worth a damn. She had tipsied out.

Jesus, Quinn wondered, what was she making him do?

Rita's eyes opened slowly, and the first thing Quinn saw was her fear. "Hi," he said, patting her hair.

"I'll take a shower," she said.

"It's almost five o'clock," Quinn answered. "I flew in late, remember? I'm dead tired. Push over, let me on the bed."

Quinn pressed his backside into her tummy and she wrapped her arm over him in a favorite sleeping pose, but she could sense his eyes were open and Quinn always knew when she was staring at him from behind.

"I need to hear it, Quinn," she pressed.

"I loved you this morning more than I loved you yesterday, and I love you now more than I loved you earlier tonight. Isn't that what really matters?"

"And with three you get egg roll!" Quinn felt the violent jerk of the comforter being flung off as she ripped it away from him. Quinn rose on an elbow as the end table lamp blared on. Rita stood over the bed, disheveled and rocking back and forth. Obviously, she had been awake and seething to a boil.

"It's actually very good," he said. "I don't want to go into it point by point until I have a few hours' sleep and can get my thoughts together."

"Liar!"

"There's some fine writing there," he said. He closed his eyes. "But most of it stinks!"

It was not Rita standing before him but a pained, contorted creature who had pushed herself beyond the edge. In that single instance of truth Rita heard what she had avoided for a decade and a half.

"It's not the end of the earth," Quinn said.

Lord, he'd never seen her like this! She was an angry Gypsy, disconnected from herself. "Two things, two things, just two things," she hissed. "That was all I wanted. I wanted to write, and I wanted to be perfect for you. I'm neither."

"Let me hold you, darling."

"No, you can't hold me anymore."

"Rita, get a grip—"

"I wanted to be perfect for you, Quinn. I was not perfect. Do you know what I mean?"

"How could you be? We were never promised to each other. You grew to be a woman while I was gone. I know you must have had lovers. It doesn't matter now."

"I thought," she moaned, "that by becoming a great writer, you'd forgive me for my imperfection. I'm neither."

Rita moaned low, all that beauty fallen into wreckage. "I did what I did in the hope you would learn and be jealous and pay attention to me. I did it to anger you. I did it . . ."

"What?"

"Carlos and I."

The pain of his head wound came alive, and he fought for his feet and staggered around the room. Her sobs were loud and followed him until he turned to her and pushed her away.

Rita heard the screen door slam.

Vroom . . . vroom, vroom, vroom. The Jeep screamed away.

TWENTY-ONE

Denver—Early 1980s

Bloody secrets! Bloody lies! The church, the ranch, his parents, the whole goddamned valley seemed to conspire.

This was far worse than losing Greer Little. Greer never betrayed him. He had seen truth in Rita. But what the hell, Quinn thought, he had been away at El Toro Air Base shagging the ladies, breaking hearts. She couldn't make promises to him, for there were no promises to be made.

But Carlos? Hot and deliberate. Aimed to gore him! Why hadn't she come to him with this before the wedding? Why did it have to be a part of the goddamned secrets and goddamned lies?

Reynaldo Maldonado returned from Cuernavaca after Rita had fled. He was shocked and hurt almost as deeply as Quinn.

"Sorry it took me so long to get here," Mal told Quinn. "I made a couple of stops along the way."

"Did you find her?"

"The day before yesterday she went to Carlos in Houston."

Mal watched his son-in-law shudder.

"Apparently, she arrived in bad shape. She wouldn't see me. Quinn, I had no idea they were carrying on. When a woman deceives, she can carry it off so smoothly. Only, she got caught in her own web."

"I thought she loved me more than this," Quinn said.

"She does, beyond all reason. Don't jump on me. My throat is dry from the salt from my eyes."

"What kind of destructive logic consumed her with the notion that she had to become a writer to atone for a sin she never committed?"

"If anyone is responsible, I am. I should have seen it coming," Mal said.

"Why didn't she tell me? Why Carlos?" Quinn cried.

"Desperation from warped logic. Confusion. Quinn was the Quinn she could never really have. Carlos was the Quinn who loved her."

"Stop it right now. I don't want to hear his fucking name, right? I've got nasty images in my head. I could kill him."

Mal unearthed his hash pipe. He found a bottle for Quinn.

"Rita grew up surrounded by dozens of drawings and

wire figures and polished marble of her mother. Every pose of Mimi sang out that she was perfection. I remember Rita trying to imitate her mother. Maybe it all made her feel inferior to Mimi. When Mimi died, Rita wanted to supplant her mother in my heart. I couldn't paint or sculpt her, and that probably cut her even more deeply."

Quinn poured. Mal puffed.

"Then came a never-ending parade of women. What was I searching for? My dead wife. Poor Rita, always in an adjoining cabin on a cruise while daddy, next door, was banging some rich widow or some adulterous married woman. I didn't even see her growing away, tucking herself in a corner writing poetry. Soulful, deeply hurt. That's why I found Troublesome Mesa, so she would gain her self-respect."

Quinn poured himself a neat double and closed his eyes. After he had gone off to the Corps, he had tolled up the difference in their ages. It was not the number of years that counted. When a young man in Troublesome getting urges, Rita was still a little girl in the second grade. When Rita blossomed, Quinn was at the university, engaged in his flame-out affair with Greer Little. When he went into the Corps, Rita was just beginning Wellesley.

As his image of Rita had grown in the semi-isolation of the RAM unit, she had crept into his mind more and more. He equated it at first with missing the mountains. He was Colorado. She was Colorado. He looked forward to her letters and photographs. Yet he continued to correspond with her as he would a younger sister.

In a full, rich moment Mal had told Quinn what he had not seen. Rita was a glory among women, and she had waited for Quinn patiently. By the time of their marriage, he had begun to realize how deeply Rita had woven herself into his fabric.

"She's my daughter," Mal said. "I have to go to Houston and see what I can do."

Quinn nodded his head that he understood.

"I'll probably have to reach Carlos. Will she ever be able to come back to you?"

"No," Quinn answered. "As for Carlos, if I see him, I'll blow his face away."

Siobhan broke her tour off and rushed back to Troublesome. She immediately grasped that the only thing she could do for Quinn was to leave him alone and be there, should he ask for help.

The ranch and other business had backed up so badly that Juan Martinez had to seek the boss out. When Juan entered the ranch office, he had to contain his shock at Quinn's appearance. Quinn settled on the other side of the big partner's desk and emptied his briefcase.

"These checks have to be countersigned," Juan said. "The new fencing along Silver Alley Creek looks very good. I want you to inspect it before I order more." He studied a paper. "I don't like the Mountain Feed bid. I'm for sending ten or twenty head to the feed lot and see if we aren't spending too much per animal."

Quinn studied the propositions, rubbing his beard and catching Juan's eyes piercing him. "I guess I look like ten miles of dirt road," Quinn said.

"Fifty miles," Juan said, "after a thunderstorm."

Quinn managed a smile as Juan rolled a cigarette, biting on the label of the drawstring to close the sack. A few of the Marines on the RAM team had rolled their own.

"Anything else?" Quinn asked.

"A lot else," he retorted. "Siobhan and I have taken care of everything we can without you. So, what's it to be?"

"I'm bleeding, man," Quinn rasped, "valley of deceit, valley of lies, present company exempted. You don't lie, Juan. I have lied for the honor of the Corps."

"That's not lying."

"You're his brother, you tell me, Juan."

"I certainly sensed something was happening. But I don't spy on my brother. It was none of my business. You had kept Rita longing for you for far too long. It happened in a moment when they were free. Now? Jesus, I don't know. He is my brother, and I must come down on his side. The Martinez family is ready to leave the ranch."

Quinn felt himself sinking, deflated.

"Carlos could not resist Rita. He can't now," Juan went on. "Even if it meant betraying you. You were younger than him, but you were his hero."

"Why? Carlos did everything better than I. Macho, fists, sports, women, guitar strumming."

"Carlos," Juan interrupted, "worshiped you because of the quiet way you stuck to your ideals. You would not let the gringos and Mormons gang up on any Mexican kid. When Carlos ran away and took your father's car, it was you who stood between Carlos and the sheriff. And your father came, and you made him take Carlos back."

"Funny," Quinn mused, "for years I thought of Dan as another Archie Bunker."

"Dan was reactionary as hell," Juan said, "but he was a man of principle. He not only gave us a good life but he made us belong in this valley." Juan picked up on Quinn's desire to keep talking. "What is it, amigo?"

"Carlos could have said no."

"How could he resist Rita Maldonado? Look, there are very few of us who know about this."

"I don't give a fuck who knows," Quinn snapped. "One by one the valley unearths its dirty little secrets." The delayed punch of Juan's possible leaving the ranch hit him now. "Where would you go, Juan, what would you do?"

"My parents are enjoying their old age, except for the aches and pains. As for me, there's enough in the Martinez kitty for me to start up a small ranch."

"Does the idea appeal to you?"

Juan hesitated. He stood and his spurs jingled. "How do you feel about it, Quinn?"

"I want you to stay," Quinn answered, and rose from his chair. He gave Juan a big *abrazo.*

"This is my home," Juan said.

"You did the right thing by not ratting on your brother."

Denver had a nice flow to it. It was not a glorious or dynamic city, but it was friendly and had lots of elm trees. The O'Connell condo on Chessman Park afforded a lovely view to the state capital and the foothills into the Rockies.

Being the state capital and a town of Western tradition, there were always circles of lively ladies about.

Quinn eventually took up with Helena Baxter, a sharp CEO of a Denver-sized public relations firm. She was twice divorced, with no children, and a pleasant and striking companion. They went into an "easy does it" relationship. It grew in warmth as six months passed since the disastrous night. Helena knew the ache in Quinn was dimming but would never totally go away. She was great about it, made him start to feel good about himself again. He reacted to her kindness with kindness of his own.

In the beginning Mal saw or called Quinn often. There wasn't a lot of information about Rita. He saw her only once in six months. Quinn buried his loss in his vault, and Mal seemed to grow more distant. With Quinn in Denver a good part of the time, they grew somewhat as strangers to one another.

An aging showed in Reynaldo Maldonado's eyes, and his work was hovered over by dark angels.

A moment of truth came with startling speed and completely unexpected. Quinn and Helena were at the breakfast table, checking the papers, making calls, trading little nothings when the lobby desk buzzed.

"Morning, Mr. O'Connell. Someone to see you. I sent him up."

Quinn knew. He pulled himself together. His doorbell insisted. Quinn opened it and looked into the eyes of Carlos Martinez. Carlos entered without invitation, took a pistol from its inside holster, and placed it on the pass-through kitchen counter.

"Oh, my God," Helena cried.

"No, no," Carlos said with a barely audible voice. "I leave the pistol in your hands, Quinn. It is loaded. Kill me, or otherwise speak with me."

Quinn took up the weapon, opened the chamber, took out the bullets, and put them in his pocket. He set the gun down and turned to Helena.

"We'll be all right," Quinn said.

Helena looked from one to the other. Carlos lowered his head and nodded in confirmation.

"I don't think I'd better leave."

"No, we're going to be fine. I'll call you at your office in about fifteen minutes."

"Uh-uh," Helena said. "I'll wait in your study."

She bussed Quinn's cheek, glared volcanic at Carlos, and retreated, leaving the door slightly ajar.

"Nice lady," Carlos said. "Can I take my coat off?"

"Sure, sit down."

Carlos stared blankly through the big sliding windows. "For a lawyer I've lost my golden tongue," he mumbled. "Let me try to get out what is shuttered in me as best I can."

Quinn nodded.

"First, Rita is all right. She is all right. Better, much better." He asked for water and sipped. "I must let you know how much I hate myself—"

"Save that shit."

"All right, all right," Carlos answered. "Then let me go point blank. When she arrived at my place in Houston, she was in a bad way. Hysterical, incoherent. A bad way. Yes, she had phoned me. Yes, I told her come to Houston. I sent away my fiancée and told her not to come back. I'm not going to lie to you, Quinn. You can't hate me any more than I hate myself. I, uh, was in exultation that Rita was coming, in exultation. It overwhelmed any sense of decency, and sense of honor—"

"Save the shit!" Quinn snapped. "I *know* how you've suffered."

"She was in a bad way. For the first days she was

under sedation and watched 'round the clock. I travel a lot."

"So I hear, a regular traveling laundry."

"I'd be a septic tank for the fees I am paid. My point is that Rita had care day and night and the best professional help in Houston. I'm not going to try to lie to you, Quinn. I did this for me, Carlos. My desire for her has always been unbalanced."

"Fuck it, get out, Carlos, before one of us gets killed."

"No," Carlos said.

Quinn felt Helena's hand on his shoulder. "Let him speak," she commanded.

"No."

"Look at him, Quinn. He's already a walking dead man. You're not far behind. Let him speak."

Quinn fell into an easy chair and stared at the carpet.

"Rita was awakened from her bad dream. For a time I was so thrilled by her restoration. But then, without sinking back into madness, she also began to die. Every day, every night. She wished for death. She does not love me, Quinn. I love her almost enough to try to keep her, but I love her too much to see her die."

"Got a bundle of hot cash," Quinn spat, "on your way to some quaint little offshore island. Offshore Martinez. Cash Carlos. Cocaine cash Carlos offshore Martinez."

Helena realized that her days and nights with Quinn

might be fast coming to a close. Thank God, she said to herself, she had not lost her soul to him. All that could be heard was their grunting breaths.

"We knew we couldn't live with it anymore," Carlos croaked. "Her head is clear now. She is very much on top of things. She called Mal a few days ago for him to come down to Houston."

Quinn passed through the French doors to the balcony, easing back from his rage. A thousand sighs were released in a single sigh. He could not form words. Helena did. "Does Rita know you're here?" she asked.

"Yes."

Helena winced. Damn the lonely nights without that man.

"I'm fucked up now," Quinn rasped. "The ebb tide and the high tide are ripping through my middle. Didn't she know this would kill me?"

"She was sick. She is more well now than I've ever known her," Carlos said.

"I'm not the only guy in the world who's gotten stiffed. So what's the proffer, what's the tender? Lose my dignity—forgive? Can I set eyes on her again?"

"That's up to you. Rita and I can't go on together. Send her away if you must. Mal will be close by."

"Can you?" Helena asked.

Quinn burst apart, sobbing. "I want children with her. I want to go to my end with her. It's no time for mendacity. Maybe I can find forgiveness. I don't know."

Carlos knew what was coming, yet he took it bitterly. But Carlos was of Mexican stuff, and he had betrayed his friend and it would claw at him forever.

"Will it ever come to pass that you'll forgive me?"

"We are men, Carlos. We are different from a man and a woman. I could not forgive you if you committed treason or committed a hate murder or raped. Your crime is . . . not even a crime, yet there was a single moment in all of this it could have been prevented. You could have said no. I would have said no. Men who love each other cannot betray that trust. That's worse than death."

Carlos made aimlessly to a place where he could lean. He slipped into another chair. His body needed support. All about him, every day, he saw a parade of "honorable" men he did not trust and who did not trust him: politicians, border patrols, dealers, kingpins . . .

. . . this was not only a game of boy and girl. This was mistrust because he was not to be trusted and those he dealt with were likewise ready to betray.

How could he tell Quinn that God had not made him into a Quinn? Carlos made the profound gesture to send her home, but only because he could not have her. And he would plunge back into his life of chartered jets and offshore sleaze, covering a pile of manure with a blanket of roses until that fucking day Carlos Martinez made the wrong move or the worse of two bad choices.

He needed to be alone to sort it out, and he went into the study. Helena watched Quinn, sadly, hopefully.

“SOME PEOPLE SPEND AN ENTIRE LIFETIME WONDERING
IF THEY MADE A DIFFERENCE IN THE WORLD.
THE MARINES DON’T HAVE THAT PROBLEM.”

Ronald Reagan, President of the United States

MARINE CORPS
HERITAGE FOUNDATION

CAMPAIGN MEMBER 2016

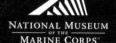

NATIONAL MUSEUM
OF THE
MARINE CORPS™

3800 Fettler Park Drive, Suite 104
Dumfries, VA 22025
1-800-397-7585

www.marineheritage.org

Carlos returned in time. "It's all set," he said. He looked to Quinn, hoping desperately that Quinn would give him a flicker of respite. He gave a quick smile to Helena, took up his coat and went to the door, then stopped for a few seconds.

"Be sure to take your pistol," Quinn said.

TWENTY-TWO

New York, New Year's Eve 1999

It was still four hours to midnight. The party was jumping. The great cruise ship *pepsiGENERATION* passed the *nasdaqTRADER* partway up the Hudson toward the *tropicanaGEORGE WASHINGTON BRIDGE.*

Both ships were fully lit, and their noise-making capacity was in full blare. All of Manhattan was lit, a light to remember.

As the witching hour approached in each time zone, there would be big bangs from planet earth to announce to the heavens that we were still here.

NasdaqTRADER had been chartered for the occasion by T3 Industries. An invitation to the party became one of the *must* celebrations in the country. The guest list was loaded with a Who's Who in politics, industry, the banking behemoths, media kings and emperors, Nike and Addidas leapers, a deep scoop into the black leadership, movie and TV actor/gods and a few celebrity mobsters given amnesty for the occasion, right-wing Baptists who called off the war on alcohol for this night, and a few Jews who were geniuses at T3 Industries. They had emigrated from Russia.

Thornton Tomtree bundled into an overcoat and stepped out of the wheelhouse. Darnell was by the rail, staring at the mega-sight of Manhattan. He was alone, in reverie, unaware of the blowing horns.

"It's been a hell of a life," Thornton said with his breath darting downriver. "You know, I'm rather slow in giving credit to anyone but myself. It was your guidance and keen judgment that got us here, Darnell."

"My daddy, God rest his soul, told me, 'Darnell, take care of that white boy. He's major.' Lord Thornton, am I really standing here? Will everything turn into a pillar of salt?"

"I came to tell you something very important. You'd never guess."

"Well, let's see, it's almost ten years ago that you creamed Senator Garbowski and became the big enchilada in Internet regulation. Our guest list on this pleasure boat controls a very large percentage of the national Republican apparatus. There's a conga line of Baptists who can swing the balance of power in seven Southern states. Mr. Jefferson here is the number one exhibition in the black community. You're fixing to run for president of the United States. You're laying the groundwork for the election of 2004."

Thornton blinked and gaped.

"Does Pucky know?"

"I just told her. She said it should be great fun."

"You've sure got your ducks lined up. Your recognition factor is right up there with Madonna, Seinfeld, and Saddam Hussein. You're holding IOU's from a lot of powerful folks."

"Because you alone have understood and have conducted the most brilliant public relations campaigns in American history, I want you to stay on for this. The media is our key to a nomination."

"There are too many correspondents, too many networks and mininetworks, and too many super-cable stations, too many news-slurping sources, and those panels of experts reciting their dreary litanies. So, they dig lower and lower in the Dumpster."

"You've outfoxed them, Darnell, and kept them sympathetic to me for over a quarter of a century. The American people will never have a scandal involving me. I am cleaner than Nixon in bed. And the public doesn't give a fiddler's fuck about who is between the sheets with their leader, so long as the economy is good. Besides, the media is still recovering from the Starr-chamber years of Clinton's second term."

"Oh, they'll recover real fast for a presidential candidate. Scoop! Thornton Tomtree makes the *Guinness Book of World Records.* He was masturbating at two years of age. However! He lied about it later and subordinated *perjury* and those are mortal sins, rickety, tickety, tin."

"How much are we spending on this party?" Thornton asked.

"You know. With the gifts, the employees blow-out in Pawtucket, chartering this little rowboat for over three thousand of your closest friends. We must be in close to twenty million."

"Don't you get it, Darnell? This party allows me to spend twenty million non-campaign dollars and get a four-year running start."

"I figured that out."

Now silence between them. As the noise grew in decibels to shattering, the river hopped. Ashore, the tall shafts of buildings seemed to sway—blinding, deafening. There only seemed to be Thornton and Darnell in the quiet darkness at the railing of some ship.

The din and blasts and blinding light shower found its way to the *nasdaqTRADER.* Darnell Jefferson clamped his hands over his ears and turned his eyes away. President Tomtree and "Uncle Tom." It's all flipped over. Listen, listen, he thought. The world is going mad.

TWENTY-THREE

Troublesome Mesa—Early Evening December 31, 1999

State Senate Minority Leader Quinn Patrick O'Connell braked the Sno-Cat and squinted through the swishes of the windshield wiper. His son, Duncan, jumped out of the Cat and sank down to his waist in snow.

His sister Rae operated the searchlight from inside the vehicle. Duncan came to the short log bridge and shoveled around, examined it, tested its weight-bearing capacity, then returned to the car. He opened the door, allowing a blast of frigid air to come in with him.

"Dad, the bridge looks solid to me."

Quinn thought aloud. "We've got an awful heavy load in here. I think we'd better unload and sled the supplies over."

This was a little conservative for the children, but

Quinn always played on the side of caution when it came to them.

"Three sled loads should empty the cargo."

The four of them worked like old packers filling the sled and, with two on the front and two on the rear, pulled it over the bridge, unloaded it and repeated the procedure two more times till the cat was emptied.

Rita and the children waited across the bridge as Quinn pumped himself up and turned on the ignition. "Not too fast over the bridge," he warned himself, "no slip-slides into the creek." He applied the gas, released the brakes. The iron monster clawed its way over. The bridge did not give so much as a wobble.

Cheers!

Relief. They reloaded the Sno-Cat, and it purred a half mile uphill to Dan's Shanty, the cabin in the sky.

It was anything but a shanty. The roof covering the living room and two sleeping lofts was a dome made of Plexiglas, and when filtering clouds gave way, one could see great pieces of the universe.

Lest we forget, Semper Fi, the essence of German shepherd, had already made the run to the cabin and greeted them. Man, he had a lot of guarding to do this night.

As Christmas approached, there had been rising apprehension that their long dream of seeing the new century in together at Dan's Shanty might not happen. Senator Quinn and Rita were heavily in demand around the state. Grandmother Siobhan was confined to a wheelchair from a hip-replacement operation. She was in Denver and slated to be wheeled into a half dozen celebrations.

Snow covered the giant bubble, but as the fireplace and the heat of the cabin rose, it melted and slowly opened up the heavens to them.

Quinn mixed a weak concoction of champagne for the kids and a stiffer one for Rita and himself. At an altitude of twelve and a half thousand feet one did not need too much alcohol to get its message.

While the kids made up sleeping quarters, Quinn engaged in his second most favorite sport, watching his wife move. The years had been delicious to her, and she adored cavorting for him. She glided in concert with herself, with her breasts always a bit loose and her hips swaying like a Mexican village maiden at the water well.

He had watched her thus for twenty years, and for twenty years she had known it. Their mutual redemption from her affair with Carlos had given them an incredible strength.

Rita capped her kitchen duties by brushing past Quinn while bearing groceries and treating him to her devastating toss of the hair.

Life had been attacked as a new gift each morning. Although the need to find his origins never went away, it dulled because of their family success.

The years had given them peace and rewards. Through enormous love and plenty of hard work, their long-held dream had come true.

Dan's Shanty was up to snuff, warm and filled with the aromas of a high mountain beans and meat meal. Semper Fi lowered his nose under his master's champagne glass and gave it a quick flip, then backed off as though he were going to be beaten to death. Quinn pounced on him, and they wrestled till overcome by the smells and sounds of sizzling steak.

"Is this great or what!"

After the meal was devoured, it was still a few hours to the new century.

"I know by the gleam in your eye, Duncan . . ." Mother said on cue.

"I've got the springs cooled down to a hundred and four," Duncan answered.

Well, she really only had to run twenty feet, but it was zero outside and this would be Semper Fi's big moment.

Attired in string bikinis, the women ran screaming from the cabin to the springs.

"Hero! I'm a hero!"

"I am the bravest!"

"Jesus!"

Quinn served wine in paper cups as Duncan threw the ball for the dog. As each confirmed this was really the grandest thing in the world, they watched in awe and silence to let the comets put on their acts.

"And now!" said Quinn, "we separate the men from the boys and the people from the people." He leapt from the springs, rolled in the snow, and returned to the steaming water as Semper Fi's whiskers turned white with frozen moisture. Rita demanded respect from her children, who dragged her out into the snow, and she howled and Duncan howled when Rae tackled him and Rae howled when Rita plopped a load of snow on her back and all the coyotes in Troublesome Mesa howled.

Thank God, Semper Fi was there to protect them.

Duncan would soon be heading for the Colorado School of Mines to take two years of basic geology to better understand his turf. From there he would go to Colorado State, a ranking veterinarian school, and study to be a vet.

For years Duncan had fretted in silence about his desires. Every time he walked into the living room, he had to pass through two great guardians of the gate. On one side on a round table, a photograph of his grandfather, Dan O'Connell, receiving the Silver Medal and Purple Heart.

On the mantel, a photograph of his father, Quinn Patrick O'Connell, in dress blues. Even his name, Duncan, was after a great Marine as the name Quinn had been after another.

Quinn got his son's drift. The boy was struggling to decide whether to get in a few years of college before his Marine hitch, or do the hitch first.

"Son," Quinn told him, "follow your own desires. Half the shit in this world comes from parents trying to bend their children into living as their alter egos."

Rita spent her maternal efforts on Rae to always make the girl feel good about herself. The pixie should not and did not go into a beauty contest against her mother. Whenever Rae got down on herself or self-doubt seeped in, Rita would take her daughter and go off someplace for a few days, just the two of them.

They were close.

They had the tears, the rebellions, the pain that people living with people must endure, but bedrock was their family unit and it was powerful.

Neither Duncan nor Rae had a serious relationship at the moment, so they were thankful that only the four of them would be involved at Dan's Shanty.

Quinn had his family in a safe place to live and grow from. He never cared to travel too far without them. His second office was in Denver. He shone as a Minority Whip in the Colorado Senate and many of his legislative positions were treasures. The last great liberal of the Rocky Mountains.

Rita learned from her mother-in-law the nuances of

running the ranch, and with Juan in the saddle, the ranch had continued to prosper.

Rita's main concern was that Quinn was wasting his talent in a position far too small for him. His Denver office had become a place of social and political ideas, a think tank for interns, a confessional, a place where rival Republicans could come in and argue, a place where adversaries could arbitrate.

The press spread Quinn's name beyond Colorado borders. Quinn had a divine secret. He was not on the take, he did not lie, and he admitted to mistakes. Quinn's space in Denver took on the feel of a local shrine.

He was a charming speaker with a mix of mountain and clean Marine humor, much in control and a very cool hand at his senate position.

Rita knew that his Colorado anchor was set because she and Duncan and Rae came first. It was time, she prayed, for the family to give him something back.

They ended the meal fat and sassy, sitting on a pillowed floor in long johns before the fire.

Duncan rambled on about the large animal hospital he planned to build on the ranch with a research facility for disease control and breeding.

Rita figured that Granddad Mal and Grandmother Siobhan had deliberately taken themselves out of the trip up to the Shanty so the four of them could spend this incredible event together.

Mal? Reynaldo Maldonado was somewhere in Mexico or Paris or Manila being lionized with a thirty-something-year-old lady on his arm.

"This is the happiest day of my life. The other two happiest days were seeing you two born," Quinn said.

"Who are you thinking about, Quinn?" his wife asked knowingly.

"Dan. It took us half our lives to figure out that love will cause pain. The worst of it was how some of us can go through life never hearing the other. We are so involved with our own world we do not hear the cries for love and help. We just don't get it."

"You get it," Rae said. "If any dad in the world gets it, you do."

"Keep loving," Quinn said.

"So serious?" Rita asked.

"I'm so filled, I'm liable to start bawling," Quinn said.

"Hear! Hear!" Duncan said.

Quinn stood, jiggled the fire, and balanced on the hearth. Rita knew her man. "I think your dad wants to tell us something," she said, "and he's having trouble."

After a silence Quinn said, "Jesus, you can't even hold a private thought with this crowd. I don't want to sound like a freaking martyr who made sacrifices for you. The joy of my life has come to fruition at this moment. The happiness and well-being of the three of you outweighed any ambitions I might have had. Well, now you've grown up, and I believe you can bear the public crucifixions that go with public office. I've come under a lot of pressure from the party lately. They are bound and determined to have me run for governor in two thousand and two."

"Shit, man, that's great!" Duncan erupted.

"Cool!" noted Rae.

"Let's tickle the governor," Rita said, grabbing his ankles while Duncan bear-hugged him and Rae shoved him off the hearth.

"You people know how ticklish I am, so cease! I say, cease! Seriously! And get that bloody dog out of my face. Defend your master or you're raccoon meat!" Semper Fi decided the best way to defend his master was to lick his lips, nose, and eyes.

"Dessert!" Quinn cried, howling. "What do we have for dessert?"

"Well, there is apple pie, pumpkin pie, brownies, carrot cake, and Häagan-Dazs . . ."

When it was midnight, they held hands, cried a little, and wished one another well. They talked until the fire died, then wearily crept up to the sleeping lofts. Rae and Duncan had nice thick featherbeds beneath them and comforters to cover them.

Mom and Dad, on the other side of the Shanty, tucked into a double sleeping bag.

Quiet lovemaking so no sounds would reach the children. Slow dancing, passionately slow, skilled. It took two hours to play it out.

They held onto each other as they arose and flew into space and over the millennium bridge. The star show seemed to move down to earth. Each star became a flake of snow as it drifted down to the bubble.

"Can't you sleep?" Quinn asked.

"No. There's never been a night like this."

She breathed hard and wiggled a bit, signs that Quinn read well. "Something is weighing on you. You can talk about Carlos," he said.

It had been nearly twenty years since she had returned to Quinn. Ten years had gone by since Carlos disappeared on a chartered jet in the Caribbean. When his body floated ashore, the autopsy showed a gun wound to the back of his head and severe bone shattering. He had obviously been thrown out of the plane over water.

Quinn brought Carlos's body home and set him down in the Troublesome Mesa Cemetery.

"When I was in Houston, hovering between sanity and madness," she began, "I knew even then that the key to my recovery was in the pages of the Venice book. My guilt about my affair with Carlos, be it before our marriage or not, eroded me. God strike me down if I ever harbor another secret like that . . . well, I'm building a case for myself," she said suddenly, and stopped talking.

"Please let go of it," said Quinn.

"Some kind of a miracle took place. One day in Houston I picked up the hundred and fifty pages of

Venice that I had given to you to read. The first time I had heard your comments I went into a rage, but I did not realize then that I was literally forcing you to reject me."

They were tight now, lying in the same direction with his arms about her. She was calm, and her voice sounded like fine wine.

"What happened?" he asked.

"I picked up my own pages and dared to read them. Suddenly, this vast mystery of writing began to fade like the sun burning off the morning fog. At least now I had some insight to comprehend my work. Through introspection I felt that any true dormant talent in me was emerging. I could clearly judge my own errors and understand your comments. The miracle came when I understood that a large part of the writer's being, of his talent, could only emerge through hard, hard work. And maybe if I worked hard enough, I'd raise the talent level enough to succeed."

"What did you learn?" he asked.

"I rewrote those hundred and fifty pages. Someday you'll read them maybe, maybe not. I'm not afraid for you to read them anymore. Again, I learned that doing those hundred and fifty pages took more endurance and willpower and raw strength than I believed a human being could possess. Well, these new pages were good, Quinn, but what a price."

The woman was kissed as she loved it, over her neck

and back, and his hands were smooth of touch and she whimpered with joy.

"So," she said, "what was it that I really wanted? Was I really ready to give it all to be a writer? I used writing as a baby blanket. The fear, the enslavement to that bloody typewriter, the isolation, the numbed mind and scarred soul, all those things that make a writer. I wanted Quinn," she said, "and I wanted Quinn's children. In the end loving you was by far the more powerful of the two forces, and I've never shed a tear over the abandonment of the writer's siren song. Thank you for taking me back twenty years ago."

"I hope I can love you as much."

"You do."

"Wow!" he whispered at the wonder of it.

"Yeah," she said, "wow!"

Quinn pulled her tush into his tummy and kissed her shoulders.

"You kidding me, Quinn?"

"I don't think so."

"Mind if I find out?"

"I thought you'd never ask."

TWENTY-FOUR

The Alamo, Maryland
Mother's Day, 2002

AMERIGUN was a show dog with a single trick, the unimpeded promotion of gun sales. It swore to a single credo. Namely, that any American of any age could buy and own any weapon in any numbers without accountability . . . as *guaranteed* by Second Amendment rights in the Constitution. Anything less was unacceptable, including baby locks on pistols.

Central to AMERIGUN's credo, anchored in bedrock, immovable, was to portray gun owners as victims for trying to defend themselves as they were being hounded by a government conspiracy.

The nation had undergone too many bombings, too many drive-by and schoolyard shootings, too many church burnings and too many grown men playing weekend warriors in the woods.

In Bill Clinton there was finally an American president ready to stand up against the violence and its chief perpetrators. Once one of the most feared lobbys in Washington, AMERIGUN's bite-and-rip bully-boy Doberman tactics were not working quite so well now.

The Clinton reelection in 1996 forced AMERIGUN into a defensive posture. Unable to compromise or think in any new direction, the organization began to sink in its own muck.

What had been unthinkable a decade earlier, newspaper articles and editorials, magazine pieces, and TV specials now catalogued the perils of reckless gun ownership. A big shift came as the American people solidly supported gun control. The issue was out in the open at last.

Bill Clinton, Southern boy from a Southern state, became the first American president to stand for gun control. He brought his message home by as many executive orders on gun control as he was able.

However, the American Congress defaulted on backup legislation. AMERIGUN used the time-tested stick-and-carrot method on the Congress. Donations to the campaign fund or face defeat in reelection. Because gun control crossed party lines in "traditional" gun states, the political parties were equally timid.

It fell to city councils and state legislators to enact the measures that Washington had defaulted on. In local situations the call against arms had such public support as to allow dozens of new gun-control laws to get on the books.

By 2000 AMERIGUN had been badly battered, having lost tens of thousands of members. Its headquarters in McLean, Virginia, was a dinosaur with a kaput eight-million-dollar computer system. It was crawl out or die.

AMERIGUN's secret handlers formed a super committee to "guide" the future destiny of the organization. These nine men and two women innocuously called themselves The Combine. Their names were not known to anyone, including AMERIGUN. They represented the weapons makers, lobbyists, and financial controllers.

Weapons makers were always nervous over the seamier sides of their product: gun smuggling, arms dealing, and massive domestic illegalities. Although AMERIGUN was somewhat diminished, it was necessary for The Combine to keep the organization going as a "clean" shield defending a dirty trade.

New AMERIGUN headquarters, the Alamo, were set up, out of harm's way, in western Maryland with a view to the Blue Ridge Mountains. The Combine reduced AMERIGUN functions. They could carry on shooting seminars, publish the magazine, *Weaponry*, conduct mailings and competitions, and rise up and scream when ordered.

Longstanding leader of AMERIGUN, King Porter, understood that without The Combine's financial support the organization would collapse.

Once King had been a terrifying predator who

gained his spurs in Congress by fear tactics. His fall from grace only lathered up his innards for the moment of revenge.

For two decades King Porter had been the "rock of ages," cemented into bedrock with a fifty-foot-high, twenty-foot-thick brick wall enclosing his brain.

King didn't stand very tall in actuality. Most people looking at eye level saw the naked crown of his head with an occasional upright hair from the horseshoe fringe. His skin was stretched tightly over his face, flattening his cheeks into a mouth set with the left side of his face a fraction higher than the right.

His dress, by ancient tailor, had a Western swag to it, back snug and straight with heavily seamed outlines. Heels of Western boots pumped him up a bit. King's eyes and ears allowed little humor. Not infrequently had he envisioned himself a Confederate general about to lead a cavalry charge when he appeared before a House or Senate hearing.

King Porter was bred and brewed as the middle and smallest male of nine stunted hillbilly kids. In order to survive he had willed himself an aura of power through intimidation. No one doubted he'd set them afire if angry enough. With rage always near the surface he was able to gain mastery over his siblings. The level of rage was usually close to a boil, as was his memory of hunger and its pains.

Porter was at once an unpleasant person, bully, and righteous defender of the Second Amendment.

What really ticked King Porter off was that the names of The Combine were held secret from him. He had to deal with a single person representing The Combine. He loathed her.

Maud Traynor was the lawyer and sole contact to The Combine. She was a middle-aged, expensively dumpy bitch. Her language could startle a drunken sailor. She cracked her knuckles and blew foul cigarette smoke in his sensitive eyes. Maud Traynor, King was certain, was a practicing lesbian.

From his window he could see her pull into the circle in her vulgar red Ferrari. King greeted her at the elevator door with the stiffness of a Prussian field marshal. She pinched his cheek in passing. He smiled through locked teeth.

"Beautiful ride up here," Maud said. "Saving your booze for the Fourth of July?" She was a no-nonsense rye drinker. King Porter slid into his seat tentatively.

"We've got a problem," she said right off.

"We have?"

"It's this off-year election. The polls show us clobbering the dirty dozen we tagged for defeat. But this cowboy running for governor of Colorado is opening his lead."

"O'Donald?"

"O'Connell. Quinn Patrick O'fucking Connell. It was made clear, King, that we can't have a gun-control freak in the middle of gun territory. He could poison all the states around him."

King shook his head. "Too bad his daddy, old Daniel O'Connell, passed on. Dan was a real shooter." King called for his records. Colorado had been saturated with infomercial tapes to three hundred radio talk shows in the region. Six hundred thousand pieces of literature had been mailed. Two or three weekly leaks to the tabloids had been accomplished. AMERIGUN's website carried out a gnashing attack.

"Look at this," King said.

. . . O'Connell is the son of a death-row inmate and a prostitute.

. . . possible fetal alcohol syndrome.

. . . severe learning disabilities.

. . . what is the true story behind his Navy Cross? A cover-up was needed for his cowardice.

. . . suspected drug addiction.

. . . wife abuser.

. . . his father-in-law, Reynaldo Maldonado is red, left-wing professor and creator of pornographic art.

. . . Maldonado probably committed incest with daughter when she was ten.

. . . O'Connell suspected of sodomizing sheep.

. . . Quinn's Mexican wife cavorted with drug kingpin.

. . . marital infidelity.

. . . hit-and-run charge covered up.

. . . tried to give state park concessions to Jap companies.

. . . caught in woman's rest room.

. . . non-churchgoer.

. . . satanic rituals on ranch during full moons.

. . . 666 tattooed on his penis.

. . . O'Connell ranch a transit point for Mexican illegals, who are sold to farms for eight hundred dollars a head.

. . . often seen in the company of Jewish money lenders.

. . . son, Duncan, a campus radical and suspected gay.

. . . daughter, Rae, badly retarded.

Maud took off her glasses and rubbed her eyes. "You know what we've got here, King?"

"Well, he refuses to answer these charges publicly."

"Well, fathom that. I said, do you know what we've got here?"

"What?"

"A shithole, and we've just poured six hundred thousand dollars down it. Your stupid campaign is only making people flock to him."

"This stupid campaign has worked time and time again," King argued.

"Can't you even understand a man who can't be intimidated!"

"You go with what works," he answered reactively. "Our education programs have always been successful. Be patient, because eventually some charge is going to stick to him."

"I'll tell you what's stuck. AMERIGUN and The Combine are stuck with a fucking Democratic liberal for the next four years."

"You were the one who signed off on this Colorado strategy," King retorted.

"Well, it's not working," she grunted. "Close down the Denver operation, phone banks, ads, talk show and media handout sheets, and slink off quietly."

King pounded his little fist on his desk and wheezed in discomfort.

"As of now," Maud said, "The Combine wants you to plan a post-election party for O'Connell. Our thinking is that we should move our 2003 convention from Dallas to Denver. What I mean is, we come in blazing and go after the legislators. We bring in Hank Carleton and every kid who ever owned a squirrel gun who has risen to fame. We bus in demonstrators from Utah, Wyoming, Oklahoma, et cetera, et cetera. We show them how unpleasant life is going to be if gun-control shit is enacted. Your campaign has got to have smarts this time, King!"

"Convention in Denver. You bet it will!"

Maud unzipped and popped open her alligator/lizard/twenty-four-carat gold-trimmed briefcase and tucked in her papers. "Battlefield, Denver 2003. Concentrate your plans on the legislature. I want everything run through me for approval."

Maud consumed another belt of rye and said, "Ahhh." She didn't move. It wasn't all over. The phone rang mercifully. It was for Maud. Probably her lesbian bitch partner, King thought, or maybe she'd brought a pretty boy to oil himself up in front of her.

"My granddaughter," Maud said after she hung up. "We've a long horseback ride in the hills tomorrow. Ow-ee, I'm getting a bit of a buzz. I'll bet you'd like me to drive off one of those curlicue roads back to Washington."

"No such thing, Miss Maud. Do we have any more business?"

"Yeah," she said, "we've got to do something about this fucking magazine," she said, reaching to an end table and throwing a half dozen copies of *Weaponry* on his desk. She read the covers: "357 Sig, Colt 380, AR–15 keeps gaining fans despite media attacks, Springfields, H&K USP .45 ASP, Savage, how to carry concealed, protecting freedom, more guns less crime.

And on page five the smiling face of King Porter on his continuing 'to the bunkers' sermon, rewrite one hundred and twenty. 'We're under siege, clean decent Americans are being stripped of their birthright by the United States government in defiance of our forefathers who gave us the right to bear arms under the Second Amendment,' cha, cha, cha!"

Everything that could stretch and stiffen did so inside King Porter.

"Here's a good one," Maud said, "God made man. Guns made man equal. Guns are the legacy of liberty."

"Just because . . . just because our magazine doesn't feature a naked woman on the cover!" he cried.

Another belt of rye. "Hell, no, there's no naked women. The sickos would rather squeeze a trigger than a woman's breast. Guns are good old boys! They got them wham-whap two-fisted names, like . . . like Savage, Colt, Ruger, Baretta, Sigs, Winchester . . ."

Porter's eyes widened. "Springfield!" he cried.

"Browning!" she exclaimed.

"Luger," he cried.

"Smith & Wesson," she said.

"Remington Viper," he cried.

"Glock. Don't forget Glock!" she said.

"Markov, Walther!" he retorted with a double.

"H & K," she said.

"Mauser parabellum," he cried.

"Anschutz," she sang.

"Magnum! All sorts of mags," he cried.

"I quit, you win," Maud said. "Mags are it."

King Porter was breathing hard and smiling at winnership.

"You start thinking about a few Sandis, or Debbies or Tracis on the cover."

"What about Dixie?" he said, miffed. "I'm not turning *Weaponry* into a pornographic sex magazine."

"Sex?" she said. "What the hell do you think this is all about, King? Guns are the little people's sex machines. Hell, they are nothing more than the extension of a cock. Bang! The ultimate orgasm! Guns make pissants at the end of the bar as big as Hulk himself. Guns equalize the oppressed in his never-ending battle with the oppressor. Guns are empowerment!"

For a moment King Porter was in a little clapboard church in a gully by the creek at a foot-stomping tirade by its preacher. He snapped back to consciousness.

"The Combine is sending some designers to work on *Weaponry*. Maybe we'll have a miss bang-bang beauty pageant. Let's sell fifty thousand of them from newsstands and not hide them inside our raincoats. Let's get ads from Ford trucks and Seagrams and AT&T instead of all those chewing-tobacco ads. Let's have stories written by real writers."

Maud was tipsy. She managed to get into the elevator. King watched the circle. The Ferrari took off at a volume that shook the leaves on the trees. Maud Traynor's red Ferrari screamed down the Alamo's long driveway and onto the highway. King stood watching on his balcony and taking a few puffs from his inhalator, his baby blanket for years. Hope the bitch is found in scattered pieces at the bottom of a ditch, he wheezed to himself. Suppose she doesn't run off the road, he thought; maybe I'd better tip off the state patrol there's a dangerous drunk on the road.

The red tide of liberals was poisoning the country. No longer was he able to use "friendly persuasion" to make certain commies didn't get on university teaching staffs and the subjects were kept pearly clean. No longer could he visit the local sheriffs and see that things were open for the gun clubs and shooting programs. It was even getting difficult to sway local and state government officials.

The colors outside flamed along with his red orange mood. His capacity to terrify had slithered away. He was in eternal battle, often with his own board.

And came the final humiliation, of exiling AMERIGUN to a puny reconverted hundred-year-old hotel. The Alamo! He had named it, and the Alamo would be heard from again.

King stared out to the land sloping down from the Alamo. He had plans of his own for the acreage he'd optioned all around. One day the Alamo would be the center of an AMERIGUN heritage park!

Great battles of our history would be reenacted. He, King Porter, would lead the first charge up San Juan Hill. *Charge!*

Kiddie rides on trains or a river would take them through virtual battlefields; Belleau Wood, the Normandy invasion, Iwo Jima, where a kid could plant a flag, Yorktown, and well . . . even Gettysburg.

And . . . and . . . and the Hall of the Great Gunfighters. For a dollar a kid could buckle up and fast-draw with a laser pistol against Wild Bill Hickok and Wyatt Earp and Pat Garrett and Billy the Kid and . . . and . . . and . . . Doc Holliday.

And . . . and . . . a very subdued, shrouded building depicting the demise of John Dillinger and Bonnie and Clyde and Pretty Boy Floyd and a scad of Mafia gangsters including Capone and . . . and the guy in the Texas tower sniping people on the ground . . .

And the heroes, the buffalo hunters and men who tamed Indians and the West. John Wayne, Jesse James, Davy Crockett!

And the kids could buy a replica only at the museum store with a host of AMERIGUN knives and grenades and pistols. And the crowning glory would be an amphitheater which would give a nightly replay of the Alamo!

TWENTY-FIVE

Denver, 2002–2003
Quinn Patrick O'Connell Wins Governorship of Colorado in Off-Year Election

Governor O'Connell stood as a lone pine in a burned-out forest. The Republican sweep took the state house in Denver and a majority of the national delegation to Washington.

Tuesday follows Monday. Quinn awoke to the reality that a sensible gun-control law didn't have a chance. He would take his time, build bipartisan coalitions, push the easy legislation first. Once he had a sense of his statehouse, he might unwrap his gun-control bill. That would be a year off, anyhow.

Quinn did not face automatic Quinn haters. His father had been a shooter, a Republican, a Marine hero. Quinn was a hero of the state, a successful rancher and state senator and a die-hard Coloradan.

For years the O'Connell office in Denver had been a place of civility, debate, and compromise. The Republicans relaxed, as long as Quinn didn't push a liberal agenda too hard.

The mansion on 8th and Logan was too stilted for the O'Connells. They used it for state functions, Girl Scout troops, parties, and photo ops, but home was their Chessman Park condo a few blocks away.

During the first months Quinn traveled in the state's King Air to get a pulse of the people and to prioritize his legislative program and win new constituents as a hands-on leader.

His first goal was to balance the state's resources for the coming century. Land and water laws were needed to protect the ranches and farms, for mining, housing developments, and the enormous tourist industry.

Quinn's blue-ribbon panel contained a cross section of ideology, but at his personal behest they worked in a professional and intelligent manner. Quinn had imposed on them the canon that if one segment of the Colorado economy defaulted, the nature of the state could be lost.

He took on commencement speeches, town hall meetings, a semimonthly TV show, business lunches, union picnics, ribbon-cutting ceremonies and, mercifully, he was a judge in the Miss Colorado beauty pageant.

Quinn ended his day's work in the evening, phoning all over the state to congratulate the day's winners or to express sorrow over deaths.

Denver was a legitimate small-time big city with generations of character and livability while retaining its cowboy gait.

He and Mayor Cholate formed a Coming to Denver committee. Gateway to the Rockies! Most sports-loving city in America!

The state supported the city in hiring a top museum curator to scout the world and put together exhibitions from Mongolia to Brazil to France and have their grand openings in Denver.

Likewise, he won support, with powerful persuasion, for the funds to upgrade the Denver Symphony Orchestra.

The Coming to Denver committee purchased a small hotel, large enough for the cast and crew of a Broadway musical. Quinn and the mayor hounded New York producers to stage their big shows.

Playing on Aspen's glitz, a series of events were telecast from skiing to the Aspen Music Festival in the summer. In a smaller way, Telluride's film and country-western festivals reached millions.

Some of the ski areas had gone "soft" as the number of skiers dwindled. Quinn convinced the newly rich entrepreneurs of China and Russia to build vacation towns for their countrymen. Little Moscow and Little Shanghai came into being and resulted in an open door for the state's export products.

Quinn Patrick O'Connell created a feel-good atmosphere.

But always hovering over him was the coming AMERIGUN convention. AMERIGUN sent shock waves through the state capital with their announcement that a regional AMERIGUN office was being established in Denver.

AMERIGUN was picking a fight, making a power play. It was a defeat that Governor O'Connell could not abide without throwing his delicately balanced program into a heap.

As the year of 2003 rolled on, endgame was near.

The Alamo—Maryland 2003

In the Alamo, King Porter seethed and wheezed the hours until the convention.

Deep down and not revealing it to a soul, King had prayed that Quinn would win the governorship. AMERIGUN and himself could prove their mettle by "victory at Denver."

In the meantime, Quinn burned the midnight oil to try to craft some way to blunt the AMERIGUN assault.

Mayor Cholate simply did not want a rumble involving his police. Peace at any price. He conveniently booked a seminar in Tokyo during the gun group's stay in Denver.

With limited knowledge, limited forces at his disposal, and limited legal options, Quinn was simply outgunned. The helplessness of his situation crashed down on him when AMERIGUN mailed flyers announcing the exhibition of a new weapon, *The Colorado Blizzard,* at the convention.

An Australian invention, the Blizzard, touted as the first great weapon of the new century, was a souped-up double-barreled twelve-gauge shotgun that was fed cartridges through a machine-gun belt. Fifty times faster than the semi-automatic "street sweeper," it could fire thousands of pellets a minute.

And, no law was broken to put it on exhibition!

Duncan unsnapped a Coors and flung himself onto the big couch.

A dying sun in the foothills and a rising night rubbed past each other, and one could nearly hear the cracking baseball bats from Coors Field.

"Dad, I was hoping," Duncan said, "we'd take in a ball game."

"Sorry. I gave our box away tonight. How about tomorrow?"

"Sure. Mom and Rae coming?"

"If we hold a gun to their heads. Speaking of guns, I hear you're starting a terrorist cell at school."

"Oh, shit," Duncan moaned, "who ratted?"

"God save the whistle blowers," Quinn said, "ski masks, lead pipes, a regular commando unit. You may be the answer to AMERIGUN's prayers."

Duncan was out of his seat. "Dad, haven't we taken enough shit?"

"It comes with the territory. No one forced me to run for governor."

"I'm glad this is on the table," Duncan said. "I'm pissed at hearing how you fornicate with animals, and I'm pissed at hearing that Rae is a junkie and my mother is a lesbian prostitute."

Bang, the fridge door slammed. *Pfizz* went another Coors top.

"Before you drown in your righteous indignation, Duncan, let me present you with a little scene. Opening shot, all newscasts: tear gas flying over the capitol lawn as Colorado state National Guard troops fire rubber bullets into an innocent crowd protesting the governor's son Duncan's hooded mob. Close-up, the governor's son. Wreckage and fire around him considerable. Pan to shot of a bleeding King Porter. We cut away to Washington, where enraged senators are screaming for O'Connell's ass. Denver loses a hundred million dollars in convention bookings, and the state has the mark of Cain on it for a generation. Thanks a lot, Duncan, nifty."

"You knew who these people were! Why the hell did you have to run for governor?"

"At this moment I'd be hard pressed to give you an answer."

Mal had been roused from his room by their yelling. He entered and snatched up the flyer on the Blizzard.

"Because he wants to do something about their efforts to legalize this weapon. Maybe he did it because somebody has to stand up against evil."

"Pardon me all to hell," Duncan said sarcastically.

"All of us wonder," Mal went on, "what are we doing here? This is your father, your family, and your state, Duncan. We don't need your pouting. Either stand with us or go back to Fort Collins and play with your Rocky Mountain oysters. Your daddy is the poster boy for AMERIGUN, only he is outlined like a target. Ten points if you hit him between the eyes."

"It's like judging the beauty contests, Duncan. Somebody has to do the dirty work," Quinn said.

Duncan laughed and cried at the same time, his cheeks reddening with shame. "I'm pretty naïve, aren't I?"

"Yep," his grandfather agreed.

"Anything I can do, Dad?"

"Yep. I need help. I need it badly."

TWENTY-SIX

"Governor's office," Marsha sang.

"Hello, Marsha, this is Dawn Mock. Is the governor in for me?"

"I'll put you right through, Dr. Mock. Governor, it's Dr. Mock."

"Quinn," Quinn said.

"I must talk to you right away," she said.

"Jesus, I've got a parole board meeting in ten minutes, and after that I'm loaded."

"It's urgent, and it won't take long. I'm on my way." The line went dead.

"Marsha."

"Yes, Governor."

"Push the parole board meeting back a half hour. Cancel dinner with Assemblyman Bonnar at the Ship's Tavern. Send Dr. Mock right in and hold all calls."

Quinn wondered what the hell could be so urgent.

In her ten months in office, it was the first time she had done this.

He smiled. Dr. Dawn Mock had been his first appointment and had bucked a nasty confirmation hearing. She had performed brilliantly.

The position of Colorado Bureau of Investigation was open. The glass ceiling was lowered for an African-American woman.

Dawn Mock, a mother of three and grandmother of six, was married to a retired detective who now ran a regional claims office of insurance adjusters.

Dawn's reputation on the Chicago police force had been gained as a forensics wizard. Dr. Mock's books, speeches, seminars, and appearances as a trial witness outshone the people above her. The powers to be took Dr. Mock for granted, even though she spent a fair part of every year on loan to other police forces.

The Colorado Bureau of Investigation was a compact unit of about fifty persons, mainly a support system for investigations in those towns that could not afford forensics labs or a staff of detectives.

State bureaus are rarely noted. Dawn Mock changed that. Quinn gave her a free hand and infused the bureau with new funds. Dr. Mock did the rest.

"Hi, Dawn," he greeted her.

"Governor."

Dawn rated a big smile. At fifty-something she had remained extremely attractive, belying her years of police work. She gestured to Quinn that she wanted secrecy. To one side of his office was a private room with a couch, a kitchenette, and small conference table. He closed the door behind her.

"You know Arne Skye?" she asked.

"I've met him a few times. Roving special agent for the Bureau of Alcohol, Tobacco, and Firearms."

"He's been working out of the Chicago office," she continued. "Arne flew in to see me today. He wants to talk to you in total one-on-one secret."

Quinn mulled this over. "What's your experience with him, Dawn?"

"I've had a lot of contact with him through the years. He's a legend in the bureau, good people. Arne's always been up-front with me."

"You know I don't like this back-alley crap," Quinn said, annoyed. "What do you think is on his mind?"

"Well, it's either alcohol, tobacco, or firearms."

"Maybe the AMERIGUN convention?" Quinn murmurred hopefully.

"I don't want to speculate, Governor. I've been with you a year, and I've never seen you draw a card from the bottom of the deck. Sorry about putting you on the midnight rendezvous circuit, but—"

"Breeds mistrust," Quinn interrupted.

"But," she interrupted right back, "no public office in America can exist without its dirty little secrets."

"Thanks for sharing that with me, Dawn."

"Quinn, Arne Skye is one of the big hitters in police world. You'd have to be crazy not to meet with him."

"God forgive me, where and when?"

"Have you got an unmarked car?"

"No problem."

Dawn took a room key from her purse. STARLITE MOTEL, the tag read, 11965 SANTE FE DRIVE, ROOM 106, and she slid it over the table.

"Santa Fe Drive. I haven't cruised that street since I was a freshman at Boulder. This Arne Skye got a sense of humor or what? When?"

"Tonight, ten o'clock. He'll be in the room waiting."

"No tricks, no bugging, no video," Quinn said firmly.

"You boys better start trusting each other."

At nine-fifteen Quinn left the condo garage in Maldonado's Cherokee.

Was this the break he had to have? It smelled of promise. Alcohol, Tobacco, and Firearms was a small agency, some fifteen hundred agents, but they could be potent.

One of the nation's oldest bureaus, it had been formed after the American Revolution. In those days of yore, there had been no such thing as personal income tax. The new nation had to finance itself largely on taxes from alcohol and tobacco collected by the bureau.

Later, firearms and arson were added to the bureau's mandate.

Like the Marine Corps, the ATF managed to fight off attempts to dissolve it. The bureau proved time and again they were uniquely empowered. They returned to the government in collected revenues twenty to thirty times their operating budget.

Quinn turned onto Santa Fe Drive, a diagonal truck route from the interstate to downtown Denver. He passed the train yards. The street had been once filled with truck stop cafés and hot-sheet motels. Swingers tacked their assets onto motel bulletin boards before partaking of the waterbeds and porno flicks.

The street now had a "safe" area with a strip of cantinas, musty bars, and restaurants where undocumented wetbacks gathered. Immigration raids were rare because too much of the agricultural economy and tourist industry depended on stoop labor and busboys.

As Governor, Quinn could do poor little about it. It was a federal problem. Quinn felt that corruption in Mexico and bleeding the underclass were beyond his powers to dent, much less change.

The Starlite Motel had seen better days and better days before that. Quinn wiggled the Cherokee into the lot and waited. The Starlite was a one-story affair about a hundred feet removed from a corner cantina. There was an intermittent but steady line of men going to one of the rooms in the motel and returning to the cantina.

Ten o'clock.

Quinn's shoes crunched over broken glass. His key fudged on him. He shoved the door and it broke open. The room was totally dark.

"Come out, come out, wherever you are," Quinn sang.

After a beat a dim lamp clicked on. Quinn could not be certain who was behind the lamp. "Hello, Governor. Is anyone listening?"

"Not unless he's one of yours," Quinn said.

"Dr. Mock called me and vouched for your veracity. Nice to meet someone in office with veracity." The voice came from behind his cover. Everything about Arne Skye was medium-sized, except for his face. It was a roadmap of past raids, of one who had spent a life in purgatory. He studied Quinn, trying to search for clues beyond the governor's unrevealing expression.

Arne Skye produced a bottle of vodka and small-sized Dixie cups from the bathroom.

"You going to do anything about AMERIGUN?" he said abruptly in a high voice of Norwegian influence.

"I thought you'd never ask," Quinn replied.

"Dr. Dawn says the state has hit a brick wall."

"These gun folks are artful dodgers," Quinn said.

"You've hit a brick wall because it's not your business. It's mine. What have you learned, Governor?"

"That you're a crusty character."

Skye's roadmap changed as he broke into a smile. "Where are you with this?"

"Well, let's see. There are up to five thousand, give or

take, gun and knife shows held countrywide each year, almost anonymously. The exhibition tables are leased so AMERIGUN is clear of any illegal sales by the exhibitors," Quinn recited. "AMERIGUN is renting out fifteen hundred exhibition tables in the convention center. Largest number ever."

A loud customer next door announced himself. The dying dove song cooed over to them.

"What else?"

"Many exhibitions carry illegal weapons. Contact is made at the show by a buyer, and the transaction is usually carried out at a trailer court. There other categories of dirty weapons exhibited hilariously as 'antiques.' And to avoid dealer licenses, they can sell weapons for cash under the guise of selling from a 'personal collection'! No record of sale required and no registration.

"Twenty to thirty percent of guns in the hands of criminals and street gangs were purchased at these gun shows. If the state canvasses the exhibition floor, we might catch a few dozen street-level dealers. If they're caught, it's no skin off AMERIGUN's ass," Quinn recited.

The customer next door was vocally aroused.

"Shit," Arne opined, "we can't go on meeting like this, Governor. Now, who have you spoken to confidentially about AMERIGUN?"

"Dr. Mock and my attorney general, Doc Blanchard."

"That's it?"

"Well, my wife and father-in-law."

"If there is any course of action, and I'm not saying there is, any operation has to be a dead-bolted secret," Arne said.

"What about your bureau, Skye?"

Arne shook his head. "It must be a Colorado operation. Even the ATF can be penetrated. It's like this, safety locks on guns have just been voted down by the Congress for the fifth time. Any leaks to the gun people would be a disaster in this kind of hit. Now, let me ask you, Governor, what kind of people you have leading the Guard and state troopers?"

"Reb Butterworth is adjutant general of the Guard. Colonel Yancey Hawke is chief of the troopers. I'd split a secret with them. In fact, both are seething to make a raid."

"I like your chances with those three people," Skye appraised. He inched closer to Quinn.

"Could you order a special two-week training course for seventy guardsman and thirty troopers?"

"Training courses and seminars are ongoing. We're always plucking some stupid climber off the top of a mountain, tracking forest fires, drug busts at the state lines, dusting for insects."

"Crowd control?" Arne asked.

"We practice that drill regularly. Will the people in these courses have any idea of what we're after?"

"No," Arne said. "Anything you don't understand about it?"

"No," Quinn said.

"If you want to bust AMERIGUN's ass—" Arne began.

"I want to bust AMERIGUN's ass," Quinn replied.

"We are bypassing the FBI, the United States government, and the Denver police. As far as the ATF is concerned, we don't know nothing. *Capische?*"

"*Capische,*" Quinn repeated.

"We may have the stars in perfect alignment," Arne said. "Number one, it has to be a big haul, hundreds, maybe thousands of weapons. Second, it has to show up in Denver during the convention. Third, someone of rank in AMERIGUN has to be connected to the weapons. Finally, the action must be swift and bloodless."

A ruckus broke out in one of the nearby pleasure rooms. A half dozen men stormed out of the cantina and hauled off one of their buddies lest the police arrive and detain them all.

Arne Skye got up. The low ceiling made him look taller than he was. "If you'll have Butterworth and Colonel Yancey form up a hundred men for special training, I'll contact you, through Dawn Mock."

"We've got no deal, Arne."

"You do need help, right?"

"You're hedging your bets. I want you to show me that card you're hiding up your sleeve."

The governor had it figured out correctly. Arne would stay in as long as he wasn't exposed. He would give the signal for a bust, maybe not. If the bust worked, there would probably be no investigation, for it would shut the mouths of Congress. If it went sour and was traced to him, so long career, and the governor might as well go back to Troublesome Mesa and stay.

Thirty years at the bureau, Skye thought, coming down to a single moment, possibility of gunfire, maintaining secrecy, and going over the head of his director. Shit!

Arne Skye had spent his life on the edge, sometimes completely ignoring his superiors, their mandate, and sometimes bypassing the odds, but a miss here would mean the guillotine.

"You look like you're in need of religious help," Quinn said.

"I know why I came to Denver," he shot back defensively. "If I knew what I know and failed to try to prevent it, it would end up as my legacy. I'm an honest cop, Governor, but I don't mind cutting a few corners."

"When I took office," Quinn replied, "I thought I was going to come out Maytag sparkling. It doesn't work like that, does it?"

"It's hard for guys like you and me," Arne said. "This is the most important potential bust of three decades in the bureau. What do you know about the VEC–44?"

"It's some kind of machine pistol," Quinn aswered.

"You betcha," Skye said. He took an arms case from his suitcase, unzipped it, and laid the weapon on the table. It was tiny and lightweight, had a three and a half-inch barrel, and weighed under three pounds. Modified to become fully automatic, it used powerful 9mm hollow-center ammunition, and had oversized clips holding a thirty-five-round capacity.

The weapon had been developed by Belgium as a NATO policing gun. Several thousand had been produced. NATO ultimately rejected the VEC–44 as inaccurate over forty yards and extremely dangerous when troops were dealing with civilians.

"It is worthless for target shooting or as a hunting weapon. The barrel gets so hot it becomes squirrely fast, and so the military rejected it. VEC–44 converted into fully automatic operates as an in-close kill machine designed for mean streets."

The vodka bottle lowered by two cups.

"When NATO dropped the weapon, Belgium sold the licenses and patents in Panama in the forbidden city of Colon. Colon is impossible to penetrate and is a world hub for drugs and arms smuggling.

"The package was finally taken over by Roy Sedgewick's Ark Royal Arms Ltd., a Canadian manufacturer, always slightly ahead of the government. VEC–44's were converted into a cash crop. Small case lots drifted into the gun shows and under the counters of gun stores.

"Sedgewick siphoned off three thousand VEC–44's and spirited them to his farm near Toronto. They were encased and hidden in a huge barn under bales of hay.

"When the Canadian government caught up with

Sedgewick and Ark Royal, he had made preparation for his old age.

"In the paradoxical world of arms smuggling, Sedgewick hooked up with Hoop Hooper, the 'commander' of a two-hundred-man militia, the Grand Army of Wisconsin.

"If Sedgewick could get the guns over the border, Hooper would stash them somewhere on his 'national military territory.'

"With the wrath of the Canadian government close behind him, Sedgewick didn't have many choices, despite his doubts about Hoop Hooper. He loaded his hidden arsenal onto a semitrailer and wheeled it down to Sault Ste. Marie, where it was reloaded onto a Great Lakes barge.

"The cache was enhanced by three and a half million rounds of ammunition, twenty thousand long clips, and a potpourri of grenades, rockets, machine guns, and mortars.

"Sedgewick estimated a street value of over three million dollars. Hoop Hooper was positive he could quickly move the guns to militias clear to the Pacific coast and as far south as the Mexican border."

Quinn had become mesmerized at the tale.

"I waited for those VEC–44's to move out of Canada for a year. Sure enough, I got tipped on a shipment of bonded crates to be passed through customs *uninspected*, apparently as a favor to a high American official."

"Yow! Why the hell didn't you seize them, Arne?"

"The guns were more valuable being traded in the States. I wanted to find out who the official was, and I wanted to learn their routes and the names of their customers, their communications, websites.

"The case was my baby, so ATF Washington laid off. The guns were held in the bonded warehouse until they were to be collected. Next day I opened a number of cases, confirmed the content, and implanted a GPS system. You know the GPS?"

"Ground-positioning satellite," Quinn answered, "I have one in my plane."

"We followed signals right into the Grand Army of Wisconsin's training camp between Madison and La Crosse. There they sit. We can remotely switch the GPS power off and on and randomly check the position. As soon as the GPS reports back, we turn off the power."

"What about Hoop Hooper?"

"Alas, poor Hoop," Arne said. "The FBI, which generally gets in our way, nabbed Hooper on mail fraud, money charges, income-tax evasion, illegal weapons, and criminal Internet scams. He pleaded guilty to get a reduced sentence but said nothing about the VEC–44's. The guns would be his stake when he gets out of the penitentiary."

"Jesus, what a story."

"Hell, this is a fairly easy one," Arne said. "Some of these schemes get really complicated."

"Why are you doing this, Arne? It's brinksmanship for you."

"You might as well be asking why I spent thirty years of my life in ATF. I don't want those fuck heads to dump three thousand murder weapons onto the streets and woods of my country."

"Arne, I belive you and thank you, man. Well, last question, who is the man who got the guns over the border?"

"A United States senator. Big in appropriations, major patriot in the red, white, and blue department. A real Yankee doodle dandy. Half his state owes him favors. He told Customs in Superior that it was a load of urgently needed Swedish farm machinery."

"Good Lord," Quinn whispered. "You're talking about Senator J. Richard Darling!"

"Bingo," Arne Skye said, "Dicky Darling."

Denver and the Alamo, Maryland—A Week Before the AMERIGUN Convention

" Good afternoon, Governor's office, Marsha speaking."

An officious throat clearing. "This is King Porter calling from Maryland. May I speak with the governor?"

"Hold, please," Marsha said, going to the intercom. "Governor, King Porter is on the line."

Quinn was struck by the sudden call. "Put him on," he said unevenly.

"Governor?"

"Yes, sir."

"King Porter here."

"What can I do for you?" Quinn asked.

"Well, Governor, I thought it would be neighborly for me to contact you. We have our differences, of course, but AMERIGUN is going to spend several days in your beautiful state, and I'd like to think, as Americans, we can call a truce during our visit. I may add, we are expecting over ten thousand delegates, you know, plus the exhibitors."

"You will be greeted with open arms, Mr. Porter."

"King, call me King. We have a very active membership—"

"No problem. Denver knows how to throw a party."

"Yes, well, we certainly do not favor or anticipate any problems."

"And we shall do our utmost to make you welcome."

"Governor, I wonder if I can beg a favor from you. It seems like Denver's mayor will be out of the country. Could I impose upon you to welcome the delegates?"

"Where and when, King?"

"We officially take over the Convention Center on the morning of the eleventh. The balance of that day goes to registering delegates and helping get the exhibitons set up. The welcoming ceremony takes place at six in the evening."

Quinn jotted a note and passed it to Marsha, who had entered the office.

"We've got a date, King. Looking forward to meeting you."

Quinn banged his fist on the desk and snarled.

"Well, he did hold out the olive branch," Marsha said.

"You know where he wants to shove it. That slimy little son of a bitch! He's dragging me up there like . . ."

"Ancient Hebrews being marched through Rome in chains," Marsha said.

"Something like that."

"Don't worry, Governor, you'll be a big hit. Dr. Mock dropped in and wants a few minutes with you. She's waiting."

"Have her come in, and hold everything."

"I need good news, Dawn," Quinn greeted her.

"You remember that big wheel of cheese you ordered from Wisconsin?"

"It never came."

"It's on the way," Dawn said. "We're all hooked in. I can monitor its progress from my office."

Quinn cupped her hands in his, sighed, prayed, and kissed her fingertips.

"She's on interstate ninety heading west, about to cross into Minnesota, beep, beep, beeping merrily along her way."

TWENTY-SEVEN

WELCOME TO COLORADO!

AMERIGUN SILVER ANNIVERSARY CONVENTION—DENVER

SEPTEMBER 13–17, 2003

"Hee-Haw!"

It looked as though the late shows at Branson, Missouri, had emptied onto the interstate and all headed straight for Denver.

In Denver the bars had spare kegs piled up in their alleys, the hookers staked out their saloons, the gangs protected their drug turfs. Fun in the Rockies!

A lot of wholesome family events on the menu. Three thousand utterly priceless tickets would be raffled for a game between the Broncos and the *dreamworksKANGAROOS*, the latest Los Angeles expansion team at *intelELWAY* Stadium. Out in the mountains the billion or so aspen trees began their dance of gold. A thousand basketball tickets for the *mcdonalds-NUGGETS* had few takers.

WELCOME AMERIGUN DELEGATES

"Hee-Haw!"

The autumn air was crisp and gentle. Glorious deep breaths ensued.

Rae O'Connell watched her brother, Duncan, amble over the parking lot toward the entrance. Lordy, what a cowboy stud, she thought, a good thing we were all raised with morals.

"Hi! Over here, Duncan!"

They hugged. "I've got tickets," she said.

"What time is Dad speaking?" Duncan asked.

"Six. We've got a couple hours to look around."

Three hundred thousand square feet, filled with fourteen hundred ten-foot tables, burst open before them. The tables sagged under the weight of handguns, rifles, shotguns, night-vision apparatus, knives, laser attachments, ammunition presses, sniper scopes, lock picks, burglary tools, surveillance bugs, T-shirts.

It was the devil's fairyland.

A double table held three hundred separate and individual fake law enforcement badges where a man could button on the rank of sheriff, sheriff deputy, detective, U.S. Marshal.

There were tables of Kevlar vests and spy craft kits.

And

A tattoo artist.

And

Steroids, faintly disguised, and brass knuckles and lead-filled sap gloves and blackjacks and body vests and pepper and mace spray sets and stun guns and electric cattle prods and police clubs and handcuffs.

The main aisle tables exhibited stealth climbing equipment and barbed-wire cutting tools and pistol magazines and SWAT carrying bags designed to disguise automatic weapons.

The hall was filling up now. Untrusting exhibitors stared suspiciously at untrusting customers. Word had been passed that the Denver police were on "live and let live" orders.

Camouflage uniforms closely following Army and Marine Corps specs took up a five-table area.

Next to it were bayonets, shooting earmuffs, bi-pods, machine-gun tripods, combat boots, and bird shot.

Targets holding outlines of human beings.

And

Confederate flags.

And baseball caps bearing such identification as SWAT, ATF, FBI, SHERIFF, BORDER PATROL, U.S. MARSHAL SERVICE.

There was a table with a rainbow of military medals and ribbons on display, from the Order of Lenin to the Victorian Cross. Step right up and show the folks how courageous you were—in case you misplaced your own citation. All of the armed services military medals from the Spanish-American War to the present were on sale, except for the Congressional Medal of Honor, which had to be special-ordered.

Duncan and Rae retreated for a hot dog and Coke, munching listlessly, saying nothing, talking to one another with their eyes. If this is legal, then what is illegal? All disguised to defend liberty. All bitter, frightened people who had abandoned joy and laughter early on.

They were not exactly sterile, Duncan thought. Here, among fellow gunners, they were empowered by their numbers.

"What time is it?" Rae asked.

"Twenty to six," Duncan answered.

"Let's go into the hall."

"I want to look at those book stalls."

"I'll go in and save us a seat, on the aisle near the rear. Is Mom coming?"

"Dad insisted she go up to Troublesome."

"She'll be here."

Stacks of books, six tables long, stacks of pamphlets, three tables more.

The Turner Diaries was the major title, the book that had inspired the most infamous terrorist in American history, Timothy McVeigh. It had been his bible for blowing up the Murrah Federal Building in Oklahoma.

There was a how-to table.

Terrorist Explosive Source Book

"Folks!" called the loudspeakers, "be sure to register

whether you are a delegate or just an AMERIGUN member visiting. We'd like to show just what kind of support we've got. Registration tables are at . . ."

How to:
Create Your Own Home Workshop Guns
How to Build Claymore Mines
Grenade Launchers
Blow Guns—The Breath of Death
101 Weapons for Women
Beat the Border
Counterfeit ID Made Easy!
Disguise Techniques
The Outlaw's Bible—How to Evade the System by Using Constitutional Law
Just Say No to Drug Tests
The Poisoner's Bible—Deadly Concoctions Through the Ages
How to Avoid a Drunk-Driving Conviction
Got to Get Money $$$$$—New York Street Con Games
Fugitive's Guide—How to Run, Hide, and Survive
Man-Trapping Techniques
Detonators
Slash, Thrust, Strangle
Booby Traps
Hostage Taking
Forgotten Legions—Obscure Combat Formations of the Immortal German Waffen SS
Protocols of the Elders of Zion—The True Story of

How the Anti-Christ Gutter Religion Conspires to Take Over the World

And the winner is!

Body for Sale: An Inside Look at Medical Research, Drug Testing and Organ Transplants, and How YOU Can Profit from Them

"Over here, Duncan!"

He slumped in beside her. The auditorium noises heightened in anticipation.

"Those so-called antique guns," Duncan whispered to his sister, "are World War Two. Both the carbine and M–1 garand are used today for hunting, and the World War One 03 is still one of the most accurate rifles in the world. Man, they're twisting and distorting every law."

"Every law and human decency," Rae said. "Christ, I feel like I'm on a different planet: Mars, war, blood."

He patted her shoulder. "Thank God for men like our Dad," he said.

"Ladies and gentlemen! Folks! Shooters! Can I have your attention? The welcoming session of this great conclave will take place in fifteen minutes in the *unitedairlinesAUDITORIUM.* Preferred seating to delegates and AMERIGUN members showing their registration badges. Governor O'Connell has agreed to personally welcome you all himself. Make certain he gets a rip-roaring ovation."

Duncan thought he was going to get his first asthma attack.

GOD SAVE THE SECOND AMENDMENT declared a banner on the balcony railing. Every seat was filled. Hall Carleton, a hall of fame football player turned actor in times past, filled his days with after-dinner speaking to agitated, hopping-mad groups of an immoderate Christian fellowship.

Hall mumbled toothily, a problem he had had with his acting. As the celebrity spokesman of AMERIGUN, he rose among them like a giant. Five, six, seven thousand people and growing were in the embrace of the protector.

King Porter shuffled his feet and gnashed his teeth, motivating himself for his upcoming hell-bent, Katie-bar-the-doors sermon.

The day of the gun had arrived in Denver.

Six o'clock. Hall Carleton banged the gavel and declared the convention open and smiled an ivory smile to the delegates.

"Fellow shooters! Please take your seats and let us prepare ourselves for the serious work ahead in the next three days. Now, we're all 'Mericans here. We love our freedom and our children, and we treat our women with respect. We are known for our fair play. My daddy," Hall continued, choking a bit, "gave me a Daisy BB gun when I was five years old for picking blackbirds off the telegraph wires. I got so good, we had bird and rabbit for dinner whenever I went a-hunting. This old dawg can hunt!"

Cheers, whistles, stomps, drumroll.

"When I was chosen to star in some of the great film epics, I never forgot where I came from and *why*. And I thank God—yes, you liberals, there is a God—I thank the Almighty for allowing me to spend my twilight, my declining years in the service of decent citizens asking only for their God-given just rights. That's all we ask of a government turning more and more against these just and constitutionally guaranteed rights."

Cheers, whistles, stomps, drumroll. Both arms spread like a Moses parting the Red Sea.

"Now, I can't say," Hall Carleton said, "that everybody agrees with us. But we are tolerant. The man I am about to introduce may not support us on the various issues, but he will learn to. Because he is a fair-play man and he is a great 'Merican hero, a great Marine, a great . . . rancher and governor. So, stand up and cheer our honorable opponent, Governor Quinn Patrick O'Connell of the great state of Colorado!' "

Rae and Duncan turned to the entrance of the *unitedairlinesAUDITORIUM* and saw their father and their mother beside him, calm as a whisper.

The band struck up the Marines' march, "Semper Fidelis—Always Faithful." Quinn strode slowly into the waves of hands reaching to be shaken. He nodded quickly to his children. The cheering intensified as he was greeted at the steps to the platform by Hall Carleton and King Porter. Be gracious in victory, King told himself. Down the line of board members Quinn went.

He stopped for a long handshake and shoulder slap

from Senator J. Richard Darling, then came to the microphones. The cameras moved to close-up, and a pan shot as a banner rolled down the balcony rail, COLORADO GOES AMERIGUN.

Order at last. "With enemies like you," Quinn began, "who needs friends?"

The *unitedairlinesAUDITORIUM* convulsed.

TWENTY-EIGHT

The governor and his family snuggled into a booth at Daddy Bruce, the renowned purveyor of spare ribs, long deceased. They chomped.

"What's the matter with those people?" Rae asked.

"You can't paint a single picture and call it universal. If there are common denominators, it would be poverty in youth, perhaps corporal punishment, dust and cactus life, or places of raw exploitation. They grow up to be losers and band with other losers in losers' bars and losers' trailer courts. Together, they flesh out who caused their birth-to-death misery. Few people have the guts to really look into themselves, so they go for the cliché villains. The government is the big, bad demon in their lives. They dream of being warriors, they play at being warriors. Their rationale is warped logic, but logical to them nonetheless. They stay as persecuted outcasts, a role they fit into, and therefore everyone is out to get them. So, enter the weapon, the equalizer, and shout out about fantasy rights they do not have . . . pass the sauce. The rest of the entire male world, from kings to commoners, have always been and always will be enchanted by the power of the gun. Sooner or later we lose our civility."

"I'm glad we're out of that hall," Rita said shakily.

"So am I," Quinn said.

"Are you going to be able to do anything, Dad?"

"Possibly," he answered with a wink.

"Don't do anything crazy," Rae said.

"Tell him that," Rita pressed.

Quinn waved a pair of gooey hands. Rae cleaned them off with wipes and napkins. Duncan pointed at his father's chin, and she dabbed it.

Rita took her husband's hand and pressed it against her cheek. "You son of a bitch," she whispered, "please be careful."

"Most of these gun people in town are just after a good time." Duncan said.

"It's the other ones I'm worried about," Rita added.

Reynaldo Maldonado came in and pulled up a chair at the end of their table. He had eaten. He had seen his son-in-law's welcome on TV. Gutsy.

Quinn checked his watch. "Take Rita and the kids back to the condo. I'll commandeer the Wagoneer."

"Can we know where you're going?" Rita asked.

"I'll be in Dawn Mock's office at the CBI. I have no idea how long the meeting will last."

"Honey, please, no heroics," Rita pleaded.

"You were there tonight. We've got to put a stop to this shit, or we're going to start losing our country."

They sat staring at the empty paper plates and empty paper cups as he left.

Quinn entered Dr. Dawn Mock's office. Colonel Yancey Hawke, head of the state troopers, came to his feet and shook the governor's hand.

"Hell, Governor," Reb Butterworth, the Colorado National Guard commander said, "you could have won the governorship of Louisiana tonight."

"Where is the mother lode now, Dawn?" Quinn asked.

She brightened the screen and fed in a road map of Minnesota and made a face. "Nothing. Let's run in an Iowa map." She punched in coordinates and hummed, "I—ooo—way . . . here we go."

A fuzz ball on the monitor pulsated: *peep . . . peep . . . peep*.

"You'll pardon the expression," Dawn said, "they're really truckin'. They've bypassed Des Moines and are heading west on eighty for the Nebraska state line."

"Their speed tells me that there are two or more drivers, rotating," Yancey observed.

Dawn Mock punched a number of keys. "At present speed they will hit the Nebraska-Colorado state line by morning. Colorado . . . Colorado . . . here we go. The interstate changes to Route Seventy-six. Four hours will get them into Denver, plus a food break."

"They've timed this out to reach Denver by late afternoon," Yancey concluded. "At dark they'll go into the prearranged site."

"Dr. Chin?" Dawn asked her CBI Internet buster.

"We are listening to a hundred of the most active gun websites," Harry Chin said, checking his notes. "Nothing regarding a destination has shown up. However, there appears to be spirited activity for the purchase of VEC–44's at the convention."

"How many?" Reb asked.

"In the low hundreds," Chin answered.

"Which says," Dawn Mock said, "they're going to a prearranged location and deliver the VEC's that have been sold. They won't let the individual buyers pick up the weapons. The dozen or so dealers will retrieve the VEC's and disperse them in their trailer camps and motels."

"Yep," Quinn agreed.

"They're going to shag ass for the Utah line, maybe Four Corners. That's where the big dealers play."

"Why all this brouhaha about the dump site? We can't foul up on the destination. The little bouncing ball on the screen will lead us right into it. As for our forces, Reb, your people will be tucked into Elway Stadium within spitting distance of the convention center.

Yancey, split your force into a triangle, use high-speed vehicles, and converge once we have the exact location."

"And where would that be?" Yancey said.

"My primitive guess," Quinn answered, "way out on West Colfax near the foothills. The strip is loaded with warehouses and factory outlets. Colfax will put them right on the interstate for Utah."

"Governor," Yancey moaned a bit, "I realize you want these people caught in the act, but we're going to have better luck by nailing them right inside the Colorado line."

"We know there is one or more relief drivers, but we do not know how many of them are in the trailer riding shotgun," Quinn answered. "As soon as we slow them down, anywhere, anytime, anyplace they may go for their weapons."

"What!" Reb said. "Crash a roadblock and drive the length of Colorado? Not rational."

"Gunrunning isn't rational," Yancey said.

"Are you in contact with Arne Skye?" Quinn asked.

"Afraid not, Governor," Dawn said. "He set up the GPS here and signed off. He's taken himself out of the loop."

"Rightfully," Quinn answered. "We're not to reveal his name on pain of death." The governor held up both hands to create some thinking space.

"A roadblock is not what we want. If so, we could

have seized them in Wisconsin or Iowa or Nebraska. A roadblock crashing and a high-speed chase will create a real mess."

The heads of the troopers and the National Guard were a bit peeved, as was Dawn Mock. Harry Chin played it neutral. The other three perspired, and their fingernails fidgeted on the desktop.

"Denver is filled with late-night shopping traffic and tourists and conventioneers and forty thousand baseball fans all in the vicinity of the convention center. Governor, it could end up looking like the beach at Normandy if the bouncing ball ends up there."

"If you are wrong, Governor, and believe me, they could have faked us out of our jock straps, we are in major shit," Yancey warned.

"Yancey, put a video and still photographer at the state line. Let's see if we can make a double confirmation by getting some plate numbers and what advertising they're carrying on their sides."

"We're close, but no cigar," Dawn said. "Suppose we rip into a warehouse filled with recliner chairs and Serta perfect mattresses?"

"Dr. Chin, do you have anything on Roy Sedgewick, Ark Royal Arms?"

"I've got two detectives at the airport covering passport control," Chin said. "The Canadian government is breathing down Sedgewick's neck. My information is that they are going to commence an audit at Ark Royal within a week. This could be the moment for him to flee, and he may need the money to be generated in Denver."

"No." Quinn mulled it over. "There aren't many flights from Toronto to Denver. He'd use Chicago as his port of entry—there's no passport control there—or he's on his way to South America. No way Sedgewick will show up."

"We'd better have some shithouse luck," the adjutant general moaned.

"Amen," Yancey said.

Quinn rolled his head about and cracked the bones of his spine and neck. "I love you guys. Dawn, do you have a place where I can crash for a few hours?"

"There's a big couch in the hall outside the morgue. Hart's people will report if they have anything new. I'll be at the monitor here through the night."

"Okay, you guys, you know the drill," Quinn said.

"You've got more guts than brains," Reb said, giving the governor a warm *abrazo.*

"Ditto," Yancey Hawke said.

Dawn Mock slipped a pillow under the governor's head and laid a blanket over him. She mussed up his hair and wrapped up his feet.

"Cool Hand Quinn," she said softly, "have it your way. My way or the highway. Dirty decision time. You're my hero, Governor."

"Not me. Arne Skye."

"Good night, man. I'll be following the beeping ball."

"Dawn, call Rita, will you? She's at the condo."

"Okay, get some sleep."

TWENTY-NINE

"Yuck!" Quinn said, smacking his lips together. He unscrambled himself from his blanket, came to sitting, and held his face in his hands. "Yuck," he repeated. "My name is Quinn Patrick O'Connell," he told himself. "Now where am I . . . what is that strange odor? The morgue!"

"Morning, Governor," Dr. Dawn Mock said.

"Jesus, what time is it?"

"Past ten."

"Huh, guess I must have been tired. Morning, Dawn."

"Good news first or the bad news?" she asked.

"Good news."

"There is none. Roy Sedgewick has disappeared into thin air."

"He could be here in Denver, using an alias," Quinn said, groping for his shoes.

"Or," Dawn added, "halfway to somewhere. The

Canadian government has put him on an Interpol alert. Interpol would cough him up in Europe. That leaves South America and Asia. I'd guess China. Sedgewick has a long history of gunrunning for the Chinese. I gather the Chinese financed him on getting the licenses for the VEC's. If China is his route, forget it. He's too well connected, and they'll let him in and hide him."

"Damn, so we scratch him, huh?"

"For sure we won't find him today."

Quinn stretched hard, yawned, excused himself. "I'm going to run to my condo and clean up. I'll be back in an hour."

Dawn gave a double thumbs-up sign, and a look passed from one to another that said, "Are we crazy or something?"

Rita smiled broadly to cover up her sleepless night, as did Rae. Quinn stood under an ice-cold shower until he could handle no more. An infusion of coffee awaited him as he exited the shower stall.

"I'm thinking," Quinn said with a good feeling of putting on clean clothing, "you and the kids ought to move into the mansion. Take Mal with you."

"Why?"

"Don't give me a hard time."

"All right. Duncan called earlier. He's at the convention. I gave him my cellular in case you needed to reach him."

The great "fairness" theme had evaporated with Governor O'Connell as he left the auditorium. One after another, the row of front benchers of the board came to the pulpit and roasted the demons of the anti-gun, anti-American, anti-Christ charlatans who ruled the government.

A basket of pro-AMERIGUN proposals and "whereas-es" was passed unanimously. Underaged gun owners, anti-children's safety locks, anti-limitation of twenty guns per family, anti-parental responsibility, antiwaiting periods, were all branded as violations of Second Amendment rights.

On this morning, King Porter made damned certain that last night's resolutions were remembered. The basic AMERIGUN strategy was now to silence the major gun-control freaks and particularly one in a Western state. With Quinn O'Connell put in his place, the rest of the state houses in the nation would think twice about gun-control legislation.

King Porter whipped himself up into a lather with a romping, stomping revival sermon.

"Hello, Duncan, it's Dad."

"Hi, Dad. They just hung you. That Porter guy was frothing at the mouth."

"So, what's new?"

"I've canvassed the exhibition hall with four of Dr.

Mock's detectives. They estimate there may be several hundred illegal weapons in the hall, but there's no way to get to them. By the time we get the legal search and seizure papers, they will have scattered."

"Duncan, don't lose the faith," Quinn said. "I want you to get back to the condo, pronto, and move over to the mansion . . . and no fucking arguments!"

"Okay, Dad, I hear you."

The instant Quinn saw Dawn Mock, he knew that something terrible had taken place. Harry Chin, usually expressionless, suddenly looked ancient. Dawn pointed at the GPS monitor.

"It stopped transmitting about fifteen minutes ago," she said.

"There's nothing I can do, Governor," Dr. Chin said. "The batteries inside the crates have lost power, and the GPS has stopped transmitting."

"They were supposed to last three years!"

"Batteries can be funny," Chin answered.

"Dawn, get me Yancey."

"Colonel Hawke here."

"This is Quinn. Did you get any photographs of the truck last night?"

"Just going to call you, Governor. There was a bitching thunderstorm around the state line. Neither the video nor still photographs are able to identify anything."

"We've lost contact with the truck," Quinn said.

"Oh, Jesus. What do you want to do? Call it off?"

"Let me think for a minute, let me think," Quinn mumbled to himself, trying to retread a plan. "Here we go, Yancey. Hold your triangle. I still say West Coster will be the target area. I'll leave it to you to contact Reb and make sure he keeps his people undercover at the stadium. I'll get back to both of you soon as I can."

"If it weren't so tragic," said Chin with a straight face, "it would be hilarious trying to find an unidentified semi truck and trailer in Denver."

"Governor, let's chuck it in. If we pull out of it right now, there won't be any damage to you. None whatsoever," Dawn pleaded.

"None whatsoever except a fucking AMERIGUN office in Denver telling us how to live our lives and three thousand more murder weapons on our streets."

"Man, we tried," she cried. "You've got to consider the careers of the people who have gone all the way with you."

Quinn wound up as if to punch the monitor but only cursed it instead.

"We've got a long day coming up," Quinn said at last, "at least four or five hours to run out every option."

"We can't keep it secret much longer," Chin said. "It's going to leak."

"All right, give me two or three hours. I need you people here."

They both nodded tentatively.

"Dr. Chin, find out for me who is the top man in the federal penitentiary system. Find out his military service, i.e., which branch he served in. Keep lowering the search by rank until you find me a Marine."

"Highest-ranking Marine in the penal system."

Quinn was about to punch in the number for Hoop Hooper's attorney, A. Wayne White, but stopped. "I'll go to him last, Dawn. Once we start dealing with lawyers, our security is compromised."

In the interim, Dr. Dawn Mock had pulled herself together and organized the bureau's regular day's work with her assistant in the outer office.

Harry Chin returned in six minutes. "Highest-ranking penitentiary official is George Appleton, First Deputy Director, Marine Corps, 1978–1986, rank of major, Viet combat, decorated."

"Am I speaking to *the* Governor Quinn O'Connell?" Deputy Director George Appleton said excitedly into the phone.

"Yes, sir," Quinn answered.

"Gunner O'Connell?"

"Yes, sir," Quinn repeated.

"I am honored! I was in rapid deployment on my hitch. Now, what can I do for you, Governor?"

"This conversaton is Marine to Marine," Quinn said.

"I understand," Appleton said softly. "I think we'd better shoot a little verification."

"Sure. There is my wife, Rita, in Denver and my secretary Marsha at the Capitol. You don't have to tell them who you are, but that you need to speak to me about some cheese coming in from Wisconsin. Both of them will give you the same number. I am in Dr. Dawn Mock's office at the Colorado Bureau of Investigation."

"We will be Marine to Marine," Appleton assured himself.

"Absolutely."

"I'll be back to you on a secure line."

Second by second tension ensued. Not a word passed between Quinn and Dawn, but she could almost see smoke coming from his ears as he pumped his brain for direction.

"Governor O'Connell here."

"Appleton."

"Semper Fi time?" Quinn asked.

"Semper Fi time," Appleton pledged. "What do you have in mind?"

"There is an AMERIGUN convention taking place in Denver."

"Yes, I'm aware. A very angry one."

"We have intercepted a plan to dump up to three thousand VEC–44's and millions of rounds of 9mm ammunition. We lost contact with the delivery truck. You have a prisoner in the system who is our last hope of giving us the destination of the weapons."

"I see . . ." Appleton's voice trailed off. "Does he have a lawyer?"

"He has a rat's nest full of them. We have been able to make this exclusively a state of Colorado caper. Actually, only six people know anything about the target, one of them my wife. Time will not allow us to deal with the lawyers. If I have to negotiate with them, we'll probably be too late to apprehend the cargo, follow me?"

"Yes."

"It will take the media months, if ever, to figure out how we pulled it off. And in that time we will fade into thin air."

A scent of procrastination seemed to flow from Appleton's phone. Quinn could hear the man breathing, weighing. Was it fair for the governor to use the federal system on an operation from which they had been bypassed?

Undoubtedly, Appleton thought, O'Connell had gotten tips along the line from the FBI or ATF. Appleton was about to decline when the big picture of a great hero, Gunner Quinn O'Connell, loomed before him. After all, what the hell was O'Connell doing? Putting his ass on the line in the service of the people. On the other hand, the rancor between federal agencies would ensure a media convulsion. Why the hell does he have to give me that gyrene shit?

"What do you need?" Appleton said at last.

"I want to speak, one to one, with a prisoner on a secure line."

"Oh, hell, we do much worse," Appleton sighed. "Bury my name, for God's sake."

"Hey," Quinn said, "we're on death-before-dishonor vows here. Your name will not emerge from this end."

"Who do you want to speak to, and what facility is he in?"

"Herman Hooper, aka Hoop Hooper, Atlanta Penitentiary. Former leader of the Wisconsin militia. Bundle of charges. He's pleaded guilty to get a reduced sentence, which has been lowered to twenty years from forty."

"I'm on it," Appleton said.

"And, George, we are desperate for time."

Senator Dick Darling closed the morning's session by pointing his finger toward Washington and shouting "thou shalt nots." Hall Carleton was elected president of AMERIGUN, by acclamation, unopposed.

Carleton smiled so broadly his teeth shone clear to the last row as he and the senator held up each other's arm in victory.

King Porter announced the afternoon's business and an evening fare of barbecue and folk dancing.

Reb Butterworth spirited fifty guardsmen and troopers into Elway Stadium, one truck at a time. He was positive he had not raised alarm or suspicion.

The troops were housed in a wide corridor between the field seats and the balcony. Bedrolls and boxed rations were the order.

They would remain fully clothed and could reach their trucks in two minutes, with another four minutes bringing them to the convention center.

A report from Yancey Hawke. He had established his triangle, three positions that could converge at an instant's notice. Each apex had some fifteen troopers and guardsmen all in secluded areas.

"Hi, Rae, it's Daddy. You're all in the mansion okay?"

"There seem to be twenty guards outside. Are we going to need them?"

"I hope not."

Hours of midday dragged by, the longest of their lives. A pair of half-eaten pastrami sandwiches died on Dawn's desk. Quinn was knotted up. He could barely get his teeth unclenched to drink his Coke. Dawn had been staring at the empty monitor. Tears welled in her eyes.

"We've been stiffed," she said. "It's four o'clock."

"One more half hour," he mumbled.

"You've been saying that since noon."

"Never mind," Dawn said to herself. "Why argue the point now? The governor had played it skillfully and bravely, but neither skill nor courage was the game. And no one has ever figured out how to stop time."

Both of them clicked on as the scramble phone buzzed. Dawn nodded to Quinn. He lifted the receiver.

"Hello," Quinn said.

Dawn put a headset on to listen.

"Hello," the other end said. "Who am I speaking to?"

"Governor Quinn O'Connell, Marine Gunner O'Connell."

"Tell me, Governor, who was your commander at the Urbakkan raid?"

"Major General Jeremiah Duncan."

"And he won the Congressional Medal?"

"Yes, as a fighter pilot in World War Two. He received a posthumous Navy Cross for Urbakkan."

"About how tall was Jeremiah Duncan?"

"He was on the short side, like five eight."

"George Appleton here, Governor. Sorry to put you through the quiz. I flew to Atlanta after we spoke to set things up myself. Who is aware of my participation?"

"Dr. Dawn Mock, chief of the CBI. She's been involved from the beginning. And Dr. Harry Chin, our Internet specialist."

"I'm speaking to you on a secure phone? No tapping?"

"Of course not."

"And I'm just doing you a favor, and I don't know what it's about."

"Yes, sir," Quinn said.

"All right, here's your man."

"Hoop Hooper," a voice growled.

"This is Quinn O'Connell, governor of Colorado."

"Yeah, I know who you are."

"Good. I'll cut right to the chase. A semi and eighteen-wheeler left the Wisconsin Grand Army two and a half days ago carrying three thousand VEC–44's and a lot of massacre trimmings. Destination, Denver."

"I don't know what the hell you're talking about, Governor."

"We've lost the truck in the Denver environs," Quinn plowed on, "and we may not find it here. But we sure as hell are not letting them out of the state. Roy Sedgewick was going to set up a nest egg for you with the Denver sales. Sedgewick is gone, probably en route to China. Hoop, you've got to know that Sedgewick was going to beat you out of a couple hundred grand either way. He fled because everyone's hot breath was on him."

"Well, who in the hell is Hedgehog?"

Quinn ignored the remark. "Dickie Darling is going to pocket all your hard-earned money."

Bingo! Quinn heard Hooper wince.

"I'm on the fast track, and we've got time to make a bust. Where are they going to deliver the guns sold at the convention?"

"I don't follow you."

"You have a forty-year sentence that has been reduced to twenty by your guilty plea. Give me the information, and I'll do everything in my power to reduce your sentence to ten or twelve. That means, with good behavior you could be out in six."

"You should be speaking to my lawyers, Mr. Governor."

"No way. I'd have to expose the operation and my associates, and there's not time to argue with attorneys. It is you and me, Hooper, you and me, us."

Hooper ran over the governor's figures. It meant going in with a forty-year sentence, coming out with six. I have to take his word that Sedgewick has fled, and he sure has his facts right on the VEC's. "How do I know you'll deliver?" Hooper asked.

"You don't. You're going to have to trust me."

"I ain't never trusted nobody and never will."

"Well, today is a real fine day to start."

Hooper huffed, grunted, and snarled. The tattoos reading MOTHER COUNTRY GOD on his left arm pulsated. He looked over at George Appleton, who was fixed on him with hatred. Hoop knew hatred when he saw it. Sure did. He knew if he rejected the governor, prison life was going to be brutal.

"Give me some time to think about it," Hooper said.

"Sure, you've got thirty seconds and I hang up."

"Hold on, Governor. The gun run from Wisconsin to the Denver convention was planned seven months ago, when we were unable to sell them. I've been in prison for five months. They sure as hell must have changed the delivery location."

"What was the former location?" Quinn snapped back.

"Friehoff's Furniture Outlet, somewhere out on West Coster. Can you get me a single cell?"

"Maybe. Tell me about the truck and the drivers."

"They're crazy, man. Three brothers and a cousin named Jensen. They've been running contraband out of the Great Lakes ports for years. On this run their pay will be on delivery."

"What are they advertising on the side of their truck, and tell me about their plates."

"Governor, I don't know. They're probably driving a hot rig they stole recently. On a few runs I know they put up Old Milwaukee beer sheets with magnets. I don't know."

"All right, give me a solid gold name of an exhibitor at the convention who is dealing in the VEC's."

Jesus! Hooper had already exposed the Jensen brothers, and he'd exposed himself. Chuck it in and pray, he told himself.

"I want to get moved to another facility," Hooper whispered hoarsely.

"Why?"

"I, uh, ran into a number of militia boys and Klan people. All of a sudden I'm organizing them against the niggers, and the niggers are out to get me."

"Hoop, it's not in my power. Let me speak with the deputy director," Quinn said.

"Hello, Governor," George Appleton said.

"Hoop is about to give us the key piece of information, but he thinks he's been fingered by the black prisoners. He'd like to be transferred to a facility where he isn't known and can be isolated."

Appleton blew a long whistle. "You'd better pull this off or God save us all. Here's Hooper."

"Well, now," said Hooper, "I've met two guys I don't trust in the same day."

"Let's have it!" Quinn said abruptly.

"It's me or him," Hoop Hooper thought. "If he was in my place, he'd snitch on me." "There will be an exhibition table belonging to Chad Murtha. He exhibits plastic, Teflon, titanium handguns, ammo, and clips."

Lovely, Quinn thought. Everyman's weapons to beat the metal detectors!

Dawn Mock was at her door jotting notes for her assistant: *Get a layout and index of the exhibition tables . . . Chad Murtha is the exhibitor . . . Call up Detective Boedecker and draw ten thousand dollars in marked bills, mixed . . . Try Tennessee penal system and drivers license bureau to see if we can bring up a photo of Chad Murtha . . .*

"Okay," Quinn went on. "Does Murtha's exhibit have any kind of identification sign or banner?"

"Yeah, the back banner reads 'Glock Almighty!' and a smaller one under it reads 'Glock 'Em All!' "

"Now tell me about you and Chad."

"Me and him been on the circuit twelve years or something. He hit on the plastic weapons because they're a big-turnover item. They'll only shoot up a few clips when they start to crack."

"All right. After I find the Glock Almighty sign and I'm talking to Chad Murtha, what do I say?"

"Say, 'I think I got the wrong table. Billy Joe said I could get some real metal here.' Chad's gonna say, 'I ain't seen Billy Joe in a coon's age,' and he's gonna ask you where you last saw him. Then you say you seen him at the gun show last year in Fort Smith, Arkansas."

"I follow you," Quinn said. "What does Chad look like?"

"Heavy guy, big gut, used to wrestle professionally. Blond hair, he dyes it, like sixty years old and usually wearing a baseball cap."

"Can we get a photograph of him?"

"Probably. He's done some time in Tennessee."

"Continue, Hoop."

"Chad's gonna say something like, 'What kind of metal you looking for?' and you say, 'Swedish metal.' He'll want a ten percent deposit. Then he'll give you the location of his camper park and the number of his parking space. He'll probably tell you to show up at two or three in the morning."

"Couldn't he just take off with the deposit?"

"No, not and deal in gun shows for a dozen years. Honor among thieves. That's the standard time when the deliveries take place."

"Hmmm."

"See, he's got to keep his exhibits open at the convention hall until they close, usually around ten-thirty to midnight. Then he has to get the guns."

"And, in theory, he'll lead us to the mother lode."

"That's the ticket, Governor."

"Next," Quinn said, "there is a special parking lot for exhibitors at the convention center. What's he driving?"

"A light blue Ford pickup, trades it in every other year for another light blue Ford pickup. It has a stainless steel camper shell over the truck bed. He'll have Tennessee plates."

"Hoop, think hard, are there any other exhibitors who can be as helpful to us as Chad Murtha?"

"No, he's the main man. He'll look over the exhibitors, and if there are some who have worked with him, he'll select maybe four or five, depending on how sales are going."

Hooper was unaware of pressure in his chest. He had always thought the pain was a part of his being. As he spoke, he blew out words coming from his deep interior, and it was like a relief from a tremendous crushing machine.

"Let me speak to George," Quinn said.

"Appleton."

"I'm setting some things into motion. Can you put Hooper in a holding cell so I can stay in contact, if needed?"

"The present setup is very secure," Appleton answered, and gave his phone number. "We'll be here. For Christ's sake, don't forget to inform us."

"Semper Fi, buddy," Quinn said.

"Semper Fi," Appleton said.

Quinn grabbed the stale bread on Dawn's desk and bit a hunk off it, starved. In a moment Harry Chin spread out a map of the exhibition hall, and they scoured it with magnifying glasses. Quinn went down the list.

"Bingo! Murtha, Chad, Knoxville, Tennessee, plastic handguns and paraphernalia. Side booth on west wall, stall number seven hundred twenty-three.

"Dawn, I need a half dozen detectives in three two-man teams to locate Murtha's pickup truck. I know we've gotten burned with signals from the big truck, but can you slap something on Murtha's vehicle to give off a radio signal?"

"I've got a dandy, and it will work."

"All right, your three CBI cars will follow Murtha some time after ten-thirty. As soon as his signal gives us a general direction, I can set Yancey's team into motion. Wait a minute, wait a minute, wait a minute!" Quinn said, slapping his forehead. "Position a plainclothes pair in an unmarked car near Friehoff's Furniture Outlet so he has a bead on 10101 West Coster. I've a wild hunch these people may not have changed the drop-off location."

"It's sure as hell worth a shot," Harry Chin said.

"God, I wish I could go in with Yancey," Quinn said.

"With all due respect, Governor," Chin answered, "keep your ass right where it is."

* * *

Chin made a log at Dawn's computer.

1800 Glock Almighty! reads the banner at the back of booth number 723. A second small banner reads Glock 'Em All.

1822 Photo of Chad Murtha arrives CBI. Description, excellent.

1830 Detective Lieutenant Mary Boedecker contacts Quinn from convention hall. She has located booth. Description of Murtha equals man at the booth.

1835 Mary Boedecker proceeds to booth.

Her appearance belied her profession. Mary Boedecker was thin, fifty-something with black and gray hair pulled back in a penny-plain knot. She wore no make-up and was dressed ranch style. Mary pointed at Chad and said she'd like to look at a pistol. Murtha unlocked chain from trigger guard.

Mary made a sour face and set the pistol down. "I think I must be at the wrong table," she said.

Chad scrutinized her so keenly, Mary could nearly feel heat from his glare.

"I'm looking for Chad Murtha," she said.

"I'm Chad."

"I ranch some up in Lodgepole County."

"Pleased to meet you, ma'am."

"Billy Joe said I could obtain some real metal from you."

"Billy Joe."

"Yes, suh, Billy Joe."

"I ain't seen him, must have been a hundred shows back. I thought for sure he quit the circuit," Chad said.

"I saw him a couple months ago in Fort Smith, Arkansas," Mary said.

"I missed that show. I was doing something around Helena. Just what kind of metal are you interested in?"

"Swedish. The best Swedish."

It connected! The lady was talking major money.

"Well, now, top-grade Swedish is hard to come by," Chad gurgled, counting dollars as he spoke.

"I want ten of them," she answered, opening her large purse and giving him a flash of her bankroll. Chad Murtha's eyeballs clicked.

"That's a mighty big order," Chad said.

"You ever tried to get anything done with the United States government?" she snapped. "Me and some of my neighbors had our grazing rights on public land terminated. For two goddamn years we tried to get it reversed. It was like walking in hell and trying to argue with the devil."

"Government is at the root of all evil," Chad sympathized. "What's your name, ma'am?"

"Mary Decker. My neighbors and me think that if

we form a militia unit, we could change the government's mind."

"Sounds like a plan, Mary. Could I have your phone number and the name of someone who might be at the ranch?"

"Thank you, Chad," she said, smiling broadly. She gave the number slowly. "My husband, Harry, will be there."

"You realize, now, the class of weapon you're looking for is top-of-the-line fully automatic and pretty near fingerprint-proof. Ten VEC–44's, new, ten thousand rounds in long clips. We're looking at around a thousand a copy."

"Get them," Mary ordered.

1802 Detectives locate Chad Murtha's pickup truck in exhibitors' lot and attach a radio signal under its tailgate.

1831 Photograph of Chad Murtha arrives at the CBI. Record shows some small-time robbery convictions. He has been fairly clean in past five years.

1840 Detective Lieutenant Mary Boedecker contacts Dawn Mock. From description of photo, Mary is certain they have the right man.

1841 Detective Hymes has security point a camera down from roof to tape Chad Murtha's booth.

Murtha checks the deposit for marked bills. He is satisfied. Murtha proceeds to pay phone and dials the number.

The number is routed into Dawn Mock's office on phone line two. Harry Chin lifts the receiver.

"Hello," he says, "Harry Decker speaking."

"Oh, hello, Harry. How are things going on the ranch?"

"Shitty. Who am I talking to?"

"Just a friend down at the AMERIGUN convention. Thought I might get to see you."

"I sent my old lady down."

"I'll keep an eye out for her."

Chad hangs up with a big "cat in the fishbowl" smile. Motherfucker, there is going to be a big old payday!

1900 State trooper Sergeant Hap Cronin in plain clothes and unmarked car takes up vigil in sight of Friehoff's Furniture Outlet at 10101 West Coster.

1930 The evening's "Barbecue and Bash" opens its doors to the microsoftGRAND BALLROOM.

2001 Detective Mary Boedecker returns to Chad Murtha's booth.

"I've got some good news for you, Miss Mary. I managed to find the last pieces in Western America. The

VEC–44 is a beauty, a real man-stopper. Aren't you worrying about all that money you're carrying?"

"Well, now, don't you fret, Mr. Chad. I can hit a mosquito's ass at forty yards with my little Beretta 25."

"I sure bet you can," Chad said, feigning what might be a chuckle. "Here's the way it works. Don't write none of this down, just remember it. You be at the Foothills Trailer Camp on Lawson Street at two in the morning. You'll be observed, so come by yourself. I am in space number eighty-four, in a small mobile home."

Mary repeated the numbers, then asked, "What kind of vehicle do you have? I don't want to go knocking at the wrong door at that time of morning."

"Blue Ford pickup, Tennessee license plate. Maybe we can split a beer or two."

She gave a noncommittal shrug that didn't exactly say no.

2014 Mary Boedecker contacts Dr. Mock's office, reports on gun-delivery instructions, and confirms the blue Ford pickup truck as vehicle to follow.

2100 Ribs and chicken and beans proliferate as the bash rolls into motion at the microsoft-GRAND BALLROOM.

2134 State trooper Sergeant Hap Cronin reports that a single automobile with driver and one passenger is buzzed through the main gate

at 10101 and parks near the loading docks. Automobile is this year's Mercedes and appears to belong to a top-echelon person.

2145 Quinn ups the ante, deciding that 10101 is still the designation. He orders Yancey to move his people very quietly to within a mile of 10101 and hold.

It was the best damned evening AMERIGUN ever put on. There were lots of country and western performers, some Nike all-stars, sitcom stars, and finally, Senator Darling moved the crowd to tears.

Line dancing up to forty yards long pounded the deck and skirts flared, showing the ladies' legs, and the bars damn near ran dry.

2200 Chad Murtha secures his booth for the night, departs convention center, has two beers at the Londonderry Bar.

2235 Chad Murtha repairs to convention parking lot, locates and drives off in Ford pickup.

2226 Detective Solomon at parking lot catches signal, alerts other teams, and pursues Chad Murtha at a distance.

2236 Three CBI teams depart parking lot in

unmarked cars and have Murtha under surveillance as he drives west for the interstate.

"By God, Governor," Harry Chin said with uncharacteristic emotion, "you were right! It's going to be 10101."

"What kind of stupid fools are they?" Quinn thought aloud.

"Repetition," Dawn Mock said. "If a mode of operation works ten times, it will work the eleventh. All criminals leave a signature. Maybe no one was certain who was supposed to be in charge of changing locations, so nobody did."

"Folks, could I have your kind attention?" the loudspeaker boomed. "There's a line of yellow cabs at the main entrance. They have been provided for your safety. If you feel you've had a couple of drinks too many, take one of these tipsy taxis. You will be delivered to your lodging without charge, compliments of the Colorado Tourist Board."

A sweet and hurting voice continued singing. The revelers were beginning to get weary, soaked, and grow heavy-legged. Quick action by the police stopped a fight before punches were thrown. "Don't you go looking at my wife that way."

"Well, tell your wife not to look that way."

The police nudged them into separate taxis.

As the wearies trod from the microsoft GRAND-BALLROOM, the singer was closing out with slow dancing, loves lost, losers, loves strayed, loves betrayed, all in heartache three-quarter time.

"Ladies and gentlemen, fellows and gals. Shooters! Tomorrow night is the grand awards banquet . . ."

Could I have this dance,
For the rest of my life,
Will you be my partner,
Eeevverrry night!

"Give me the governor!"

"Quinn here."

"Detective Solomon. Chad Murtha has turned off the freeway. He's heading for 10101."

"Hang on."

Quinn, Mock, and Chin spread the map and returned to the phone. "Have your teams come in steadily on Petroleum Boulevard. Park your cars in the Colo Computers' lot and proceed by foot three blocks east to Oakdale and Bancroft. Trooper Hap Cronin will be advised you are coming and will update you. And remember guys, no casualties if humanly possible."

2330 Chad Murtha in blue Ford pickup stops before the gate at 10101 and flashes headlights. He drives immediately inside the gate, which remains open. In the next seven minutes, four vehicles

driven by dealers are waved in by Chad. Gate is clicked shut. Vehicles drive to loading dock.

2340 Eighteen-wheeler bearing Old Milwaukee sign is buzzed in and maneuvers to loading dock.

2342 First units of Yancey Hawke's people make connection with Hap Cronin. State troopers followed by guardsmen surround the entire chain-link fence, set up tear gas, spotlights and a loudspeaker system.

2343 The rear of the Old Milwaukee truck is opened.

Owner of Mercedes identified as Franz Friehoff, owner of the furniture outlet.

Franz Friehoff and Chad Murtha check off an order sheet.

"Morrison."
"Here."
"Seventeen pieces, seventeen thousand rounds."
"Trinowski."
"Right here."
"Sixty-five pieces, sixty-five thousand rounds."
"Here's my own order," Chad said. "I've got two

hundred and seventy pieces. I'm buying the beers. I've been looked up by a dozen militias."

"Spotlights!" Yancey Hawke ordered.

Friehoff's warehouse and grounds lit up as though an astro from outer space were making an earth landing. Blinding!

"Now hear this!" Yancey Hawke boomed. "You people are surrounded and cannot escape. If you resist or open fire, we will shoot to kill!"

First to leap off the loading dock screaming, "Don't shoot," was Jessup Jensen, the trucker's middle brother. He had run a few steps toward the gate when his younger brother Darren shot him in the back.

"First volley," Yancey Hawke ordered.

A number of stun grenades arched over the fence, followed by a barrage of tear gas that hit the loading dock and crashed through the windows into the warehouse.

"Shall I bust open the gate, Colonel?"

"Hell, no, they are penned in. Just leave them penned in."

It seemed that everyone among the gun runners reached for a weapon at the same time and appeared to be shooting at each other.

"Drop your weapons! Walk to the fence with your hands over your heads and stand, holding the fence facing us, or we will fire. This is not Waco or Ruby Ridge or the Montana Freemen! You have thirty seconds to raise a white flag. Anyone who tries to hide in the warehouse will not come out alive! You now have twenty seconds!"

2415 Mary Boedecker contacts Dawn Mock. The ballroom is an empty mess. Clean-up crew and a dozen security guards are it.

2425 Reb Butterworth and his force in intelElway Stadium dash for their trucks and roll the short distance to the convention center.

Unloading and setting up a picket looks as though it were an illustration from the Army manual. Twenty state troopers and CBI detectives enter exhibition hall and move the night watchmen aside.

"Now hear this," Butterworth said to the empty ballroom. "This facility is hereby seized under Colorado statute six-oh-four-A as a clear and present danger to public safety, and other crimes."

THIRTY

BREAKING STORY BREAKING STORY BREAKING STORY

"We take you now to our Denver affiliate. Don, are you there?"

"Yes, this is Don Fender, CNN, Denver. In the late hours of last night and the early hours of this morning, Colorado state troopers and the Colorado National Guard carried out a lightning raid intercepting a gun-running scheme. A second task force seized the Colorado convention center where the national AMERIGUN conclave was being held."

"Can you tell us—"

"The operation apparently depended on secrecy and speed. Details are very slow coming in . . ."

BREAKING STORY BREAKING STORY BREAKING STORY

". . . interrupt this program to bring you a breaking story from Denver."

"This is Anita McGlore, MSNBC, Denver. The cock has crowed and Denver citizens are waking up this morning to the electrifying news of a major gun bust and the closure of the AMERIGUN convention. Governor Quinn Patrick O'Connell has scheduled a news conference for one o'clock this afternoon, Rocky Mountain time. It will be held at the historic Brown Palace Hotel."

Rocky Mountain News GOVERNOR QUINN PADLOCKS ARMS SHOW

Denver Post MAJOR ARMS CACHE RAIDED

USA Today TWO KILLED IN ARMS RAID. A PAIR OF BROTHERS, IDENTIFIED AS DRIVERS, DIE IN SHOOTOUT

New York Times (See story inside, section A, page 31)

> A truckload of assault weapons was captured by the Colorado State Patrol and a small unit of the Colorado National Guard. Two drivers were killed in the operation and several hundred guns recovered.

New York Post GUN MUGGERS MUGGED

The "historic" Brown Palace buzzed with anticipation. Its atrium lobby soared nine stories to a glass roof which held an American flag four stories long.

By one o'clock some sixty print journalists and a dozen camera crews had assembled, each with their own rumors.

Deadly silence. One could hear people parting as Governor O'Connell made his way to the rostrum. A smattering of applause. A half dozen journalists came to their feet cheering. Now, sustained applause as Quinn fooled with the microphone.

"First, I want to sing you all a little song," Quinn opened. "I've never been involved in a press conference of this magnitude, and it's a little frightening. Half of you I don't know, so please give your name and organization. We okay with that? Thank you."

BREAKING NEWS BREAKING NEWS BREAKING NEWS

". . . switch you now to a press conference at the historic Brown Palace Hotel in downtown Denver."

Announcer in a whisper: ". . . that is Governor O'Connell at the rostrum. The three people sitting at his left are identified as Adjutant General Butterworth, commander of the Colorado National Guard, Colonel Yancey Hawke, chief of the Colorado troopers, and Dr. Dawn Mock, head of the Colorado Bureau of Investigation, a well-known figure in law enforcement circles."

Quinn held up and waved a sheet of paper. "You all have received a rap sheet like this. It brings us up to an hour ago, noon. Questions?"

"Vernon Creech, *Rocky*."

"Hi, Vern, I thought you'd never ask."

"Governor," Creech went on, "the rap sheet says your initial tip was anonymous. Are you saying, sir, that it wasn't someone in the federal government or that you didn't have assistance of the FBI or BATF?"

"First, we aren't going to blow our sources. Second, the operation is still going on, and third, we might want to use the same sources again in the future. It was my belief that the entire AMERIGUN invasion of Denver was meant to be as intimidation, a warning about future antigun legislation. If any of you listened to the rhetoric at the convention, you'll understand my drift. I considered it a crude attempt to bully Colorado out of its sovereign rights. This was a state operation from beginning to end. My colleagues and I felt we could only be successful if we held the secret to just a few people. I determined that we had sufficient state forces to do the job. The weapons are Canadian-made VEC–44's of Belgium origin and were smuggled into Wisconsin via the Great Lakes. Apparently, the drivers, the Jensen brothers, had been running contraband for several years."

"There must have been middlemen, sir," Creech said, not yet sitting down.

"The manufacturer, a Roy Sedgewick of Toronto, has disappeared. Friehoff, whose warehouse was the drop spot, has been placed under arrest, and we also arrested five weapons dealers working from the exhibition tables."

"Governor," Chita Mendez of the *Pueblo Chieftain* said. "It sounds like no officials of AMERIGUN were involved."

"Just one," Quinn answered, "Senator Richard Darling of Wisconsin."

BLAM

* * *

BREAKING NEWS BREAKING NEWS BREAKING NEWS

"Governor O'Connell has named Senator Darling of Wisconsin as the chief operator of a longstanding smuggling ring from Canada. Apprehended at the Denver International Airport, the senator has vociferously claimed his innocence. We switch you now to the Denver International . . ."

When the press conference regained its sanity, Len Sanders of the *New York Times* threw the question:

"Did you use computer surveillance, and how did you follow the weapons from Wisconsin to Denver?"

"Yes, we used computers. Our entire operation was covered by appropriate court warrants. Moreover, we took abnormal caution to see that there were no casualties. The two Jensen brothers were apparently killed by their own gunfire. I'm not totally free to give you the method we used to trail the weapons to Colorado."

"Can we have some more dope on the VEC–44's?"

Quinn held up the assault gun. "Here she is. It's a 9mm, about .38 caliber, fully automatic machine pistol using thirty-five round clips. She only weighs three pounds, and the barrel is a few inches. You couldn't hit a bull in the ass at twenty feet with one of these little buggers. They are designed to be in close and personal killers particularly for street gangs and burglars."

"What is the current status of the operation, Governor?"

"Well, let's see. Three thousand VEC–44's have been

logged and impounded. Some five or six hundred weapons were due to be delivered to buyers last night. They are part of the cache. The dealers have been taken into custody. More important, we have a search-and-seizure warrant in effect. Our teams are in the convention center checking all the weapon ID numbers. So far we have turned up well over a hundred laundered guns. In addition, a dozen exhibitors are wanted by police elsewhere."

"What you going to do with all these weapons, Governor?"

"Melt them down for sewer lid covers. Let me say that any exhibitor selling legitimate material can have it returned by merely going to the Exhibition Desk."

"You don't expect any dirty dealers to actually try to claim an unregistered gun, do you?"

"Stranger things have happened," Quinn said. "I wish to apologize," he went on, "to the AMERIGUN delegates and directors and exhibitors of legitimate items. The vast majority of folks are honorable, law-abiding citizens. Unfortunately, an ugly element pervades any gun show, and there are hundreds of them every year. There is always an aura of fear and danger emanating. This was a rare opportunity to inspect all the contents of the exhibition tables."

"You rat!" a voice screamed from the rear of the room. King Porter was held at bay by his confederates. "You entrapped us!"

"Ladies and gentlemen," Quinn said, "that is King

Porter, CEO of AMERIGUN. King, you are free to come up here and join the news conference."

"What! To your Goddamned fucking liberal press! This is war!"

"You bet it is," Quinn answered.

In the days that followed, Governor O'Connell was deluged with messages of approval. The raid rang a note that a peaceful people had at last given the neighborhood bully a punch in the nose.

Quinn pressed forward with a gun-ownership bill, the sane bill for sane citizens that encompassed provisions that would have been defeated a few weeks earlier. It was to be a model for other states.

The polls in and out of Colorado showed high approval ratings on the governor's action.

Polls showed 78.6 percent for, 21.4 percent against.

J. Malcolm Dunlay, a former attorney general, appeared on two dozen panels of experts in the following fortnight as part of the 156 TV panels to discuss the pros and cons of the sting.

The Civil Liberties fanned the fire by declaring that the gun dealers had been denied their civil rights.

Others accused O'Connell of usurping the federal charters of the FBI and the BATF.

More panel shows.

Quinn and his people withdrew as a ravenous media

started searching through the capital's trash cans and toilet stalls.

A count total was lost as to the number of Internet communications, but it appeared that they ran 78.9 percent in favor of the operation.

The public was smitten. Replays of *High Noon* abounded. Governor Quinn Patrick O'Connell was thrust into national prominence.

At the end of the month, the AMERIGUN bust and cowboy O'Connell dissolved and were replaced when a star of one of sitcom's royal series chopped up his wife with a carving knife.

Homicide panels replaced weapons and legal panels, although J. Malcolm Dunlay slid from one to the other effortlessly.

Even though Governor O'Connell was out of the immediate spotlight, a buzz had started around him. Instead of taking the glory road, he seemed to withdraw, dazed and wondering.

Rita was finally able to tear him loose from Denver and lure him to Troublesome. They would stay at Mal's, where they could enjoy more isolation than at the ranch.

The rain plopped hard on the skylight, perhaps the last rain before the snows. Rita's knowing hands rubbed out his sore spots. At first he was not even up to making love.

Wind misted with rain and bombarded threateningly, then softened to a mellow tattoo of little raindrops. A moment for resurrection was at hand.

Rita and her father rocked on porch swings, watched the storm drift south, and smelled the freshness of after rain.

They stopped talking as Quinn, in floppy bathrobe, yawned his way out to them. He had crashed, for this particular nap, for four hours.

"Well, my wife and father-in-law seem to be in a conspiracy . . . what? And assassinate the cruel governor with daggers and gain the state house?"

"You are, my dear son-in-law, a victim of your own success. Anything not clear to you, Quinn?"

"Like what?"

"Like I saw you on your knees at the family chapel for the first time in the four decades I've known you," Mal said.

"It was between me and God," Quinn said. "Please tell me, Lord, who I am and what do you have in mind for me. Do I have veto powers? Be still my heart."

"You know what's going on," Mal said. "Rita and I have fielded calls from every big hitter in the Democratic Party. They've a golden boy. Get used to it."

"I love the people's politics—" Quinn started.

"And are the most beloved governor in Colorado history," Rita said.

"I was thinking maybe an embassy. Maybe Australia or New Zealand. No cabinet posts, just a non-trouble-making embassy."

"Well," said Mal, "why not try to open a consul general in St. Barth's and lie on the beach and look at tits all day?"

"And I'd get to look at peckers," Rita said.

"Out with it, Quinn," Mal pressed.

"First the Urbakkan raid," Quinn mumbled, "now this AMERIGUN bust. All the sudden adoration is bound to fade, and they will say, Quinn's a man of violence. Who needs him? The good life depends on peace and prosperity. Moral imperatives like the defeat of slavery come at too high a price. So long as we remain fat and free, we will avoid the lingering festering issues. At any rate, I am not going to be the one to gather up the people on a moral issue. It makes for a dull person."

"You're anything but dull," Rita said.

"And what about you and Duncan and Rae? Are you ready for a million maggots at your door every morning?"

"What I am worried about," Rita retorted, "is that if you walk away from the call, we'll spend the rest of our lives in our own form of self-imposed hell. I knew this was going to happen even before you ran for governor."

"Don't raise the stinker that you're retreating because of your family. They know their daddy is a great leader . . ." Mal said.

"Mea culpa time," Quinn said. "I wanted clean in and clean out. Before the bust I made up my mind that I would stand for reelection if I had a chance to get this legislation through and impound about eighty-five percent of the guns in Colorado. When plans for the raid became a reality, I treated myself to massive doses of mendacity, the ancient art of lying to oneself. I lied, I made dirty deals, I was very selective of people's rights, I put a lot of folks in harm's way, I endangered the careers of some very gifted people. I went into Urbakken clean and escaped by a miracle. I went into AMERIGUN tainted and again escaped clean, except for those sad Jensen brothers. Am I cursed to have to always ride in on wings of a raven? Must I blow up half of the state to prove my point? Do the people really want a cowboy?"

"Well, right now they've got one," Mal snapped back.

"You are their hero, Quinn," Rita said.

"I love you guys," Quinn whispered, "and I know what you are thinking but dare not say. Play it cool for your next term, Quinn, then go take a shot at the presidency." Quinn had balled up both fists. "Nothing," he banged out, "nothing can happen, no disaster can befall so great as to go through the agony of Bill and Hillary Clinton. Nothing," he said, "nothing, nothing, nothing."

PART THREE

THIRTY-ONE

The White House, 2007

From the get-go Thornton invoked a formal operation of the White House. It was a more serious place with a serious dress code. No more inline-skating in the halls outfitted like a member of the chorus of *Guys and Dolls.*

Serious young people were nominated for internship by serious Republicans. No more liberal punk kids. No more showing of thigh or cleavage and improper hairdos.

Intimacy among staff was more risky.

Under control, the hordes of legislators, consultants, media, public relations hired guns, and lobbyists entered a correct and hallowed place.

Daringly, the press facility near the Oval Office was exiled to the nearby Executive Building. The media went into a rage. Darnell knew that this was one the President could win. After the media debacles at the end of the last century, the public was delighted that the press was learning manners.

Thornton Tomtree was the first fully computerized president. He installed a crew of the finest computer analysts. No matter what the chore, background on a political appointee, weather in Alaska, cabinet meeting, they could dissect and translate information faster than any like team in the world. Tomtree went into his meetings with up-to-the-second data, the sway of public opinion, every nuance of the financial world.

Darnell Jefferson had the run of the place. He pulled together a public relations staff of rare genius to counter any idea that the Oval Office was rigid.

With his first years scandal free, the nation's social agenda was soon overtaken by power bestowed on the corporate world, allegedly to keep America as the only superpower.

If Thornton was smart about one thing, it was human greed. Every American owned some. His programs were designed so the public saw a payoff for them.

Pucky had grown into a stylish sixty-year-old. She and the President had been long unfamiliar with one another's bed. This did not result in her anger, but in a strange sense, it gave her freedom. She did all the First Lady things, often adding spice and humor and throwing the most elegant banquets in memory.

Thornton understood her value and rewarded her by endowing the cultural scene.

* * *

I am sleeping and I can't wake up! I can't wake up! Where the hell is Pucky? Where am I! It will be daylight, and O'Connell is addressing the nation . . . enormous consequence.

Where the hell is Pucky?

"Mr. President," my steward, Eric, repeated, pulling me out of a deep, confusion-filled sleep. I pointed at my mouth. He handed me a glass of mouthwash and held a spittoon, then put drops into my eyes.

"It is four A.M., Mr. President, two o'clock Rocky Mountain time."

That got my attention. I asked for Darnell's whereabouts. Eric had hunted him down before he awakened me. Darnell was tied up for ten minutes or so in the press room. "Hold my calls until Darnell can brief me," I ordered.

Come on, Darnell, God dammit! That's funny. The first time I said those words to him was when we were teenagers.

Darnell Jefferson, the first black billionaire in American history—he who sat on three dozen corporate boards, he who endowed the black community and colleges handsomely, he who personally went to Moscow as the Soviet Union was breaking up and snared the twenty best computer scientists in the country for T3, he who talked me into building a pleasure palace for my workers which became the model for all industry, he who, he who, and so forth and so forth.

Well, I've done damned well for Darnell . . . and he's done right well for me. He is the only one whom I can trust in this vacuum I carry. I trust no one in there but him. Suppose we had never met? Suppose he had decided not to spend his life keeping my public image pure and dynamic?

On New Year's Eve of 1999 I told him I was going to make a run for the presidency in 2004. Darnell was way ahead of me and charted out a brilliant campaign.

We rode to the White House right after the turn of the century. The care, feeding, and control of the Internet had created great answers and greater confusion.

All of a sudden the world had potentially three billion would-be writers, not only with free and unfettered access, but hidden by anonymity.

The great computer firms were bent on speed and shrinking chips. Packaging, marketing them were the berries. Competition had become slaughterhouse-mean and fighting off an antitrust suit the most noble form of corporate life. No one seemed to have a vision of the future, or where this electronic colossus was taking us.

Darnell took a team of experts and science writers and crafted a manuscript: *The T3 Commonsense Guideline for International Internet Ethics: A Primer for the 21st Century.*

I wrote the final draft and subsidized a major publisher to put it on the market. Damned if it didn't sell over a million copies in the bookstores and another million over the various web sites. I made *T3 Commonsense* a must in every convention and salesroom at sweetheart prices and sent hundreds of thousands of copies to schools and universities.

Like *According to Hoyle* and *Burke's Peerage* before it, *T3 Commonsense* established the rules of the road on a road sorely needing them. I had taken my first step on the golden carpet which climaxed with my election as president of the United States.

All the above may sound funny to you in light of the nation coming out of the closet by the end of the nineties. However, many of the things we let out of the closet would serve us better if they were shoved back in.

The point of this is to say, I myself, Thornton Tomtree, am a clean, moral, progressive, self-made entrepreneur.

The Four Corners Massacre was not my doing, but it happened on my watch. Darnell Jefferson and Pucky literally forced me to travel a nation in mourning and share the people's grief.

Awkward and stumbling in the beginning, I learned the art of compassion. Even though I never personally knew or understood it. I acted it out, people responded to my "sincerity" . . . I never felt the depth of their anguish. Isn't that what a leader is all about: not to go down in an ash heap, but demonstrate strength and ability to endure after a tragedy?

If a leader felt pain in every flood, hurricane, shooting, epidemic, school bus overturning . . . he would cave in and no longer be a leader.

Darnell and Pucky forced enough of the mundane stuff into me to help me regain my position for reelection.

Speaking of tragedy! I was gaining on Governor O'Connell in the polls, and at the Great Debate I expected to bury him. I blew it! As for Pucky's part in this, it is history better left, unwritten.

We are now less than two weeks away from the presidential election of 2008. I'm not doing so well. Or am I?

Why, out of clear blue sky, did O'Connell call for national TV coverage of an announcement?

Darnell came in with a handful of pages. He glimpsed at the dark suit Eric had laid out. "Put away that mourning outfit," Darnell ordered Eric. "I want the President to wear a green sports jacket and open collar."

"Darnell . . ."

"A lot of folks downstairs need their morale lifted."

No use arguing over so trifling a matter.

"What's the latest?"

"We have some data from the NYPD. This Ben Horowitz visit seems to have set off some kind of chain reaction in the O'Connell camp. Ben Horowitz is a detective lieutenant, thirty years' service, semi-retired or detached to teach at the John Jay College of Criminal Justice. Horowitz's father was a professor of Russian studies at NYU. Horowitz's own expertise is missing persons."

"Got any photos?"

I lifted my magnifying glass, studying the pictures. "There may be a resemblance, there may not be. I can't tell from these. What else?" Tomtree asked.

"I've spoken personally to our main man inside the Church hierarchy. There are no official records in Church adoption files about O'Connell's birth. Two people were intimately involved in the adoption, namely, Cardinal Watts of Brooklyn and a Monsignor Gallico, both deceased. They did this on behalf of a priest who was Siobhan O'Connell's brother but gave him no details. He is also deceased. The convent that raised and delivered O'Connell to Colorado could not give us any information as to the child's biological parents."

I liked what I was hearing. Some kind of moral blister was ready to pop, the kind the media could seize on to devour whomever. Sure, Horowitz and O'Connell were connected. Yes, I have turned a corner, and the polls in a few days would see me back in the lead. The miracle of my reelection would happen. It would be an upset even greater than Truman's defeat of Dewey. I was chomping at the bit. Was there a way to find out what O'Connell was going to say before he went on? If so, we could be planning our counterstrike right now.

"You're drooling, Thornton," Darnell said.

"You bet I am. If Horowitz senior was an academic teaching Russian, there has to be an FBI file on him."

Darnell gave me a "shit for brains" look. "Wait, for Christ's sake. Do not fart with FBI files. Do not jump the gun and step into a pile of shit. We will know in a matter of a few hours. I believe O'Connell has painted himself into a corner. It has to be good news for us."

THIRTY-TWO

Colon, Panama, 2007

The free-trade zone at Colon was a long hour's drive from Panama City. The zone sat plunk in the middle of the north-south axis of the Western Hemisphere and was the transit point of anything and everything going up to North America and down to South America. Anything, everything.

The town itself epitomized a thieving, seedy, peeled, steamy, muddy-floody, baking, dangerous Central American place where eyes and ears seemed behind every corner and wall in a greedy hunt for deals.

Red Peterson, an old West Texas wildcatter, was scarcely moved to perspire even though the overhead fan grunted its last days.

Across from Red sat Moshe Rosenthal in earlocks, beard, yarmulke, and prayer shawl. He took an envelope from his safe and handed it over the desk to Red.

The envelope contained a blue-white seventeen-carat diamond, in a diamond cut. The stone was a blinder.

"Now, which South American dictator's wife did this little gem come off of?" Red asked.

Moshe held up his hands in innocence.

"Did you set your price on this?"

"You have an idea, Red, what this is worth?"

"*Mas* o' minus."

"For you and only you, a hundred and fifty thousand."

Red replaced the diamond in its envelope, folded it securely, placed it in his top shirt pocket, and buttoned it. He signed an IOU marker to Rosenthal which the jeweler could cash later at Villa Hans Pedro Oberg, one of the main clearinghouses and banks of Colon.

"You made a good buy," Rosenthal said. "It might be a little risky to sell it as one stone. If so, it could fetch over a half million. I'll give you the name of a tip-top merchant on Forty-seventh Street in New York. He can figure out the cuts like no one else. He'll double your money."

"Moses, you know I don't deal in this crap. This is just a little present for the big, tall Swedish bombshell I'm married to."

"Such a stone for your wife! Well, it will look beautiful in a necklace setting."

"It's like this, Moshe. I got her this G-string."

"A G-string, you know, a G-string?" Red said tentatively.

He stood up and pretended he was wearing a G-string. "Up the left side, I call that first base, the string has a row of little rubies. Up the right side, I call that third base, a row of emeralds. This diamond is going right in at home place."

"You're such a romantic," Moshe said.

The teakettle whistled. How the fuck can he drink hot tea? Red always wondered. He never winced, but it annoyed him whenever he saw Moshe Rosenthal's concentration camp tattoo. Moshe produced a bottle of Red's stuff. They clicked on the deal; prayers would be said tonight at shul.

"You delivered a hell of an order here. Some guys were around this morning looking for your pilot, Cliff Morgan. Apparently some kind of parachute drop."

"Smells like CIA, doesn't it, Moshe?"

"The guns are going into the Sierra Maestra Mountains in Cuba to a half dozen anti-Castro guerilla bands. Strange, I remember in fifty-nine or sixty when the Americans parachuted guns to Castro back in the Sierra Maestra."

"Nothing changes," Red said. He looked outside. It was darkening for the daily downpour. "Guns coming out of the United States, sold to the CIA in Colon, and flown into rebel Cuban camps. At the same time I'm going to buy Bulgarian AK's for shipment from Colon to the United States."

Red caught forty seconds of hard rain and reached Kelley's Klub dripping. Cliff Morgan occupied a table with a half-dead bottle and a dancer on his lap. Christ, Red thought, that little *concita* reminds me of why a fellow can never go on a diet of straight blondes.

"Aren't you going to introduce me to your little friend?" Red said on entering.

"This is Choo-Choo," Cliff said. "Her and her sister, Candi, do a real artistic number together. They'd like to be broadened by a mature man."

Red took his hotel key out and handed it to Choo-Choo. "Arrange to get off about nine or ten o'clock," Red said, "I'll square it with Kelley."

She took the key. Red's hand felt the beautiful curve of her hip and she left.

"Thanks," Red said to Cliff.

"My treat," Cliff answered. Red wished to hell Cliff Morgan had paid the installment on his jet.

"I hear the CIA was looking for you."

"Yeah, they want me to fly our delivery in a transport and drop them in the Sierra Maestra. Fifty thousand in it."

"You take the job?"

"After I finish up our charter. When we leaving?"

"I've got a little business at the Villa. Was going to leave tonight, but Choo-Choo and Koo-Koo . . . well, tomorrow morning. File a flight plan for Lubbock."

The guards passed the Villa Pedro Oberg's limo through the gates. Red emerged and with Hans Pedro disappeared into the safe room that had no eyes or ears.

It was one of the most protected civilian buildings from the Rio Grande to the tip of Argentina.

The fucking little Swiss banker, Claus Von Manfried, was at hand to pick up droppings of the deals. Could he operate! He spread the large accounts into a half dozen to a dozen banks, all numbered and inaccessible accounts.

"Let's see what I've got here," Hans Pedro said. "I have a verification of the pieces you sent down. Payable to you in the sum of two million, seven hundred and fifty thousand dollars. Minus four hundred and seventy thousand you owe for the Bulgarian AK's."

"Yeah, I owe Moshe Rosenthal a hundred and fifty thousand."

"Have you verified your purchase?"

"Yeah, I checked this morning. They're all there. They'll be going up on a Greek freighter, *Kaspos.* What have I got left over?" Clauf Von Manfried's calculator added in bribes, transportation, Hans Pedro Oberg's clearinghouse fees.

"Slightly under a million."

"What're my total deposits?"

"Thirty million in eight accounts."

Red scratched his head. "Bank a half million of the new money and give me the rest in cash."

"I'll prepare it, sir."

You bet your sweet ass you'll prepare it, you Swiss fart, Red thought to himself. "I'll pick it up at six in the morning."

Handshakes and curt nods all the way around.

Red smirked as he left the villa. Bunch of thieves, he thought. But then Coo-Coo and Du-Du would be . . . waiting . . . and,he broke into his first smile in days, Greta would wear the G-string. Not a bad deal.

THIRTY-THREE

Hosanna Corner in the godforsaken outskirts of godforsaken Lubbock had ministered to the righteous and the sinner in its alternative histories. Hosanna Corner had come into being after the Civil War as the last watering hole before the wagon trains plunged into the southwest desert.

Nearly a century later, during the heyday of the West Texas oil strike, it naturally evolved into a saloon with gambling and prostitution amenities. When the oil patch collapsed, thousands lost it all and were left with land that could scarcely grow a crop.

Lubbock turned into a mean and nasty place where the American dream had betrayed the wildcatters, roughest of all men.

Hosanna Corner returned to a sense of grace as a local gathering house where a variety of Christian sects tried to gain a foothold among the discontent.

This was a big meeting night. Passwords and identification were required. Red Peterson entered and spotted a lone chair in the rear. The big main floor had been reconfigured with tables removed and chairs set up in auditorium style.

Red seated himself, alone, tilted his chair against the wall, and squinted at the cast of characters. On one side of the bar, a poster of a lynched Negro. On the other side, a photograph of the Waco burning. The bar served as an altar, bearing a standing cross. Klansmen unhooded themselves, feeling relief to be among their own. More secret greetings.

Now a half dozen Oregon skin heads tacked a poster of Adolf Hitler on a wall.

Words across the back bar mirror told them that YAWEH IS HERE!

A dozen men wearing silk shirts adorned with an orange cross and an orange quasi-swastika took their seats in the first row. These were the new preachers to be sworn in to the White Aryan Christian Arrival, WACA.

The room lowered to dim light, a reminder that most of their work was carried out in darkness.

Members of the West Texas Militia, sporting tattoos and Uzis and gigantic mustaches and red bandanas, encircled the chairs.

"This is an important meeting," a Klansman opened. "We are gathered to swear in a dozen new preachers of the White Aryan Christian Arrival."

As the Klansman lay fist against heart, the room

leapt to its feet and returned the salute. The chant of "White power!" resonated, shaking the Hosanna Corner to its foundation.

The dozen new preachers took their oath of office.

". . . we will cleanse this nation of ethnic adulteration. We will defend the purity of our women against mongrel infestation and our children from heathen perverts and homosexuals. We swear all this in the name of Jesus Christ and the memory of His forgotten son, Adolf Hitler."

"White power! White power! White power!"

"And now the moment has come to hail our spiritual leader, the moderator of the White Aryan Christian Arrival . . . Pastor Ed Jenkins . . . Pastor Ed."

Cheers, half bows, arm-thrusted salutes welcomed Pastor Ed to the altar. They hoorayed a small bespectacled man, everyone's Uncle Ed dressed in polyester civilian clothing, frayed and unkempt, a tireless worker for the movement.

Red Peterson snuck a drink, as did a fair number of flask carriers about the room.

"There are government spies here tonight," Pastor Ed began. "Look at your neighbor. Is he one of them?"

"No!"

"As you know, brothers, I have been discharged from prison when the foul and dishonest government dropped their sedition case against me. But for six months I moldered in a stinking cell amid sexual deviates, drug addicts, Mexicans, rapists, and murderers, all for the crime of trying to defend my blessed wife and our four blessed children from a government terrorist raid in the middle of the night by the so-called Bureau of Alcohol, Tobacco, and Firearms."

The hissing and booing zoomed round and round the room, and the stomping and pounding caused the place to rumble.

Pastor Ed held up his hands for silence.

"I was beaten unconscious by the ATF people, who then planted drugs and firearms around my house, ripped the place to pieces, and carted off my legal weapons that we must have to defend ourselves from governmental tyranny."

The whiny-modulated voice now opened into that of a rasping serpent with flicking tongue:

"In that dark and dangerous prison cell, at the lowest point of my life, Jesus Christ came to me. Pastor Ed, Jesus said, I come to you in the name of my Father, and my Father wants you to tell the truth about the government conspiracy against the decent people of the white race."

Pastor Ed drank from his water glass as he commanded silence. Red Peterson yawned.

"Listen up, Ed, Jesus told me. Jesus told me that at the beginning of 1900 the czar of Russia instituted a series of fake pogroms against the Jews . . . which never happened. It was a ruse to ship millions of Jews to America and infiltrate and infest our beloved country. When Jews got to New York or other hymie cities, all they had to do was draw cash from Jewish bankers and move into every town and village."

"White power! White power!"

"*Seig Heil!*"

"Them Jews took over the press, they own all the department stores, and they own Hollywood—and look where Hollywood has taken us. And the banks and financiers, the Goldmans, the Saks, the Lehmans, the Rothschilds, and television, and the web of secret Jewish societies has choked off the air from decent Christians. The Jews got ownership of companies to feed us poison any time they want to. And the Jews got the niggers all riled up so that the niggers were put into high places to do the Jews' work . . . that is, when the niggers weren't looking for white women."

Pastor Ed held up his worn copy of *The Protocols of the Elders of Zion.* "Here speaks the truthful exposé of the international Jewish conspiracy to take over the world. Got it? The kikes bought their way into American colleges. And the Jews won all the Nobel prizes because their committee was made up of Swedish and Norwegian Jews."

Pastor Ed had brought the room to rage. Now to tears.

"See, they look down on you and me as scum. You don't see no Jews as poor dirt farmers. You don't see no Jews in the wasteland of a dried-up oil patch. No Jew kids picked cotton and peanuts or fished for shrimp . . ."

Now came the big sweat. Off came Pastor Ed's wettening jacket.

". . . and Jesus told me in my prison cell of the shiftiest conspiracy of them all. Adolf Hitler was a Christian, a nationalist, a man who loved his country. Rather than see his own country collapse by Jewish putrifaction, he sent his small and proud and humble and unarmed brown shirts into the streets to cleanse the nation. The Jews, children of the Devil and Eve, cringed as Hitler moved to rid the world of them by attacking Russia."

"*Seig Heil!*"

"Franklin D. Roosevelt, the greatest traitor this planet has ever known, sent American boys to war fighting on the side of Jews and communists. When the Jews vomited out of Europe at the end of the war, to set up an advance base for world conquest, it gave the world the biggest of all lies, the so-called Holocaust! By now the kikes had infiltrated every branch of the government. The only thing sad about the Holocaust is that it didn't happen."

He waited for a retort of rippling laughter.

"You are here," he said, "because you've seen the plot unfold. With all the Jews and government traitors in place, farms of decent Americans like me and you, farms that had been in the family for a hundred years, were foreclosed in Nebraska and Kansas and the Dakotas. Them little shit-ass local banks done it on direct orders from the big Jew financiers. And they moved in with giant food-growing corporations. You got the picture! Jews control the press. Jews control the money. And soon they will control the food!"

Now the sweat of a hundred men gave their rage a smell. Pastor Ed was speaking of Yaweh again and his prison visit from Jesus Christ.

"It all comes down very plain. I've seen with my own eyes, NATO trucks and artillery in a warehouse in Houston. I seen with my own eyes the interplanetary space people who landed in Roswell, who were snatched and hidden by the federal government. I've seen reports from our Canadian brothers that their border is filled with NATO and Russian troops . . . ready to move in the name of the New World Order. Brothers! There is only you and me to rise up and stop them and save this nation."

THIRTY-FOUR

Providence—the Week Before Labor Day—2007

What was it that annoyed President Tomtree about Labor Day? After all, he had once built a model work-force environment. Or was it Darnell Jefferson? No matter, it was the proper move to make at the time. T3 had felt far more at home in the boardrooms.

He'd travel to Detroit, make a "read between the lines" speech extolling the partnership of labor and management, and slip out of town without offending anyone.

Today, though, was a day to laze on the water, which was unusually calm near Noah's Rock. The mini-yacht *Yankee Pride* was rigged for serious fishing. There were not too many days the President could drop a line in the water.

In a moment he heard the sharp report of the yacht

club's cannon, indicating that the sun was under the yardarm and, most important, the bar was open. The President ordered the outriggers to be reeled in and once again reviewed the report of his brother-in-law, Dwight Grassley.

In the years since Dwight Grassley had first bet on young Thornton Tomtree, he had risen from family donkey to family patriarch. Inside the Republican Party, Dwight took on a role of what might be called a hatchet man.

Grassley was a superb fund-raiser who bent and twisted the soft-money rules to their limits. Not that T3 needed funds. He could draw from his own accounts, and legally. Tomtree insisted that the widest net was cast to have each and every individual CEO make their contribution.

Soft money had become a basic canon of American politics, protested by all but stopped by none.

Napkins with the presidential seal were laid on a cocktail table with assorted yum-yums. Eric, the steward, offered hot lemoned towels to deodorize the fish smell from their hands.

"Black Label on the rocks with a side of Black Label on ice," Dwight said. His fringe of hair was white, yacht club white, a waxy silver white that growled at his plaid pants and startling crested jacket. Tomtree pontificated on the beauty of soft money . . . to let every big donor feel he had an insider's look . . . soft money was just a way of covering bets . . . soft money was soft graft with a three-thousand-year history. Throw it out the front door, it will return by the back door. If Tomtree turned back soft contributions, the CEOs would hold his feet to the fire for the next five years. T3 knew them all. All of them had Bulldog networks operating from his great computer center in Pawtucket.

"Goddamned Labor Day," Thornton growled and sipped. "My daddy was drowned on one of those Labor Day weekends. Seems to always bring bad news."

"Well, the news can't be better," Dwight interrupted. "We have our coffers filled. We can channel funds on joint advertising to our candidates, *and* the economy is great. You're going to be reelected in a landslide."

Eric brought the news that the commodore's skiff was on the way out with Mr. Jefferson aboard. Well, get on with it, T3 told himself.

"Dwight," he began, "we are planning to formally announce after Labor Day. It is the best tactical time, before Christmas and the January doldrums. Announcing early will have any other candidates scrambling for money and key people. We'll have it all. However, I want to enter the campaign with no lingering shadows hanging over my head."

Dwight froze. In all their years, he had never felt fully comfortable with Thornton. In his years of serving the man, Dwight wanted only a small reward: second or third man at Justice or Treasury.

The President was fully aware of Grassley's value. He

commiserated. "There are things you cannot do," he said, "even as president. I can't keep the pope from overrunning the planet with scrawny diseased little brown people with perpetual hatred in their eyes. I cannot stop the annual flooding of Bangladesh. I can't stop the corruption of Mexico and Indonesia."

Thornton stalled out and scanned the ocean and his trappings of power: helicopter overhead, a picket of Coast Guard craft, the finest sailors and Secret Service the nation had to offer, electronic equipment that could reach Moscow in three seconds. And out there, a launch filled with media. He had positioned *Yankee Pride* so that the press boat would catch a nasty rip tide and have them all green and queasy.

"You seem in a hurry to leave," the President said. "Got a date?"

"That doesn't sell papers anymore," Dwight said. "Who cares?"

"I care," Thornton answered. "Get rid of him."

Dwight squelched his desire to scream out as he had always squelched it.

"Look, not that I'm gay bashing or have homophobia, God knows. We have a lot of guys who've done Trojan work for the Republican Party. So, God knows I'm not into gay bashing. You'll thank me, Dwight. I personally have never allowed passion with either sex to rule me. You know, Dwight, I can tell the minute a man walks into the Oval Office if he's into adultery."

Dwight wept.

"I take it," Thornton pressed, "that you do not want to resign as my financial chair."

Right now, goddammit, Dwight thought, stand up and tell him to shove it! The sonofabitch has never felt anything in bed. Ask my sister!

"So, tell Bruce to move out of your New York condo."

"His name is Randy," Dwight whimpered. "I'll tell him."

The commodore's launch pulled alongside. Darnell Jefferson, now a white-haired and distinguished gentleman, hit the boat's ladder like a point guard slashing to the basket, quick and graceful. Darnell was greeted by a pale number in Dwight, who winced out a smile and greeting, then was helped into the launch.

Darnell downed a catch-up drink as T3 studied the political atlas.

"What the hell's the matter with Dwight? He looks as though he was shot out of a cannon and missed the net."

Thornton punched that sweet-sounding little bell and pointed at his drink. Darnell knew when Thornton had one drop more than allowable, sometimes drifting into forbidden territory. Darnell reckoned it was the President's fourth.

"Christ, don't glower," Thornton said. "You're getting like those Navy doctors. They're on automatic. Cut down on the booze, Mr. President. You know what the Navy doctors remind me of—a sidewalk filled with wind-up dolls all going in different directions and yakking, 'Cut down on the booze.'"

"You and Dwight have words?"

"I had words for him. Get rid of that sweet thing, Rodney or Rudy or whatever the hell its name is, or resign the party."

"Dwight Grassley is your devoted slave, and he is family."

"Sure, the same kind of family Jimmy Carter had with that hee-haw brother of his."

"What about me? I bring white girls to the White House banquets."

"You are not currently married."

"Dwight and Brenda have not had sex in a quarter of a century. Both of them are entitled to their lives. You know, fucking A, when Dwight suggested a divorce twelve years ago, you flipped out. For the first time in his life, Dwight has a sweet young man to love him."

The President's face screwed up in disgust. "That is very ugly."

"Mr. President, the American people don't give a big rat's ass if Dwight Grassley is fucking rattlesnakes."

"Oh, sure," Thornton answered, "take a look at the press launch. You think the Clinton scandal has put an end to our prurient curiosity?" He changed the subject. "Anything in your reports that needs attention?"

"No. A few small blips. I don't want to sound cocky, but unless there is an unforeseen disaster, you can't lose the election next year. Neither volcano nor ice storm can knock you off the mountaintop."

"That's what George Bush thought after the Gulf War." Lifting the phone to the bridge, "Captain, have we got a few rays left?"

"We should be heading in in forty minutes, Mr. President. The Secret Service wants us to land before dark."

Thornton stared at the sea pensively. "We don't get to see many sunsets, Darnell. It's been a long time since we sat here watching sunsets with our daddies."

"Why did you change your Labor Day itinerary?" Darnell asked.

"I didn't like it. Besides, I like to outfox the press. From Detroit we fly to Kirkland Air Base in Albuquerque and helicopter to Glen Canyon. Three columns of Eagle Scouts are converging for a twelve-hundred Scout jamboree. We will sing, "Under the Spreading Chestnut Tree," pin on a few merit and bravery badges, and address them as the new leaders of the new generation."

"What the hell has that got to do with Labor Day?"

"I hear say," Thornton answered, "that architects will soon be redundant . . . obsolete. In fifteen seconds a Bulldog can put up on the screen detailed plans of every major structure that has been built in the last two thousand years."

Thornton Tomtree stared at Noah's Rock in puzzlement. To Darnell he looked like Orson Wells about to say the word, "Rosebud."

"Architects are done. Writers are going. We can put every known piece of literature on the screen in seconds. Creative arts were once the beacon of civilization. But now the people have come to realize that the one perfect and infallible mechanism on earth is the computer," the President said. "I am the man who can control the Internet. The people know that."

In his Nanatuck study, the President etched out his Labor Day speech. Who could he offend by going to the Eagle Scouts? What the hell! These were lads who knew to get a sane haircut and wear a necktie and polish their shoes.

Eric brought dinner to his desk, and Pucky came in. She looked rather interesting. Thornton had never seen her in his office in exactly this kind of configuration.

Pucky had a gossamer-draped material over her breasts, which had remained surprisingly young. She was otherwise flashy and elegant, her height allowing her to wear whopping jewelry.

"I'm off to the Van Aldens'. Some new Vivaldis have been unearthed. The Juilliard String Quartet will be playing. Are you all right, Thornton?"

"I've a rotten week coming up."

"You are always in a snit when you go out to Noah's Rock."

"Is that a fact?"

"Should I stay in with you? I'd like to."

"No, no, you run along," he said reflexively.

THIRTY-FIVE

The worst part of this job, Maud Traynor thought, was moments like this, flying into a smuggler's redoubt in a single-engine penny glider. All of them were hidden in jungle and scorched mesas. The Cessna woofed up on a sortie of hot air off the desert floor. Now ponderous, brooding rock formations of dull color flipped quietly beneath their wings.

She tried to rest and closed her eyes, but the plane's motion made it impossible. Maud lit up.

Already ten years she had been "special counsel" for The Combine. She had been working in a massive Washington law firm as a labor lawyer, married Morton Traynor, also a labor lawyer, and settled into dulldom.

Yet her appearances at legislators' offices on the hill had gained her a measure of notice. The Combine had offered her a position that assured her a life of creature comforts.

Her husband had objected. With The Combine she

would be immersed in secrecy, among sleazy characters, and straddling the line of legal and illegal.

One thing was for certain. Morton had to go. She divorced him.

A short while later, Maud proved her mettle to The Combine, and she purchased a horse farm over the state line in Virginia.

Maud's daughter, also divorced with a pair of children, became the centerpiece of her life. Maud did not struggle long or hard to make peace with the morality of her work: three hundred fifty acres, a very rapid sports car, eye-dazzling finger rings, and a roustabout's lust.

Maud always had a tall and handsome and manicured Washington first-stringer after her short and uncommonly plain body. She seduced whomever at will. Earthly rewards? The devil pays mighty wages. Maud didn't let morality compromise her lifestyle. Once in a while, when a jet carrier was bombed out of the sky, she winced.

That was the way of things, straddling the line. Legally, America exported more weapons than any other nation. Below the line in the gray and black world of gun runners, America exported more weapons than any other nation. Fall into wrong hands? Who decides wrong hands when you put Stinger missiles in the hands of Afghans to shoot down Soviet planes, then have to buy them back from the Afghans?

That was the way it worked. Morality was best kept at arm's length.

Maud mulled over the coming meeting with Red Peterson, who had become a major player. The Combine had decided it would be best to ally with Peterson, who had gained inside control of the distribution point in Colon, Panama. Two of The Combine's top dealers had been erased, one tossed from a helicopter at sea. No one had accused Red Peterson. Yet no one failed to get the message.

Maud's Cessna blessedly set down on a baked dirt strip on the far side of the mountains from Los Alamos near Yucca Bend.

The plane turned and taxied back to where a Wagoneer waited.

"Maud Traynor?" Red asked.

"Red? Do I call you Red?"

"Christ, I don't even remember what my Christian name was."

They sized one another up quickly. That old bird will fly, he thought.

Maud had looked into the eyes of the cruelest men in Afghanistan and Guatemala. Red Peterson was in their league. His skin was spotted and wrinkled from too many years in the oil fields.

"Here, let me give you a hand."

Strong old bastard, Maud thought. Red was put together in quality tailor-made shirts and jeans and the prerequisite turquoise and silver trimmings. His voice was politely soft. He could let his eyelids drop in such a manner as to block him from looking on another's eyes but at the same time look directly at you.

Peterson's villa was halfway up a thousand-foot butte, negotiated by a series of switchbacks. The building was unevenly integrated into the natural contours of the hill. A smashing flying wing seemingly hung way out with no apparent support, its vista nearly to infinity.

Maud took quick takes. Five-car garage. His and hers Mercedes. Furnishings a daring but easy mix from ultra-modern to staunch Western. Paintings were expensive, partly Western and the balance from Impressionism, nearly to modern.

Maud had not seen a more magnificent suite since the Peninsula Hotel. Marble floors with soft Navajo coverings, huge and fluffy monogrammed towels, hot jets, seating for two or more, and every electronic convenience imaginable. It's going to be interesting, she thought.

They took drinks on the flying-wing veranda. Staff, well-trained and silent. Maud lifted a pair of binoculars and scanned beyond the valley where a set of book cliffs threw off their covers to take a vibrant fling before the sun dropped. She picked up a car ripping around the curves to the house and into the garage.

In a moment, Red Peterson's wife, once among the most beautiful show girls in Vegas, appeared with a pair of preteen girls.

Maud watched him turn into an affectionate pussycat daddy. "My wife, Greta, and my daughters. Joan is named from my momma and Tammy after Tammy Wynette."

They found their presents in Daddy's pockets and traded talk to catch him up. He's just like I am with my grandchildren, Maud thought. Maybe they will be both of our salvations.

Greta gathered them up and moved them to their desks for homework. Greta was still extremely beautiful, a *Walküre*, an Amazon. She had little to say as she curled his long gray hair with her forefinger.

It certainly did not appear to be a dysfunctional house. What a show girl Greta must have been, not a high kicker in the chorus line, but at six feet she stood on the platform of the ascending staircase, arms out, breasts out, and packing forty pounds of glitter.

The daughters were animated and seemingly at ease with themselves and strangers.

It all broke up the snarling, leathery image of Red Peterson. And Greta? What the hell! A six-foot Swedish lady comes to Vegas to find herself a Red Peterson. He pampered her, and she knew what to do in return.

Not a bad life, winters in Mexico and high-roller trips to Vegas or a New York or Paris spree.

Red's hand slipped between his wife's legs.

"I'll let you two talk," Greta said. "I'll have dinner served on the veranda."

"Sure, Swede," Red said, "and maybe you'll join us

for dessert." He patted her backside as she arose. "The donkey is going to ride tonight."

Now, not to get it mixed up, Maud thought, is Red making a pass at me by getting a rise out of me? Maud realized that Red had held her hand just a little too long and tried to get a peek up her leg in the Wagoneer. That should have delighted 'most any sixty-year-old divorced grandmother, except that Red was threatening.

"This cognac is magnificent," Maud commented.

"Ought to be, it cost enough. You'd think it was biblical."

Red had started life as a son of a Gulf shrimper and went the daring way by taking his best shot at the oil fields of Tyler. In the fifties and sixties it was strike and boom, boom, and bust. He went through three fortunes, and he sang the wildcatter's song of big winner to broken-hearted loser.

Red smelled a coming collapse of the oil fields early in the sixties and sold off his equipment and leases.

What hot spot remained for an old wildcatter? Mexico for a time. Venezuela for a time. Hell, these countries had so many crooks in office, the guy out in the field didn't have a chance.

Immigrant smuggling from Mexico showed promise. He knew every bend in the Rio Grande. It led to drug smuggling.

During the Clinton years the North American Free Trade Association reversed the established pattern of traffic at the borders. In the old days Mexican vegetables and fruits and cheap goods had flowed to America. Now America was exporting heavily to Mexico.

American weapons, in eighteen-wheelers, lay under the false bottoms. The trucks went through without sincere inspection.

Once on the Mexican side, a few friends had to be taken care of, and passage was open to Central America.

An incredible dinner on the veranda followed, but the air turned cold instantly when the sun dropped, and they retired to Red's office, a tucked-in little room to remind him of the bitter past, complete with rolltop desk and big pictures of oil men and oil strikes. Red had been a wiry and handsome young man in those days.

"Got any more of that thousand-year-old cognac?"

They sparred until Greta led Joan and Tammy in to say good night. Maud thought Greta a tiny bit condescending, indicating a feline bent. Or was it that Red went for all women, despite age and configuration?

Promised once more the donkey would ride, Greta departed.

"Well, now, Miss Maud, what brings you to the fleshpots of New Mexico? I've been trying to reach The Combine for more goddamn years than I'd like to think."

"It's a closed club, Red. We reached you because we feel we can deal with each other now."

"What kind of deal?"

"There have been virtually no Bureau of Alcohol, Tobacco, and Firearms stings since Thornton Tomtree has been in office."

"Yeah, he sure likes unimpeded commerce."

"Red, we've been looking into your operation since some of our top agents started disappearing in Colon."

"I heard about it; cut to the chase, Miss Maud."

"Smugglers' routes have changed. Contraband moves north and south. Vancouver is practically an oriental city. Once an eighteen-wheeler gets into the States, the way is through Route 99, inland California. You've put a lock on the border and through Mexico. It's not friendly to us anymore."

"You'd think The Combine would be happy enough supplying the new NATO armies."

"We're all greed heads in a greed head business," she said.

"I like that, Miss Maud. I'd like to be on a slow boat to China with a load of weapons heading to Colon and pass a sister ship on the high seas with a load of American guns heading for the Philippines. What level deal are we talking about?"

"Top level. Partners from Vancouver to the southern tip of Argentina."

Oh, my goodness, Red thought. The power of The Combine was awesome.

"All supplies?"

"Uh-huh. Fifty-fifty split after expenses. Cash. It includes ack-ack, fifty-caliber machine guns, dynamite, water-treatment plants, medical supplies, field boots, you know, you know . . ."

Red was silently adding zeros to his potential take. All the hard work had not been in vain.

"Why?" he asked softly.

"You've got a very fine reputation, and you also have what seems to be foolproof access into and through Mexico. You're a man who is well thought of, a straight shooter. The Combine sees enormous growth in the Southern Hemisphere marketplace. There are now three opposing guerilla groups in Cuba, restless bands along the Amazon, weapons for the dealers, and a half dozen spots in the Caribbean ready to pop."

"What do you think you're going to be able to do for me?"

"We can supply you with American weapons, no limits."

"You supply, I run them over the border."

"That's right. And, uh, we go on a handshake. No letterheads, lawyers, websites, contracts. It has to be a matter of trust, Red."

"Trust among the polecats," Red mused. "Is that it?"

"You must produce one key element. Not all merchandise can move at all times like a conveyor belt. You have to produce a fail-safe secret depot for storage."

If Red Peterson wanted to make a stand, The Combine could construct parallel routes and get rid of him. But that would cost The Combine a fortune. Red had it down, to the permanent key officials to be paid off.

He knew that Red Petersons would come and go, but The Combine would be there forever, because greed is eternal. Come drought, famine, earthquake, collapse of government, come what may—guns were the currency.

The two went through a long list of figures. Red was coming to realize that in relatively short time he could put upward of a hundred million dollars in his pocket. He offered his hand.

"We've got a deal when I approve of your depot," she said.

"I'll take you there tomorrow. Want to get laid tonight?"

"Never on the first date, Red."

THIRTY-SIX

Red Peterson groped, caressed, patted his wife's backside, then hopped up into the pilot's seat of his Queen Air. Greta touched cheeks with Maud, giving her a mandatory "Ummm" but knowing full well her old bastard was on the prowl.

The rattlesnake knew he was good, Maud thought. They had blended into a merger that would corner the expanding Latin weapons market. Maud had slept with one eye open and one ear trained on the bedroom door, hoping he might pay her a visit. He was menacing, like the men in The Combine.

Red moved with certainty to hold the sassy airplane in check, as though he could see the wind.

That morning after breakfast, Red gave her a briefing of the Hudson Mining and Cattle Co. on the White Wolf Ranch. It lay in southern Utah and was one of the few militia able to keep some full-time "freedom soldiers." These men were carried on the payroll of the copper mine and ranch.

The White Wolf Brigade commander and ranch owner was a retired Army officer, Oswald "Wreck" Hudson. The mine and ranch barely broke even. Big monies came from Red Peterson, drug and immigrant smuggling, and web-site scams. White Wolf was also part of an underground network supplying a safe haven for criminal militia on the run.

They flew west into Utah past one canyon after another, mesas holding a few determined trees, stone chimney rock formations of a phallic nature, agonized peaks, tan desert and, always, a stone edifice to a sleeping Indian maiden.

Red set the Queen Air down at Cortez, as anonymous as an airfield could be without being illegal.

Maud had pictured Wreck Hudson accurately. Thin man, handlebar mustache in a struggle to get attention and to be brave. He greeted them in civilian garb but packing a pair of ivory-handled pistols finished in silver.

In a Land Rover, Wreck settled in behind a field marshal's panel. His tutored hand flipped dials, punched buttons, and picked up a microphone.

"This is Rover One to Rover Two," Hudson said to a second Land Rover nearby filled with a guard detail.

"This is Rover Two to Esteemed Personage. Rolling right behind you."

"Base One, this is Esteemed Personage."

"Go ahead, Esteemed Personage," the ranch called back.

"Base One, we are rolling from Cortez. Do we foresee any security problems en route?"

"Negative."

Wreck bullied his vehicle like a heavyweight hitting the big punching bag. As yucca and thistle and tumbleweed flashed by, Wreck rambled, as would a braggart.

After a long dirt run through Navajo country, they came to a halt at a guard shack. Three surly members bearing Uzis approached the car and upon recognizing Esteemed Personage snapped to salutes.

"Inform Base One of my entry."

"Yes, sir."

The guard placed a pair of four-star pennants on the fenders and waved them through.

Ten miles later, an oasis loomed in the form of a huge Iowa-style Victorian ranch house, where Wreck was greeted by three barefoot Mexican women, all twenty-something or younger. The guard vehicle pulled up behind them.

"Clean up the fucking command car," he ordered. The women quickly took Maud's and Red's luggage, each getting a pinch on the cheek from Esteemed Personage as they passed him. Wreck took Red off to a side: "Can we show this broad everything?"

"Yeah."

"Anything more I should know about this?"

"No, but put us in adjoining bedrooms."

They settled into a powerful Mexican lunch in a huge tiled kitchen, attended by the women. Red's eyes followed the sway of their hips and rear ends. Wreck joined them, having changed into a military uniform of sorts: a hodgepodge of crossed sabers, gold epaulets, and scrambled eggs.

The lunch, tequila and beer, hit home with a thud, accompanied by Wreck Hudson's never-ending intoxication with his good self. Between shifts in tales of Wreck's imagined past, Red popped up. "We'd better get a move on and have Miss Maud look over the facility."

Miss Maud indeed! Who the hell was she, anyhow? Wreck played with the console of buttons near his chair. "This is Esteemed Personage calling Ranger Two. We are about to embark on a tour of inspection. Is the fucking car clean?"

"Positive."

"I want four guards to follow in Ranger Two."

Red had liked the White Wolf setup from the get-go. It abutted Navajo land on three sides. Underpaid Navajo police received innumerable perks and lots of booze to act as an advance warning system. Even if the government was to mount a raid on White Wolf through the reservation or even if helicopters were used, the Navajo would have to be warned in advance.

The other opening into White Wolf Ranch was

through Six Shooter Canyon, a five-mile defile whose path was punctuated by sheer walls of stone up to two thousand feet high. Once past a wide spot in the canyon called Bloody Gulch, it ran another two miles into the rear of White Wolf.

On the mesa, near the ranch house, Wreck Hudson had installed a horseshoe ring of gunfire to cover the two miles of canyon visible to them.

There were six multi-use .50-caliber machine-gun nests and 37mm ack-acks to down helicopters, and another six 150mm mortar posts and four artillery pieces of various measure.

Down in the canyon, every narrow spot past Bloody Gulch held up to a hundred yards deep of barbed wire running from wall to wall.

They had night-vision gear and homemade fire bombs.

All of this played into Red Peterson's hands. Certainly, government forces could take White Wolf, but the risk of high casualties was too great in a nation that did not like casualties. Losing a hundred- or two-hundred-man army was not going to sit well with the American people. Moreover, there was a lack of government initiative, a hands-off policy.

They drove to the mine entrance, a mile from the ring of fire over the canyon. Hudson had built a spur rail line from the reservation on into the mine.

Enough salable ore, with copper and iron the main metals, justified the operation. The ore cart tracks moved slowly downward inside the cliff entrance. At an unlit, hidden juncture a rail switch moved some tracks into what appeared to be a black hole.

They all climbed into ore carts, the tracks following the narrow tunnel some two hundred yards.

And there before them burst open a humongous cave. With its sister caves, it could have held the *Titanic.* Weapons of all kinds and apparatus and apparel for war lined the cave walls.

At this point Wreck confided they also had a dozen Stinger missiles, purchased back from the Afghan rebels, the brand that had half destroyed the Soviet air force.

At the ranch, the basement under the cellar was a cell of megalomania for Esteemed Personage. Huge survey maps of the Four Corners region hung on the walls with troop markings to indicate a never-ending mock battle.

A computer on a rudimentary system kept in contact with a plethora of patriots: the White Aryan Christian Arrival and wooded militias. It also tracked gun sales, gun shows, gun legislation, and their inventory of hate literature.

Maud counted a dozen to two dozen men who were probably on the payroll. She distrusted Wreck's boast that he could pull a thousand patriots onto the ranch on any given weekend; nonetheless, how many festering sore spots like White Wolf existed?

Oswald Hudson dismissed his communications people and ensconced himself behind an enormous desk decorated with phones of different colors. Behind him, a blown-up poster of Tim McVeigh.

One of the Mexican women served coffee and pastry and opened a hidden cart of booze. Red grabbed the woman's backside as she dared brush past him flirtingly close.

Maud threw questions, trying to get past her feeling that she was in a netherworld of the impossible.

"I got me this little country to run," Hudson went on. "My men would follow me to hell. These patriots are as good as Army Rangers, Marines, Seals. With a dozen militia ranches in the Four Corners under my command, and another hundred around the country, we could coordinate an attack on the Golden Gate Bridge, the Lincoln Tunnel, the Capitol, the Superdome, the harlot film studios."

He poured a bunch of cognac into his glass and wiped the fallen drops on his mustache with the back of his hand.

Maud was damned good at covering her disbelief. "So, tell me, Wreck, what is your target?"

"Hoover Dam," he answered, not skipping a beat.

"How?" she asked.

Hudson cleared his throat, lowered his voice to

"highly confidential." "I am in the process of designing a radio-controlled submarine torpedo. We will launch it, when the word comes, into Lake Meade and set it to blow up at the dam footings."

Now to Nam. Wreck confided that he should have been made a full colonel in Vietnam. "My battalion was sent into a large gook village near Phen Dok. As we advanced up the hill for Phen Dok, can you believe it, my fucking knee gave out. Old football injury at Michigan. Some sports writers said the knee kept me from being one of the great all-Americans. This time, taking the hill, it cost me a Congressional fucking Medal of Honor. My men just broke down and cried. They'd follow me to hell."

Maud spent the afternoon pondering mightily. She sensed a presence. Red Peterson had entered through an adjoining door and taken up the rocking chair close by.

"He's not as crazy as he makes out," Red said. "He does the drill because his people want it and because felons need a place to hide."

"You knew this White Wolf would shade my thinking," she said.

"Got a better depot and transit point? No? Then you have to deal with the mad hatter who runs this one. Besides, Miss Maud, you'll never have to see Wreck Hudson again. Remember, I own him. Like you said—or was it me who said it to you?—it all boils down to trust between us."

When did I last trust? Maud wondered. She'd built a

firewall between her activities and the ultimate end of a gun barrel. The dirty bunch, the dusty road bunch, the busted pickup truck bunch, the beer-sucking bunch at the roadside hell saloon, the bunch who could never face their own failures.

So, what did the bunch do? They created that hovering monster, The Government, who was really responsible for their misery.

"Wasn't it inevitable, Maud, to come to this place?" she thought. Thank God, Red Peterson was with her. Lust and all, she felt safe with him now.

"Maud, every once in a while we stop, we think, we dislike ourselves. We don't fire these weapons. Shut us down and ten more like us will pop up. Men were butchering each other with sticks and stones till they discovered bows and arrows. War is intrinsic in the human race, driven by the most passionate of all human drives, greed."

"Spoken like a true Jeffersonian. Have you ever looked in the mirror and spit?"

"Yeah . . . once. I got a hymie friend in Panama, a jeweler. I saw the tattoo on his arm. What we are doing by comparison is just keeping the boys amused."

Maud spent the balance of daylight pacing her little porch in contemplation. The White Wolf Ranch was perfect. Red Peterson was some brilliant piece of personnel. She had to weigh that against the questionable mental balance of Oswald Hudson.

Furthermore, who were these people around?

She had trained herself not to be at home when moral issues came knocking at her door. This time they pounded through to her.

Moral issues cause people to think of their grandchildren and become all teary. Red had explained it perfectly. She and he were only a pair of folks servicing a human need for blood lust.

The lunch and liquor caught up to her. The sounds of her wretching brought Red into her room. On her knees over the toilet bowl, Miss Maud just wasn't all that sexy.

"Deep and abiding love," he said, adjusting the angle of her throw, "means holding each other's head over the bucket. You gonna be okay?"

"Ughhh."

"Shit," Red thought, returning to his own room and lighting up his hash pipe. He heard the shower going from her room. Now, that's a good woman. She don't want to smell bad.

Maud came to him scented in creamy, dreamy stuff. He'd have to get the name of it for Greta.

Colors!

In the courtyard Esteemed Personage gathered at the flagpole, and while the White Wolf flag was lowered, they all howled "Aaahhhhweeee! Aaaarhaweeee!" after which Wreck, damaged from cocaine, shot off a few clips. Wreck staggered . . .

"Aaaaahhhhhhhuuuuuuwwweeeeee!" his patriots answered, and began shooting off clips of their own.

From a distant place, a coyote responded.

Maud and Red excused themselves from dinner, taking a stomach-settling diet in his room. It made no never mind, because Wreck was unconscious.

"I saw the devil today," she said, "and I'm part of him."

"Speaking of the devil, how about a 'lude?"

"Is that a 'lude or a lewd proposition?"

"Take it and find out." Down the hatch with a back of hashish. And soon the devil was all gone. Red set her up on the high bed and kicked off his boots.

"I've got to say, Red, you feel good."

"Crocodile skin and all."

"Yeah . . . cowboy . . . yeah . . ."

"Aaaaahhhhwwweeee," he crooned.

"Assssahhhhhweeee," she responded.

THIRTY-SEVEN

Four Corners-Labor Day Weekend
Saturday, September 1, 2007

Sun's first rays slithered over the rocky bivouac as the hated reveille sounded from a bugler. A groan rose en masse all over the Eagle Scout encampment. Four hundred of them ran, shoeless for the most part and naked, to where Montezuma Creek trickled past under a bluff.

Scout masters hustled them. The sun went up high, quickly. Sounds of splattering urine as four hundred young men took turns over the slit trenches.

The column had been in the desert for three days, planning to reach their destination of Mexican Hat at the tip of Glen Canyon day after tomorrow.

Two other columns of Eagle Scouts traversed from different directions toward Mexican Hat. When they converged, twelve hundred, one fourth of the total national number of Eagle Scouts, would hold a jamboree: boating, rafting, a thousand contests of skill and endurance, songs, camp fires.

The President of the United States was due to fly in and address them on Monday!

Hank Skelley, a revered old scout master, sat in a circle of his company leaders, pondering a map. Hank was a lean rod of spring steel with dedication to the movement emanating from every move and gesture. Around him, a smell of bacon to revive any flagging spirits.

Hank looked at his watch. Five A.M.

"We didn't pull our weight yesterday. Those trucks breaking down screwed up our entire transport. Darned if we can make it into Mexican Hat tomorrow if we skirt this row of canyons as originally planned."

Hank's long, thin, arthritic finger traced an alternative route. "We can cut off about nine and a half miles if we go straight up Six Shooter Canyon."

"Where does the end of the canyon lead us?"

"Into the rear of an outfit called Hudson Mining and Cattle, a big tumbleweed ranch."

"I heard that Hudson Mining has some Utah militia training, and they are none too friendly."

"Well," Hank answered, "I tried to reach them by cellular phone to get permission to pass through, but their phone didn't answer.

"Webster," Hank said to the chief master of Colorado. Webster Penrose inched to the front. "I don't think anything goes up Six Shooter Canyon anymore, but I've flown over it constantly and had occasion to go for three miles to a wide water hole . . . right here . . . Bloody Gulch. Now, I don't think it's dangerous, except in a winter flash flood that sets the rocks spilling down."

"Suppose we go in as far as the ranch and are turned away? What about that, Hank?"

"Then we go back to Bloody Gulch and pick up a goat trail out of the canyon. It will put us on the Navajo reservation, and we still will have saved several hours."

"Possible injuries, Hank?"

"Nothing we can't deal with," Webster Penrose interrupted. "We have a helicopter on standby in Farmington."

At the rear of the circle a clicking sound accompanied by bells binging turned attention to Brad Bradley, trying to raise White Wolf on his personal computer.

"What kind of shit is this?" Hank Skelley exploded. "Trucks to carry off our bedding and kitchen, ground-control satellites, computers, evacuation helicopter. Excuse my obscenity, but we *are* Eagle Scouts and we aren't ready to come in out of the cold."

Agreed. No one had disagreed with Hank for five years, maybe longer.

They broke camp. Bedrolls, the kitchen, and dead weight were piled to be picked up by trucks. Each scout had a two-canteen limit of water for the five miles through the canyon, and each hoped to find sweet water at Bloody Gulch.

Fall in! Pep-talk time. Ranging back and forth with megaphone, Hank Skelley yelled out that this column held more boys from more states than the other columns. "We will reach Mexican Hat first or croak trying!"

"Let's hear it for Hank Skelley!"

"Hip-hip-hooray!"

"Number one to Mexican Hat!"

Chester Skelley, Hank's grandson and one of the most decorated scouts in the West, was called front and center to take his place alongside Hank to lead them into Six Shooter Canyon a few miles past the stream.

Chester felt faint and of throbbing heart as the pride in him swelled. He knew it was probably his grandfather's last forced march. Getting there first would take daring. Chester knew about courage. He had fought his way back from a near-crippling childhood disease with superhuman determination.

Singing stopped as they faced the sheer walls and narrow path of Six Shooter Canyon. A huge sign read: CLOSED; DANGEROUS; DO NOT ENTER, and accordion barbed wire covered its mouth.

"You sure about this?" Brad Bradley asked.

"It's public land and we are American citizens," Hank responded. He knew it was his last jamboree. He knew he had to get there first even though the other columns had easier routes. This five-mile push through Six Shooter would end up in legend and song.

Fifty yards in, a boulder blocked the trail. Chester scatted up, found the footings, and extended his hand to his grandfather. As the young man pulled the old master up, it became a golden instant. Their eyes met for only a blink, and their smiles were just as quick. One generation was making, one generation was taking its passage.

And on, into the valley.

The red alert phone in Wreck Hudson's room rang unmercifully. Wreck was flung awry onto the couch, buck naked. The phone persisted. Wreck jerked the cord from the wall, threw the phone through the window, and stood up wavering.

The girls were gone. Second time this week. He'd have to see about assigning a male orderly. Like today, he was having a difficult time with the arms and legs of his clothing.

Wreck felt better when he strapped on his pearl-handled pistol. Shiiiiuuuuut! He didn't have pants on, and the pistols fell to the ground.

A pounding on his door. Wreck managed to put both legs in one pant leg and fell flat on his face as he reached for the doorknob.

"You dumb son of a bitch!" Wreck greeted Sergeant Floyd.

"Sorry, sir, I got a call from outpost number seven over the center of the canyon. Dust is rising at the far end."

"Why didn't you say so!"

"I tried to phone you, but . . . you shot up the outside phone lines last night."

"Call all stations, a double-red alert and move all personnel to the horseshoe posts."

"I did that, sir."

"What the fuck—who authorized you?"

Down the corridor, Red Peterson came out of his reverie. Maud was gone, but Jesus H. Christ, did that old girl give me a time when the 'lude kicked in. Was there any way Maud could teach some of that screaming and cursing to Greta? Sometimes Greta acted like the statues she portrayed on the stairs in Vegas.

The Continuous sound of a racket filled the hallway. Maud, showered and dressed, came in and nodded toward the sounds of confusion.

Wreck blammed open their door. "We've got a problem!"

"Well, Christ, let me get my pants on."

"There's dust blowing up the canyon."

"Hey, Wreck, dust is always blowing through the canyons."

"Maybe it's a herd of buffalo," Maud ventured.

"There ain't no goddamn buffalos, and there ain't no goddamn wind."

"Esteemed Personage," Grand Militia Sergeant Floyd said, "maybe it's cattle rustled from Mexico and being hidden in the canyon."

"I don't think so," Red said. "You can't drive a herd of

stolen cattle clear through the state of Arizona and into Utah without being spotted. You there, Sergeant, get Wreck's vehicle warmed up. We're right behind you."

They halted on the steep trail fifty yards below a rock-strewn summit. Wreck shifted into compound low to scale the hill. The hill won.

He came to the guard post where a dozen White Wolves had gathered and screamed at them to take up positions.

Red Peterson, meanwhile, scanned through binoculars. His wise old eye always searched for the patch of black gold. "Yeah," he said softly, "I see them. They're taking a rest stop at Bloody Gulch."

"Who? How many?" Wreck cried.

"Wreck," Red said softly, "I think you'd better get down there and meet them and either turn them back or let them through. Get rid of all that crap you're wearing and look like a rancher."

"You dumb son of a bitch," Wreck screamed.

Red seized him and with one hand lifted him off the ground and held him, nose to nose. "No goddamn commander is going to run troops into a box canyon in broad daylight. If this was an attack by armed forces, you'd be obliterated in five minutes. Now, you get down there."

"You!"

"Grand Militia Sergeant Buck Jones, sir!"

"Get your ass down there and turn those people around."

"No, sir, I ain't going." Jones quivered. He was

silenced by Wreck's .45-caliber slugs. Wreck turned to the other patriots, who slunk off to their posts.

Peterson led Maud a few feet away. "We're getting the hell out of here," he whispered. "I'm grabbing one of their Uzi guns and clean this post out. When I open fire, get down the hill and into the Land Rover. He left the keys in the ignition."

In the next agonizing moments, the cloud of dust stirred up again and spewed. Wreck was frozen . . . immobile. As fast as a lizard's tongue, Red snatched the Uzi from a patriot and tried to slam a bullet into its chamber. It was stuck!

"You motherfucker!" Wreck Hudson screamed.

Red threw the weapon to the ground and shook his head, crying, "I brought in two hundred thousand of these guns, and I've got to get the one that jammed."

"Kill the motherfuckers," Wreck ordered.

The five other patriots poured gunfire into Red Peterson and Maud Traynor, shot up until body parts came loose.

Deep in the canyon below, the formation of Eagle Scouts closed up and tested the water in Bloody Gulch. Addition of iodine and a chemical packet would make it potable but terrible tasting.

Fortunately, the canyon walls shut out most of the sunshine and the rocks had a cooling effect on the adventurers, but it was hot!

It had been a hell of a morning! Skating over rocks, clinging to side walls—slow, torturous movement had sucked them fairly well dry in those first three miles.

Chester Skelley now limped slightly in deference to his weaker leg. His grandfather met his eyes. Both of them rolled a glance heavenward. No songs this break.

Chester Skelley knew that if they had to climb a goat trail out of Bloody Gulch, old Hank would be in some kind of trouble. Hank was chilled by the thought he had made a bad decision.

An advance party of scouts went a half mile and returned with good news that the final two-mile stretch seemed flat and friendly.

The scout masters argued respectfully. One of three choices: two miles up the canyon to the ranch or take the goat trail and climb on cliff sides two thousand vertical feet, or return to Montezuma Creek and truck into the jamboree.

To turn back would be heartbreaking. Perhaps prudent, but heartbreaking. They had gotten through, thus far, without a major injury. It had nothing to do with prudence but with pride.

The other masters communicated without words the feeling that Hank Skelley could never make the high climb.

"Form up the column. We will continue down the canyon to the rear of Hudson Ranch. Double file, when possible, and tell the lads, it's only a short way now."

* * *

From locking fear to a mad euphoria, Wreck Hudson seemed to float over a great battlefield with mighty legions at his fingertips and an impenetrable defense . . . as he transformed himself into a George S. Patton.

"Here they come," Wreck whispered. He contacted his ring of machine gun, artillery, and mortar posts.

"Christ, it looks like a division of them down there," Floyd said.

"We take no prisoners," Wreck replied.

On they came, an ant line trudging out of Bloody Gulch toward White Wolf.

"I don't see no weapons," Floyd reported.

"They've got their machine pistols in their back-packs."

"Looks like some of them are wearing short pants. Hey, looks like Boy Scout uniforms."

"It's a disguise," Wreck growled. "They're either Marines or Rangers."

Now into the steep and narrow defile. Wreck looked down on the entire double line. He rolled his crazed eyes—he had them bagged in a deep well. "I've got less than twenty men . . . there were fifty last night at White Wolf! Where the fuck is my fucking brigade!"

"They shagged ass out of here."

Wreck emitted his animal howl, fell to his knees, and held his face in his hands. Two patriots helped him to his feet. They were coming close, down there.

"Fire!"

Machine-gun fire crackled into the narrow rift, ricocheting off the walls like tennis balls. Some of the invaders went down!

Now they'll know about Wreck Hudson! Glory! God! Glory! Jew plot foiled. Look at them fall! Fire! Fire! Fire!

The echoes of the bullets were as loud as the bullets, a hailstorm from four machine guns . . . mortars swished down and flamed and the earth bounced and heaved . . . now cannon fire far down range to blow the walls in and seal the canyon from retreat.

This is war! This is fucking war, man! I'll get my Congressional Medal now!

The racket was so immense, it seemed to be a kind of rumbling that must have happened at the birth of the planet. A burst of small rocks spewed into the defile as machine gun bullets loosened them. Now the mortars fired into the narrowest part of the canyon, and down came boulders from basketball size to Greyhound size.

"Surprised you fuckheads! Look at them running around and screaming!"

A huge slab skidded down, bounced off the cliff wall and behind; rocks poured down like a waterfall.

The Eagle Scouts were trapped and machine-gunned and a blizzard of rocks poured down on them and a dozen avalanches ran amok . . .

. . . higher and higher the debris piled on the canyon floor, twenty, thirty feet . . . far over any scout.

Waves of concussion stirred up with angry dust and

dislodged thousands more tons of rock. The waves careened through holes and fissures . . .

. . . and found the cave with eight hundred tons of dynamite.

The mining operation was lifted from the ground and hurled over space. Now a torrential rock fall as the canyon gave up great hunks.

The ranch house was eviscerated.

The last of the screams came from the patriots as their horseshoe of gun emplacements simply skidded off its moorings and plunged down.

Now the artillery shells and missiles and ammunition in the storage cave belched thunder after thunder after thunder.

Now death . . . now death . . .

THIRTY-EIGHT

Naval Air Station–South Weymouth
At the Same Time

Air Force One moved to South Weymouth so that its departure would not gum up the air traffic around Boston and Providence.

President Thornton Tomtree boarded and went directly up to his office to put final touches on his Labor Day speech to the Eagle Scouts.

Darnell Jefferson oversaw the placement of personnel and that all systems were functioning. Working in a tighter proximity than the White House, the people aboard seemed doubly busy. Beyond *Air Force One* and two thousand feet lower, a long white plume trailed from the press plane.

Chief of the Secret Service presidential detail, Rocco Lapides, opened the door of his outer station to allow

Darnell Jefferson in. Darnell was extremely wobbly, Lapides noted, as he knocked on the President's door.

"Lapides, don't answer the door until I tell you. We have to keep the lid on some news for ten or twenty minutes," Darnell rasped.

No inquiries, ears, eyes, and mouth covered, the Secret Service man took his instructions.

"Mr. President," Darnell said, addressing Thornton formally, as he always did in the presence of a third party.

"Everything in order?" Thornton asked.

"Not exactly."

"You look horrible. What did you do? Tie one on last night?"

"We have received confirmed reports of a cataclysmic event. One of the columns of Eagle Scouts moved up a canyon, and the canyon walls collapsed on them."

"Jesus! How long ago?"

"Maybe forty minutes. The Navajo police say it struck like a nuclear bomb. They flew a chopper to it, but there was such a cloud of dust over the area, they were prevented from taking a close-down look."

"Oh, my God!" Lapides said, breaking his vow of silence.

"Just how many of these scouts were involved?"

"We don't know, sir. We're trying to glean a number. So far the news is frozen, except for a Four Corners emergency network in to us. Mendenhall and I set up a communications system. The press plane smells something—"

"They always smell something!"

"Mendenhall is holding them off. As soon as we have a hint of any casualties, you should have a tactic for announcing it to the people."

Tomtree tried to screw down his focus to laser sharpness, winging through a dozen possible scenarios to hold the information from pouring over the floodgates. Thank God it was an accident! Tomtree immediately thought of his personal position in all of this. In a week he was to announce he was running for reelection in 2008 in order to short-circuit any overly ambitious Republicans from the Baptist crowd.

Mendenhall, who could perspire on an iceberg, was drenched as he came in.

"CIA satellite confirmation," he rasped. "The canyon walls collapsed along a two-mile stretch. The path is under millions of tons of fallen rock."

They all feared the next question:

"How many scouts were in the canyon?"

"We aren't sure, Mr. President. There were three columns converging on Mexican Hat for a total of fifteen-sixteen hundred Eagle Scouts."

"Well, goddammit, divide fifteen hundred by four. That's four hundred in that column. That doesn't mean, by any stretch of the imagination, they've all been hurt. In any event, it was a natural disaster. I should be able to rally a great deal of sympathy."

Good Lord, Darnell thought, he's acting like divine providence was taking him to the Four Corners. Maybe he could make his presidential reelection announcement right after they reached Four Corners.

Darnell Jefferson had all but collapsed in his armchair. The President and Mendenhall turned *Air Force One* into a flying White House, sizzling out instructions to the armed forces and connected agencies.

. . . Information went in and out from a dribble to a rush . . .

"Christ, Mr. President. The Internet is running pictures of the canyons near Hovenweep National Monument, Utah. *National Geographic* is leading the charge."

"Mr. President," Darnell said hoarsely, "you've got to talk to the press plane."

"Mr. President, confirmation from the scouts' supply truck drivers that plans were changed in the morning and the column entered Six Shooter Canyon!"

"How many?"

"We don't know, sir."

"Mr. President, Boy Scout Headquarters confirms the column entered Six Shooter Canyon with four hundred scouts and masters. They are from thirty-seven states."

"Sir, we are hooked up to the press plane."

"This is Thornton Tomtree. An avalanche of unknown origin apparently took place in one of the canyons near the Hovenweep National Monument in Utah. It appears that a number of Eagle Scouts hiking to their jamboree at Mexican Hat might have been trapped. *Air Force One* is now en route to Albuquerque, where I was to give a Labor Day address. I ask our beloved nation to join hands and pray."

The emergency team of White House Chief of Staff Tony Rizzoli, Darnell Jefferson, Mendenhall, and political strategist Turnquist had free access to the President.

. . . Get a list of names of the people in that column . . .

. . . The President needs a legal staffer up here to give us a picture of possible government responsibility . . .

. . . Also send up Jacob Turnquist, the political spin meister, to set up damage control and estimate political fallout. Better to announce for reelection now as a calming gesture to the public, or better to announce after the first of the year? . . .

. . . "We can't say until we have all the facts."

Admiral Wall, the President's personal physician, checked blood pressure and pulse rate. "High, but okay."

"Where in the hell is the vice president?"

Mendenhall eased into the crowding room. He leaned over and whispered in Tomtree's ear.

"I'm going to ask everyone to clear out for a few minutes except the emergency team. I don't want to be called until I give you orders. So?"

When the door closed Mendenhall's expressive face showed terror.

"I just spoke to the Navajo chief of police by cellular. He rounded up a half dozen helicopters and landed at a place called Bloody Gulch inside the canyon. A party of ten pressed down Six Shooter . . . and they ran into a fifty-foot-high wall of fallen rock.

"They climbed for a better view and saw no signs of life. Further here, apparently hundreds of people in the region heard voluminous gunfire around zero seven three zero this morning."

"Are you saying," Darnell said, "that the explosion was set off?"

"According to the Navajo police, the adjoining property, a White Wolf Ranch, was headquarters for a Four Corners militia group."

Admiral Wall gave the President another blood-pressure check, quickly prepared a syringe, and asked the President to lower his pants so the shot could go into his butt.

"Which camera crew is aboard?"

"CBS from the pool."

"Have them wait in the hall. I'll be making a statement in ten minutes."

"Latest report, Mr. President: Navajo police report is confirmed. It is possible, even probable, that no one in the canyon escaped alive."

"Ladies and gentlemen, this is Larry Merton aboard Helicopter One, KTM, Salt Lake City. The clouds of dust over Six Shooter Canyon seem locked in. In a matter of moments medical teams and mountain rescue will try to enter the canyon. There have been no signs of life. The canyon continues to rumble and slide. We are going to try to fly under. Oh, my God! It is a catastrophe down there. All buildings at the site of the ranch house and mine have been eviscerated—"

"We interrupt to switch you to *Air Force One*, en route to Albuquerque, New Mexico, to bring you the President of the United States."

"My fellow Americans, a great tragedy has befallen our nation. A column of approximately four hundred Eagle Scouts and their scout masters from over thirty states were hiking to a jamboree at Lake Powell. As they passed through a deep ravine known as Six Shooter Canyon, the walls imploded on them. First reports tell us that there appear to be no survivors. I am sorry beyond measure to have to report to you that we believe it was not an accident, but a deliberate attack by a Hudson Mining and Cattle Company. Information on this may be scarce because all signs of life and property at the ranch were destroyed as well. We, our nation and its people, have entered a terrible period of grief and of outrage. We must rise above our grief and our outrage to be able to make clear decisions.

"I have ordered the largest and most thorough investigation in history to commence forthwith and to issue a preliminary public report within a matter of weeks.

"America is a great and strong nation, the longest existing democracy, and such greatness was not gained without constant challenge and bloodshed and sacrifice.

"Our enemies will play on this tragedy to try to prove the fall of American greatness. Yet we have prevailed where others have fallen into the mists of time, and we shall prevail again.

"As your president, I beg you to open your arms to the families of those young men who have been killed. They must feel the strength and the prayers and the sharing of their sorrow.

"How could such an event happen? Well, we must look back, perhaps generations, to find the link. I believe the link will take us back to our very roots.

"Yet this catastrophe occurred during my watch, and I must bear the responsibility.

"Lord, let a light stream out of this darkness and tell us that these brave young men will light the way to our future."

"Henrietta Joslin, CNN, Denver. The government has set up the following toll-free numbers for families of the expected casualties. All airlines flying into Albuquerque and Santa Fe are issuing complimentary tickets to the families. Shuttle service will be in effect by tomorrow morning to connect from Denver and Salt Lake City. Lodging in the Four Corners will be provided by the hotels and motels in the area."

* * *

The President was finally able to carve out time for himself and Darnell. Darnell had suddenly become ancient-looking, going through waves of being stunned over and over. What in the name of God am I doing here?

Thornton Tomtree, sitting over there, having given his moment of grief, was torturously trying to think how to wiggle his way out of the catastrophe.

There had to be finger pointing. Already fingers were being loosened by the media, and Democrats were giving middle-finger salutes.

The gun issue was always kept low-key, but T3's laissez-faire attitude on guns and militias was a matter of record. Darnell had argued the gun-control position regularly with the President in his first two and a half years.

"You can't stop bootleggers, you can't stop drug dealers," Tomtree had answered. "What the hell makes you think we can stop gunrunning?"

"They are evils," Darnell had argued. "Because you see an evil, an overwhelming evil, and say, 'nothing we can do about it, old chap' and let it run wild—this is not the behavior of a civilized people. Evil must be fought at every level."

"So, what are we to do, Darnell, go holy on this subject and watch China or the damned French take over our arms commerce?"

"But we are the United States of America!"

"Exactly my point," Thornton had responded. "I couldn't even move the Congress . . . even if I had a notion to. So, looking at the reality of the situation, we must then look at the bottom line."

Darnell was exasperated. He knew that somewhere along the road with Thornton, a bridge would be down. Time and again during their corporate years, Darnell verged on leaving in anger. Always, the lure of T3 pulled him back into the cycle. Thornton was a genius, a great man, and he, Darnell, would be sackcloth and ashes without him.

Thornton grasped the enormity of the tragedy and sensed he was going to have the most intense scrutiny in history. Did Darnell want to try to save this man?

"We need a plan, we need a plan," Tomtree said.

Darnell didn't answer. Thornton looked at him suspiciously. "Are you—"

"I don't know!" Darnell answered.

"We must be careful," Thornton said, "we are on thin ice."

"Tell me about it," Darnell said.

"We need a plan."

Mendenhall came in with several sheets of paper. Tomtree winced that he was not wearing a jacket but perspiring like a man on a chain gang.

"Mr. President, here it is! Spot polls, raw data."

"Who got it so fast?" Darnell asked.

"Warren Crowder. Ten minutes after the explosion he had reporters polling gatherings like bus stops and bowling alleys and malls and firing the information back to Crowder–Washington—"

"That means that bitch, Greer Little Crowder," the President snapped.

". . . The printout isn't bad, sir," Mendenhall said. "Let's see: Gravity of the event—serious 97 percent, don't know 2 percent. Blame current lack of gun and militia laws—don't know 62 percent, yes 33 percent, no 7 percent. Believe President shares responsibility—yes 30 percent, no 30 percent. Believe Congress shares responsibility—yes 50 percent, no 37 percent, don't know . . . et cetera. White males over forty—"

"Hold the phone," Darnell Jefferson said. "Thanks, Mendenhall, just leave the rest of the data here."

"Here is the way we go, Thornton. We make a two-pronged attack. Attack number one is an attitude toward the Congress. We admit we put these issues on the back burner because the Congress was not going to be moved on them, *including* dozens of Democrats. That, if done subtly, opens the Congress to a populist outburst. Congress will know what to do when they get the heat—"

"We will offend our own power base, Darnell. You've got to remember we assumed majority with a fragile coalition."

"That's where the second prong of the attack comes in. Remember when we spent twenty million on the millennium party? It was campaign-free money, and it went a long way to get you into the White House. All right, try this one on. You and only you can soothe this anguished nation. Use this next period to travel to twenty, thirty gatherings of the parents. It will be covered by national and local press. The polls will let us know when it is enough. But as their president you will display compassion and strength."

"Huggy-kissy is not my long suit."

"We'll teach you compassion. Once you get the drift of it, you can turn the shaky voice and the tears off and on in a blink."

Thornton Tomtree had much to weigh. Move quickly to get the onus off the White House and shift the burden to Congress. It sounded like a plan. The compassion stuff? "Well, I got to the White House once," he told himself, "I'm sure I am as compassionate as Nixon was."

Darnell shrank back. An hour ago, a half hour ago, he had been filled with disgust, and he had arrived at the moment to tell Thornton to go to hell. In the flip of a poll, he was going to use any and all means of getting Thornton reelected. The disgust now was with himself.

Neither he nor the President had made mention of the Eagle Scouts—just how to spin the story.

THIRTY-NINE

Iowa Caucus–Waterloo, Iowa
February 2008

"Hey, good-looking, how about buying a girl a drink?"

Quinn heard her, smelled her, and felt her touch on his shoulder. He turned on his bar stool and smiled apprehensively. Greer Little-Crowder, wearing exquisite pearls, wore no man's tailored jacket. Her dress was soft and luscious, see-through violet, and gold bracelets anchored her wrists. She was still very slender in her fifties, and had never forgotten how to focus on her endowments.

Quinn's eyes flashed on her tiny, volcanic breasts, then the hair, not straight anymore, but coiffured with stunning highlight streaks. Quinn opened his arms, and she tucked in. Thin girls wrap up so neatly, he thought.

"Jesus," Greer said, "you look lousy."

"You look absolutely delicious," he replied.

Greer touched his cheek and let her fingers run through Quinn's hair. Was she saying, "Fasten your seat belt?" Not necessarily. The two on occasion had been at political or media or civic affairs. Otherwise, neither attempted to contact the other on a personal basis.

Greer Little-Crowder had risen to be one of the top women executives in the country. She was a media wizard, a CEO of Warren Crowder's conglomerate, a queen of the world.

"Can I get you something, ma'am?" the bartender asked.

"Vodka rocks with a twist," she said.

As some reporters and photographers drifted in, Quinn pointed at a booth out of their sight line. The bartender became so excited, he half spilled her drink. "Hey! You're Governor O'Connell!"

Quinn held his finger to his lips. Their secret. "Your money is no good here, sir."

Greer dipped the tip of her little finger into the vodka and slowly traced it about her fawning lips.

"Knock it off," Quinn said.

"Quinn, have you forgotten we did it once in a little hallway between the bar and the kitchen . . . what was the name of that restaurant?"

It still rang a bell. "There's a buffalo herd of media coming in looking for someplace to stampede," she went on. "Did you think I might show up?"

"Always passes through one's mind. But Waterloo?"

"That's where the action is, bubba."

"Run, Quinn, run," he said. "See Quinn run . . . see Quinn jump . . . jump, Quinn, jump. I am acting out the role of reluctant candidate . . . or am I that reluctant?"

"Glad to see me? Mad? Sad? Thinking bad?"

"All of the above," he said, taking her hand but avoiding her eyes. "Mostly sad," his voice croaked.

"It's been ghastly," she said. "You should have been in the news room over the holidays. The land is permeated with fear and grief. It has been as though one of those black holes in the universe sucked us in. This tragedy was so terrible you start thinking that the day of a nuclear bomb has got to follow."

"We lost thirty scouts and scout masters from Colorado. In the middle of singing the anthem or at a cocktail party, people suddenly break into convulsive weeping. It was when the parents begged me: 'Governor, is there anything left of my son? Just a finger, anything?' I, uh, got a little bit unsteady, I have to admit. You remember Dan's Shanty? I just sat crumpled in a corner, getting close to the edge of losing it. I was a madman in a cell tying on the biggest drunk in the *Guinness Book of Records.* I told Rita I wasn't coming out until I could walk out and function as their governor . . . look, you hear this story all over the country."

Greer caught sight of the bartender heading toward them with another man and patted his hand to be quiet.

"I just had to tell the boss," the bartender said.

"What an honor," the owner said.

"My pleasure," Quinn said, giving him a hearty handshake.

"Governor," the man said, "you have to get us through this Four Corners Massacre."

The words blistered Quinn's ears. He managed a sigh and a wan grin.

"Governor O'Connell, the restaurant will be filled with press people soon. I would be honored if you'll let me prepare a special dinner for you and the lady. I'll bring it up to your room."

Quinn looked at Greer, who nodded.

"You've got a deal."

"And I've got to tell you something, Governor," the owner said. "This here was my father's booth, God rest his soul." He pointed at a photo on the wall. "Nobody's got their picture on this wall except for my father with Joe DiMaggio. I want yours, too."

Quinn scribbled the owner's address and promised a personalized signature.

"Go by the side door. There's an alleyway to the hotel. Leave your drinks, I'll send up a couple of pitchers."

"Thanks, buddy," Quinn said.

The penthouse suite of the Millard Fillmore Hotel was not all that corny. Old, deep window seats and high molded plaster and mahogany furniture and clanking radiator pipes all seemed in rhythm with a new snowfall outside. It was lovely.

Quinn changed into a running suit and woolly slippers. In a few moments Greer appeared in chic comfort. She went to him and deployed her body against his for maximum contact. They kissed deliciously. Her hand took his and guided it down, between her legs. Quinn held up his other hand weakly to stop.

"That's got to be it," Quinn said.

"Before we won't do again what we won't do," she said. "Oh, brother, could we create a scandal."

"I had hoped that after the humiliation of Clinton, America might have gone beyond such things, but oh, boy, would we sell newspapers. I say, not with a great deal of pride, that we of the boomer generation wanted American society to come out of the closet: stop hypocrisy, be politically correct, no N word, no heroes, no goals, except money. Well, my son understood what homosexuality was in the fourth grade and listened to language on TV that the Marines wouldn't even use. I think we'd better go back into the closet on some things. Greer, you own a piece of me, forever, but Rita is my life. That's the real reason."

The rebuff to Greer was soft and simple but, she knew, final.

"So how's life by Greer?" he asked.

"Mrs. Warren Crowder or Ms. Greer Little-Crowder? I've always given you a wide berth because moments like this one can lead to self-destruction. Anyhow, when your mother and father came to New York and patched me up, years ago, there was no stopping me. Brilliant as he is, Warren was an ignorant innocent about a lot of things, including the birds and the bees."

"Hadn't he shed a couple of wives?"

"That's right, but Greer baby came to play and to stay."

Pitchers of martinis and vodka came with a lovely bottle of Chianti. Greer sipped and looked sad like a torch singer at the piano. "Warren wanted a tour guide through the hellfire clubs. I was better than good. I did things to please him and fetched my price: Mrs. Crowder, stock options, and the top woman in media in the country. You cannot imagine how rich I am, Quinn. Actually, Crowder owes more money than most third world countries . . . but wealth is counted not by what you have, but by what you owe. You see, his banks have to keep him solvent because if he ever defaults, he will take down a dozen banks with him and shake a number of economies."

"Well, now, that's power, isn't it?"

"I care for Warren. I love his ruthlessness. So what if he found a little of his lost youth in *ménages*? He was a voyeur and we touched the edge of the drug scene, but Warren didn't want anything that would fuzz his mind. After a while, even my dance of the seven veils became a bit static, so we drifted into a real marriage with a real calling, making hundreds of millions. I'm pretty straight now. I go into heat every once in a while. Maybe I'm still looking for Quinn."

The food arrived with a robust aroma, as if to say in

Waterloo there was something in the world other than meat and potatoes.

Quinn poured the Chianti. "Bang!" he said.

"So what brings you to Waterloo on this snowy night?" she said as she prepared the table.

"Greer, I came here kicking and screaming, and I'm not talking false modesty. All right . . . I came here because so goddamn many people told me to come here. So, I'm here, I'll look around and say, include me *out.* I've been to Waterloo, folks, and there's no way I can make the presidency."

"You're full of shit," Greer retorted.

"No, ma'am, I'm not going to be meat for buzzards. I'm not putting my family through it. During my first campaign for governor, AMERIGUN threw the book at me, including the rumor that I was buggering sheep. Truth can be a little pebble that gets washed over a roaring dam. Yet some of those lying, rotten stories will stick on me to the day I die. Is there life beyond the presidency, or do they all leave office as dead meat?"

"I see snow out of the window," Greer said. "I'm afraid you see acid rain. A tidal wave is forming up and could become unstoppable. You have rung the bell on an issue whose date is due. You are gun control to a nation pleading for it. You can't walk away, man, no matter how it intersects your own life. Your country is bleeding, and that's all the reason you have to know. There is another reason you won't back out. You crave for your birth mother and father to look down from heaven and be proud of you: 'Our son is running for president!' "

Quinn paled. "Is that why I'm doing this?"

"Yes."

"I thought I had a grip on it."

"You lied to yourself."

Greer responded to a knock on the door with movements that had been polished over the years to gain and hold the observer's attention.

"Professor Maldonado, I do believe."

"Greer!"

Mal came in, bussed her slightly, and made for an inspection of the bedroom and bathrooms . . . and the big walk-in closet. "So, what brings you to Venice?" he asked on returning.

"The same thing that brought you," she said.

Mal went right at their dinners. "The veal is like butter." He had grown old lovely.

"What's going on out there?" Quinn asked.

"A phenomenon," Mal said. "I'm being contacted by several Democratic governors who are interested in your candidacy. The party is lining up quickly behind you."

"Do not count Quinn as a shoo-in. T3 is no pushover," Greer said. "He has done a masterful job of distancing himself from the Congress. Fewer and fewer people hold him responsible for Four Corners, particularly with this new humility, stiff back when the flag is lowered, occasional teary eye, and those gripping hugs to the parents. And Pucky Tomtree has done just as good a job."

"They say that Darnell Jefferson has engineered it," Mal said. "He and T3 are like non-identical twins. Whatever he's done, the President has fought his way back."

Quinn noticed a quick, mousy smile from Greer. "You run with that crowd," Quinn said.

"Well, I did have an interlude with Jefferson a few years back, on Martha's Vineyard. He was on a diet of white meat," she purred.

"I thought Tomtree's humility schtick was transparent," Mal said, tossing down the tiramisu.

"People want transparent," Greer shot back. "Look at the lineup of sitcoms. English not spoken here. Back up the garbage truck and carry off this week's show. No! It's worth billions in syndication. We recycle more shit in a year than the Chinese dump into their holes in a decade."

"Yeah, get the children out of the room," Quinn said softly. "Some kids today say 'fuck' so much they think it's their middle name."

Mal pushed his chair back, patted his feel-good stomach, and checked all the pitchers. The vodka looked promising.

"What we have shaping up here," Mal began in a professorial manner, "is a recurring cycle. The human race is no less cruel, no less murderous than it was ten thousand years ago. Yet every so often it runs into a moral imperative that it has to overcome for civilization to advance. In America? The revolution against England was a moral imperative. The destruction of slavery was a moral imperative. The decision to fight Hitler and commence with atomic energy were moral imperatives."

"You're talking about Washington, Lincoln, and Roosevelt," Quinn said, laughing.

"And maybe Quinn O'Connell. A great moral imperative ended in bleeding tragedy in Six Shooter Canyon. AMERIGUN isn't going to roll over and die easily, but you're the man who faced them down," Mal said. "So how are you going to live with yourself without giving it every ounce of fight you have?"

"The nation is ready to do some serious gun control, and the people know they will have a tough-ass president taking it on," Greer added.

"Thanks for sharing that with me," Quinn said.

"Wait, there's more," Greer jumped in. "It's nine months till the election, and you have no national, state, or local campaign machinery, no money, no endorsements. But you are the king of the hot-button issue. Can you take the lies and taunts? Can you lead? If you think you can, I want to play!"

"Thanks for your glorious offer, Greer, but, baby, the American people may not be as sophisticated as you believe, and this won't fly."

"That's a point," Mal mumbled.

"I resigned from Crowder Communications yesterday."

Her thunderbolt knocked them speechless.

"What? How? You're a married woman!" Mal said.

"Oh, I'll bet Warren Crowder likes this," Quinn said. "It will bring his illustrious lady's career to a crescendo."

"Warren's a player," Greer said. "And he knows I'll be back."

"You two have got to behave yourselves," Mal said. "I mean, really behave yourselves. If we can put Greer in charge of the nuts and bolts, she knows every political person in the country. She knows all the hired guns. She has access to money overnight."

"I'd have your national committee in place in five days," Greer said, "and in a week I'll have a strategy on the table."

"The voters will take a long second look at me. Better stay in Colorado, cowboy. Every time they've heard of Quinn O'Connell, it's been the result of a fight. Urbakkan . . . AMERIGUN . . . and now the Six Shooter Canyon Massacre," Quinn espoused.

"Slight difference," Greer said. "The people may have the political will to follow a moral imperative."

"I'll call Rita," Quinn said. "It has to be dead right for her."

"You don't have to call her," Greer said. "I talked it over with her before I got my air ticket to Waterloo. Rita said, 'Thank God you're going to him. At least you'll give him a fighting chance.' "

Maldonado answered the phone. Senators Ebendick and Harmon were in the hotel and wanted a few minutes. "Phew!" Mal said, "some real big hitters just blew into town."

"Who?" Greer asked.

"Ebendick and Harmon."

"That is a statement," Greer said.

"I'm going down and enroll them," Mal said. He wanted to say more about hoping he could trust Greer and Quinn. Once they had melted cannons with their heat. How can an odd moment of stress or passion or joy not hurl them into one another's arms? But Rita believed. What game was God playing putting a decent man like Quinn into the shredder as he slouches toward Jerusalem?

Governor Quinn Patrick O'Connell walked to the rostrum in a crammed ballroom at the Millard Fillmore Hotel. A blast of TV lights blared while still photographers ate up film.

"Hi," Quinn said when it quieted. "I'm Quinn O'Connell, governor of Colorado. Any national recognition I may have is pretty much based on my penchant for gun control. There is a long list of serious issues on the American agenda, and if my candidacy continues on, I will issue my position within days."

Greer laid her head on Mal's shoulder and she cried a little.

"But we're here today because much of America's bright hope lies silent in the box end of Six Shooter Canyon. It could have been avoided by the political will of the people, and it will happen again without the political will of the people to change it.

"I stand before you, not as a saint running for sainthood or as a sinner dodging hell. I intend to live my private life privately, and I intend to bring back a great measure of dignity and authority that has been missing from the presidency for almost a decade."

Quinn became silent, and the room suddenly fell under his spell. He opened a small book on the rostrum.

" 'Article . . .' " he read, " '. . . A well-regulated Militia being necessary to the security of a free State, the right of the people to keep and bear arms shall not be infringed.' "

A murmur of disbelief buzzed about the room.

"When the Second Amendment of the Bill of Rights came into being, our new nation had no standing army to contend with hostile neighbors, England, France, Canada, Spain. We also were fighting many Indian nations, and part of the population was still loyal to the king. *Therefore!* Each colony, each new state set up their own militia. These militias were not very good.

"Now look at this Second Amendment. It has nothing to do with the rights of the citizens to own guns, but the formation of *well-regulated* militias."

Quinn was parched, but he feared his hand would

tremble if he held a water glass. To hell! He took a swig, steady as a rock.

"If anything in the entire American panorama has been distorted and convoluted, it is the Second Amendment. The militias failed. After the Civil War many state units were converted into a national guard. A *well-regulated* national guard, as required by the Constitution, with their weapons under government control.

"For far too long, men of questionable intent have hidden behind the skirts of the Second Amendment, claiming it as their divine commandment to own guns.

"Bull! Because of federal inaction on gun control, many towns and cities and counties and states, including Colorado, have legislated their own gun-control laws. But the gun lobby is powerful. One gun comes off the assembly line every seven seconds, and during that same seven seconds another gun is imported into the country.

"I intend to cut to the chase!" Quinn belted out, "because most of the court cases in the states and towns could be eliminated with the passage of a single national bill. The right of gun ownership is not and has never been a constitutional guarantee, and in order to get it right and get it clear . . . the Second Amendment of the Constitution must be repealed."

FORTY

Washington, February 2008

If tears had been stars, there would have been enough shed to double the size of the universe. The nation passed to the new year with darkness at noon, in a fetal position. No ball had dropped from Times Square; half the bowl games were rescheduled or canceled. Only the Super Bowl went on bravely, bravely. There was just too much money involved. The stock market plummeted, and soon finger pointing began in earnest. Panel shows of experts begat panel shows of experts.

The Four Corners Massacre was a unique event in American history. No one really knew who to turn to, but Thornton Tomtree was there and made a strong case of distancing himself from Congress. He began to take delight in his new mode of compassion.

After the Superbowl, T3 had emerged as the "tall" man, the shepherd, the big father.

Then came the dispiriting initial findings of the investigation.

All evidence on the ground in the vicinity of Six Shooter Canyon and the White Wolf Ranch had been obliterated. The perpetrators had all been killed in the blasts.

The FBI hunted down White Wolf Patriots who were not present in order to fashion a line of events. The more the FBI pieced the story of Wreck Hudson together, the more it fell in the realm of fantasy. The existing White Wolf patriots faded into an underground run by the White Aryan Christian Arrival.

As for resolving the fate of Six Shooter Canyon, there was a terrible rub.

In the deepest pit of his life, President Thornton Tomtree moaned over the recommendation on his desk. The investigation commission, which included the breadth of the society from engineering genius to religious leaders, had made a rapid first finding, and it made its way to the Oval Office by late February of 2008. The President had no choice but to take it to the American people.

"My fellow Americans. The report which I am about to render to you was previously communicated to the families of the Four Corners Massacre. The commission has now come to an initial recommendation . . . please bear with me . . . I must conjure up some horrible images.

"We cannot get earthmoving equipment into this narrow stretch of canyon. The alternative would be to dynamite the walls to widen access. After that, we would be embarking on an earthmoving project the size of several Hoover Dams, which would take years to complete.

"Test bores indicate that the victims were crushed by the initial avalanche and then buried under ten to twenty feet of rock. Another forty to ninety feet of rock came down atop them.

"The test bores also tell us we will probably not retrieve sufficient remains for individual burials. The forensics experts and the DNA experts feel that no one is truly going to be identified, as the remains are so interlocked and pulverized.

"If an excavation was ordered, we would remain in the grip of this tragedy for many years. In the end, it would be a futile gesture. The survival of our nation depends upon overcoming our national grief. Therefore, I have asked the Republican and Democratic leadership for a bipartisan bill to seal the canyon and erect a suitable memorial."

"Some promising news, Mr. President. Three-fourths of the families are in agreement, right from the get-go. On your telecast . . . sixty-two percent of the editorials in the hundred-thousand circulation class think that the closure and monument are right on . . . only eight percent think we ought to remove the canyon . . . On your message, seventy-two percent of the CNN/TIME/CBS/*New York Times*/*USA Today* polls said we should get on with the life of the nation . . . CBS/*New York Times* has a seven percent of 'don't know' . . . If this sampling holds, we're through the worst of it!"

Thornton Tomtree felt blood circulating through his body again.

"And, sir, a little cream on the pudding. The Iowa Republican caucus wants you to run for reelection by over seventy-three percent."

"Who took the Democratic caucus?" the President asked.

"That yahoo, the Colorado Kid . . ."

"Quinn Patrick O'Connell?"

"Yes, sir."

Would/could the American people ever trust another politician, even if they knew of his warts in advance? They gathered about Thornton Tomtree. At that moment T3 was all that was left. He was super calm, and much in control.

And along came Quinn.

"Savior" was too strong a word, but a nation desperate to get off its knees had moved him onto center stage. An enormous media focus on New Hampshire bespoke the arrival of a new force.

In Denver, down by the railroad tracks, a big old warehouse was donated for use by the O'Connell for President committee. It had long been derelict as a warehouse and later went belly-up as a disco. Greer corralled an overabundance of volunteers and opened a bank account.

Contributions of office furniture and computers arrived from Chicago to Salt Lake City.

Quinn's midnight arguments with Maldonado, Greer, and Rita, his most inner circle, took on a legend of their own. The three of them came to realize that with Quinn, it was "the campaign will be my way or the highway."

Half a candidate's time was consumed with fund-raising among the high and the mighty. No serious candidacy could go far without the major contributors . . . who found unlimited, ingenious ways to bypass the legal donation limits. Quinn made a daring decision on the night he left for New Hampshire.

"I will not take contributions from PACs. I will not accept soft money. Soft money is slimy and difficult to catch, but you know what soft money is and I know what soft money is. I want my candidacy to be supported mainly by contributions from ordinary people. I'm being asked to do a difficult job, and if you think I'm the man, then let me hear from you."

For the first of many times, one was certain that O'Connell had shot himself in the foot.

However, by the time he hit New Hampshire, a deluge of pledges came in to Quinn, conveniently charged on Diners Club, MasterCard, VISA, Discover, and American Express cards.

BROTHER, CAN YOU SPARE A DIME read the headline. I AM THE PEOPLE'S CANDIDATE.

Quinn held up his daily press bulletin. On the top were several boxes giving donations of the past twenty-four hours, expenditures, and total in the bank. This degree of openness chilled the American house politic down to the marrow.

At Manchester there was a sudden and urgent feeling of in-gathering of people from Maine and Vermont. They just had to see this fellow. Please, God, make him real. In the winter drearies, the streets were thickly lined, and an unlikely scene unfolded of New Englanders showing public passion.

The pundits dug deeply into the history of the American presidency to find more of a "down-home" candidate: witty, environmentally brilliant, sound on his issues, and completely modest and at ease among the people.

Quinn and Rita skied a treacherous run known as the Oh Shit Trail and ended up on their feet.

Look at that couple!

Was he too good to be true? Have we forgotten the

terrible besmirchment of the president's office in the Clinton era? Have we forgotten the pain? Can we ever trust another politician?

Surely the voters could be venting their pent-up hurt, and surely they could be gambling their own future aspirations. But don't stop the carnival!

In his town hall meetings, Quinn often shocked with his common sense and candor. He spoke the truth, more than once, to criticize his own failings. Quinn ignited the rebirth of many values thought flown from the society.

The result? Startling! Quinn Patrick O'Connell polled more votes than five other Democrats combined and went head to head with the Vermont governor, running as a favorite son.

Less than a month after the Iowa caucus he had established a legitimacy, even though his insistence on populist financing barely kept the campaign running. The day after New Hampshire was a good day for collections. And, well, it had to be, for there was no time for a pit stop. Quinn and his staff suddenly stared at Fat Tuesday, a few days off.

Fat Tuesday was a coast-to-coast twelve-state primary and caucus with American Samoa thrown in. Quinn might have a foot in the door, but the phone bill had not come in yet.

Quinn needed a strong showing in the Southern states of Georgia and South Carolina and the quasi-Southern state of Maryland. Unable to visit even a sampling of states, he chose to deliver his message at Emory University in Atlanta.

Through great civic pride, entrepreneurship, leadership, and a migration, the city had become the power center of the South, sophisticated, dancing far into the night, ambitious, and a wonderful place to raise a family.

In the very beginning of his career as a young Colorado state senator, Quinn had been shy as a speaker, but buoyed himself through self-deprecating wit. By the time he won the governorship he had grown into a strong and confident—but measured—speaker.

All things seemed to come together when he arrived in Atlanta as a growing national curiosity. Quinn sensed that the people were longing to hear what he would say. He felt, for the first time, he had the power as an orator to grip his audience.

As Quinn spoke, softly at first, he felt the vibrations, and he fell into a rhythm, dancing a ballet, endowed with a grace, aware of what was happening to him.

Determined not to be labeled a dog with one trick, Quinn set aside the Second Amendment issue and wrote himself a visionary political essay.

Quinn's staff held their collective breath.

". . . we have nurtured a mighty forest of law and values and decency. We are trashing it without planting new trees. Under the disguise of freedom of expression, our boundaries of morality are pushed so far twelve-year-olds know the vulgarisms of our language, or of the explicitness of sexual behavior, or of crime and of drugs. So, have we shed the old hypocrisies, or are we caving in to the claptrap foisted on us by people who are really out to make a buck and will push and push until our sense of disgust is finally stilled?"

Ka-boom! Quinn knew the speech was flying.

"A decade ago, the American people were subjected to listening to a president forced to give a discourse on oral sex. We swore, never again. But it has happened again and again and again. The nation can no longer afford this prurient blood lust, which is already robbing it of brilliant candidates who no longer want any part of public service.

"The world prays for us, waits for us to get out of the gutter. It is incumbent that each citizen have a long, quiet talk with themselves and not succumb to mendacity."

Ka-boom! The vibrations from speaker to listener trembled in the air. Quinn departed from the rostrum, microphone in hand and went from side to side of the stage.

"Are we closing out personal relationships, and have we grown distant from one another? We surge on great waves of billions of bytes . . . but do we know each other anymore? We bank, shop, vote, play the market, purchase groceries, fly, vacation, read at the whim of an electronic device that, despite all its miraculous wonderment, has no heart, no soul, no compassion.

"When salvation comes, it will not come in the form

of a computer printout but from the Word brought down from Sinai. We must go back to one another and establish the rules of decency."

It was a strange speech. It hardly seemed political, but more from the pulpit. How did Quinn realize the public's thirst for a moral direction? Still in mourning over the Four Corners Massacre, they needed a spiritual direction.

Quinn had deftly drawn a line in the sand and taken the moral high ground. Clever or political genius?

Fat Tuesday.

The primaries said that O'Connell was in to stay. He won Maryland by an eyelash, lost Georgia by the same amount, but he polled forty percent of the South Carolina vote. Do the West and South identify with one another? Perhaps in being treated as a cultural wilderness. This stranger from a strange place was no stranger at all.

Quinn and his people staggered into New York for a hit-and-run visit. This was Greer Little-Crowder country, and she filled the Plaza grand ballroom with a bursting crowd of financial wizards, stars of the entertainment business, developers, attorneys, CEOs, tall athletes, bankers.

(Gawd! He is gorgeous!)

(Well, she's not exactly chopped liver.)

Quinn went to them as a successful businessman.

"To retain our exalted commercial status in the world, let us run a gut check on ethical standards. Hey, soft money is greed money. Greed money is soft money. Soft money erodes our underpinnings."

Just about everyone in the ballroom was uncomfortable but emptied their wallets to the limitations. Maybe Quinn was not for them, but it was nice to have a spokesman for the conscience before reelecting Thornton Tomtree.

Now for the grand entrance in a late rally at Columbia University with students bussed in from NYU and St. John's and Fordham and Yeshiva and City College.

"We can no longer afford racism. A short century and a half ago we fought a civil war to erase the ogre of slavery. The twentieth century was all about people liberating themselves, declaring their freedom and dividing the planet into a hundred and eighty-five independent nations. This new century is the century we will get rid of one of mankind's oldest scourges. We will rid ourselves of the curse of bigotry."

A hundred cameras ate up several thousand exposures of Quinn shaking hands with Warren Crowder, of Quinn shaking hands with Warren Crowder and Greer Little-Crowder.

Meanwhile, Rita had garnered a great deal of attention of her own.

The Madison Square Garden fund-raiser turned away over three thousand people. The fever was like a Lindbergh parade down Broadway. Quinn left New York with over a million and a half dollars and fifty-eight percent of the Democratic vote.

"Governor O'Connell, Charles Packard, Reuters. Would you care to comment on the *Newsweek* story concerning your campaign chairperson, Greer Little-Crowder?"

"Without Greer my campaign would have never gotten off the ground, nor could it run so well."

"Follow-up question, Governor. Were you and Ms. Crowder romantically linked?"

"We sure were. We were sweethearts at the University of Colorado thirty years ago. She was also an excellent baseball coach and raised my batting average almost forty points."

"Doesn't it seem newsworthy, sir, that Greer Little-Crowder is now a powerful person, throwing herself into your campaign?"

"Obviously, she was anguished by the Four Corners tragedy and, along with millions of Americans, believes the Second Amendment must be repealed."

"Louise Markham, *Washington Times*. Have you and Ms. Crowder had contact in the intervening years?"

"Well, not the kind of contact you are hinting at. We've met on public occasions."

"Governor, Chance Spencer, MSNBC. Did Ms. Crowder resign or simply take an extended leave?"

"Hold the phone, ladies and gentlemen. You're leading me down a dirt road to the woodshed. For God's sake, don't throw us back to the dark ages of 1998 and the damage it wrought, and the torture imposed on a great but imperfect man."

"What about the public's right to know?"

"That right ends at my front door. I hope I will be able to invite everyone into my parlor. The rest of my home is a private place between me and my wife and family, and God."

Showdown time in Dixie. Six of the eight primaries were in the South. Florida and Texas, two of the mega-states, loomed in front of Quinn. A favorite-son candidate from Florida, Governor, and later Senator Chad Humboldt, girded to stop the O'Connell train.

Quinn's family began to surface in the press and interviews. Rita and her smile and her kind ways. One had to think back to Jackie Kennedy, although Rita's beauty could scarcely be matched.

Hey, that Duncan, what a hunk! He left the daily nuts and bolts of the ranch operation to Juan Martinez. He spent most of his hours in the veterinarian and animal research facility built on the property.

It was only fitting that Duncan fall in love with a Glenwood Springs veterinarian, Lisa Wong, of Asian-American heritage. She came to Troublesome on a research grant, to positively determine the shelf life of eggs. She saw Duncan enter through the chicken coop . . . and that was that.

Duncan went campaigning and saw to his father's rest periods, filtered the in-coming communications—a lion at the gate.

Lisa remained at the ranch, seeing to the comfort of her grandmother-in-law Siobhan, who was failing to cancer.

Rae, a computer scientist at the Atmospheric Research Institute in Boulder, took a leave of absence to set up and operate the campaign headquarters' computers. She reported to Greer on everything from collections to travel reservations to advertising.

Rae tried one four-day campaign swing with the candidate, and that was enough!

. . . because everything blurred together: airports, welcoming committees, Secret Service men moving back TV cameras, shouting correspondents, "Would you mind a picture with Mrs. Gumport?" "I'd love it!" Quinn would answer . . . hamburgers, baloney sandwiches, tourist class, Big 8 motels, polls, TV studios, talk radio shows, ballrooms, school auditoriums, "Let's hear a rah-rah O'Connell," homes for the aged, beady-eyed big donors, wide-eyed girls with short skirts, throw out the first pitch, press conferences, more press conferences, short parades in small towns, Irish, Jews, Italians, Gulf Coast fishermen, Mexicans, wheat farmers, black mayors, white mayors, tan mayors . . . Sunday. "Rita, you go pray for me, honey, we've got meetings every twenty minutes" . . . Internet, outer nets, books as wisdom, "Can we get this pressed and have it back in an hour?" . . . "What the hell do you mean, I've got a fever? I can't have a fever, because I've got to be in Des Moines," "We need cash, boss," position papers, "Happy Days Are Here Again!" . . . orange juice, lots of orange juice . . . "Am I going to have time to go to the john?" . . . "Sorry, not till our next stop, Governor."

Chad Humboldt blistered the South through innuendo. The word Catholic was not used out loud, but it played in the Christian Right churches. The gist of it was that O'Connell is only pretending to be one of us, but he isn't. He's a brooding mountain man, and when he looks you in the eye it is impossible to know if he is truthful. "Let us not forget that we have had presidents who looked us in the eye and lied through their teeth."

Chad Humboldt was a generations fixture supported by a sudden coalition of politicians in Florida, Louisiana, Mississippi, Oklahoma, Tennessee, and mighty Texas. Be cautious of the stranger. Be cautious of his inexperienced views on the issues. Humboldt wove around the gun-control issue but warned of a stranger who would steal away the traditions.

Jackson, Mississippi—Monday
March 10, 2008

"You're going to the well once too often," Greer snapped. "It won't play in Jackson."

"It played in Atlanta."

"It had great surprise and shock value, granted, but that was then and now is now. No electorate is going to keep listening to morality plays. We are in Apache country, Quinn."

"Ummmm."

"Rita, Mal, help me, for chrissake."

Mal scanned the polls. "We're behind in every Southern state—well, you've got a small lead in Oklahoma, but they're a sister state to Colorado."

Quinn did not speak. He seemed to be drifting off again in some kind of narcoleptic state with an inner concentration that shut out external noises.

"If I were a gambler," Mal said, "I'd say, go ahead, make your doom-and-gloom population-control speech. This isn't a gamble. You're going to lay an egg."

"So we're going down either way! What can I do but gamble?"

"Play it safe," Greer said. "And let's get out of here with our ass intact and go crazy in the big Midwestern states. That's only a week away . . . and then California."

Duncan arrived with a late bulletin. "Dad, Denver

reports we picked up over three hundred thousand this week."

"Good, we won't have to hitchhike out of here," Quinn said.

Otherwise, Quinn was stubbornly silent and the rest, gnashingly frustrated, wanted to shake him.

"Fuck it!" Greer screamed.

"You've grown awfully hardheaded," Mal said. "Your state senate office in Colorado was a place of conciliation and compromise."

"Because," Quinn answered drudgingly, "whether Democrat or Republican we were all hard-core Coloradans. Maybe we've treated these people down here like country bumpkins for too long. There are issues besides the Second Amendment that I have to save for Thornton Tomtree. We have to hold our fire until we see him in the crosshairs. Hey, guys, love you all. I've got to get some sleep."

"And the next president of the United States, Quinn Patrick O'Connell!"

". . . one thing in this campaign has really bugged me, and that is my challengers trying to put across the idea that I come from a strange place to a place where I have no business. They go further. They say, 'What can a governor from a small mountain and prairie state possibly know about Southern history and tradition and politics? If, God forbid, a Coloradan gets to the White House, what will happen to us?' I resent the past isolation of the South, and I resent the Chad Humboldts who want to keep this isolation going.

"I resent it when I am told, do not make a doom-and-gloom speech in Mississippi. Do not bring up overpowering moral issues because the Mississippi electorate can't get it. They want honey on their hush puppies.

"I believe an informed electorate, an informed *American* electorate, North, East, South, or West, should be aware of the concerns of our leaders. I am deeply worried about a lot of things which can no longer be shoved into the closet.

"So, muffle the drums. We are gutting this planet close to the point of no return."

Greer closed her eyes, but the thumping of her heart could almost be heard. Duncan took his mother's hand. Both hands were wet. Maldonado felt a hard stab, and wanted to stand up and scream for Quinn to stop.

". . . In a word, we are taking more out of the planet than the planet has to give in order to sustain life.

"All over we see ominous signs of a lessening quality of life, bald spots for shopping malls ripped out of the evergreen forests of New Zealand . . . Indians fighting off elephants coming right to the village edge to get at the leaves in the tall trees . . . wood bearers having to go miles to find firewood that used to be on the edge of their fields . . . dead fish who can't get over the dam, crushed by generator blades . . . green slime we spill back into our waters that takes the oxygen away from millions of shellfish . . . the shark, the most ancient and perfect fighting machine, now facing extinction. Sixteen lanes of blacktop running the length of Florida, covering forever destroyed rich pastures. Deep plowing that has eroded our great prairie farmlands and blown away irreplaceable topsoil.

"Yes, I believe that the people of Mississippi understand this. And I know you understand when I say that fifty thousand people die of starvation and malnutrition every bloody day of the year. Sixteen million deaths from hunger a year—a child dies every six seconds.

"The planet, with all its great agricultural innovations, cannot feed our present world population of four billion people. How in the name of God is it going to feed eight billion, the number that will inhabit the earth this century.

"We must chart an intelligent course through these mine fields. I know that population control offends my church and many of your beliefs. I know that from the beginning of time poor men have counted their riches in the number of children they could produce. It is a luxury we can no longer afford, and it's going to happen to your children and grandchildren unless we recognize what's going on and do something about it!"

"Tell me, and I'm listening, how we are going to

survive to see the next century without population control? . . ."

"Oh, Jesus, he did it!"

Florida: Humboldt 64% O'Connell 35%

Hawaii: Humboldt 21% O'Connell 79%

Louisiana: Humboldt 53% O'Connell 47%

Mississippi: Humboldt 50% O'Connell 48%

Oklahoma: Humboldt 40% O'Connell 55%

Oregon: Humboldt 33% O'Connell 62%

Tennessee: Humboldt 45% O'Connell 46%

Texas: Humboldt 51% O'Connell 44%

Thornton Tomtree took two top White House people and moved them to his election campaign. Hugh Mendenhall, a hefty, bubbly wizard of the polls, and Dr. Jacob Turnquist, the analyst. They were close enough to T3 not to be overcome with fear in his presence. Like any great executive, Thornton allowed those close to him to take him on and speak their minds.

The nation had undergone the first anniversary of the Four Corners Massacre. Thornton had flown over Six Shooter Canyon in a helicopter and afterward laid the cornerstone of the permanent memorial.

He had done just enough on his unopposed Republican reelection campaign to keep his name high, and took the convention by acclamation.

But so had Governor Quinn Patrick O'Connell in a boisterous, bombastic Democratic convention in Detroit.

On Thornton's return to Washington, he called in Hugh Mendenhall and Dr. Jacob Turnquist and repaired with them and Darnell to Camp David.

"Ahhh!" said the President.

"Ahhh!" Turnquist and Mendenhall agreed.

"Ahhh!" said Darnell, and poured from the large pitchers of Bloody Marys. The President's steward adjusted the awnings to keep the sun off the patio.

Darnell Jefferson lay back in a chaise longue chair as a listener.

The time was here to start blazing away at the Democratic opponent. The weekend was to detail strategic warfare. There was the sound of celery stalks being crunched.

"Our jingle-jangle rope-a-dope cowboy is going to be a handful," the President said.

"I couldn't believe it," Mendenhall bubbled. "O'Connell talking birth control in Mississippi. He's got to trip and fall; he's too disorganized and reckless."

Jacob Turnquist always had his authoritative, sincere, goateed, think-tank expression. "Or," he suggested, "are we dealing with a political genius? He knows, like a bird riding the wind, just how far he can ride any issue. He is developing quasi-fanatic followers . . . and keep in mind, all he has done so far is to present himself with a soft-shoe dance. He has only touched on significant issues superficially. He has given the Second Amendment wide berth. Why? Until he got control of the party—now he can take dead aim at you. Up to the day he won the convention, he took wild gambles to gain attention . . . for example, financing through populist means . . . we are now facing close to two million voters who have invested in him, who will show up at the polls."

"Clever desperation. It worked this time. It never worked before," Mendenhall said. "We've got to look back to Four Corners to understand the trepidation the voters still have."

Tomtree spoke, and both leaned forward, Darnell still the quiet, removed observer. "What the son of a bitch has done," the President said, "is deliberately start an erosion of our Southern base. A lot of Baptist women are on birth-control pills, and a lot of Baptist women don't like the guns in their husbands' closets. His invasion was either going to blow him out of the race or establish him as a powerful new force. Now, what are we dealing with?"

Turnquist spoke keenly, sincerely, earnestly. "Quinn and Chad Humboldt barely slapped each other's wrists. Our ace in the hole, Vice President Hope, has held his end of the coalition of the right wing together for twenty years."

"It's our imperative," the President said. "The vice president will be here tomorrow to get his marching orders."

"We're still leading in the South," Mendenhall insisted. "It's still O'Connell's to take, and my money is on Matthew Hope."

"Have we got anything on O'Connell?"

"He's refused to answer questions of a personal nature," Hugh Mendenhall went on. "I think, maybe, the press has gotten his message. They now approach him with caution, even respect, one might say."

"The man has a rock-solid reputation for honesty."

"Nothing festering on the Greer Little-Crowder hump-up?" Thornton asked.

"That was thirty years ago, Mr. President. They were college students. Besides, we are in an era that flinches away from sex scandals," Turnquist said.

"Bullshit," the President shot back. "They'll stop flinching when they get another juicy one to chomp into. We're not going to lose sight of this odd relationship. If not O'Connell, Greer Little has had a reputation as a naughty girl." They all laughed and sipped, save Darnell.

"If we can find one major indiscretion to take him down off his god pedestal, we've got to push it, hard. The instant he's cut down to human status, the coyotes will ravage him."

"We'll do a rerun of his history," Turnquist said. "You are right on, Mr. President. When a holier than thou falls by the wayside, he's cooked."

"Having established his persona, O'Connell is going to switch to issues—" Mendenhall said.

"But," Tomtree said, "each time we nail him, we also bring up the gunslinger, reckless, irresponsible, dangerous side of the man. This is where the cowboy is most vulnerable."

The vice president called from Washington. He would be helicoptering to Camp David within the hour. Good!

"Should we do anything about him being an orphan . . . you know, a puzzled childhood . . . all that?"

"There could be rumors floated about his biological parents. Certainly we have friends who can raise the issue. And that wife of his. Any nudes of her around?" Mendenhall asked.

"Look into it, Hugh, but very, very carefully. Now, here's what we're going to do. TV and print ads are almost ready. There will be three takes of each ad: high, medium, low, low meaning negative, fuck the truth, innuendo or personal attack. If, for example, the low ads don't work in Seattle, we try medium and high ads in Kansas City and Chicago until we know what works where. That's a big, big job for you, Hugh. Don't make any goddamn accusation we can't slip out of!"

"Yes, Mr. President."

"I want all future ads run past Darnell."

"Absolutely, Mr. President."

"Got that, Darnell?"

"Ummm," Darnell said, refilling his glass.

"Darnell, you've been very quiet," Tomtree said.

"Just awed by the process."

"What part of this don't you like?" Tomtree pressed.

"Most of it. You've got to ride out to meet this Quinn on the mountainside. You're not going to tunnel up to him. He's breaking down our coalitions, for chrissake. He has become somewhat Churchillian in his speeches. He knows he is on the great issue of the century."

"And?" the President asked.

"Take the Second Amendment issue away from him or cloud it up. Or, for God's sake, even join him."

"Join him?"

"Join him."

"Join him?"

"It would show that you realize the time of the gun is over and you have the courage to come forth with a staggering and enlightened position. That's how to beat this guy!"

The President pressed his fingers together and closed his eyes. Ballsy idea, but mad. "What are we looking at, Hugh?"

"After the convention you had a fourteen-point lead, plus or minus three percent. It's down to eleven, but you know, it could be virtually the same."

"Jacob, do we take this campaign up into the plains of heaven?"

"It's a political campaign, and my feeling is that he has alienated the press, which will jump on your bandwagon the instant he slips."

"Excuse me, I stand corrected," Darnell satirized. "What do you want to do about the debates?"

"Well, he needs to debate me to try to catch me. I'd set down extremely restrictive terms, limitations on questions and positions. If, God forbid, my lead falls down to single digits, then we slide into serious negotiations. No more than two debates and keep the rules confusing."

"Bear in mind," Darnell said, "that if O'Connell keeps gaining, we may have to go to him for the debate."

"It will never happen," Mendenhall said.

"Never," Jacob Turnquist agreed.

FORTY-ONE

When it was apparent that Governor O'Connell was going to sweep the Democratic convention, the governors of Texas, New York, Florida, and California, hat in hand, pitched for the vice-presidential nomination.

Quinn instead pulled a rabbit out of the hat by reaching back for Senator Chad Humboldt, his main opponent in the primaries, even though there was a difference on some issues. Humboldt was, quite simply, the best man. Moreover, the senator could neutralize Vice President Matthew Hope in the South.

After a year of mourning, the public looked anxiously toward the coming election. Quinn hit the ground running.

As governor he had sought and brokered an environmental and land-use bill that encompassed ranchers, mining interests, the ski industry, developers, and private landowners, preserving open space and ranch land forever.

The University of Colorado had been upgraded to one of the top ten state schools.

Colorado was the best-managed tourist state.

Colorado had more foreign import-export deals than any state west of the Mississippi River, other than California and Texas.

The Denver Symphony had been made into one of the nation's best, and Denver became a cultural oasis.

There was an impressive list of accomplishments in secondary education, child care, welfare, and he had shut down two of the state's more obnoxious HMOs.

Leading the parade, the issue to repeal the Second Amendment now opened for business.

Denver, October 1, 2008

Greer heard the nasty sound of the phone and put a pillow over her head. The ring persisted. She clicked on her table lamp and simultaneously clicked on her head.

"Greer," she said.

"This is Darnell Jefferson."

"Hi, Darnell, what have you been doing with yourself lately?"

"Greer, you're going to have to excuse the hour, but I just got through with my meetings. Are we on a secure line?"

"You bet."

"Do we trust each other?"

"To do what?" she asked.

"Anything beyond this phone call. If we meet, where we meet, what we say is not taped or bugged or leaked."

Greer mulled a moment. "I don't know. What do you have in mind?"

"The President's kicked ass on me. We're trying to complete his campaign schedule, and we can't do it unless we agree on the debates."

Bingo! Greer thought.

"All right," Darnell said, "so we blinked first, but you know and I know every campaign pussyfoots around the debates, then always conducts them. The responsibility falls on both sides. And you know damned well, we'll end up with debates."

"Couldn't have said it better myself."

"The President is really leaning on me. He wants it settled in the next couple of days."

Darnell was calling from Washington. It was two in the morning there. Pretty late to clean one's desk. Presidential urgency. They must have gotten late polls. Quinn was running neck and neck with Tomtree. Were they soft, or was T3 trying to set Quinn up?

"So, what's the program?" Greer asked.

"Chicago is midway between Denver and Washington. We have a safe house there, or if you are too suspicious, you can set it up in a hotel of your choice. We'd send a charter jet for your negotiator."

"And yourself?"

"I'm authorized to cut a deal."

"I'll get back to you in a few hours, Darnell. If I come to Chicago, I can't leave until tomorrow evening. It should be me and Professor Maldonado."

"The governor's father-in-law?"

"Yep."

"I'll be waiting for your call. It will be nice to see you again."

Greer could not fall back to sleep, so she finally arose, yawned and stretched, and set the coffeepot into motion. Since the Iowa caucus in February, she had expected someone to tap her on the shoulder and say, "I know what you know."

Every day her secret grew, like a tumor, and every day she ignored her own sense of propriety, it enlarged. Greer walked through her arguments again, but she found herself in the same place, with the madness of holding a secret. The fear of letting it go made her shiver.

Call Warren? Christ, she knew what he would say. He'd tell her to press her advantage, as in hostile takeovers. No prisoners.

"Oh, Christ," she whispered and punched a phone number.

"Hello," a dreary voice said.

"Hi, Rita, it's Greer."

"Anything wrong?"

"Are Mal and Quinn at the condo with you?"

"Yes."

"Get them up. I'll be over in a half hour."

* * *

The three of them were draped around the living room, knowing, at this time of night, they were going to be talking "rotten apples."

Greer came rumpled, and she showed the wear of executive decision making. "I got a call from Darnell Jefferson, two in the morning Washington time. They want to get together with us and nail down a debate."

"They must be hurting," Rita said.

Greer shook her head and, although it was a serious moment, she could not help but see how voluptuous and filled with Quinn Rita was. Greer felt a pang of jealousy.

"What did you wake us up to tell us?" Reynaldo Maldonado asked.

Greer took a deep breath, closed her eyes, and lifted her face. "Pucky Tomtree has been having an affair for two years."

"Well, you've got this old boy's attention," Mal said. Both Quinn and Rita stared, puzzled.

"Go on," Quinn said softly.

"I've personally known Pucky Tomtree fifteen, maybe twenty years," Greer began. "She chaired an awful lot of community services from Boston. Committee to Save the Llamas, Committee to Bring Caruso Back from the Dead, Up the Symphony, Artists Against Starvation, Artists for Peace. She either chaired or served on the boards of a hundred national groups.

We've been on a dozen committees together. I find her to be a lovely woman."

Orange juice all around.

"Providence has a very active theater life. Sort of a bedroom community for Broadway. She loved to hang out in the garret scene. There were a few moot whispers about affairs. Nothing to write home about."

"I don't want to hear any more of this," Quinn interceded.

"Shut up and listen," Mal ordered his son-in-law.

"Okay, gang," Greer said, "hand me the envelope, please. And the winner is . . . Aldo de Voto," she said, "the reigning conductor of the National Symphony Orchestra. I worked with him before he moved to Washington, when he directed the New York Philharmonic. Events . . . committees . . . fund-raising. He's a very charming guy with wife and kids safely tucked away in Spain. No, we were never lovers, but Aldo and I were bosom buddies."

Greer went on that Crowley Media kept a company apartment at the Watergate where Aldo de Voto lived. They spent a lot of time rapping, as friends, each having the key to the other's apartment.

"Why did you think you needed a key to his place?" Mal asked.

"Because my place often looked like the interstate, with the Crowder people coming and going and a line of politicians at the door. Aldo seldom came home until very late, and I could hide out there. Washington trips ain't no fun, folks."

To this day, Rita found discussions of infidelity discomforting, but she tried not to show her reaction. Quinn seemed to be hardly listening, while Mal cleared every sentence in his mind.

"I hadn't been to Washington for about three months, and after the FCC hearings I had the bird dogs on me, even from my own network. I gave Aldo a ring, but his voice machine said he was in Philadelphia. Anyhow, his key still worked. I stretched out on his couch for a while, then went to freshen up. There was a cosmetic bag at the vanity mirror with the top opened. Have you ever noticed the jeweled Japanese fighting-fish brooch Pucky wears?"

"Yeah . . ." Mal sighed.

"It was there in the cosmetic bag as well as her lipstick, an initialed notepad, her perfume, et cetera. And, a name tag."

"It would be impossible for anyone to plant it," Mal said.

"Particularly a brooch worth several hundred thousand dollars," Greer said. "There were a few other things in Aldo's closet that a lady would wear for an afternoon tryst. Her size."

"What about her Secret Service detail?"

"She drives her own damned car sometimes. Pucky is an independent lady."

"Didn't we stop all this with Clinton?" Quinn asked in disgust.

"It's been eight years without a whisper of scandal in the country," Rita said. "Do you think the American people even care?"

"Look, daughter, the President can ball any alleycat he gets his hands on. But the First Lady! The Capitol dome would fall to the floor," Mal said.

"Adultery is a man's misdemeanor and a woman's felony," Greer said.

"Who knows?" Mal asked.

"We and the principals. They do not know that I know. My educated guess is that Tomtree is oblivious of it."

Quinn saw Rita shaken up by it all. His hand pressed her shoulder. "That's all we need to hear," he said. "We are going to do absolutely nothing except to vow to each other to do absolutely nothing. Done. End of discussion."

"That is extremely decent of you, Governor," Greer exploded. "But do you have any idea of the broadsides these people are going to fire at you on the Internet and TV and in the press? And don't tell me the American people can tell the difference."

"Quinn, if Tomtree found out, he'd want to keep a lid on it until after the election. Then he'd let it fly. This is a real ace in the hole. We squeeze just a little bit on the debate negotiations," Mal said.

"I said no, and I mean no. Maybe I've come this far on the dead bodies of those kids in Six Shooter Canyon. No, no, no, no!"

"Vintage O'Connell!" Greer snapped. "Woweeeee!"

The four of them gasped at each other, as fighters who had gone a nonstop round.

"Maybe it is vintage O'Connell," Rita said. "Maybe a lot of people out there are beginning to understand what kind of man he is. Maybe he's the last honest politician the world will ever see. Maybe the thought of hurting me makes it too difficult for him to bear. Maybe he is self-destructing. But he's a Marine. Take him or cut bait."

Oh, man, did Rita chill them out.

"I need your promise you'll never mention Pucky or your resignation," Quinn said.

"Shit," Mal groaned. "All right, include me in. You've my word."

"It remains between us," Greer promised.

FORTY-TWO

At the last moment Greer decided she needed Rae O'Connell with her and Mal in Chicago. Rae, a successful, computer-oriented businesswoman, had run the electronics at her dad's Denver headquarters. After she gleaned and analyzed the incoming messages, she gave them to Greer, in order of priority.

The last time Greer had been on the road without Rae, her work had backed up unmercifully.

Overnight bags packed and ready to go, Greer had the charter jet switch to Colorado Springs in order to avoid a possible media alert.

Their red-eye express set down in the private-plane section of Midway Airport, where a limo pulled alongside, and they drove off to the Schweitzer Mansion on Lake Shore Drive, a Republican half-way house, and site of secret rendezvous.

The mansion was century-old-mahogany- and tapestry-clad. Each bedroom held a ponderous four-poster, and each bathroom had a freestanding sink, pipes to heat towels, and crested linens. It said "robber baron" all over it. The present Schweitzers lived magnificently on the old fortune. They were Chicago denizens of high order.

Alma, a robust former mezzosoprano, greeted them and ushered each to their suites. Kurt Schweitzer was in Washington until after the election.

Darnell Jefferson would be arriving at dawn. A meeting in Mr. Schweitzer's study was called for ten in the morning.

Greer, Mal, and Rae went into power sleeps, after which they loaded up on orange juice and danish followed by a large transfusion of coffee.

Ten o'clock.

Darnell spilled out of Mr. Schweitzer's chair.

"Greer!"

Jesus, he looked great, she thought. The wiry, bubbly white hair against his milk chocolate skin. Even in relaxed clothing he appeared like a model.

"Hi, handsome," she said, running her fingers through his hair and giving him a hug and peck. "This is Professor Maldonado, and this is Rae O'Connell, the governor's daughter."

"It's an honor to meet you," Darnell said to Mal. "I have a pair of your figurines in my home."

"Really? Which ones?"

"Russian ladies."

Mal smiled. "Yeah," he said, "yeah."

"I asked Mrs. Schweitzer last night," Rae said, "to set me up as close to you as possible on a secure phone. I'll have to run messages to Greer during your meeting."

The study was pure Teddy Roosevelt, with stuffed heads of boars and lions and buffalo staring down at them and photographs of safaris, killing safaris.

. . . good trip, fine . . .

"You know," Darnell said, "every campaign plays hide-and-seek on the debate, maneuvering for an edge. In the end there is always a debate. I hope we can hash it out."

"We know you are ready to shotgun the country with ads saying Quinn was the one refusing to debate," Greer said.

"Our attitude here, now, is that you really don't want the debate," Mal said.

"I refer to one debate," Darnell said, "because two simply can't be fit in. Here is our proposal for site and rules."

"And here is ours," Greer said.

Darnell's paper ruled out university campuses. Universities were too volatile and apt to be too liberal. The cities suggested were San Diego, Portland, San Antonio, St. Paul, Baltimore, and Montgomery.

The debate would last ninety minutes, and there would be alternative moderators.

Three minutes on each new subject. Three-minute rebuttal. The last fifteen minutes, questions from the audience.

Rae came in from the adjoining office and laid a half dozen notes before Greer. She scribbled on two of them and set two aside. "This should excite you, Darnell. We have just qualified for federal matching funds for the balance of the campaign."

"The proposal?"

"Bullshit," Mal said characteristically. "Montgomery, St. Paul, Portland. Why don't we hold it in the middle of the Amazon? Besides, your October 11 date could well be during a World Series game. Otherwise, there is absolutely nothing we agree with in the balance of this proposal."

Darnell held his hand up to be able to read the counterproposal. Rae came in with a half dozen more notes, two for Mal.

Darnell set their proposal down. "Are you serious?" he asked.

"Well, your proposal was pretty sanitized."

"And yours, revolutionary."

"All we are trying to do," Mal said, "is bring the art of debate up to where it was a hundred and fifty years ago."

"Those kind of debates are won by artful dodgers," Darnell said.

"I'd say both of the candidates qualify," Greer said.

Darnell glared down at the paper on the desk. They would vie for a single three-hour debate with a twenty-minute break in the middle. Only one venue was proposed, the Celeste Bartos Forum Hall in the New York Public Library.

It would be an open debate. Either candidate could bring up any issue and argue it. Either candidate could rebut. The deadline would be five minutes. If a candidate ran under five minutes, he would be given credit for the time; if he ran over it, it would be deducted from his total speaking time.

One moderator.

"This is a prelude to a shouting match," Darnell said strongly. "It's a street brawl."

"No," Mal said, "we're talking about getting truth to the people."

"Truth is what we all seek," Darnell thought, but declined to say it. They weren't budging. Perhaps, he thought, they believed they had an edge. But wait! They have more to gain than we have. We're out to neutralize this debate by cluttering.

Rae returned with an urgent message. Greer studied it, contemplated, then arose. "I have to take care of something," she said. "It will take a few minutes, maybe more. You guys keep going and I'll catch up."

Mal faced Darnell, Darnell faced Mal. Darnell wondered if they were setting him up.

Knowing the Republicans were about to inundate the airways with nasty advertisements, Mal had formed a "Truth Squad" which had obtained copies of about half of the ads. Quinn would be ready to react instantly.

Yet President Tomtree was still the power and owned the machinery to maul and grind under his opponent by sheer weight of numbers of dollars and had little appetite to be bound to the truth.

"I don't think you get it," Mal said.

"I think you've made preposterous demands. I won't even show these to the President."

"You intend to go through the motions of a debate reduced to no consequence and unleash your media barrage and turn the rest of the campaign into a fuck fest. Just skip the gutter and go straight down to the sewer. Okay, let's play some sewer games."

"I'd rather wait until Greer returns."

"Sit still, Mr. Jefferson. Pucky Tomtree has been having an illicit affair with another man for over two years."

Darnell's mind ran a Pucky-check. If she had, she was extremely clever and careful. Would she? Little gossip bits had her with artists and writers, but that had been long ago, probably before Thornton. What seemed certain was that Maldonado would not try this if it wasn't true.

"What are your intentions?" Darnel asked grimly.

"This campaign is not going into mud slinging. We demand a full, honest, open debate, without stunts. We demand decency in your advertising."

Darnell had been scissored. He knew it. Yet Maldonado was not trying to shade his demands. Darnell had gotten to know Quinn with a lot of secondhand study. This was pure Quinn Patrick O'Connell, a sense of humility and honor that conveyed itself to the public.

"Who knows about this?"

"Greer learned about this first. She told the governor, myself and my daughter, who is Quinn's wife. We are it."

"The press?"

"*Nada*, nothing."

"You are certain to be able to keep a lid on this till after the election, provided we remain in certain bounds?"

"I'm as sure as I can be about anything," Mal said. "We're dealing with three fine people. Greer doesn't even know I'm confronting you. Quinn ordered us not to leak this at any cost. I'm taking it upon myself to offer it to you as a warning."

"If I agree to carefully inspect our advertising and I agree to your debate conditions, will you give me the name of the gentleman?"

"Do you agree?" Mal asked.

"I agree, but how can O'Connell afford this gesture, a gesture that could deny him the presidency?"

"You just don't get it, Mr. Jefferson."

When Greer returned, Darnell watched the two very closely. Were they in cahoots, in a good-cop, bad-cop play, deliberately giving Mal time alone with Darnell so he could squash him while leaving her out? There was absolutely nothing in her demeanor to indicate she knew of Professor Maldonado's revelation.

Through the next two hours of "negotiations," Darnell began to "see" more and more merit to their proposal. He wondered out loud that it might even help Thornton. Two politicians facing each other honestly. Now, that's a picture . . . or an extended oxymoron.

Darnell won a few points in quibbling over this and that, and by early afternoon they broke camp to return to Midway Airport.

The final seal would be a simultaneous announcement with both candidates praising the honesty and openness of the debate.

Rae sat in the cockpit at the navigator's desk, still directing the streams of information coming in.

The cockpit door was closed.

"You all right?" Greer asked.

"I feel very tired," Mal answered.

"You told him while I was out of the room."

"Yeah," Mal sighed, "I nailed him."

"That puts Quinn in a rotten position vis-à-vis the two of you."

"I'll save him the pain of having to fire me. I'm resigning."

Greer patted his hand. "Maybe we see Quinn in too bright a light, Mal. Maybe he knew, in his heart of hearts, one of us intended to confront Jefferson about the Pucky affair. He's that smart, you know."

Rae came back with messages and gave them to Greer.

"Are you okay, Grandpa?" Rae asked.

"Just tired, honey."

Quinn read the short note of resignation from Mal.

"This is terrible," Quinn said.

"I got you the debate I think you need. So, don't let's rehash it."

"I'm going to have to accept your resignation," Quinn said, feeling a trembling wash over him.

"Yes, I know."

"Mal. We are still family. We're only humans. I wasn't really all that surprised when you told me. Maybe I silently hung the bad deed on you. And you only did it to make the playing field level. I want to keep Rita and my personal rooms at your home. We are family, man!"

"Thanks, Quinn."

FORTY-THREE

New York Public Library—Fifth Avenue
October 15, 2008

On this day the grand repository of human existence and thought was the focus of the nation. On this day illicit lovers could no longer rendezvous at the statues of the lions, for the building was isolated by police barricades.

Forty-second and Fortieth streets and Fifth Avenue held bumper-to-bumper privileged parking.

In the rear of the great edifice, running to the Avenue of the Americas, stood Bryant Park, a pocket park. Twice a year the fashion establishment raised a tent and models slunk down the runway. Cheers for Karan and Klein.

Beneath Bryant Park the greatest of treasures—an eight-story bunker held a trove indicating human existence on the planet, from cuneiform to Stone Age arrowheads, from the Gobi Desert to Newfoundland. All of it was here, awaiting visitors from space.

The tattered elegance of the *kodakCELESTE BARTOS* Forum had received a face-lift for the affair, her imposing glass dome shined to a glitter and four hundred temporary stadium seats installed.

The overflow of media had to cover the event piped back to the *fujifilmJOHN JACOB ASTOR* Ballroom.

Carter Carpenter, a hallowed father figure of the American media, had been resurrected to moderate the affair.

It was to be a wide-open debate, with the moderator stepping in only to preserve civility.

A buzz of anticipation hummed upward as the clock moved for nine. Outside, last-minute tickets, drawn by lottery, were hustled for over five hundred dollars each.

"Ladies and gentlemen, please take your seats," Carter Carpenter said authoritatively. Controlled applause greeted the governor and the president as they took to their rostrums.

For that instant Thornton Tomtree was glad he had let Darnell talk him into the venue. His lead over O'Connell had slipped from double digits to a single digit of nine percent.

Thornton, the stoic master of a great corporation, a gigantic figure, organized and in control, now showed an addition of tragedy—Lincolnesque. He had humanized himself, somewhat, since Four Corners, after slipping the mantle of blame and gaining sympathy for "taking responsibility, because it happened on my watch."

On this night he'd be facing the gun issue as never before. He was ready.

Carter Carpenter explained the very liberal rules. "Mr. Tomtree will go first, as he won the flip of the coin."

Tomtree's opening statement said, in effect, "We are in midstream in several ways, leaving an old century behind and healing from a catastrophic event. We don't change horses in midstream. Having ascertained that Four Corners was a national tragedy which demanded of every politician and every American, to accept his share of the blame . . .

". . . what are we being offered in my place? A popular rodeo-style candidate who, in fact, is probably more at ease branding cattle."

Quinn's smile burped up to a short laugh. Tomtree pretended not to hear. Quinn knew what kind of brawl was coming up. Keep the powder dry for the last half hour, he told himself.

"The American people must not roll dice," Thornton went on. "We must not mistake my opponent as a Western hero, the sheriff in *High Noon*. This is a reckless man whose claim to fame has come about through violence.

"In the AMERIGUN fiasco Quinn O'Connell put lives in danger a dozen times with tactics illegal in our system of justice.

"Do we want a shoot-'em-up-first president? Do we want to trust the future of our nation to a man whose finger is always on the trigger?"

Strong, strong stuff and only two minutes and thirty-two seconds had passed. "Mr. Tomtree, you have credit for twenty-eight seconds."

Quinn slipped a high stool under him, found a comfortable position, and rested his arms on his podium, speaking without notes, as Carter Carpenter nodded that his time had begun.

"Thornton Tomtree has done an admirable job in the past year of helping us heal our wounds, but he has done an even more admirable job of salvaging his own reputation.

"The day on which Mr. Tomtree assumed office four years ago, the United States proliferated with a third of a billion guns, one for every man, woman, and child in America.

"Bogus militias had spread like pack rats in our forests and canyons and cities. Today, the White American Christian Arrival claims nearly two hundred thousand followers, followers of Adolf Hitler and purveyors of hate.

"From the time of his first inauguration until this day, Thornton Tomtree has never once raised the issue of gun control.

"He, like many Republicans, and Democrats, went stone deaf, dumb, and blind during the intimidation waltz played by AMERIGUN.

"Thirty thousand Americans are killed each year by guns. Match that against sixty thousand killed in Vietnam over a ten-year period.

"Each year more Americans die by gunfire than are killed in traffic accidents! More people die by gunfire than die from Alzheimer's . . . or by leukemia . . . more than are killed by cirrhosis."

Thornton tapped the bell on his podium.

"Those are pretty heavy numbers," Carter Carpenter said. "Would you like to answer them?"

"Yes, I would," Thornton said. "It is easy to bandy about superficial numbers."

"I hope so," Quinn said, "we drew them off the Bulldog Information Net, which guarantees their accuracy."

"Raw data," Thornton said, "can be manipulated to suit any argument. Private ownership of weapons has been an American tradition from the inception of the nation. They cleared the way as we moved west. Those so-called statistics all have ipso facto's connected to them. The numbers are in the eyes of the beholder. We may have come to that point where there has to be new thinking on the subject. But we must wait until the investigations are done and all the information is in. We must not rush to judgment and in so doing endanger a basic American right."

"Hold on, sir," Quinn interrupted. "What about the monumental investigation you promised? It has been a year, forty-four million dollars has been spent, and there is no report.

"It is a matter of American justice that we get all the information in. When I received the Four Corners commission's preliminary report last February, I had to go before the American people and tell them that Six Shooter Canyon had to become a permanent mass grave. I sensed, as president, that our people needed more time to heal. If we had released the thousands of pages of documents, it would have only served to intensify national pain and make the American people relive the incident over and over.

"No matter our history and traditions, the tragedy in the canyon was a three and a half billion to one shot. It cannot and will not ever happen again, no matter what resolution we come to on gun ownership."

"Both of you gentlemen have stated your basic positions. Should we hold this data in mind and move on to another subject?"

"No, sir," Quinn said quickly. "This is the issue that brought me here. Yesterday, today, and tomorrow, fourteen children daily will be killed by guns. In addition to the thirty thousand slain, another hundred thousand are wounded, filling our emergency rooms with blood. Each gun death costs us $395,000. We are the shame of the civilized world. One of the richest forty nations in the world, the United States alone is responsible for half of all gun deaths."

Thornton Tomtree felt his first blip of fear. He knew that Quinn had gotten a foot in the door of his Christian Right. He had known exactly what statistics Quinn would throw out. It was the pulsating manner in which Quinn delivered his message, without bullying. Thornton knew he could say the exact same words and never achieve the same effect. Thornton glanced at Darnell. He was a statue. The overall debate strategy now evolved in Thornton's mind. To spring the trap? Yes? When to spring the trap?

Thornton smoothly shifted gears into his achievements, as immortalized on the Bulldog Information Network. Trade deficit down, budget surplus; Social Security funded for the century; great medical achievements; full employment; *and* world commerce, commerce in which the United States was the power that was!

Quinn's list of achievements was paler stuff, but the kind of stuff which had held Colorado up as a light of the nation.

Thornton jumped on Quinn's opening fusillade of helter-skelter statistics as another example of his recklessness.

Now to hit Quinn with the "doom and gloom" speech Quinn had made during the primaries in Jackson, Mississippi. The two major elements of it were world population control and the finite resources of the planet.

Tomtree was almost overwhelmingly tempted to bring up the birth-control issue. But birth control and pro choice was a chancy subject. Most Americans, by a wide margin, favored and practiced both.

If somehow Thornton could drive a wedge between the issue and the fact that O'Connell was a Catholic. He caught a glimpse of Darnell, whose eyes told Thornton he might be setting a trap for himself.

Okay, then, the second part of the Mississippi address.

"Mr. O'Connell paints a brooding and grim assessment of the future of the earth's resources. During my administration the United States has stood at the head of a consortium for the exploration of the seas. Using the great gift of computer science, we are in the process of mapping the bottom of every ocean, sea, bay, polar cap, and lake.

"Treaties have been concluded with most maritime nations in which America will do the searching and the mapping. Treaty nations will receive a share of the eventual profits.

"What have we found under our oceans? We have discovered hundreds of thousands of chimneys, maybe millions of them, spewing up a variety of basic metals and ores, from inner layers of the earth. If we keep exploration focused on our seas, I believe we will discover what we will need to sustain future life. So, let us drop our doom and our gloom. Our computer science is becoming so advanced, we know it will show us that the planet will continue to prosper."

Carter Carpenter cleared his throat, sincerely. "Would you care to respond, Mr. O'Connell?"

"Yes, sir. I think that the intense underseas exploration may have some merit, but we cannot bank the future of the planet on it."

Thornton's bell rang as he sensed Quinn hesitating. "Do you have a position on this, Mr. O'Connell?"

"I sure do," Quinn answered. "I've been briefed on this by Scripps Institute, Woods Hole, and Long Island University School of Oceanography. While we have gained enormous knowledge of the universe, we really don't understand the lay of the land a few miles down. Space exploration feeds the human drive to explore, to learn, to have a romantic contact. Perhaps, in this century, we will make contact with intelligent life out there. But under any equation, we will never be able to replenish the earth's shrinking resources. God does not run a trucking company from outer space. As for inner space, the chimneys on the ocean floors are truly God's handiwork created over tens of millions of years. Heat from lower layers beneath the earth's crust spouts from under the bottom of the sea, spewing minerals through the chimneys. Will we find infinite new sources of materials? If we tamper with these chimneys, which indicate fire below, then we are setting the table for underwater volcanos and the tidal waves they will create. We could be setting the table for a heating of our waters that would risk worldwide coastal flooding and a century-long El Niño.

"Does not this underwater exploration indicate a sense of desperation to replace what has been lost? Have we not done enough damage to our waters?"

Quinn went deeper into the perils of underwater

mining. "Exploration is primitive. To take something from the bottom of the sea would cost a hundredfold more than surface mining."

Thornton felt a surge of raw fear. O'Connell was explaining something in Thornton's realm with utter clarity. Thornton could fire back with esoteric computer data, but it could well fail.

Thornton had believed himself incredible, close to godlike, the way he had fought his way back from the Four Corners. But more, the people believed their president had added a dimension to his character.

Thornton had toyed around to come up with a probe for the debate, one that would catch O'Connell cold. In actual fact, Thornton had grown a little sour on much of the underseas probing. Yet it was a good, tricky subject to show up his opponent's ignorance.

Thornton glanced at the time-keeping apparatus. Quinn had built up a reserve of ten minutes while he, Thornton, was on borrowed time.

T3 had not come into the Great Debate without a hidden ace. He could wait till the clock wound down to five minutes. Meanwhile, Quinn had skillfully maneuvered him into an unwanted question-and-answer game.

"Mr. Carpenter," Thornton said, turning to the moderator. "My position is that we need a study."

"Mr. Tomtree, there is no restriction or limitation on any subject. Mr. O'Connell can revisit anything he cares to."

Thornton grimaced inwardly. That son of a bitch, Carter Carpenter, was at this moment the most powerful man in the world.

"What about child locks?" Quinn went on.

"That's reasonable," Thornton answered.

"How about a national gun registry, of which our police and other law enforcement agencies unanimously approve?"

"We are floating into the potential of a massive bureaucracy."

"We have registration in Colorado. The bureau has forty people in it who also double as instructors for certification of a weapon. What about the limitation on the number of personal arms a citizen can buy?"

"You can buy as many gallons of gas and chocolate bars as you want and need."

"Well, it's all right if each citizen purchased fifty guns, as have many citizens?"

"If we spell out numbers of guns, we may be endangering freedom of choice. Yes, there can be a ceiling, I suppose."

"I have two pairs of skis, two tennis rackets, and between myself and my ranch manager we have three weapons. Sir, are you aware there are a hundred thousand licensed gun dealers in the U.S.?"

To let this run its course or not to let it run? Show dignity, Thornton told himself. The damned point of all this was that as president, he was protecting both

Democrats and Republicans who received huge contributions from AMERIGUN and its allies. Dammit, they'd never support any national gun law with teeth.

Quinn was going on about the Colorado gun law, saying that the provisions he was bringing up were commonsense matters.

"Tell me, Mr. Tomtree, do you believe the Second Amendment in the Bill of Rights of the Constitution should be repealed?"

"I am going on record with our moderator to say that your line of questioning is more like a prosecutor in an inquisition. But I'll answer you, Mr. O'Connell. We do not play politics with our Constitution. It is like toying around with the Ten Commandments. A repeal will never happen because too many Democrats hold our belief that that could cause a domino effect on the Bill of Rights. What then? Attack freedom of worship? Freedom of the press? Freedom of expression?"

"Why so contentious about the Second Amendment?" Quinn asked. "Let us read the words: 'A well regulated Militia, militia being necessary to the security of a free State, the right of the people to keep and bear arms shall not be infringed.' Can you tell me, Mr. Tomtree, why is it that the gun advocates never quote the first part? The great banner on the wall of the AMERIGUN convention read, 'The right of the people to keep and bear arms shall not be infringed.' Well, where is the rest of it, and why is it missing from all your propaganda? Could it be you are hiding the first part because it is not a gun rights amendment but an amendment about forming militias?"

Thornton checked the clocks. O'Connell had used up all but two minutes of his time and they were coming up on intermission. Now to pull one out of the hat! Now to blast O'Connell before intermission so people will be hit by his words and level the playing field.

"Mr. O'Connell, I would like to get your input on the weekly newsletter published by the highly esteemed Longacre Institute."

"I haven't read their most recent bulletins, but to inform the audience, the Longacre is a Washington think tank closely allied to the Christian Coalition, the Falwell, Robertson people."

Thornton held up the newsletter. "And I quote. 'The truth behind the Urbakkan raid,'" he said. "According to the Longacre Institute, sir, the Urbakkan raid, which occurred in 1977, was a myth. What actually happened? A rapid-response team, of which you were a member, was testing a prototype aircraft on a NATO training exercise in Turkey. You were testing various systems, and you went off course into Iranian air space. A tanker plane had been following you for an air-to-air refueling, and the cockpit spilled fuel and caught fire, killing five Marine officers, including a major general. They were burned to death. The Corps, desiring several hundred of these planes, made a cover-up story. That cover-up story was the Urbakkan raid. The raid was a sham. The legends of bravery about yourself and others were likewise a sham."

A murmur arose from a shocked audience.

"For years," Thornton said, "I've heard rumors about Urbakkan. When I went to research it, I learned that the report on the raid was sealed and under lock and key. Now we know why," he said, holding up the Longacre newsletter.

Jesus, Quinn thought, keep your cool! The bastard thinks he can create confusion that cannot be clarified until after the election. Quinn scratched his jaw as Tomtree continued to thunder.

"I respectfully request that you lower your tone, Mr. Tomtree," Carter Carpenter admonished.

"On behalf of my courageous buddies who gave up their lives, I cannot dignify you."

"Sham!" Tomtree repeated. "Convenient of you not to answer."

"There are seventeen survivors of the Urbakkan raid," Quinn said. "We have remained close down through the years. We have never missed an annual reunion. I have been stalked about Urbakkan since I first ran for state office over a quarter of a century ago. I knew this was going to come up. Fifteen of these Marines were able to come to New York and are in the audience. Both the former commandant of the Marine Corps and the former chairman of the Joint Chiefs of staff are now in the process of issuing statements to answer the Longacre Institute's terrible lie. The reason the facts of Urbakkan were kept secret was because of the raid's success. We did not want the enemy to learn how we did it. Moreover, the plane itself and many of its systems were kept secret for national security reasons. In fact, the surviving members of Urbakkan will hold a news conference in the McGraw Rotunda directly after the debate."

Darnell hustled Thornton into a side office at intermission. A string of damage-control people trailed in. Darnell sat the President down. The President was a tombstone with eyes, staring at the floor. Darnell hovered over him like a manager whose fighter has undergone a beating.

"Mr. President, according to a snap poll at the Oyster Bar—" Mendenhall began.

"You, Mendenhall, out!" Darnell commanded. "And you, Turnquist, out, and you, you, and you—*out*!"

"Mr. President—" Turnquist demanded.

"Out!" Darnell yelled.

"Do what Darnell tells you to," Thornton rasped.

Secret Service Agent Lapides moved everyone into the corridor quickly and closed himself in with Mr. Jefferson and the President.

Thornton looked up, crestfallen. "I fouled up," he mumbled.

"Big-time."

"Why, how did I do wrong?"

"You tried to turn this debate into a search-and-destroy mission," Darnell snarled.

"It's hard to get a handle on O'Connell," Thornton went on.

"Yeah, he can beat you to death with the truth. If we are on a losing slide, you go out with dignity, Thornton. It's liar's poker, and you got called. You walked into a couple of sucker punches with your fucking ocean floor and Urbakkan raid. Who the hell at Longacre did you assign to write this newsletter?"

"It doesn't matter."

Darnell turned to the door. "Lapides, the President is soaking wet. He has a clean shirt in the bathroom."

Thornton was led to the sink and mirror. The damage was not beyond repair. He freshened up. Darnell tied his tie, watching his man's mood go from self-pity to anger.

"Five minutes!" they heard a voice from the corridor.

"I think I'll go back in early," Thornton said.

"I know by your expression what you're thinking," Darnell said. "You can't do it."

"It's legitimate!" Thornton said, gaining authority by the instant.

"You will not bring up an affair Rita O'Connell had thirty years ago."

"She left her wedding bed to run off with a drug cartel lawyer!"

"You will not bring that up," Darnell cried.

"I'm the president. I can do any goddamned thing I want!"

Darnell held him by the lapels. "Pucky has been having an affair for two years. O'Connell knows about it."

Thornton tried to brush Darnell's hands off him, but Darnell held on tightly. Thornton blinked, and blinked again.

"Was this affair with a male or a female?"

"A man."

"Well, thank God for that. Do you think O'Connell will sit on it till after the election?"

"I warn you, don't go after his wife."

"I see," Thornton said. "And you've known about this all along and didn't tell me?"

"I learned about it when I meet with Greer Little and Professor Maldonado in Chicago."

"Greer Little!" Thornton spat. "That bitch!"

"You've got it backward, Thornton. Greer uncovered Pucky's affair. O'Connell made her swear to keep it a secret. Maldonado was the one who spilled it to me. When O'Connell learned, he fired Maldonado on the spot, his own father-in-law."

"Who the hell is this O'Connell?" Thornton moaned.

"One minute!" the voice called from the corridor.

"Darnell, what should I do?"

"You have to apologize. You say that in Longacre's

zeal to get O'Connell, they fed you disinformation which you disavow!"

Thornton nodded his head. "Darnell, are you going to leave me?"

"No, I won't leave you, Thornton."

For the first time in their long years, Thornton threw his arms about Darnell and hugged him strongly, then went to the door.

"Thornton."

"Yes?"

"Don't you want to know the name of Pucky's . . . lover?"

"What the hell's the difference? How could Pucky have done this to the presidency?"

Thornton Tomtree had a hundred seconds to resurrect himself, and he did. He spread his options out. The news of Pucky's affair was annoying. Who the hell could have wanted her? That's not the point, he told himself. How much damage would it do before the election? If O'Connell showed enough desperation to make an attack, Thornton's spin people could throw it back in O'Connell's lap and show the American people his Democratic opponent would stoop to anything. With the knowledge out Thornton would get to play "the wounded Lincoln" suffering.

Even as he followed Darnell to the door, a plan

evolved. The Urbakkan raid still had enough mystery to it to cause confusion over the real facts.

The crowd had thickened in Times Square a few blocks away under the great news screen.

In this home and that, the intermission chores were closed up with a final flush of the toilet, snap of the Coke and beer bottles, and gathering in about the television.

America's downtowns were empty.

This land, so diverse, realized that a particular moment of epiphany was about to take place.

"Thornton," Darnell whispered, "the people know you are still the president. There is a fear of O'Connell. This next hour is the moment of your life."

Thornton nodded to Carter Carpenter as he cozied to his lectern.

"Mr. Carpenter," Thornton said, "because of the nature of our debate before the break, I'd like to make a statement."

"It is not your turn, sir," Carpenter said.

"I'll cede to Mr. Tomtree," Quinn said.

"It's a rock-bottom humiliation for a politician to look in the mirror and see egg on his face. This Longacre report was only published today, and because the issue of the truth about Urbakkan has become vital to this election, I accepted it because of Longacre's decades-long devotion to the truth."

The loved ones in Quinn's section paled. There

seemed to be loved ones in Thornton's seats besides Pucky, but they were faceless to a father who didn't know their birthdays.

"Why did this spring up now? If Longacre published this account and it is proved false, then I would be greatly embarrassed. But, my fellow citizens, Urbakkan has been sealed for three decades. I believe the truth is that someone on O'Connell's staff deliberately fed disinformation to the writer of this article. What media power fits the bill, and will she answer?"

"Mr. O'Connell?"

"Mr. Tomtree's reference was to my campaign manager, Greer Little-Crowder. The Longacre think tank has marched to T3's drumbeat for twenty years, fed by your generosity of over three million dollars."

"You see there, how you are trying to distort—"

"Longacre didn't verify a single fact, Mr. Tomtree. It was a hatchet job to create suspicion over the raid. There are only one or two persons who could have written it. We'll know soon enough, and it won't hold till after the election."

Well, now, he had dared O'Connell and O'Connell had not thrown out the Pucky affair. Even if Quinn attacked, the revelation would backfire on him. O'Connell could then easily go down as a raider and a shark.

On the other hand, if Quinn misses this opportunity, he will show he is too weak to duke it out with me, Thornton thought.

"The American people will have an answer on this in a few days," Carter Carpenter said. "I think it propitious to move on to other issues."

Just what Thornton wanted, to create doubt and confusion, leave it unsettled, challenge O'Connell's hero status.

Thornton was now wired with charts and graphs—over the hills and down to the dales, to grandmother's house we'll go—lines and colored bars and round pieces of pie all sliced to percentages. Thornton was in a boardroom posture where he could lay a hundred and one booby traps with the figures distorted, omitted . . . and with three you get egg roll.

"I've got a real problem with your charts," Quinn laughed.

"Yes, I know, of course you do," Thornton replied. His blood circulated faster as his full strength returned. Thornton hung tenaciously to the visuals, unfinished portraits.

"Gentlemen," Carter Carpenter said, "we are running low on time. You both have enough for a three- to five-minute summation. Mr. Tomtree."

"So what if the Urbakkan article proves to be wrong? All it proves is that after three decades under seal, someone in O'Connell's court was able to slip disinformation to us, using an honorable institution as a dupe. It is this kind of confusion that the American people will be facing from the White House if this man is elected."

"Hot damn!" Thornton congratulated himself. "I whacked him good! Now, nail it on, T3."

"Is it not fitting," Thornton continued, "to have had this debate in this great library? Nothing could better explain the difference between us. I am of the new American breed who has made possible transmitting every piece of information in this library anywhere on earth, in a fraction of a second. Since this new century began, we have moved to the cusp of forging a great electronic world. Men like Quinn Patrick O'Connell would rather carve in stone than have a printing press. Yes, there is greed and sin and garbage on the Internet and on the cable channels.

"When has the human face been free of greed? Every time a new invention comes into play for the betterment of the human race, greedy legions pounce on it.

"I know that. I also know who of the two of us is better suited to deal with this complicated new world technology. Quinn Patrick O'Connell has shown himself to be a one-issue candidate. The sophistication and needs of man's new electronic age cannot be mastered by him."

"May I?" Quinn asked.

"Yes, Mr. O'Connell," Carter said.

"Thornton Tomtree will indeed keep us busy regulating the two-bit stockbrokers, children's porno, scams, and slap a wrist for the massive invasion of American privacy. There will be sensational trials and rigid regulations. That will be for the greedy little flies buzzing around a dead carcass. But Thornton Tomtree will leave the big players alone. T3's seven hundred and forty industrial, commercial, shipping, banking networks are the greatest instruments for greed this world has ever seen. He'll use his power to ride shotgun on the little fish while, at the same time, he covers up billions of dollars moving daily in utter secrecy."

Quinn had weighed carefully but quickly, and the words seemed to tumble out of his mouth.

"This is not a Tut's tomb or an obsolete dinosaur. This is my father's generation who gave more of themselves for the betterment of this nation than any other."

A great door opened between speaker and listeners.

"I've lived on a ranch most of my life. My parents and I took a lot of trips. The moment of glory was entering this building and the Library of Congress in Washington. It was like coming into a sacred place. I knew, early on, that the writer afforded me a window to our past, an understanding of human relationships that set me on a bridge to cross and participate with my own generation. I was often lonely. It was not till I read *Of Mice and Men* that I realized I was not alone and that loneliness was a universal sadness of man.

"I've spent a lot of time with John Steinbeck. He bared his soul to bring light to me. He bared human frailty in his pages and in his own life—as did a hundred . . . no, a thousand other authors who knew what one little boy was going through and who stood tall for the dignity of man."

What the hell is he getting at? Thornton wondered. He's rambling. But would you believe the quiet in here? Believe it?

You ought to see Times Square silent. Taxis pulled over into parking lanes, and twenty-five thousand people, or more, watched the great screen.

"We tore down buildings like this not long ago," Quinn went on, "in our everlasting hunt for the mall and the skyscraper. What the hell! The legacy of past generations can now be kept on a piece of software and flashed up on the screen with a tweak of the mouse.

"Something is missing from that. What is missing is the personal relationship, the love between writer and reader, all the hope and all the horror the writer has to tell you. It is you and the writer alone, together, that will give you understanding about the joy and fear, the jealousy and love you have with your parents and your sisters and brothers.

"I glory in the electronic age, but do not tear this building down. I believe that the salvation of man will not come from an IBM printout, but from the words, on stone indeed, that came down from Sinai. Let us not abandon all the great thought in these rooms to the proposition of putting all our faith into an impersonal machine. By so doing, we will become something less than human beings ourselves."

FORTY-FOUR

After the debate the ground shifted, radically. The Tomtree campaign seemed to run out of energy. O'Connell had splintered away part of the hard Right, not by politics alone, but by the growing charisma of the candidate. Is O'Connell too good to be true?

In Los Angeles, Quinn spoke to the Mexican-American community with a candor they had not heard. "We have no right to interfere with Mexican internal affairs, but for Mexico to be a good neighbor of the United States, its institutionalized corruption must stop. No better example of that is the exploitation of Mexican labor in factories along our borders."

It was another of Quinn's daring speeches, but some people finally heard out loud what they had been saying in whispers.

The following night was a gathering in the Hollywood Bowl for a two-hour telecast from the community of stars. It was a love-in.

Rita knew the instant her daughter-in-law phoned. Siobhan had pulled herself together for coherence every night when her son phoned. For the last two nights she had been unable to speak to him.

"She's in and out of lucidity. We just don't know how long."

Mal and Quinn had been able to keep up civil contact, a new bend in their years together. The pressure was taken off when Mal phoned first.

"I've been visiting with your mother," Mal said. "She is in a bad way, Quinn. If you can get back, you and Rita still have your wing at my place. I can book enough rooms in Grand Junction to fairly well cover the entourage."

"It's your dad," Quinn said to Rita. "I need to go back."

"Siobhan?"

"Yes."

"We've got your mother in a quiet place, adjoining the south veranda. Beside Duncan and Lisa, and Rae, there should be other rooms open at the ranch house."

"Rita and I will fly directly into Troublesome. We should be there after midnight or so. Mal . . . Mal . . ."

"Don't say anything, Quinn. Get it straight that I am not sorry I told Darnell Jefferson what the President's wife was up to. If I hadn't, Tomtree would have attacked my daughter and your wife. No job in the world is worth how they can ravage and savage. But, asshole that thou art, you are my son-in-law. Now, where do you want me to put Greer?"

"Greer, Greer. She stayed in New York to see her husband and clear up some business. Will you have room at your place?"

Mal laughed. "The room where Rita kept her stuffed animals. I'll have Juan and a couple of the hands get it cleaned out. I'll install what electronic and computer shit there is around to keep the wires buzzing."

"Mal, thank you, man."

"You're a stupido bastardo, but I love you."

Rita was on another phone. She canceled Quinn in the Northwest, then directed a press aide to put out a simple bulletin to the effect that it was family business.

Rita kicked off her shoes and stretched on the chaise longue. Quinn sat on the ottoman and massaged her feet.

"How are you doing, honey?" she asked.

"*Media y media.* Dan, Siobhan, and Father Sean are the only family I've ever known. I feel detached and floaty."

"You're very close to completing an American wonder work. You've restored a lot of faith, and you've come through intact."

"Am I, Rita? All that clean? I knew when I sent Greer and Mal to Chicago to negotiate the debate with Darnell Jefferson that one of them was going to threaten him with Pucky's dirty laundry. I warned them not to and I fired Mal, but I was not all that unhappy with what he did."

"From the moment you shared your darkest and

most dangerous secrets with me, I realized you were the only whole man I ever knew or was apt to meet. Hey, you haven't presented yourself to the voters as all silver-plated and shiny. You've told people a lot of things they didn't want to hear. They get it. You don't hide behind the Constitution, you stand in front of it. Your failings, your unbelievable courage in admitting to them—that is what they want."

Quinn established a mini-office near his mother's bedside. Even in those times when she was alone with her terrible pain, she seemed to know of his nearness.

Duncan and Rae alternated in bringing him messages.

"I need Greer," Quinn said.

"Headquarters has made contact with her charter. She'll be on your cell phone," Rae said.

Quinn jotted notes on the communications, handed a couple for Rita to take care of. He looked from his mother to his son to his very pregnant daughter-in-law to his daughter . . . to his wife. God help me, he thought, it's mad, but Rita looks so sexy!

From the whine over the phone, Quinn knew the caller was in an aircraft.

"Quinn," he said.

"It's Greer. How is Siobhan?"

"She's hanging in. She asked for you, Greer."

"Look, I'm going to fly directly into Grand Junction.

I'll be there by noon. Have a car meet me. Something extremely important has come up."

"Can you say what it is?"

"No. We should have a secure room to talk in."

"I'm at Mal's. His studio will be safe."

From the studio porch of Maldonado's villa, Rita could see to the cutoff road from Troublesome. A motorcycle escort led a car up their hillside.

Greer emerged with a stranger. Quinn and the man stared at one another.

"Come in, Mal, you're a part of this," Greer said, closing them all in a place flooded with sketches and wire statuettes and a work that had been in progress until the campaign began.

"I want you to meet Mr. Horowitz," Greer said.

"Sir," Quinn said, extending his hand.

"Governor O'Connell?" the man asked.

"Yes."

"I am your brother, Ben."

FORTY-FIVE

The Soviet–Polish Border, 1945— The End of World War II

In the mid-twenties after Lenin died, Stalin took power. The Communists set out to destroy Jewish communal life. Religious life, educational institutions, the theater, the press, were forbidden. Jews were reduced to second-class citizens.

The Soviet borders were sealed, and tragic isolation ensued. Would there be an identifiable Jewish community at the end of World War II?

Small groups of Zionists in Russia kept a thin thread alive to the outside world. Zionism was a cardinal crime, akin to treason. The Zionists, the only Jews to survive intact, were mostly in partisan units in the forests.

Yuri Sokolov was a teenager when he escaped the Warsaw Ghetto and found his way to Jewish partisans operating in White Russia, east of Warsaw. At the time the war ended, he was twenty-two and in command of four companies, and a whispered legend.

Yuri knew about the liquidation of the ghettos, the massive slave-labor camps, and, later, of the genocide. As a surviving Zionist, his mission changed to finding remnants of his group and starting them on the perilous journey across Europe, then running the British blockade into Palestine.

Marina Geller was not yet twenty when she met the fabled Yuri. She had survived the war more easily. She had been taken in by an aunt in Minsk who had married a Christian and converted.

Marina had also come from Zionist stock. At the instant of peace, she set off to find her parents and brothers and sister. After a futile search, she realized her family was just another tiny blip among the millions of murdered Jews.

Marina threw herself into working with the small Zionist units who were now desperately engaged in getting the survivors out of the graveyards of Russia and Poland.

She established a safe house near the Polish border, at Bialystok. They came in twos and threes at first, mostly Zionists who had fought the Germans as partisans.

Now and again the trickle included an orphaned child or one too ill to continue the hellish journey. She turned part of the house into an orphanage, giving a cover to the emigrant-running operation. Marina was able to cull food and medicine as a "legal" orphanage. Soon she had twenty children.

Yuri and Marina were married in a partisan wedding, and even before their passion was spent, they went back to their bitter work.

They vowed, as couples vow, that if Yuri was ever captured by the Soviets, she would make a run to Palestine and wait for him.

It happened in quick order, by the hatred of an informer. Yuri was captured, taken to Moscow, and charged with Zionism. It was a good day for the Soviets, for Yuri Sokolov's name was known far and wide. He would serve as an example to the Jews that they had to conform with the regime and not attempt to establish Jewish contact on the outside.

Although viciously tortured, Yuri refused to stand down. He was sentenced to twenty-five years in a labor camp in the Gulag Archipelago, a frozen waste on the White Sea. He was swallowed up, vanished, and all contact broken.

The time came to close the orphanage in Bialystok. An illegal emigration agent, a Palestinian Jew named Shalom Katz, set up a daring plan to evacuate Marina, her two helpers, and twenty children.

They rode out of Poland in a closed passenger car ostensibly holding high-ranking German prisoners. By the time they had reached the Czech border, the ruse was discovered, but they dashed into Czechoslovakia.

The Soviets demanded the return of the train to

Poland. The British demanded the escapees be taken to refugee camps. The Czech president, Jan Masyryk, son of the father of his country, refused and granted safe passage through his country.

Marina arrived in Palestine by refugee boat just as the Palestine Jews declared independence and were attacked by the Arab nations.

Marina was a rarity, the wife of a great Jewish hero, a hero in her own right. Ben-Gurion himself and Golda Myerson believed she would best serve in America, to wake up that nation's Jews.

Marina traveled the American landscape endlessly to spread the message of the Holocaust and to plead for help in getting survivors to Israel.

Her husband, Yuri, had disappeared in the tundra of the north. Only the occasional rumor surfaced, but no direct word.

Traveling in America on the low side in 1948, she had the same mildewed hotel room, seemed to meet the same welcoming committee, speak to the same small but earnest audience, eat the same homemade meal, fly in the same jerky little airplane, until it all looked like a blur. San Francisco blurred to Oakland blurred to Los Angeles blurred to Phoenix. In those days before jet travel, none of the grand airports had been built. It was a smattering of daredevil pilots' shows at jerkwater landing strips. The roar of the jet lay yet in the distant future.

She traveled with a huge, neatly wrapped poster

depicting her husband, which was unfurled and hung across the back of the podium. Her open-ended tour took her into small towns in Pennsylvania and Oregon, where the few quiet Jewish families wanted to listen.

A year passed during which Marina made over four hundred appearances, building a small but active following. She simply burned out. Her life had been one long struggle. And God only knew what news of her beloved Yuri.

A friend from the Israeli embassy convinced her to remain in America. When she had gotten her vitality back, she would be a strong resource among the Jews. For now she just wanted to be alone.

Marina resumed her maiden name of Geller and vanished into a studio apartment in an area of New York City known as the Village. She was unable to make ends meet on her dole. Her knowledge of the Russian language and Russian history made her attractive for a position when she applied at New York University.

Professor David Horowitz, head of Slavic studies at New York University, thought that Marina was an excellent find.

Safely housed and able to meet her bills, Marina allowed the wonderment of New York to seep in. A bit of anticipation arose whenever she knew she would spend a bit of time with David Horowitz. Kind . . . soft . . . his smile and concern penetrated her depression. Soon it was lunches together, right? Just lunches. A social meeting.

Lunches expanded into dinners. Marina was exposed to the gem shows that played in shoe-box off-Broadway houses that dotted The Village. Four months into their acquaintance, a new sound emerged when she broke into laughter during *The Fantastiks*.

David was much the scholar. No siblings, both parents gone. He had married, had a child, and divorced. His three-year-old son, Ben, was his weekends.

What reached Marina most deeply was the sense of peace that emanated from David. He was so unlike her bombastic Yuri Sokolov.

"Why am I comparing?" she cautioned herself. She had known a few men when she was on her speaking tour, but always awakened in the sludge of guilt. What was stirring her up about David was putting her into a compromising situation. She was married and promised, and promised to return to Israel.

Word reached her that all trace of Yuri had vanished. One of his fellow prisoners thought surely that Yuri was dead.

The woman was on the brink of madness when David Horowitz took her into his arms tenderly and led her into a safe place. Yuri was a fighter. David was a lover. She required love.

David's loft in the Village was a little kingdom of laughter and music and heated scholarly discussion. Teachers knew the place. Students knew the place.

David's great, great friend was a rogue priest, Father Mario Gallico, who taught Latin and ancient Greek at the university. Father Gallico was at their table twice a week, uninvited but always welcome.

Cardinal Watts of the Brooklyn diocese wanted desperately to mend his priest's wayward ideas. The cardinal needed him as a strong arm in Brooklyn, a fixer. After watching Father Gallico make a non-pastoral advance at an adoring secretary, the cardinal shipped him to Manhattan and the lady was returned to her husband.

Marina had completely lost her mantle of freedom fighter. David totally filled her. Thoughts of marriage, of children, were not possible. When his son Ben came for Sunday visits, she hugged and loved him like her own . . . but was that enough?

How many years had gone by without a single word from or about Yuri? Over five years. The promise to go to Israel to meet her husband had lost its rationale. Must she grieve forever for a corpse?

She became pregnant, and she and David chose to have the baby.

Alexander was born to them in 1950. The bliss of being, of existing, was theirs. On the weekends and for short trips, Alexander's half brother, Ben, was there. The four seemed family, close and loving.

"Marina!" a man's voice called.

She turned to see Shalom Katz coming toward her.

She smiled and greeted him warmly, covering up her apprehension. He took her arm and pointed at a park bench in Washington Square.

"It's been years," she said. "Are you still running emigrants?"

"I've retired from Alyiah Bet," he said, referring to the central underground organization. "I'm an Israeli diplomat at the United Nations. Second secretary, or something like that, in the mission."

Marina smiled. Shalom was a cop. Cops looked like cops and acted like cops. The Israeli underground cops were a tough bunch.

"What to do?" Marina wondered. Tell him about her new life, as if he didn't already know? Surely he was bringing her the news of Yuri's demise. At the same time she wept for Yuri, she would scream out her new freedom.

"Why am I so honored by your visit?" she asked.

"With a real government, we are able to accomplish things impossible in the old days. I can speak to you, of course, completely confidentially?"

She nodded.

"We captured a high-ranking Soviet KGB station chief in Jerusalem. He was disguised as a priest in the Russian Orthodox Church. The Russians wanted him back. I was a negotiator. I gave him a list of Zionists they had imprisoned to exchange. Yuri Sokolov is alive."

She leaned against Shalom and shook. "How long have you known this?"

"I wasn't going to inform you until we got an absolute confirmation. We are going to bring out Yuri and two others in exchange for the KGB spy."

"How is he?" she asked shakily.

"The gulag neither killed him nor broke his spirit, but he is a badly damaged man. He has been brutalized. It is a question of your being in Israel to meet him."

"Meet me here tomorrow, same time," she said, and moved away quickly.

Damnable Russian tragedy, the mournful music, the endless dull winters, the bleakness, the walls of cold stone, weeping women in babushkas, the drunk on the street, the listless eyes of a thousand men and women on the escalator coming out of the Metro underground.

Oh, David, what have I done to you? You are my love, greater than anyone. Yuri brought us together, and now he is taking us apart.

Yuri! I have been an unfaithful wife. I have betrayed you. When I had David's child, I wanted to hear news of your death. What the hell, David and Alexander and Ben were nothing more than a dream. Russia is real. No matter what, she had to keep her rendezvous with Yuri in Israel. This great man could not be further broken with a scandal. Secrets had to be kept.

The safety of the child was a need greater than Marina and David's agony. Alexander had to be put up for adoption, and she would return to Israel. But how? Through the Jewish agencies her name would surely be discovered.

Father Gallico was now Monsignor Gallico, a strong servant for Cardinal Watts. His relationship with David Horowitz remained.

"My dear friend, my dear, dear friend," Gallico comforted him. "So, here we are. I will see how I can get it done."

Alexander was a year old when Marina handed him over to Mario Gallico. The child would disappear inside the Catholic bureaucracy.

From that moment on it seemed that death played a hand in silencing those people who had knowledge of the plot.

First to die was Marina Sokolov. She and Yuri knew a moment of peace. They were given respite on a beautiful kibbutz on the Sea of Galilee.

But Yuri was a wreckage of a man, blind in one eye, one leg amputated, violent headaches from his beatings. Marina poured her life into him, but as she did, her own life ebbed from her. She continued to live the big lie, frightened every day that her secret would be discovered. Always wracking her, the terrible longing for Alexander and her beautiful lover, David.

Marina went silently, they said of congestive heart failure. It was a broken heart. Unable to go on without her, Yuri followed her to his grave a year later.

The little convent of St. Catherine held many secrets. One of their unspoken duties was to care for certain "nameless" orphans. Sometimes, these were children of priests and now and again a nun. Other children were sent there to protect them from the notoriety of revelation.

The less the mother superior knew, the safer for the child. "Baby Alex," without a surname, became "Baby Patrick." Parents, unknown. For the next two years Patrick was a centerpiece of the convent, a greatly gifted and adored infant.

During this time the priest Sean Logan had pleaded with Monsignor Gallico for a special child for his sister, Siobhan O'Connell, and her husband, Dan, to adopt.

David Horowitz, sucked of will to live after the loss of his lover and child, succumbed to pneumonia, brought on by neglect of himself.

At first Quinn didn't want to hear the story, felt invaded, exposed in a manner that would bring the walls down on his head.

As Ben spoke, it changed. It turned into a moment he had dreamed of and played out ten thousand times. That moment! That exact moment!

"I was thirteen when our father died," Ben continued. "We had become very close, although any mention of Marina and Alex was simply forbidden. Grief wore him out. Guilt finished him off. He knew nothing about where you were, who you were with, how you were faring. The last year of his life was pitiful. When I reached my bar mitzvah, he revealed to me the circumstances of your disappearance, and he told me that Marina Sokolov had died in Israel, bearing their secret."

"Hell of a bar mitzvah," Greer said.

"Our father told me that I was a man now, and had to assume a man's burden. I only remembered my half brother in veiled tones, and somehow the name of Alexander stuck in my mind."

The melting away of fear in Quinn changed to a flooding gladness as Ben stopped for a drink, noting that the altitude made him dry. He took a small photograph album from his overnight bag and opened it.

"This is our dad."

Quinn felt Rita's hand grip his shoulder as he stared, and said nothing.

Ben drew a deep breath, turned the page. "This is the only photo I have of your mother."

Quinn spun out of his seat and turned his back to them, mumbling to himself in a jerky voice. Ben gulped another glass of water.

"I'm sorry, Ben, I'm being very selfish. Lord, what you must have gone through."

"I knew I'd find you. The search became the hub of my life. I went into police work to specialize in missing persons. After I made detective lieutenant, I joined the faculty of John Jay College for Criminal Justice. For years only cold trails—here are my kids, two boys and two girls. Well, they're not kids anymore. And these are the grandchildren."

"I'm an uncle. God, that's strange, Uncle Quinn. And I'm going to be a grandfather, and my daughter will have cousins and an aunt and an uncle . . ."

"Maybe I could have picked a more appropriate time, but Ms. Crowder convinced me it would be disastrous to hold on to this information . . . so I came."

Ben related the rest of his odyssey. All the principals were dead, and Alexander had disappeared as if into thin air. Ben had vague memories of Monsignor Gallico's visits, but these stopped.

"When Dad died," Ben said, "I was his main survivor. I was there with the family lawyer when we emptied the safe deposit box. There were a few things of value, some stocks, jewelry, certificates of ownership, insurance policies. What I did not know was that Dad had sent a sealed envelope to Monsignor Gallico and his successors. The front read: *Not to Be Opened Until the Year of 2000 by Benjamin Horowitz or His Immediate Heirs.* Here are the contents."

Quinn looked at photos of Marina and David and a birth certificate for a "Baby" Horowitz.

"I tried to play the Catholic card but didn't even get as far as the convent door. It's a deep, dark, mystical world in there, with an understanding of God that is strange and different."

"God sure has a weird sense of humor," Mal grunted.

"It became a matter of numbers: matching footprints on the birth certificate. The FBI had hundreds of millions of prints, but computer clarification had not caught up to them. Footprints of a newborn infant can change, so I went by probable birth dates. Well, everyone gives up a print sooner or later. When yours popped up, it was a very close match to the one on the birth certificate."

"My footprint? How the hell did anyone get my footprint?"

"I didn't, but a certificate told me your name, the time you were born and where. Then I researched Catholic adoption records covering a five-year period. A single line said, 'Baby Patrick, *parents unknown.* Adopted by Daniel and Siobhan O'Connell, Troublesome, Colorado, February 17, 1953.' The rest of it? Baby Patrick grew to be Governor Quinn Patrick O'Connell."

"But how did you confirm your connection with Quinn?" Rita asked.

"Quinn has given innumerable pints of blood to the Red Cross to be used as a bank for a family emergency, and otherwise, he is a regular donor. I was able to get a hold of a pint and run a DNA on it, then one on myself. To make utterly certain, I had Father's body exhumed and took enough to test him as well. The three of us are a match."

"We don't need DNA results," Rita said, lifting off Ben's glasses. "Just look at the two of them."

They drifted down from the tale of fantasia back into Mal's studio.

"Thank God, Ben reached us when he did. If the

public learned after the election, it would be a prelude to a national nightmare," Greer said.

"Am I privy to this?" Mal wanted to know.

"Of course you are," Quinn answered.

"All right, then. We must put this before the American people at once," Mal said. "But no matter what approach you make, you've entered a mine field."

"He'll tell the truth," Rita cried.

"Truth is in the heart of the beholder. Them that wants the truth will believe him. No truth can penetrate them who can't comprehend the truth. They will cry wolf about a Zionist conspiracy. In ten minutes I can find someone in the media down in Troublesome and tip him off that a left-wing Catholic priest planted a Jewish child as part of a Zionist plot. You think that's crazy? Nothing among the haters will be too far-fetched."

Mal looked at the brothers and shook his head. The resemblance was remarkable. "The problem is, Jew hating has always been close to the surface throughout the last two millennia. It's the perfect system of bigotry, time-tested—the Roman sacking of the nation, the divorce of Jesus from the Jews in order to make a new religion, Islam, the ankle-deep blood of Jews by the Crusaders on the Rhine, the Inquisition, Martin Luther, the pogroms of Eastern Europe, and lest we forget, the Holocaust."

"Is the human race forever in a prison of bigotry?" Quinn whispered.

"Quinn, I don't want you or Rita or the kids to have

to walk into a blizzard of hate. Withdraw from the race," Mal said.

Ben once again berated himself for his bounty-hunter zeal. Greer answered him that he had to do what he did. Neither Quinn nor Rita spoke of the terror they had endured before and after the AMERIGUN convention.

"We Jews are the most outstanding example of a patriotic minority," Ben said. "At only two percent of the population, we've created great industries and writers and musicians and doctors. As I teach my students, there are over seventy Jewish American Nobel prize winners. Goddammit, we deserve the respect of our countrymen!"

"There has been no crime . . . no conspiracy," Quinn said.

"Depends on who is telling the story and who is listening," Mal said. "They're all in place, waiting for the news."

"And if I quit, the Second Amendment will never be tested."

"Remember what was done to the Clintons," Rita said. "Destruction, sheer destruction." Her quavering words were her first. She knew what lay ahead if he went on. Quinn was deeply jarred by her less than enthusiastic support. His strong allies in life were becoming his reluctant allies. Greer? What about Greer? She'd be too clever to slip one way or another at this point.

"It's your call, boss," Greer said.

"Like my old commander Jeremiah Duncan said, 'If blood bothers you, don't go on this mission.' Greer, buy some network and cable time. I'll read a statement from here to the American people at one o'clock," and then he laughed, "Rocky Mountain time."

"Call me if you need me," Mal said, and left the studio.

Rita hedged. She'd give no further resistance. She would come to his side. Only, it was shaky knowing what was ahead. Greer saw through it. She took Rita's arm and spun her around.

"Here's truth," Greer snapped. "Quinn Patrick O'Connell cannot and will not walk away from this fight. Never has, never will."

"I know," Rita said with tears streaming down her cheeks. "I know."

"What will you say to the voters, Quinn?" Greer asked.

"Straight up and down, I think. I won't plead or defend. I won't grovel. It's going to be up to the people."

"Oh, Jesus," Greer sighed. "Ben, come with me. We have to sequence your story correctly for the press."

"My nieces and nephews, Duncan and Rae?" Ben asked excitedly. "Isn't Duncan's wife due?"

"Their dad will tell them. You'll be able to meet them in an hour. Excuse me, we've got work to do," Greer said. She and Rita exchanged hard glances.

BREAKING NEWS BREAKING NEWS BREAKING NEWS

"This is Lou Luenberger, MSNBC Denver. We are in Troublesome, Colorado, the home of Democratic candidate, Governor O'Connell. The air around his traveling headquarters has been rife with rumors. The O'Connell people have kept a lid on things, skipping the daily afternoon press briefing. The center of this appears to be a new player on the stage, who flew in from New York this morning. He has been tentatively identified as Detective Lieutenant Ben Horowitz, also a professor of criminology. The governor will make a statement at eleven Eastern, two Pacific Coast time."

Quinn sat, naked to the world. No notes, open collar, no flags, no mantel filled with photographs, no busts of Lincoln or statues by Remington.

"My fellow Americans," Quinn said, "today I experienced one of the most joyous events of my life. As you are aware, I was orphaned at about the age of one year and was raised in a convent until I was three. I do not remember the names of any of the nuns, and I do not know the name of the convent or its location.

"At the age of three I was adopted by my mother and father, Dan and Siobhan O'Connell, ranchers near Troublesome, Colorado.

"My family and I were no more or no less dysfunctional than the average American family. Being Irish, we got into our Eugene O'Neill mode from time to time. In the end, we came back to a most loving relationship.

Dan is gone. Siobhan is very ill. I am the most fortunate person in the world to have been their son.

"Yet for every orphan there is a dual life of fantasy. You cannot separate the orphan from this dream. The need to know your biological parents is a need to know yourself. Who am I, really? Where did I come from? God puts you on a relentless search. You are never a complete person if you do not find your roots.

"Today, I met my brother, Ben Horowitz, who has been searching for me for nearly half a century."

Quinn briefly told the tale of David Horowitz, Marina Geller, and Yuri Sokolov.

Herein lies the rub," Quinn said. "I believe the American civilization has reached a challenging moral plateau. We have made a powerful attempt to rid ourselves of bigotry. We still have a long way to go to rid our nation of racism. If I had been Alexander Horowitz, I believe I would have been elected governor of Colorado. I also believe that Governor Alexander Horowitz could have won the Democratic Party nomination. And I also believe that Alexander Horowitz could win the presidency.

"I am the same man I was yesterday. I have not changed. I will carry on with the same issues I had yesterday. Along with my other commitments, I will fight for the repeal of the Second Amendment.

"I was raised as a Catholic. I will remain in the

Church. Yet I cannot help but inquire into my Jewish heritage. Where this will take me, I cannot predict.

"The human race has had a checkered existence, from the beginning unto this very day, of blood and evil. Yet we come to moral imperatives, like slavery, where we must rise and create a new norm. The issue of guns, I believe, is such a moral imperative. I also believe that the crushing of anti-Semitism is such an imperative.

"I have come to you speaking the truth. If you believe me, if you want what I want for the American civilization, for American decency, then we will carry the day.

"Good day, God bless you, and God bless America."

FORTY-SIX

Balancing a bucket of ice and a bottle of vodka and glasses, Rita backed her way into the guest room and closed the door behind her with her foot.

Greer sat on the bed, back against the headboard, watching another gathering of pundits on TV. Her face bore a rivulet of tears dripping off her nose and chin and carrying down the colors of her makeup. On the nightstand, a dead pint of vodka.

"I'm a fucking mess," Greer wept.

"Mal told me he is plugged into Denver. They've called for volunteers to man the switchboards."

"Quinn?"

"He's with Mal fixing a plan for the balance of the day. No press conference till tomorrow."

Rita set the tray down, poured another for Greer and a double for herself. She left and came back from the bathroom with wet and dry towels, sat on the edge of the bed, and wiped Greer's face as one might a kindergarten pupil.

"What about Duncan and Rae and Lisa?" Greer said, still weeping.

"We saw them before Quinn spoke to the nation. They're with their Uncle Ben now. He's a really nice man."

"I'd better get my shit together," Greer slurred. "Lemme see. Too late to get back to Denver. Then . . . I better be here in the morning. You and Mal pissed at me?"

"I knew Quinn wasn't going to quit," Rita said, "but I just got damned frightened for a moment. I'd better get my attitude straightened out. I'll not live in fear."

"I, uh, got to work out some damage control . . . this can run out of control like a wildfire," Greer said.

"Take a deep breath, Greer, and let's get drunk."

"Hey, two *shiker sikas*!"

"The first reports from Denver and DNC are not that bad."

"Well, now," Greer said, "we have thirty channels of talking-head experts taken out of cold storage and given electric shocks to get their batteries surging. Frankly, I get my in-depth news from E! Channel and Comedy Central. Oh, that goddamn Quinn is a bastard."

"How well I know."

"He's so wonderful," Greer wept. "I called Warren and told him to shag ass and get the yacht up from Florida. I'm going to spend five million dollars on myself in Paris. Son of a bitch . . . we came so close. Now, I've got to leave pretty soon . . . I mean, for all time." Rita dabbed a new downpour of tears from Greer.

"I'm a fucking mess," Greer repeated.

"I want you to know what a courageous thing you have done, Greer. It was the work of a genius. And it was overflowing with love. I think I know how much you love him."

"I love you, too, Rita. Only a very secure woman would have left me alone with Quinn Patrick O'Connell. As I grew to love you more and more, it made things bearable for me."

This was followed by another slug from the bottle, which Greer scarcely needed. The women embraced and hung onto each other. Greer was feather-light. Rita rocked her back and forth and let her blurt.

Rita fluffed some pillows and stretched Greer out and lay beside her so that she held Greer as her baby, and she stroked Greer's head and whispered a Mexican lullaby.

"I love you both," Greer managed.

A moment later there was a knock and the door was opened. There stood Quinn. Rita held her finger to her lips for him to be quiet.

"Some rioting has started," Quinn said. "Birmingham. Chicago is simmering."

"Hadn't you better try to reach the President?" Rita asked.

"He knows what happened and how to reach me."

"Quinn, I'm with you, man."

FORTY-SEVEN

Washington

Marine Corps Helicopter Number One swayed from its Camp David pod and swished urgently for Washington. The President tried his earphones and switched on his mike.

"It's a miracle, Darnell," Thornton said. "I've never believed in divine intervention because it doesn't have a website or a printout. Can we get the election turned around?"

"A lot is going to take place in the next seventy-two hours. You'll have to play it statesman and big daddy."

"Darnell! The man has left us an opening!"

"You've walked into his openings before. Don't even think 'nasty.'"

The President picked up his White House phone. "Martha, this is the President. I want Jacob Turnquist and Hugh Mendenhall in the Oval Office, pronto. Better run down Lucas de Forest," he said of the FBI director. "I want to meet with them in my study alongside the Oval Office."

"Don't you think we'd better have Pucky attend this meeting?"

"Do you know where she is?" Tomtree asked.

"Unless she's away on a campaign speech, she pretty much locks herself in her suite at the White House," Darnell said.

"As a matter of fact," Thornton said, "keep her at the White House. I think it would be wise if she and I made several campaign appearances together."

He looked away from Darnell, lifting the White House phone again.

Darnell became awed for the thousandth time at how the Capitol rose from the dark and dazzled with white, blaring focus on the dome and the monuments. There, the White House ahead. A crowd was gathering in Lafayette Park over the street. What would they chant this night?

Marine Corps One touched down silkily. With neither dog nor wife to greet him, Tomtree stretched his long legs over the lawn toward the portico. "Here they come!"

"Mr. President . . ."

"Mr. President . . . will you tell us . . ."

He turned at the door and held up both hands. "Ladies and gentlemen, as soon as I'm fully briefed, I'll have a statement for you."

"Has Governor O'Connell tried to reach you?"

"How is this going to affect the outcome . . ."

"Mr. President, were you aware . . ."

Thornton disappeared inside. Darnell glanced down the driveway, where TV trucks and the cars of correspondents were hurtling themselves onto the grounds.

Jacob Turnquist was in place as Mendenhall, shirttail askew, entered the Oval Office with a stack of late data.

"Martha! Where the hell is Lucas de Forest?"

"Just got a cell call. He'll be here in ten minutes."

Thornton nodded for her to leave and shut out the world. He pointed at Mendenhall.

"The buzz words," Hugh Mendenhall said, "are general confusion and disbelief. Too early for any kind of reliable polls, but the cable stations are filled with constitutional experts, you know, the musical-chair crowd. The only piece of hard information is that O'Connell is not playing in Birmingham. The KKK is burning a cross before a Jewish-owned department store. One synagogue trashed in Atlanta and inner-city rumblings all over: Watts, Oakland, Harlem, Detroit, East Saint Louis."

"All black?"

"Yes, sir, seems like the Muslim preachers are really trying to get them stirred up. While the new data is pouring in, I'm trying to canvas tomorrow's newsprint editorials."

"Are any in yet?"

"Yes, sir," Mendenhall answered, and reluctantly passed a special edition of the *New York Times.*

IS GOVERNOR O'CONNELL TO BE BELIEVED?

"There is nothing in O'Connell's ancient past or recent candidacy to even hint he has ever lied or deliberately deceived the public. The *New York Times* finds no reason to withdraw our endorsement of him for president."

"Jesus Christ!" Thornton said, hitting the desk.

"Mr. President," Jacob Turnquist said, "don't read in too much. The *New York Times* is a Jewish newspaper catering to an enormous Jewish population. We can expect a number of his endorsers to defect to us."

"Mr. President, Director de Forest is here," Martha said over the intercom.

Lucas de Forest, the nation's first black FBI director, was Tomtree's showpiece nominee. He had returned the New Orleans Police Department to a position of respect and then done the same in Philadelphia. Only thing about him, he was too damned assertive and at times played a bit loose with citizens' rights. He and Thornton had bucked heads on Internet issues. The FBI wanted to be able to break into lines such as the Bulldog Network. One of the reasons Thornton was in the White House was to keep that from happening, and do nothing to fog up business transactions.

Nonetheless, de Forest was a great cop.

"What's your read, Lucas?" Tomtree asked after they were bolted in.

Lucas looked like a cop, and even more like a boxer, whose face had caught its fair share. Yet he was a rock. He turned to Hugh Mendenhall.

"We're only a couple hours into this thing," Lucas said. "Hugh, what's going on on the Internet?"

"Every little neo-Nazi and White Aryan Christian Arrival website is beating the keys. Real puss stuff."

"What about the TV media?"

"Utter confusion amplified by their panels. No one has called O'Connell a flat-out liar . . . yet."

"For the moment, I think we are in good shape," Lucas went on. "If the outburst is confined to the hate groups, we'll have no problem dealing with them . . . and I don't feel any of them has a great reach into the mainstream, or the stamina to make a continuing fight."

"What worries me," Jacob Turnquist said, "is the inner cities. The conditions are in perfect alignment to have a black pogrom against the Jews, Cossack-style. 'Now is the time, brothers, to vent all your frustrations against Jewish slum lords,' et cetera, et cetera."

"You're right," Lucas answered directly. "We can't allow brush fires to flare up in the inner cities."

"Do you believe the situation will deteriorate that much?" Tomtree asked.

"Mr. President, a riot takes on a life of its own," Darnell answered.

Mendenhall whispered over the phone in the attached pantry. Knee-jerk reaction was coming in from the Christian Right, careful criticism with a tinge of rancor. Yet no one outside the hate groups had branded O'Connell as a flat-out liar. More hot spots were developing from the Aryans and the Klan.

"I think we'd better make a statement," Darnell said.

"Press or TV?"

"Right now a press release will have to do," Tomtree said.

"Those news dogs are hunting out there," Mendenhall said.

"A statement will hold things for a while," Darnell reckoned.

"Jacob?"

"You are on to the events of tonight," Jacob said as he stopped to ponder. "Something to the effect that nothing has changed, *if* O'Connell is telling the truth. Then go on to say you hope all the facts are in *before* the election."

"That's accusatory," Darnell said.

"I don't think so," Turnquist answered. "He doesn't say Jew, he doesn't say liar—"

"He says," Darnell interrupted, "if the dog hadn't stopped to take a shit, he'd have caught the rabbit."

Thornton closed his eyes and mumbled lightly as he ran through the words.

"*Wall Street Journal* editorial, Mr. President." Mendenhall read, "The waters have been muddied. The safe course is to stick with the President."

A thump of delight, of tension falling.

"Jacob, jot out my announcement. *If* O'Connell is telling the truth, and we hope we can learn that *before* the election, we can save the nation from a perilous direction."

"Dammit! Cut the last part," Darnell said, "we don't have to issue a warning citation. Everyone knows what we're talking about. Mr. President, you have a chance here to make a statesmanlike, brilliant, meaningful pronouncement . . ."

"Such as?"

"Well, try this on," Darnell answered. "I've read the Constitution, and nothing in it says it is illegal for an orphan to find his parents. The question has no part in this election."

Turnquist winced. Mendenhall winced. Lucas de Forest was politically noncommittal, but Thornton seemed unable to stop himself from taking a free kick at his opponent.

"We'll go with *if* O'Connell, *before* the election. We'll cut the part about saving the nation, for now," the President said.

"Mr. Director, what kind of contingency plan do we have for this?" he asked Lucas de Forest.

The director took a large three-ring binder from his worn old briefcase, put it on the coffee table, and bent down to it.

TOP SECRET—OPERATION JOY STREETS, the title page read. "In the event of civil disobedience by antigovernment groups—this is not a plan that includes students."

"Don't the damned campuses always erupt?" Tomtree asked.

"Mr. President, there is no occasion where a campus has rioted against the Jewish population," de Forest said, "but we can't rule them out. This is a unique situation."

"Run this Joy Streets past me," Thornton asked.

"Phase One, alert FBI; Bureau of Alcohol, Firearms, and Tobacco; U.S. Marshal Service; establish local communications to Washington headquarters."

Lucas buzzed down the page with his finger, omitting the details.

"Okay, here we go," he read. "This is also part of Phase One: Contact our moles, informers, spies in suspected groups. This is key to Phase One . . . namely, ascertain from our infiltrators if their cell, group, Klavern, et cetera, have preselected bombing targets or persons to be assassinated. Name and address of cell leaders."

"How many moles have we planted?" the President asked.

"A couple a hundred," Lucas answered. "Of these, two or three dozen have totally infiltrated and are reliable. The rest from luke cold to luke warm."

Thornton waved for Lucas de Forest to continue.

"Mr. President, let's take a look at this Phase One. If we

can have our people at the controls and if we can stop three or four bombings, it is going to disrupt their attack."

"I disagree," Thornton said. "If we initiate this first call-up only on the suspicion of what might happen, then the people will think we are trigger-happy, overplaying our hand and the like."

"But the call-up is secret," de Forest argued.

"Hell," Hugh Mendenhall popped in. "Five minutes after you initiated Phase One the press would know it."

"You see, we've branded O'Connell, with some success, as being the reckless gunfighter," Thornton said.

"But, sir," de Forest persisted, "if we hesitate in putting Phase One into motion, it could entirely lose its effectiveness. The idea behind Joy Streets is to beat them to the punch."

"Keep reading please, Mr. Director," Tomtree ordered.

"Phase Two, deputize all urban police forces and county sheriffs to round up and detain suspects. Phase Three, call up the National Guard in threatened locales. National Guards to maintain a peace-keeping posture."

"It's starting to sound like the Keystone Kops," the President said.

"How, sir? Once we have a list of priority people and buildings to defend and have the National Guard on the street and we have rounded up their leadership, we'll snuff it by the middle of the day, tomorrow."

"Let's hear the rest of this plan," Thornton said, knowing he'd made up his mind.

"The rest of the phases deal with a full-court press on the streets—curfews, ultimatums, finally call up the Army and Marines for martial law."

"Bad news," Mendenhall interrupted. "Jewish community center in Los Angeles was just bombed."

"We can't count this as a trend," Jacob Turnquist grunted academically. "Just sporadic incidents."

"If we do not put Phase One into motion, we'll be playing in a game we can't win. If we allow fires to erupt, the fires will consume everything until they burn themselves out," de Forest warned.

"And I say that jumping the gun sends a bad signal to the American people. It might be all over with by dawn," said Tomtree.

"I wouldn't count on that," de Forest said. "This is a matter of public safety, sir . . ."

"Mendenhall."

"Sir."

"Run off a copy of this Joy Streets for my personal use. You've got to know when to hold and know when to fold. What else have you got there, Mr. Director?"

"Release form, Mr. President. An executive order to be signed by you to put Joy Streets into motion."

"Just leave it here. Thank you, gentlemen," Thornton said, nodding to each. "Mr. Jefferson, remain, please."

The three left, consumed with apprehension. Hugh Mendenhall ran Joy Streets through a copier. A note was handed to Director Lucas de Forest.

"Shit. Synagogue torched in Baltimore." He glared at Mendenhall, who threw up his arms.

"I don't know why," Hugh said defensively. "The chief plays a mean poker hand."

Thornton unlaced his shoes and rubbed his feet. He'd never seen Darnell Jefferson suddenly become so haggard. "I think we're on the right track, Darnell, but you looked like you were ready to explode."

"Because," Darnell said hoarsely, "I know something that I didn't know before."

"What would that be?"

"I really don't think you can comprehend what I've got to say, Thornton."

"It's too late to speak in riddles, and we've got a bitch of a day tomorrow. I'm wondering now, how do we approach the last days of the campaign?"

"Well, just travel right into the riot spots."

"That could be messy. I think . . . I think we buy two thirty-minute time slots a day, one at noon, one at eight in the evening, and we'll do a combination infomercial/up-to-the-minute report."

Darnell Jefferson turned on his heel. "Darnell! Do not leave!" Darnell's hand dropped from the doorknob. "Now, what is it you know you didn't know before?"

"All about my life," Darnell said. "It isn't very interesting."

"Sit down, have a drink," Thornton said. "This thing could be volatile, because—"

"Because you want it to become volatile," Darnell

said, looking down, then into the President's eyes. "You want some more bombs to go off, cemeteries desecrated, synagogues burned to the ground, *Kristallnacht*, you want a *Kristallnacht.* Then their big daddy president will move in and save the day. You want to deliberately start Joy Streets late so you can take on the role of savior."

"Are you trying to say I'm orchestrating these riots?"

"You knew they would happen, brother. And you knew you could have stopped them dead in their tracks a half hour ago. But there is more. You want some blood on the streets as well. Every time someone is killed or wounded, the pressure mounts on O'Connell to quit and withdraw."

"That's diabolical!" Thornton protested.

"It sure is. Thornton, stick this in your craw. Every casualty that puts pressure on O'Connell puts even more pressure on you."

Thornton turned his eyes away.

"It's down to simple math. If the people believe O'Connell, they will vote him into office next week," Darnell said. "If they believe you, they will vote to reelect you."

Tomtree averted his eyes from his friend's piercing glare in a manner he had not done since they were teenagers.

Darnell became a bundle of sweating, pleading. "God, man, stop these riots!"

Knowing that Thornton was not going to budge, Darnell backed off, broken, to whine: "I've been following a black-hearted man all my life. My daddy believed there was a bright star in the east the night you were born. Like Jesus! 'Thornton's mind can go into places where no one can follow. He will achieve ultimate greatness for himself and for the human race.' I believed that, too. I believed you would never make a decision that knowingly put America in danger."

"That's enough, Darnell."

"No, it isn't. The reason you are doing this tonight is that seed already planted in a gangly, pimply excuse for a basketball player in Pawtucket. You were pissed then, and you're pissed now. World! T3 is going to even up the score for his friendless life."

"I said, that is enough!"

Darnell ignored him. "The Bulldog Network, absolute secrecy guaranteed. A paragon of human achievement. Why did Thornton Tomtree love that? Big-time greed is where the power is, where the big bucks play. Greed is the curse of making yourself a deity in your own eyes up to a point where you cannot manage a human relationship. Greed is justifying any and all means of control. You're an electronic monster! We have a president uncaring of how many people are killed on the streets so long as he wins his reelection."

"I knew you'd end up weeping on your knees, big-time, when the going got tough. You didn't know what the presidency is all about," Thornton said.

Hugh Mendenhall slipped in.

"Muslims stirring up a riot in Detroit. That's a very incendiary place. Michigan governor Grayson McKenney has just called up the National Guard."

"Goddammit! Grayson's a Republican. He should have called me first!"

"At the moment AMERIGUN is setting up for a TV and website blast starting in the morning. Otherwise, these brush fires continue to pop up."

"Colorado?" Thornton snapped. "Has O'Connell called up his guard?"

"Negative. Nothing seems to be happening in Denver."

"Any idea how we might set Denver off?" Thornton asked.

"I don't fucking believe this!" Darnell cried.

"Sit down and shut up, Darnell."

More news of rioting. The downtown areas of a dozen cities began to flame to the beat of broken glass!

Kristallnacht!

Thornton moved to his study, adjoining his bedroom, where he had a setup of a dozen TV monitors. Snips were arriving of tear gas, swinging batons . . . now water cannons!

"Okay, buster," Thornton said to himself, "so let us play chicken, O'Connell, let's play chicken!"

Ben Horowitz was damn near inconsolable, taking the blame for turning the devil forces loose.

Quinn's calm calmed them all. No chinks in the armor, no wringing hands, no shouts to God. He spoke softly as the news reached him and gave quick, thoughtful responses.

"Nebraska has just called up the Guard," Greer said.

"I didn't think we were doing that well in Nebraska. How many call-ups?"

"Nine states, six states pending. Twenty-eight states report no rioting activity . . . but, Jesus, if the President doesn't issue an order . . . how long?"

A car bomber plunged into the plate-glass window of Feldman Toyota on the auto mile of San Francisco.

A gunman entered the Lew Singer Deli on lower Broadway and sprayed the place with automatic fire. Six are known dead, twenty wounded.

A bonfire of books from the Judaica sections of the Jacksonville Library licked the sky while encircling neo-Nazis saluted and chanted.

Ketchum, Idaho, Bank hit by a dozen militia. Half million dollars taken. One dead.

As the night settled in, the question at hand was the upcoming day. Bitter O'Connell haters watched how the authorities were responding to see what situations would be ripe for daylight exploiting.

And the governors and mayors watched, to use their forces gingerly and not get into a situation of putting a thousand of their citizens against their own arms.

And the sound of *Kristallnacht*!

The Reverend Amos Johnson was the surviving icon of the early civil rights movement. He had risen to challenge for the presidency twice in primaries and walked off with eighteen percent of the vote.

His personal ambitions chilled by the white establishment, Amos became a dynamic wellspring of hope for his people and gathered in a large Hispanic following as well.

There was a time of separation between a liberal Jewish activism and the black community. Some African-American leaders scolded their former allies as pious do-gooders looking down with pity on their black brothers.

Into this mix crept the inevitable ancient tentacles of anti-Semitism. The slum lord, Jewish wealth, Jewish power, now grated on those downtrodden ghetto dwellers.

Amos Johnson himself took the view that the Jews

were patronizing them without either deep love or conviction.

Attempts to heal a widening rift by covering the issues with a Band-Aid did not help.

The Black Muslim movement fanned a constantly smoldering pall of anti-Semitism. The Jew is the enemy!

The Reverend Amos Johnson had worked closely with too many Jewish politicians and leaders not to realize that the two communities were inexorably bound together by tragedies.

The Jews, as a people, had reached many of their goals. This angered some and enraged other blacks whose gains came slower and with more pain.

A cycle emerged of black for the sake of black. Reverend Amos Johnson always gave a wide berth to the hate teachings of the Muslim Nation. Despite his high regard in the country, Reverend Amos never publicly rebuked them on any issue.

It was not as though the history, leadership, and white citizens deserved better. They had wrought a system of injustice that was ending in black-white polarization. Black juries proved as prejudiced as white juries had always proved.

The firebrand days were behind Johnson, and three of his children, two of them daughters, were members of Congress. They badgered him constantly to lead the African-American community out of perpetual victimhood.

As soon as the riots started, his children rushed to his

home, held hands, and prayed for guidance. Outside, a crowd of believers started numbering in the thousands, backing up clear to both street corners.

The media included black cable TV channels and a black press.

"Now hear me!" Amos began.

"We hear you," was the response.

"We have been driven to the wall time and time again throughout our tragic history in this nation. We are in pain!"

"Pain!"

"We are in agony! We still await our walk in the sun!"

"You tell us, Reverend!"

"Slowly, slowly, always too slowly we have crawled the crawl, feeding on crumbs of this wealthygate society. We yet await our walk into the sun!"

"Hallelujah!"

"Tonight!" Amos cried.

"Tonight!" was responded.

"We will play the role given us by Yahweh to be full Americans. We will set aside the injustices for the moment, and we will be Americans first! We who have suffered the terror of lynchings and dogs and nightsticks and hate-filled policemen . . . we who suffered all this say: we will not be used as monsters to bring down another American community!"

"Amen!"

"Do not let the forces of evil in and out of our community let us be used to do unto another what has been done to us! No matter what our personal experiences with Jews, we just set them aside, for Yahweh has commanded us to save our brothers!"

Silence swept over them.

"We who have been denied the right of full citizenship will not be used to deny that right to others. Let no black man stain himself with the blood of a Jew, because, if the carnage is not stopped, the black man and woman will become the next target. America must exist with all its little communities intact, or it will not exist at all. We must now set our own grievances aside because tonight we are Americans!"

Amos turned away from the bank of microphones into the embrace of his wife and children.

"You said the right thing, Daddy," his daughter told him.

"The hate is killing us," Amos whispered.

Milwaukee was quiet. The skin heads of Milwaukee looked time and again for police on the streets. There were none. They grew bolder. A call went out on their website for an immediate gathering.

Sixty bald heads swathed in black leather and adorned with swastikas marched toward the Beth El Synagogue singing one of the good old blackshirt songs.

When Jewish blood
is dripping from our daggers . . .

* * *

BREAKING NEWS BREAKING NEWS BREAKING NEWS

"This is Charlotte Cassidy, CBS, Memphis. Southern Grand Dragon Potter Wesley has called for a four-state convergence of the Klan at Memphis to parade at daybreak. Mr. Wesley! Sir! May I have a few words with you?"

"No."

"How many klaverns do you think can make it to Memphis by daylight?"

"What did you hear?" he growled.

"Upward of a thousand Klansmen."

"I won't dispute that, and while we're at it, let me tell you something. CBS is just another Jew network."

"I understand that some of your people will be carrying weapons—"

"This is a peaceful march. The KKK does not believe in violence against niggers or kikes. Now, if some folks want to bring along a weapon to defend themselves, ain't much I can do about that."

"The KKK show of force," Charlotte said, "will not be disturbed as long as it remains undestructive, says the chief of police. However, a survey of college campuses in the vicinity indicates that the Klan will run head-on into growing ranks of students."

BREAKING NEWS BREAKING NEWS BREAKING NEWS

San Francisco.

Eric Cardinal Mueller, a dean and often spokesman,

took his seat as the cameras honed in on him and the commentator spoke, softly giving the priest's background.

"It is the never-ending mission of the Church to find truth and speak truth even to the point of admitting Church wrongdoing in the past. No church can survive on lies. Since World War II our foundations have been rocked by the passive role of the Vatican during the Holocaust. In this search for truth, we are now investigating our role in the Spanish Inquisition.

"Only a half century ago Jewish citizens of Germany cried out in the night for their neighbors to help them. As they slammed the door in Jewish faces, the gates of Auschwitz were opened."

"A *Kristallnacht* is shaping up in the streets of our cities and in our countryside. In the end we have to earn our keep as Christians.

"We are still haunted by the Holocaust. The Holocaust is not a Jewish problem. The Holocaust is a Christian problem. We cannot permit this to happen, for if we do, we will wipe out our own teachings."

"Turn that goddamned thing off!" Thornton snapped. "That goddamn kraut cardinal now wants to slap their guilt on us. Don't forget, O'Connell is still a Catholic. And the Reverend Amos and his three kids are still Democrats."

As Thornton received the minute-to-minute reports,

Darnell all but hid himself in a corner, shriveling into a fetal position. It was befalling him to empty his head of his life and deeds. Surely, in a showdown Thornton Tomtree would come down on the side of decency. That proposition had kept them in place for over four decades. Why couldn't he have seen what he saw now?

T3 was doing no more or less than making him an extension of himself. No, he would not curve the course. No, he would not go down graciously.

Yes, he would endanger the nation!

Oh, Lord! Darnell thought. There will be a still photograph to mark the era, like the Marines raising the flag on Iwo Jima, or the little oriental war baby sitting in the middle of the road, or John-John Kennedy saluting his father's coffin. What will this photograph be? A burning Star of David? Blood on the street? Someone's stuffed bunny being clutched by a dead infant? What will be our *Kristallnacht*? Like the Monica Lewinsky–Clinton embrace, the *Kristallnacht* will bring back an ugly moment.

Dr. Jacob Turnquist did not sit opposite the President with a great deal of comfort. He squirmed.

"As the hard right groups have had a chance to organize, we can expect a renewal of street activities at daybreak. Once these incidents hop from town to town . . . I think we've reached a danger point."

That was not what Thornton wanted to hear. He needed to speak to the vice president, to ascertain that the bedrock Christian Coalition was still in place. What was Thornton weighing? Why? How much danger should he allow?

Mendenhall came in sallow, a single sheet quivering in his fingers.

"Well!"

Mendenhall cleared his throat, a signal of a coming disaster. "Editorials for tomorrow, one hundred largest markets. Front page, ninety-two. Pro rioters, so long as they protest without destroying property or life . . . twenty. Call for the President to react . . . eighty-one. Believe Governor O'Connell . . . seventy-eight. Zionist plot . . . three. Postpone election . . . yea, twelve, nay, eighty . . ."

"Shit!" Thornton mumbled.

"Some of the editorials hit pretty hard," Mendenhall said.

Thornton looked to Turnquist angrily. It was one thing to sit at a conference table espousing his political Princeton wisdom, but quite another to be in the bunker with shells flying all around.

"Vice president is on the phone."

"Thank God," Thornton said. "Where the hell did you set down, Matthew?"

"I'm in Tulsa."

"Bring me up to date."

"I have canvassed twenty-five of our largest Coalition churches. It's a very mixed reading, Mr. President. It seems that O'Connell has made very significant inroads into our solid front. The women don't seem to want guns, many of the men idolize O'Connell as a great hero, school prayer a non sequitur, and uh, right of choice . . ."

"What!"

"Well, they've always been taking the goddamned pill and visiting abortion clinics. They just feel it shouldn't be covered up any longer. You've got to make a move. All we are doing is reaching now. We have to put men on the street and go on the offensive."

"I was hoping I could hold up the process until afternoon," Thornton said. "It crosses a thin line for reelection."

"It's very dangerous," the vice president insisted.

"How do you stand personally in this!" Thornton demanded.

"We are speaking of a very disturbing image of America creeping in. Stop them now!"

Thornton slammed the receiver, then picked up another phone. "Find me Lucas de Forest," he ordered.

It was four-thirty in the morning, a few hours left before the curse of darkness turned into the curse of daylight. He noticed the devastated Darnell Jefferson, an old slave in sorrow. Couple of good shakes and Darnell would be back on board.

"Hello!"

"Mr. President, this is Lucas de Forest."

"Where the hell are you, Lucas?"

"At FBI headquarters. I'm cleaning out my office."

"What! I did not fire you."

"I resigned. I left an envelope for you on your secretary's desk."

"Well, I don't accept the resignation," Thornton said, alarmed that such news would all but seal his doom. "I'm declaring a national emergency . . . and you must stay."

Lucas de Forest throbbed, head, heart, joints, eyes. "Are you ready to order Joy Streets into motion?"

"Tomorrow at . . . say, ten o'clock."

"Mr. President," wheezed Lucas, "you are a schmuck."

"Don't hang up . . . don't hang up . . . all right, Lucas, what do you have in mind?"

"Joy Streets immediately. Phase One and Phase Two simultaneously. Yea or nay, sir?"

Darnell had uncrumpled himself, went over and took the phone from Thornton's hand.

The two men locked onto one another with a ferocity never known before. He handed the phone back to the President.

"I agree," Tomtree said. He hung up and continued his venomous glare. "All I needed was a few more hours to make this work right."

"Sure, boss," Darnell said. "So, you've gotta know when to hold and know when to fold. I'm picking up my chips, Thornton."

"What? Oh, you mean our heated little discussion? Forget it, pal. We've got a pile of work to do to get the story out straight . . . Darnell, are you listening . . . Darnell, are you really going to leave me? You won't be so godawful righteous without those humongous T3 checks coming in!" Thornton cried.

"Doesn't make any difference, man. I've given most of the money away, anyhow. Got a spin for you, free. Why don't you blame Forest de Lucas for the late start on Joy Streets. Overriding your FBI head shows real balls."

"Do you think we can use it?" Thornton asked earnestly.

"Jesus, I'm all dry," Darnell said. "Not enough to wad up a good spit in your face."

What would the photograph of *Kristallnacht* portray?

American hate? American decency.

Oh, say, can you see, by the dawn's early light?

FORTY-EIGHT

"I've never seen anyone with the will to equal Siobhan's," the doctor said.

"Five more days," Quinn begged.

"I don't see how. She sinks to a near comatose state then forces herself awake, in unbearable pain and saturated with drugs. She will fight until she has a half hour, an hour of clarity. On one of these slumbers, she is bound to go."

Quinn sat at the bedside holding her fragile hand. The sun always crossed this room lovely in January. The big mountain outside became diffused and, as the sun inched along, it made a montage of colors, then dipped below the horizon.

Her books were varied, a generations old Bible in both Gaelic and English. They read to her now, Thoreau and *Leaves of Grass.* She'd nod that she understood and one could not help but feeling their content fortified her.

Siobhan's eyes fluttered open, scared at first, until Quinn came into focus. "Son."

"Can you understand me all right, Mom?"

"Yes."

"Rita and I have to leave tomorrow. We are already two days late. But they're planning a party for you. Rae and Duncan and Ellie and the baby—Dan Wong O'Connell, named after our dads—will all be here."

"They should be with you."

"I'll have Rita and Mal, and my brother Ben."

"How gracious you all are. . . ." Her eyes rolled back and she winced, gripping his hand with what poor, little power she had.

"Bad, Mom?"

"I wouldn't wish it on Hitler."

Her pain passed through. "Four generations of O'Connells," she said. "Now, that is a family . . . that is a . . . family." Siobhan rallied for she knew she'd go under again soon. "Dan's Chinese great-grandson. Quinn," she cried, "what of you?"

"God willing, we are beyond middle-ages inquisitions in our Congress. Clinton had to stand naked before the world and take more humiliation than any human being ever had. In the end, it was he and his wife who came through it with courage and dignity. Are you okay, Mom?"

"I'll tell you when I've had enough."

"I believe in the decency of the American people," Quinn said.

Siobhan made the tiniest of smiles and indicated he should read her to sleep from one of the books on the bedside table. Quinn knew his mother was starting her journey, fighting to understand the words he spoke, hearing his voice last, as she desired.

"From *Generations*," Quinn said, "Ralph Waldo Emerson." He opened the volume to where it was marked, then closed it and recited. "'Man is a god in ruins,'" he said. "'When men are innocent, life shall be longer and pass into the immortal as gently as we awake from dreams.'"

Siobhan nodded.

"'Now, the world would be insane and rabid," he went on, "if those disorganizations should last for hundreds of years. It is kept in check by . . . by . . .'"

"Death," she said.

"'It is kept in check by death and infancy. Infancy,' our Daniel Wong O'Connell, 'Infancy is the perpetual Messiah when it comes into the arms of fallen men, and pleads with them to return to paradise.' Mom, I feel great love from the American people and they know I will brook no evil."

Siobhan's voice fell so low he had to lay his ear to her lips. "Can I say it, just once?"

"Sure."

"Mr. President," she whispered and closed her eyes.

The authors of the Constitution overlooked a January inaugural, too damp and cold for the great American street carnival.

A thousand miles of bunting decorated Washington as icing on a big cake. The National Mall ballooned with science tents and food tents and history tents and technology and discovery and art tents.

And in all the auditoriums came the sounds of America singing, singing gospel and Mormon hymns and rock and samba and, of course, bluegrass. Bagpipes and the horns of Dixieland. There was a dance tent where Irish step dancers followed a Mexican folk dancing group and children's choruses. There was a gay men's chorus and drummers from Korea and Hawaii and India.

And in the Kennedy Center the National Sympathy played lofty, patriotic music of the great plains and seacoasts and mountains and cities reaching up as fingers to God.

On they disgorged from Dulles and Reagan Airports and the Union Station until the great statues smiled from their pedestals.

There would be thirty something inaugural balls and the faithful would wait breathlessly for the five minute appearance of the President and First Lady.

As the mood of the great party filtered over the land, a king would grumble with envy of it.

January 19, 2009

Quinn had disciplined himself to be able to sleep anytime, anyplace, for however long he was allowed. Without this, few politicians could survive.

Quinn reached over the bed for Rita. *Where am I? Oh, that's right. Blair House.* He flopped back on his pillow, then propped up on an elbow as he caught sight of Rita penning something at the desk. She sat before the window, curtains open, snowflakes falling outside. He watched until she finished.

Rita folded the sheet of paper and wrote *Quinn* on it. She found the suit she had laid out for him and slipped it in his pocket. She drew the curtains and they cuddled in and lay thus until morning . . . each now so aware of the moment they could not speak.

By dawn the snow had stopped. Branches swayed and fluffed off their patches of white.

"The sun is trying to break through," Rita said, as steam rose on the lawn. "Are you sure you don't want me at the prayer breakfast?"

"It will be understood."

"I'll pray here for Siobhan. You pray for the country." Rita disappeared into the dressing room to begin her countdown.

Rita had commissioned Stetson to make them a pair of matching Western hats, not too cowboy, not too in your face, but a sort of Clark Gable riverboat gambler hat. Quinn felt very Colorado for the moment.

After the prayer breakfast he would meet the congressional leaders and Rita would join him for traditional tea with the outgoing president.

* * *

Pucky, at her most gracious, was as gracious as they came. She schooled Rita to take over the enterprise of operating the White House. During these frosty days, Thornton Tomtree scarcely left his study. No songs to cheer him, no ladies to endear him. There was the bittersweet moment Darnell Jefferson returned. They were destined to crash on a Noah's Rock, together. Tom's BULLDOG held no answers.

"I had control of the greatest single invention in the history of mankind. I thought we'd hit the ground running," Thornton said. "What the fuck happened?"

"I could sure go for a Bloody Mary," Darnell said.

"Go ahead. You don't have to be on the reviewing stand. What the fuck happened?"

The first sip was good, the second sip delicious.

"Well?" Thornton pressed.

"You know, Thornton, people are driven by this machine, our personalities. We obey it even when we don't know what we are doing. Our personality always tells us we are right. We cannot understand clashing with someone else's personality who tells us we are wrong. That's how you became a president. But, hell, your engine took you exactly where you wanted to go."

"Then why am I so overjoyed? Thornton snarled.

"That personality drove you to earning twenty-five billion dollars, the American presidency, and for a fleeting moment you nearly gained control of all the king's horses and all the king's men."

"I had it right here," he said, showing his fist. Darnell turned his eyes away. "Didn't I?"

"The people didn't think so, Thornton. Greed is endemic but when the time came to have the Lincoln Memorial sponsored by Nathan's hot dogs, they shamed."

Thornton tried to understand.

"We name our children after our father and mother, or an aunt or a hero. We bury our dead in green lawns and bring fresh flowers to keep their sainted memory. We weep on bad days of remembrance of our family. We toil for them. We are tender to our aged. And we fight them tooth and nail."

"And . . . ?"

"I haven't cried for a dead computer," Darnell said. "Men like us, who were there at the beginning, should taught have computers their proper place, before they gained control over the morals of half the human race."

"Hasn't that always been the game?" Thornton asked. "The irresistible personality in man driving us to wars. So, what do we do, Darnell?"

"We may think we're hot stuff now, but we've a lot of catching up to become as great as we have been in our past. Fortunately, there is a lot to draw on."

Thornton Tomtree paled. "And Quinn O'Connell personifies our past greatness . . . and . . . the way to the future. That son of a bitch. You said I had no control over the drive of my personality."

"That's right, Thornton."

Pucky entered. "The O'Connells are arriving. We should meet them at the front door."

"This tea is a pretty shitty tradition, if you ask me," Thornton said, creaking out of his seat. "What the hell do we talk about?"

"Oh, the Denver Broncos," Darnell said, "O'Connell is a Bronco junky."

"I, Quinn Patrick O'Connell do solemnly swear that I will faithfully execute the office of President of the United States, and will, to the best of my ability, preserve, protect, and defend the Constitution of the United States."

In all the heavens we know of and all the heavens we know nothing of, can there be a more almighty event to befall a single, lone person?

The thousands arrayed before him in chilled air did not budge.

"I have come to you for about a year to listen to your aspirations and to present you with my vision of the future. You have told me, resoundingly, that now is time for America to travel the high road. The high road requires of every citizen to lend their energy to one gigantic swell for progress and decency. . . ."

Quinn reviewed the things he wanted to bring to

America, always with reference to the most generous and decent people in the world.

And, in a few moments, because it was very cold, he concluded on his lofty theme, knowing he will be fought all the way, but daring those who would turn him back or those whose robber hearts who would take the planet down.

"The human race," Quinn said, "has functioned from its first day on the proposition that some people are superior to others and thus empowered to rule and exploit those people of lesser stuff. Humanity is often mistaken as civility. Humans have always been somewhat less than human. Well then, how do we score this game? Every so often a MORAL IMPERATIVE demands that we must alter our sense of humanity or fade into the stardust of the universe.

"Slavery and our Civil War was just such a MORAL IMPERATIVE. After the Holocaust we believed, did we not, that no such event could happen again in the family of man. But genocide by the human race to the human race has happened over and over.

"In the beginning of the last century we awakened to the invention of electric light and airplanes and the X ray and the automobile and film. And, also, the machine gun, a weapon that killed twenty thousand men at the Somme River in a single day.

"We kick the door open now and march into this twenty-first century with more promise that the human race can solve the enormous tasks before of feeding and giving a decent life and preserve this planet.

"When the sums are added, the meaning of the past century was a rising of people to liberate themselves from their masters. It was the century of Mandela.

"Yet the seeds of hatred are within us all. Along with un-rivaled progress in our way of life, we must face the demand of a MORAL IMPERATIVE with the goal of eradicating racism. Racism from person to person, tribe to tribe, and nation to nation is the greatest blight on the people of this land, of this world.

"No, we can never defeat it entirely. But we must know to recognize it, confront it, and destroy it wherever it surfaces.

"And, in this matter, we have a richness of different communities and our basic decency to say, who better than America can lead the way."

There was a long, long moment of silence as Quinn stepped away. Then from this side of the Mall and that side and from the stands a single word was chanted and swelled till the old town shook.

"QUINN!" they cried, "QUINN! QUINN! QUINN!"

Ah, it was a good thing Rita remembered to slip in a couple of pairs of après-ski boots in the presidental limo for the street was slushy. They walked to the White House as hands reached out begging for a touch, crying the chant.

Quinn saw an awed little fellow of about twelve whose clothing told him he was poor. Quinn halted for a moment, took off his new Stetson, and put it on the lad.

A few moments later they took their places in the reviewing stand and up Pennsylvania Avenue came the Marine Corps band. It stopped before Gunner Quinn and, behind the trumpet and drum roll, played "Hail to the Chief."

And on came America.

Chinese dragon dancers.

And a man on stilts dressed as Uncle Sam.

And floats with coal miners and mules from Virginia and a lobster boat from Maine.

And up the street marched the Mount St. Joseph High School band of Bloemer, New Mexico, who traveled to the capital on money earned picking crops.

And the replica of the Statue of Liberty.

And the United States Army Band.

And prairie schooners.

And a flyover nudging the sound barrier.

And minutemen.

And the fiercest posse in the West.

And the United States Navy Band.

And mountains and plains and rivers and streams and timber and paddlewheel boats and alligators and floats bulging with the bounty of the nation.

The last division of marchers were led by the United States Air Force Band just as the sun began to lose its zest.

It would be another hour before the some thirty inaugural balls would require their visit. Already the night was punctured by ten thousand fireworks.

Quinn realized he was quite out of the world this moment, but the sight of Rita dressing brought the biggest smile of the day. *Better get a move on,* he told himself as he patted his pants and jacket pockets before emptying them. He withdrew the note that Rita had written the night before.

For My Beloved

It has come to this

You beside me

This is my unwritten speech to you

Inaugural, a first poem

You found in your pocket

On this night I am my own crowd of supporters,

Which trusts so much the familiar slope of your ear

that listens to you listen,

gives a fair account of what you hear,

surrounds your every cell

as if each were its own true conviction,

and I am not afraid how many other distant from you

may keep you this way.

For the want to know you as I know you,

just as after seeing a painting of a radiant

faraway land.

You arrive there and find it unchanged.